Born and raised on the W... England, **Charlotte Hawk...** intrepid boys who love he... games with them and obje... ...ly ... the amount of time she spends on the computer. When she isn't writing—or building with blocks—she is company director for a small Anglo/French construction firm. Charlotte loves to hear from readers, and you can contact her at her website: charlotte-hawkes.com.

Zoey Gomez lives and writes in sunny Somerset. She saw *Romancing the Stone* at an impressionable age, and has dreamed of being a romance writer ever since. She grew up near London, where she studied art and creative writing, and now she sells vintage books and writes novels. A good day is one when she speaks to no one but cats. You can follow her @ZoeyGomezBooks on X and Instagram.

NURSE'S BABY BOMBSHELL

CHARLOTTE HAWKES

THE SINGLE DAD'S SECRET

ZOEY GOMEZ

MILLS & BOON

First published in Great Britain 2025
by Mills & Boon, an imprint of HarperCollins*Publishers* Ltd,
1 London Bridge Street, London, SE1 9GF

www.harpercollins.co.uk

HarperCollins*Publishers* Macken House, 39/40 Mayor Street Upper,
Dublin 1, D01 C9W8, Ireland

Nurse's Baby Bombshell © 2025 Charlotte Hawkes

The Single Dad's Secret © 2025 Zoey Gomez

ISBN: 978-0-263-32498-3

02/25

This book contains FSC™ certified paper
and other controlled sources to ensure responsible forest management.

For more information visit www.harpercollins.co.uk/green.

Printed and Bound in the UK using 100% Renewable Electricity
at CPI Group (UK) Ltd, Croydon, CR0 4YY

NURSE'S BABY BOMBSHELL

CHARLOTTE HAWKES

MILLS & BOON

To Monty, Bart and Derek

Fifty ducks, one hundred fish and a thousand seagulls…

No, wait…that one's another duck!

CHAPTER ONE

'RUBY CHANNING FOR Ivan Volkov, please.'

Summoning her brightest smile, and endeavouring to quash the kaleidoscope of butterflies that was currently performing aerobatics in her stomach, Ruby attempted to charm her way past the formidable receptionist in the prestigious Harley Street Clinic.

Clearly, however, her charm had failed if the weight of the woman's disapproving gaze was anything to go by; it was pressing down on Ruby as though about to squeeze the last bit of air from her lungs.

'*Dr* Volkov is very busy,' the receptionist corrected. Pointedly. 'Did you have an appointment, *Ms* Channing, is it?'

'Channing, yes,' Ruby confirmed, not sure how she was managing to keep her smile in place. As if the mere act of being here in the first instance wasn't enough to fill her with cold horror. As if she actually *wanted* to be here. 'And technically, *no*, I don't have an appointment but I'm sure he'll see me if he knows—'

'I'm afraid that is out of the question.' The woman cut her off with a tight, if professional, smile. 'Dr Volkov's appointment schedule is full. Several months in advance, in fact.'

Of course it was. Ruby could have kicked herself—possibly quite literally. She knew how busy Ivan was, how much of a career-driven, workaholic surgeon he was. He had fought to get an army scholarship to put himself through his medical degree at uni, honed his skills on the battlefield in numerous theatres of war, and had now become one of the foremost plastic surgeons to the stars.

It had always delighted Vivian, their former foster mother, every time he'd called her to see how she was, only for her to demand an update on his life. Not to mention the occasions—possibly once a year or so—that Ivan had actually driven back to Little Meadwood to see her.

As he should. Vivian had been the only real mother he'd ever known.

Ruby had often wondered if Ivan's work ethic was as much about making Vivian proud as it was about anything else that had happened in his childhood.

Not that she knew all that much about his past. It was something Ivan had never really discussed—not when she'd been his foster sister for all of five minutes those many years ago, nor in those fleeting reunion encounters over the decade and a half since, and certainly not in that unexpected, lust-fuelled weekend the two of them had shared fourteen weeks earlier.

Blinking back the X-rated memories that abruptly tried to crash their way into her thoughts, and pretending her skin didn't burn at the mere memory, Ruby fought to focus on the blank-faced receptionist in front of her. She cast around to try to remember the last thing the woman had said.

Ah...right... Ivan's appointment schedule was full.

With hindsight, it had been foolish to simply appear at his clinic as though she was simply dropping in off the street. As though coming here was an afterthought rather than the result of driving five hours, in the early hours of the morning, to try to catch Ivan at the beginning of his working day, just for this specific purpose. Even though there were a million other things Ruby would rather have to do than have this particular conversation with Ivan.

Still, she couldn't quite bring herself to leave either, as much as part of her welcomed the excuse to do precisely that. To be fair, if she walked away now then at least she could say that she'd tried. She'd attempted to talk to Ivan. She'd attempted to do the right thing.

Only that sounded lamentably inadequate. As though she'd just given up at the first hurdle. And this was too important for that. As unpalatable as the prospect of the conversation might be, she hadn't driven several hours to simply turn around and head back—defeated—to her home in the small rural town of Little Meadwood.

Maintaining her smile but adding a touch of self-deprecation, Ruby tried to sound suitably respectful.

'I appreciate how busy Dr Volkov is, of course.' She was careful not to use Ivan's first name this time. 'However, it really is important that I speak with him. Today.'

Still, it wasn't a surprise that the receptionist looked wholly unmoved.

'Indeed?' She didn't precisely raise her eyebrow, but the effect was much the same. 'Even so, Dr Volkov has back-to-back clinics with patients who have waited months for their appointments, and as you yourself have already acknowledged, you are most certainly not in the appointment book.'

'Really? Back-to-back clinics?' The words were tumbling out and Ruby was sweeping her arm around the empty waiting room before she could stop herself.

The receptionist pressed her lips into a thin, unimpressed line before continuing. 'The calibre of clinic, and patients, that Dr Volkov runs means patient discretion is taken very seriously here.'

'Of course.' Ruby nodded apologetically even before the other woman had finished speaking.

As a renowned plastic surgeon and a partner in a private clinic, Ivan carried out procedures for some of the richest and most famous, and they prized their privacy almost above all else. Having one patient bump into another in the waiting room would be more than a mere faux-pas—it could be career damaging.

'I sometimes forget how different it is this side of the fence,' Ruby continued, hoping she looked suitably remorseful. 'I work in the A&E department of a busy city hospital.'

'You didn't mention that before.' The receptionist blinked in surprise. 'Is this visit in relation to a patient?'

She may not have planned it, but it was the opening Ruby needed.

'In a sense.' Ruby nodded. 'I know you'll respect the sensitivity of the situation.'

'Of course' The receptionist narrowed her eyes as if trying to decide whether to believe Ruby or not.

Evidently she was going to have to offer at least a little more detail before the woman was satisfied.

'I'm sure you're aware that Dr Volkov spent a week away on a personal nature a few months ago…' Ruby tailed off, suspecting Ivan wouldn't have revealed too much about his trip back to Little Meadwood to visit his terminally ill former foster mother—much less that he would have mentioned their own far more personal encounter.

Her body burned again—even hotter this time—and Ruby began to despair of herself. If this was what mere memories did to her, she almost feared how she would react to actually being in the same room with Ivan again.

Almost.

'I understood that he had to visit family,' the receptionist said carefully, oblivious to the tremor that rippled through Ruby at the words.

'Family,' she echoed with a nod, her mouth suddenly dry. Vivian would be so proud to hear that Ivan described her that way. 'It was unavoidable.'

'Because of a serious illness,' the receptionist continued, trying to sound professional although Ruby suspected that deep down, she was desperate to know more.

'Right.' Ruby swallowed back the lump that had abruptly lodged itself in her throat. 'And now I think Ivan and I need to discuss a new situation that has arisen.'

The decision to revert to Ivan's first name was deliberate, and for the first time the receptionist hesitated, seeming less certain of herself. Even so, Ruby hated mentioning Vivian's diagnosis, especially when their former foster mother wasn't the reason she was here. But it was clear that there was no other way of getting past the receptionist.

And she felt sure Vivian would have approved. After all, hadn't her foster mother always taught her beloved foster kids that, since many of them had already had instilled in them the harsh reality that life could be unjust and cruel, they should always be prepared to think outside the box, especially when it came to people trying to deny them or exclude them?

'I see.' The receptionist looked put out. 'You didn't mention, when you came in, that your visit was in relation to a patient.'

'I did not,' Ruby agreed cheerfully, though her tone was more feigned than genuine. 'My apologies. I was hoping to remain as tactful as possible. There is no change to the family member concerned, but I do need to discuss a matter that has subsequently arisen.'

'This is highly irregular,' the woman stated tightly.

'As I said, I know Ivan will also appreciate your discretion,' Ruby added hastily, this time summoning a cheerful but apologetic smile, refusing to feel guilty when the receptionist looked cornered.

'I'll speak with Dr Volkov but I can't guarantee anything,' the woman clipped out at last, tapping long fingernails on the keyboard as she weighed up her choices—which Ruby couldn't help but suspect were more about impressing Ivan than wanting to do the best thing for the patient.

Another one of the man's groupies, no doubt. Hardly a surprise—she was all too well acquainted with the kind of commotion Ivan made when he walked into a room. Even *before* he walked in. She'd seen it the weekend a few months earlier when she and Ivan, caught up in their unexpected shared memories of their former foster mother, had ended up going for a drink together to share old memories. Then another drink. Then a meal.

Ironic how watching women vie for adult Ivan's attention had somehow made her feel like a gawky teenager again, mooning after fifteen-year-old Ivan through the unfortunate fog of her schoolgirl crush.

For almost a year, each time her beloved birth mother had gone into hospital for treatment and she'd ended up back in Vivian's care, there had been a tiny, traitorous part of Ruby that had thrilled at the prospect of spending another weekend, week, or even month, under the same roof as the inescapably cool Ivan.

Not that he'd ever noticed her, treating her and her best friend, Nell—Vivian's other long-term foster child, who was still Ruby's best friend to this day—as little more than annoying kid sisters.

Except that Ivan hadn't looked at her like a kid sister on that brief visit a few months ago, had he?

Ruby shivered at the delicious memory of their last encounter. Even now, despite her determination to remain unaffected by the great Ivan Volkov, there was no denying that spark of electricity between the two of them that had been building on those fleeting visits these past couple of years. And this time, from the moment he'd walked through the door of Vivian's cottage, it had been so palpable to Ruby that she'd been shocked that neither her astute former foster mother nor her shrewd best friend had picked up on it.

Ruby shook her head sharply, as if to empty it of the unbidden memories. The last thing she needed was for her brain to be mobbed by spine-tingling, heart-pounding images of Ivan Volkov. Six foot three inches of sinfully chiselled muscle and wickedly handsome charm, hot and naked, and all hers.

She had to stay focused. There was no room in this scenario for personal feelings to cloud her judgement, especially since she'd finally plucked up the courage to come here in the first instance. Something she'd been vacillating over wildly for the past couple of weeks.

Not to mention the receptionist's stare, which continued to bore into her, seemingly searching for any sign of weakness or vulnerability.

And Ruby felt both. In spades. Even so she held her ground, maintaining her composed demeanour.

'I appreciate that it may seem irregular to you.' Ruby fought every urge to load those last two words with accusation. 'However, I know that Ivan will want to know what I've come to tell him.'

Well, she hoped he would, anyway.

Another long stare as the receptionist clearly grappled with Ruby's professional tone and her personal connection. Then, finally, the woman slipped into the glass office behind the reception area and picked up the phone, the conversation shielded from the luxurious waiting area.

It was all Ruby could do not to scan the woman's face

for any signs of how the conversation was going. And as her heartbeat began to ramp up in her chest, she almost wished that Ivan would refuse to see her. At least she could say again that she had tried.

'Dr Volkov will see you,' the woman grated out at length, clearly disliking not knowing what was going on. She probably ran this place like the tightest of ships. 'But a word of warning, keep it brief as he is a very busy man.'

'Of course,' Ruby murmured softly.

There was no point in deliberately stirring up complications that could be avoided. Her life had enough inescapable perturbations in it right now as it was.

The receptionist bobbed her head, slightly mollified as she pressed the button to release some discreet lock on the door that led to the consultation rooms.

'Down the corridor, left at the end, and then it's the first room on the right.'

'Thank you.' Ruby nodded her thanks and made her way to the door.

But even as she walked down the corridor, each step felt heavier than the last. There were no words to describe quite how sick she felt. No stopping her legs from shaking ridiculously beneath her. Was it too late to turn around and flee?

Much too late, a voice remonstrated in her head, giving her a metaphorical shove down the corridor.

But within a few paces doubt gnawed at the edges of her fresh wave of resolve, threatening to unravel her already fragile composure. Her footsteps echoing on the marble floors didn't much help. What if she was making a mistake? What if Ivan *didn't* want to know what she had to say?

And it was all very well telling herself—for the umpteenth time—that it wouldn't matter, that at least she'd know she'd tried. But her conscience would still be there to needle her that she hadn't really tried very hard at all. The truth was that she knew all too well that something of this magnitude deserved at least a little more effort—and no matter that she would have given anything to be anywhere else but here, right in this moment.

For a second, Ruby slowed in the corridor. The sunlight filtered through a vast window that looked out onto a pretty garden she would expect to see back home in Little Meadwood rather than here, at a clinic in the middle of London.

Flowers bloomed blissfully in various glorious shades of pink and purple that were a stark contrast to the ugly streak of dark fear that seemed to be staining her from the inside out right now. The tranquillity of the space on the other side of the glass seemed to call to her, and before she realized it, she was turning slowly and stepping up to the pane, her forehead resting momentarily on the cool glass as though she might draw some strength from the serene scene beyond.

She had no idea how long she stayed like that, seeking solace in the comfort the view offered her. Perhaps it was a minute, perhaps an age. But it was only when Ivan's voice penetrated her thoughts that she sprang back, her head jerking around sharply.

'Ruby? What are you doing?'

Pushing herself slowly off the glass, Ruby turned to see where Ivan had appeared around the corner at the end of the corridor, and instantly her breath caught in her throat, her world kicking into gear and beginning to spin on its very axis.

Damn him to hell for the effect he always had on her.

Tall, imposing and undeservedly good-looking, the mere sight of him was enough to send fire licking through her veins. She hated how she noticed everything about him, from his ruffled hair, which was just a little longer than last time she'd seen him, to the impeccable Savile Row suit trousers and waistcoat he wore over the crispest of white shirts.

And she hated even more that not even a second in his presence and already her pulse kicked inside her. Hard. Stirring up that familiar, aching, yearning desire in her gut; building it up.

Ruby thrust it down savagely, berating herself for such a visceral reaction to the man after everything that had happened between them. She was not some schoolgirl with a crush anymore, but rather a grown woman who had more than held her own that passionate weekend they'd shared. The simple idea that she kept allowing Ivan to catapult her back to their teenage years together—where she had followed him around doe-eyed whilst he barely registered her existence—irritated her immensely.

Especially given the circumstances.

Lord, but how was she to even begin to discuss the...*circumstances*...with him?

'I was just admiring the garden.' She tried to summon a cheerful smile but it eluded her.

'What's wrong?' he asked as he started moving towards her. 'Has something happened to Vivian?'

'She's fine,' Ruby assured him hastily, despite her tumultuous emotions. 'At least, as well as can be expected. I did explain to your receptionist that there was no change.'

She couldn't bring herself to say any more. They both—along with all the many foster children who had returned to Little Meadwood to pay their respects in recent months—knew that Vivian's conditional was terminal.

Not that that stopped the indefatigable octogenarian from trying to care for her former charges rather than have them care for her.

'Indeed. But I wondered if you were simply trying to be discreet.'

'Right.' She nodded guiltily.

She *had* been trying to be discreet. But not for that reason.

She was almost relieved when he turned wordlessly and led the way to his consulting room, leaving her to follow. And she commanded herself to absolutely *not* notice his broad shoulders, which made her palms itch with the memory of running her hands over them.

Just as she would not consider how his short, dark hair seemed to catch the sunlight in a way that reminded her how soft it had been when she'd laced her fingers through it when his head had been buried, so deliciously sinfully, between her legs.

Without warning, Ruby let out a low grunt of frustration— at least, she told herself that it was frustration.

Ivan swung around instantly, and the familiar scent of his cologne wafted towards her and stirred up memories she had no business indulging. Certainly not with such a fervour.

'Sorry.' She feigned a cough. 'Must be the…dust.'

Except there wasn't a speck of dust in the place. It wouldn't dare. When Ivan Volkov commanded a place to be spotless, that was exactly what it was.

Squeezing her hands together so tightly that she could feel her fingernails digging painfully into her palms, Ruby instructed herself to start moving forward again and to compose herself. This nervousness wasn't her. She was usually so in control, and so capable under pressure, especially as a nurse who spent so much of her time calming panicking patients or their families.

But this was different. It wasn't usually *her* being affected by a situation. Which was probably why right now her nerves were a tangle of yarn in her stomach, and she feared that trying to unravel them would only pull at them and make them more of a mess than ever.

Wordlessly, she followed Ivan into the room, startled to

discover that it wasn't so much a consultation room as his personal office.

Did that make this easier? Or harder?

Ruby bit her lip, trying to summon the courage to state what she'd travelled all this way to say.

'This definitely isn't about Vivian?' Ivan demanded; his low voice still tinged with concern.

Ruby shook her head emphatically. 'Not at all. I'm sorry for making you worry,' Ruby told him—and this, at least, was sincere. 'For the record, she's still fighting the diagnosis every step and pill of the way, of course.'

'I'd expect no less,' Ivan rumbled, looking momentarily relieved before sliding into the captain's chair behind a stunning-looking desk.

His very essence seemed to fill the space, commanding yet comforting all at once. The room was arranged with characteristic Ivan precision; medical texts lined the shelves, but the effect was somewhat softened by the choice of warm oaks and green baize linings that soothed the eye and somehow brought inside a touch of that verdant garden to which she had been so desperate to escape moments earlier.

Her gaze wandered for a while, flickering over everything and taking it all in until, eventually, it came to rest on Ivan himself. And on his dark gaze, which always seemed to have the power to skewer her.

'Why are you here, Ruby?'

It was the million-dollar question, wasn't it?

She took a moment to gather herself, folding her hands neatly in her lap if only to stop herself from fumbling with them.

Rip the Band-Aid off, her mother had always said—even when it was the news neither of them had wanted to discuss. Like another hospital visit. Another long course of debilitating treatment. She had never shied away from telling her daughter the truth about her illness. Never pretended she was going to get better when she knew it wasn't possible. But never let the fact that she was dying make their precious time together become negative.

Lost in her thoughts, Ruby was pulled back to the present by another growl from Ivan. A growl that made her think of other things...like those wickedly sinful sounds he had made that night a few months ago. When neither of them had been in control, yet both of them had decided control was an illusion. Especially when it had come to sending each other to the edge.

'I thought we agreed that what happened between us that night—' he began in a voice that sounded entirely too thick with memories.

And need. Even now.

'We did,' she cut him off hastily with a shake of her head, not wanting to hear him dismiss their night together as a mistake or some such brush-off.

Especially not now.

'We did agree that,' she repeated, drawing in a steadying breath. 'And I was trying to respect that. But this is different.'

She was surprised at just how even and calm she sounded despite the emotions churning around inside her.

'Indeed?' Ivan frowned, the crease between his brows deepening as he tried to piece the puzzle together.

He leaned back in his chair but the seemingly casual gesture didn't fool her for an instant. The walls of the room might as well have been closing in on her; the tension was growing thicker with every passing moment, as if the two of them were the only two people left in the entire world.

Which only made it that much more apparent that she had no place left to hide, and no conversation left to throw into the space between them. She wasn't going to be able to escape the moment any longer. And so, finally, Ruby steeled her shoulders, met Ivan's too-intense stare head-on, and decided, *To hell with it*.

'The thing is, I'm pregnant.'

CHAPTER TWO

'PREGNANT?' IVAN REPEATED, rolling the word around his mouth as though tasting it.

Apparently, he didn't much like what he sampled. *Not*, Ruby commanded herself firmly, *that the act hurt her.*

Not one bit.

'Pregnant,' she confirmed. Cheerfully.

And no matter the storm inside her.

'I think not,' he concluded.

Still not hurt, decried the manic voice inside her head.

And any awkwardness she felt was mere apprehension rather than any lingering sexual tension. Which would, of course, be wholly inappropriate given the circumstances. She squared her shoulders and wondered how she was even managing to keep her voice level.

'Ah well, I'm afraid the test results say otherwise.'

His dark gaze skewered her to the spot.

'I fail to see how.'

'Really?' *Cheery, cheery, cheery.* 'As a surgeon, I would not have thought the basics of human reproduction would elude you.'

Ivan cast her the kind of withering look Ruby was sure might intimidate any other woman, but somehow only lent her a sudden, much-needed boost of confidence.

Oddly, this was the Ivan she recognized best. The distant,

guarded Ivan—not the passionate, seductive Ivan of the other month. *This*, she could deal with.

'I've no doubt your glowers work on others, Ivan Volkov.' She ran her hands down the front of her jeans with feigned nonchalance. 'You might be a top surgeon—not to mention something of a war hero, by all accounts—but you forget I knew you when you were that teen rebel. I remember all too well Vivian sitting us all around that tiny table of hers, laying down the house rules as she baked us cookies and made us hot chocolate with marshmallows.'

For a moment, Ivan almost smiled at the unexpected memory. But then his gaze dropped to her waist.

'My point is that we only had… We used protection.'

'That's true,' she acknowledged as he plunged on.

'Therefore, I can only conclude that there must be some mistake.'

And his tone held a finality as though there was nothing left to be said about the situation.

It seemed the man before her hadn't changed all that much from the hurt, angry boy who had always sworn he would never, *never* bring a child into the world. He'd always been adamant that no kid would ever endure the cruel upbringing that he had endured.

Not that he'd ever really talked about his years with his bully of a father. Not in any depth. But he hadn't needed to. Growing up with a single mother who had been in and out of hospital for years, Ruby had seen enough other foster homes to know that Ivan's terrible story was lamentably all too familiar.

How many times had she and Nell given silent thanks that their own childhoods, whilst filled with loss, had also been full of love?

Nell's parents had clearly adored their only child right up until their fatal car accident had robbed them of each other.

Just like her own loving mother, who had always made Ruby feel like the most loved kid who existed, and every time Annabel Channing had gone into hospital for more treatment, or another operation, Ruby had known she'd done so because she was fighting her illness just to have another week, month, year, with her beloved daughter.

Without warning, Ruby's eyes prickled at the memory.

How she missed her mother. Especially now—expecting a child of her own. The need to hear her mother's voice just one more time, just for one more golden nugget of advice—or even just to hear Annabel tell her how much she loved her—was almost overwhelming.

Losing her loving, determined mother had been more pain than the young Ruby had ever thought she could bear. She was only so very fortunate that Vivian had always been the most incredible foster mother. But that only made Vivian's terminal diagnosis all the more potent.

Just as it made this unborn baby all the more precious, Ruby realized with a jolt. She had to give this tiny being that was growing inside her all the love that both her mother and Vivian would have unarguably showered on such a wanted child.

Ruby blinked again, even more determinedly, as she amazed herself at her own show of calmness. Outwardly, at least.

'There's no mistake, Ivan,' she confirmed quietly but firmly. 'I *am* pregnant.'

Ivan glowered at her, even more appalled. Though for a shocking few moments, words seemed to fail him.

'No,' he rasped at length. 'I simply will not accept that.'

She almost laughed despite the fact she was shaking inside.

'Whilst I appreciate that you are able to bend many things to your will these days, even you cannot erase actual facts out of existence simply by willing them to be so.'

Ivan raised an eyebrow, those black eyes boring into hers

with even more intensity than ever, and any sense of amusement dissipated. Something shifted inside her. What was it about the man that suddenly seemed almost...dangerous?

At least, dangerous to her heart, which was worse than anything else.

'You're saying the protection failed?'

'You're suggesting there is any other explanation?' she challenged. 'You think I did it deliberately?'

To his credit, Ivan met her gaze directly. 'No,' he confirmed. 'I do not believe that.'

'That's reassuring to hear.' She blew out a deep, steadying breath. 'And you aren't about to be completely disgusting and suggest that you think anyone else could possibly be the father? Or that you would actually think I would do something as amoral as to try to pass another man's child off on you?'

Because if he thought that little of her, then what hope did they even have of salvaging something...*civil*...out of this mess?

The look Ivan cast her was one of undisguised affrontery. If she'd thought he was mad at her before, it was nothing compared to the lethal glint in his eyes at that moment.

'That,' he bit out, as if the words were being ripped from his mouth, 'is not something I believe.'

And Ruby told herself that she didn't know why that should send such a wave of relief cascading through her.

The acknowledgement was out of Ivan's mouth almost before he had fully registered the implication.

He stood frozen; time seemed to come to a standstill around him as he struggled to process the magnitude of it. Even though they had used protection, there wasn't a single cell of him that believed Ruby would ever lie—which meant only one thing.

She was indeed pregnant, and he was the father.

The ticking clock on the wall of his office seemed to reverberate too loudly around the room, though the hands appeared stuck in the same position. He couldn't move, couldn't breathe.

He sure as hell didn't know what to think.

Was it only moments ago that he'd been staring down the corridor and wondering if her turning up at his clinic was real, or just another of the feverish dreams he'd been having almost every night since the one they'd spent together a few months earlier?

As if she'd been haunting his brain—and his body—ever since.

And then she folded her arms across her chest and tipped her head to the side, and the action was so familiar, so quintessentially Ruby, with that lashing of sass and that touch of defiance, that it hit him like a physical blow to the gut.

This was no ghost.

Memories flooded back—those late nights they'd spent a few months earlier, talking, reminiscing and laughing at the inside jokes that only they would have understood. And then, that final night they'd spent together, engaged in something far more intimate than mere shared memories of a long-forgotten past.

And still, as if against his will, he found his gaze sweeping slowly, appreciatively, over her. From that silky smooth caramel-brown hair that had poured through his fingers like the smoothest of water to that wickedly hot mouth that had done such things to him over and over again.

And from those mesmerizing hazel eyes that seemed to have possessed a direct line to her very soul, to the exquisite curves of body that had fit against his like two pieces of a puzzle that had been designed perfectly for each other. Was she as molten now as she had been that night?

What was he even thinking?

Sharply, Ivan pulled up the reins on his runaway brain. His body was responding to its own memories that his mind was fighting valiantly against replaying.

It wasn't as though he was a monk—far from it, despite his workaholic lifestyle—but when had any woman made him forget himself in such a primordial way?

The answer was simple—*never*—at least aside from little Ruby Channing. Or perhaps more accurately, the spellbinding woman she had grown into. Enough to make him lose his head.

Something snagged at Ivan's thought just then.

Quite *how much* had she made him lose his head a few months ago?

Enough to forget about something as fundamental as protection?

Now he thought about it—or at least, thought about it in cool, analytical terms rather than being assailed by the kind of feverish dreams that he had pretended hadn't haunted him almost every night since—it occurred to him that they'd both almost been too caught up in that first time together to remember whether they'd used protection.

The realization brought Ivan up cold. For a moment, he floundered, trying to work out what powerful sensation was bombarding him now.

He wanted to say he was in disbelief but what he felt was far, far more complex. *Him, a father.* He, who had always sworn from the age of six—or perhaps even earlier—that he would never, *never* continue the tainted, cruel, harsh Volkov bloodline.

And now Ruby was pregnant with his child.

Guilt, fear, uncertainty…they all swirled within him. Slowly at first, but then faster, harder, beginning to reverberate within him, making him feel as though he might throw up.

And then *crash.* They collided like turbulent waves in a stormy sea, making him feel more smashed apart than any shipwreck.

He had to stop it.

He *had* to.

But every way his brain turned—spinning this way, then that—it seemed to hit a brick wall. And amid this maelstrom of emotions, Ivan felt something else stir within him.

Anger. At himself more than at Ruby, but unmistakable nonetheless. For giving in to temptation in the first instance that crazy night. For being so uncharacteristically carried away with Ruby that he had forgotten to be as fastidious about protection as he usually was. But also for the fact that when he'd stepped around that corner and seen Ruby standing there in his clinic, in *his* corridor, it had taken every ounce of willpower he'd had not to stalk up that corridor, haul her into his arms, and glut himself on this insane attraction that seemed to vibrate so frenetically between them.

Which was clearly how he'd got into this nightmare situation.

Pregnant.

No, he couldn't possibly become a father. What would he even know about raising a kid—certainly not how to raise a happy, healthy, undamaged kid?

Him, a father? Ivan wasn't sure how he didn't sneer aloud at the very title. His own had been a man who had only ever been a father by name but never by deed.

Too many of his foster fathers had been every bit as bad. And those few who might have shown a wild kid like him even a hint of kindness had soon seen the rotten streak that was imprinted through his core like a dropped apple, and soon insisted he be removed from their cosy homes.

Only Vivian had ever thought she could see something beyond his past. She was the kindest, fiercest, most generous foster mother he had never dreamed he might deserve.

Ironic that her unfailing love had only heightened his own sense of guilt that much more. Because even if he finally had someone like Vivian to care for him, and look out for him, then he'd only gained what he'd stolen from Maksim.

Instantly, Ivan stamped the thought out. Vehemently. He had no desire at all to gaze down that particular path into the past. Not even to let that name pass through his brain.

The pain and loss simply went too deep.

Even so, he had no idea how long he stood there, caught up in turbulent thoughts, until a soft cough from across the room tore him mercifully out of the maelstrom.

'Ivan?' Her hazel eyes were full of apprehension. 'Did you hear me?'

'I heard you,' he managed, his voice sounding foreign even to himself as he tried to guess what she might have been saying.

'Well, that's a start.' Ruby's voice sounded calm enough, but he didn't miss the shake in her too-tight smile.

As though she didn't quite believe him.

'Ruby…' Ivan began before stopping abruptly, whatever he'd been about to say sticking in his throat like a dry pill.

But before he could cough the words out, he was startled by the sound of his name being called from out in the corridor, along with the fast *click-click* of stilettoes coming down the polished-stone hallway. Was it relief or instinct that had him darting across the room to spring open the door and step out into the open corridor beyond?

'It's an emergency.' His receptionist was pointing urgently back up the corridor. 'Someone has collapsed outside in the street. We don't think they are breathing.'

Ivan didn't need to hear any more. He was already halfway

up the corridor before the receptionist had even turned around. Racing through the waiting area and into the crisp afternoon air as he took the steps two at a time down from his clinic to the street below, it was only when he reached the patient— blue faced and foaming at the mouth—that he realized Ruby was right there with him.

Dropping to his knees, he checked the motionless man. His mind somehow managed the shift from the whirlwind of emotions he'd been experiencing only moments earlier to the critical situation now at hand.

Though, for perhaps the first time, it wasn't as natural and easy to do.

'He isn't breathing,' Ivan confirmed to Ruby. 'I'll start chest compressions. You need to grab the defibrillator from reception.'

Then he dropped his head to concentrate on what was in front of him, throwing himself into the task yet somehow not even needing to watch Ruby to know that she would be doing exactly as he'd asked with enviable efficiency.

Later, much later, well after this moment had passed, he would reflect on why he had found it so effortless to trust Ruby. And though he would tell himself it was just the result of having known her, on and off, for the better part of two decades, a part of him would know deep down that there was more to it than that.

But in that moment, Ivan's thoughts did not wander but were instead consumed with the urgency of the situation and the relief that Ruby was already back with the defibrillator. With a brief word of assurance to him that the receptionist was already calling 999, she began setting up the machine and running through the initial checks. Meanwhile Ivan focused on quickly unzipping his patient's top and pulling open the man's shirt in preparation for the AED.

'Charging to two hundred,' Ruby confirmed after a few moments. 'And clear.'

Sitting back, Ivan watched as Ruby delivered the first shock.

But there was no response from the unconscious man, and a pulse check confirmed to Ivan that they needed to continue their efforts.

'Charge it again,' Ivan instructed as he bent back over to continue with CPR.

Not, it seemed, that he needed to. Ruby had already seamlessly begun to transition into the next cycle of defibrillation. As they worked in tandem, the intermittent blips and beeps from the machine was the only sound to punctuate the air.

'Okay,' Ruby said clearly but quietly after a moment. 'Clear.'

Instantly, Ivan straightened back up and removed all contact from the man.

A second shock. A second pulse check. And still, nothing.

'Charge it again,' Ivan commanded, dropping back to his exhausting task.

And as he and Ruby worked together for a third time, seemingly in harmony without even having to say more than a word here or there, the third and final shock was delivered. This time the man twitched.

'We have a pulse,' Ivan finally gritted out, just as the faint sound of an approaching ambulance could be heard in the distance. 'Good work.'

'And you.' Ruby nodded briefly.

Her focus, like his, was still primarily on the patient and for the next few minutes, they continued to work together in silent unison as they tried to keep their patient comfortable and ready for transport. By the time the paramedics were on scene, the now-breathing man was already waiting to simply be loaded onto the ambulance and taken straight to hospital.

Ivan offered a concise, efficient handover and then it was done, and he found himself heading back inside his clinic with Ruby.

'That was good work back there,' he managed gruffly as they mounted the steps together.

'I could say the same. We made a good team.' Ruby's cheeks flushed in her haste to explain herself. 'I didn't mean…'

Her rich, hazel eyes met his and Ivan couldn't help feeling an unspoken sense of accomplishment. Every minute had counted with that man, and Ruby was right that together the two of them had saved a life through seamless teamwork. The image of her by his side, anticipating yet simultaneously being proactive, lingered in his mind. It inevitably made him wonder what else they might be able to achieve if they pulled together in a similar way.

Like raising a baby.

But the thought was no sooner there than it was gone again. Or, more accurately, Ivan was dismissing it.

The adrenalin from their successful resuscitation was already ebbing away, leaving the stark reality in its place. Being a surgeon who was capable of saving a life on the street was hardly the same thing as being a damaged human capable of raising a tiny human being without passing on that damage.

The weight of responsibility squatted in his chest, heavier than ever.

This—medicine, surgery—was what he was good at. Perhaps the only thing he was good at.

Being a decent human being, one capable of something as complex and impactful as *love*…? Well, that was something altogether different.

No matter how much he despised himself for it, it wouldn't make it any the less true. The sooner he could make Ruby realize it, the better for her.

'Reading too much into it is a mistake,' he bit out gruffly.

Though whether he was talking to Ruby or himself wasn't entirely clear to him.

Stepping out of the corridor, he ushered her back into his office as she turned to glance at him over her shoulder just the way she had done several months earlier in her cottage doorway the night he had made the mistake of giving in to temptation.

'I was just saying—'

'I know what you were saying,' he cut her off, hating the way his body was reacting despite his brain telling him not to. 'And *I'm* just saying that the two things are mutually exclusive.'

'You really don't want anything to do with this baby?' Her voice cracked despite her obvious efforts not to let it whilst her hand moved instinctively to her stomach as if to protect the growing embryo inside.

'That isn't what I'm saying,' he rasped out instinctively before stopping himself.

What *was* he saying? He couldn't even work it out himself, which only made him feel even more of a deadbeat. It wasn't even a fetus yet, and he was already turning into a sorry excuse for a father. Just as he'd always feared.

Not that the realization should come as such a shock to him.

Had he really thought he was capable of anything better? No matter how much he wanted to be different from that cruel drunkard who had been his own father—and no matter how many long, long hours he had fought to make a success of his life—deep down, he couldn't change who he really was.

He wouldn't be any better a father than his own had been. It was how he was built, and no amount of hate and mental excoriation could ever hope to change it. The same tainted blood ran through his veins. The same distorted codes of DNA.

And he'd never hated himself more for it.

'Ivan, I understand that this is a lot to take in,' Ruby pressed on when he still didn't speak. 'It was for me when I first realized I was pregnant. But together...'

'There is no *together*, Ruby,' he heard himself grit out, though every word felt like glass in his mouth, mercilessly grinding at the soft, weak tissue. 'This cannot be. I will not accept it.'

And he steeled himself against the hurt that flashed across her gloriously expressive eyes.

He was acting for the best.

'Ivan, please...' She stepped forward unexpectedly, reaching for his arm.

'Stop!' He recoiled instantly, doing nothing to mask his horror, hating himself for the wounded expression that scudded across her lovely features.

But he couldn't back down. She didn't need to know that he wasn't so much appalled at the thought of her touch so much as at the way his skin crackled in hedonistic expectation.

As if he exerted no control whatsoever on what his body might want even now.

Especially now.

How could he possibly raise a child of his own with all that coiled inside him? Just waiting to strike. Just watching for the moment he let his guard down. He knew first-hand how destructive a bad parent could be. He knew exactly the damage such a man could do. What kind of an example would he be for any child?

It wasn't fair to them. Or to Ruby. They deserved better than him. They deserved better. Full stop.

'Having a baby with me is a terrible idea.' The words tumbled out of his mouth. 'More than that, it is unacceptable.'

She sucked in a sharp breath.

'Are you saying you want me to...not have this baby?'

Ivan startled. Something dark and sickening thudding through him. No matter what else he thought, that wasn't what he had said. And it sure as hell wasn't what he meant.

God, he was so damaged he couldn't even get this bit right.

Taking a moment to steady himself, Ivan tried sucking in a breath. But his lungs might as well have been on fire. His head was swimming. Churning. And with it, an anchor dragging him down into an abyss.

Surely all he'd meant was that no child deserved to be cursed with the Volkov bloodline?

He opened his mouth to explain, but the right words seemed to elude him.

Ruby, it seemed, wasn't having the same problem at all.

'Because that isn't happening,' she proclaimed emphatically. And if he noticed a slight edge of hysteria to her tone then, he certainly wasn't in a position to point it out. 'I *am* having this baby, Ivan.'

'No...' He worked his mouth, trying to loosen the suddenly stiff jaw and tongue. 'I can't...*won't* be a part of it.'

And he loathed himself that little bit more for that shimmer in her captivating eyes. The pain that he was patently causing.

Because that was all he was capable of doing.

'Fine,' she whispered, nodding her head jerkily. 'I only needed to know if you wanted to be a part of this. You don't, and that is your right. I'm not asking for anything from you.'

'You don't want anything from me?' he echoed instead, his jaw clenched so tight that the pain cascaded through him. 'I find that hard to believe.'

He refused to hear her gasp of shock. Or acknowledge that shimmer in her eyes.

'You can't really think that,' she managed. And he told himself he didn't hear any pain in her tone. 'I don't understand what's happening. This... It isn't you.'

He wasn't sure if what frightened him more was the thought that she was right or that she was wrong. But right now, he had found a rope and—whether it was a lifeline or a noose—it was all he had to cling to in that moment.

'You don't know the first thing about me.'

'I think I know you better than most,' she shot back.

'A few weeks here and there, in the same foster home, a couple of decades ago does not mean you know me.'

She actually arched her eyebrows at him, angrier than he had ever seen her. Though to be fair the Ruby he had known, however briefly, had never had much of a temper. She'd been more of a sulker; the memory popped unbidden into his head.

He shoved it aside, but she was already speaking.

'I know you were a guarded kid who had suffered a lot being shunted in and out of different foster homes and boys' homes, before you ended up at Vivian's.'

As if that even covered the half of what he'd been through.

The truth was enough to knock the air out of his lungs— just as his father had done over and over again from as young as Ivan could remember.

He spun away, no more able to face Ruby than he was able to face the memories of his father's cruelty. The countless nights and days spent cowering in his room in fear whilst his father raged at who knew what, too afraid to risk creeping down the stairs in a bid to escape. How many times had he shoved his little brother, Maksim, into the safety of the wardrobe, just in case their father burst in, looking for something or someone on whom he could take out his fury?

It had to have been thousands, over the years.

This time Ivan punched the memory away viciously, quickly, before the hazy edges of it sharpened and reminded him of even more details of the life he'd fooled himself that he'd left behind.

But beneath the troubled surface, her gaze held a steely resolve he had never been sure she'd appreciated she possessed.

If this baby was to stand a chance at a normal, toxic-free childhood, then Ivan was instantly convinced that Ruby Channing would be the person able to provide it. She was her own person, but with a healthy dose of their former foster mother thrown in for good measure.

As long as she stayed far away from him.

Which meant that however hard it was, he had to get Ruby to see that for herself.

'This baby—any baby—would be better off far away from me.'

'Fine...but I'm keeping it.' She took a step back, her eyes glistening with unshed tears. Yet she held herself together in a way that he could only admire.

'I would ruin it.'

Her chin lifted with a determination that transcended the apparent fragility of her emotions. It all made his chest ache with conflicting emotions that he couldn't even begin to comprehend.

'Whether you want to be involved or not is entirely up to you.'

Words raced around his head, and to the tip of his tongue, but Ivan couldn't quite grasp any of them properly. They were too slippery. Too fast. Even as Ruby turned her back on him, straightened her crease-free clothes, and finally lurched for the door.

And he should have let her go—just as he'd wanted her to do. But something made him call out to stop her.

'Ruby...'

She paused and turned, but that moment of weakness was over and Ivan was already regaining control of himself. He didn't continue, telling himself that he had no idea what he'd even been going to say anyway.

'At least you know now,' Ruby eventually spoke for him. Stiffly. Determinedly. 'You can't ever say that I didn't tell you.'

'You told me,' he echoed mechanically.

Unable to move. Numb. Though every part of his being was screaming at him.

Then Ruby reached for the door.

'Goodbye, Ivan.'

In the moment of silence that followed, a thousand, million thoughts slammed through his brain but he couldn't understand a single one of them.

And then she was hauling open the door and stepping outside, and all he could do was watch her go.

CHAPTER THREE

IT WAS SEVERAL HOURS—and multiple motorway stops for water, hot chocolate and anything else that might prevent her body from involuntarily shaking—by the time Ruby arrived back at Little Meadwood. And still nothing had quite settled her jangling nerves after her encounter with Ivan.

How could he have been so heartless? So utterly cruel?

She'd known that as a foster teen he'd been antifamily, but she'd assumed he would have changed with age. It had never occurred to her that he would want nothing—*nothing*—to do with their baby. And all right, so perhaps logic whispered that she might have been a little naive to think that it would go smoothly. After all, what self-respecting bachelor would be delighted to hear that a one-night stand had resulted in a pregnancy? But right now it wasn't her head that was firing emotions all through her body, but rather her aching heart.

Surely he hadn't needed to be quite so callous in his rejection? It wasn't as if they were complete strangers and he didn't know what her angle was. He *knew* her, well enough to know that she would never have deliberately engineered this situation anyway.

Right?

Thoughts ricocheted around her head, sending her lurching this way and that.

Admittedly, her foolish fantasy of cottage gardens and white picket fences that lurked at the back of her mind was probably a little fairy-tale laughable, but it hurt for him not to want to be any part at all of their unborn baby's life.

And as for any suggestion that she should not continue with the pregnancy...well, that stung far deeper than she could have imagined.

Except that he hadn't said that, had he? a tiny, muffled voice pointed out from the back of her head. He'd merely ascertained what she herself wanted to do, and then he had accepted it.

But she wasn't quite prepared to listen to such a voice of reason. Not when the events of the afternoon were still playing out wildly in her head, over and over, as if she could somehow make more sense of them.

She'd anticipated his shock. Even some degree of disbelief. But what hadn't occurred to her was that he would want nothing to do with this little life.

Her eyes prickled before she could stop herself; her hand moved instinctively, as it seemed to have a habit of doing these days, to cradle the nonexistent bump. As though she could somehow protect it from anyone who might want to hurt it.

She just hadn't expected that person would be Ivan.

A rush of what could only be described as *love* coursed through her in that moment.

She was going to have a baby!

As unplanned and terrifying as that prospect was, a part of her was thrilled. If she could be even half as generous and funny and strong as her own mother had been, then surely this baby could want for nothing.

She would make sure she was enough. More than enough.

Except it didn't work that way, did it? Something unpleasant snapped around her chest, making her struggle to breathe for a moment.

Because as loving and amazing as Annabel Channing had been, Ruby thought, she'd still lost her. Horribly. Because cancer didn't just hit once; it hit over and over, levelling not only its target but everyone else in its wake, too.

So how was she to explain to him or her, eight or ten years from now, why they didn't have a father? She didn't even know how she was to begin tackling that situation. After all, hadn't she wondered about her own father despite everything her mother had ever done for her?

And hadn't she been frustrated by her mother's evasiveness every time the topic had come up, hurt by the fact that she had never known even the slightest thing about the man who was her biological father?

There was a sense of a missing piece that she had always sworn to herself she would never inflict on any baby of her own. Yet here she was repeating, it seemed, the same mistake. And there was nothing she could do about it.

Until this moment, she didn't think she had fully understood her mother's reasons for refusing to answer even a single one of her many questions.

But now, suddenly, it was all too clear.

'I promise you, little one,' Ruby whispered to her belly, 'that I will never, *never* let you feel you weren't always wanted.'

Even if that meant refusing to answer a single question about Ivan Volkov.

She stabbed her key into the lock of the small cottage she shared with her best friend and former foster sibling, Nell. Ruby didn't even attempt to unravel her hurt from her anger as she stumbled through the door, grateful to be home at last.

Then she stopped abruptly in the short, narrow hallway. She couldn't pinpoint it, but something felt somehow...*odd*.

'Nell?' she called out hesitantly, though she was sure her

friend was supposed to be on duty at City Hospital, where they both worked.

Or could it just be that she was hoping her best friend would be here? Nell would listen to her, hug her, and make her laugh. And now that she'd told Ivan about the baby—for all the good it had done—it would be a relief to finally be able to share the news with her best friend. And with Vivian, for that matter.

'Not Nell,' a deep, familiar voice carried from the living room of the otherwise-still cottage.

A shiver of indignation rippled down Ruby's spine moments before Ivan's shadow filled the small doorway that led off the short hallway.

At least she told herself that it was indignation—certainly not anticipation—given that this was the man who was the very cause of her anguish. And so, in that moment, she levelled all her frustration and ire down the hall towards him.

'What are you doing here, Ivan? And who the hell let you into my home?'

He didn't appear to move even a muscle yet the controlled fury rolled out of him. Just like thunder. And she felt it rumbling around her, making all the tiny hairs on her arms rise up and setting of minijolts of lightning right through her body.

Of fury, she told herself firmly.

'Did you really think you could drop a bombshell like that and simply walk away from me?'

And she despaired of herself that her heart leaped like that, despite her own anger. But that didn't mean she had to give in to it.

'I didn't "drop a bombshell" then "walk away",' she heard herself answer. Tartly. 'I gave you the chance to discuss it and you made it clear you wanted nothing to do with me—with it. So I left. I didn't expect to walk through my own front door to find you'd broken in.'

Ivan's jaw tightened.

'I've hardly broken in. I used the spare key. Or have you conveniently forgotten that you were the one who showed me where it was hidden last time I was here?'

'I didn't forget.' She wrinkled her nose, begrudging the fact that she had to admit it.

She'd only shown him where the key was in case he needed somewhere to wait if he turned up to visit Vivian next door, only to find that she was asleep. Sometimes the treatment took it out of her.

No other reason. Certainly not that he could let himself in when all she'd wanted to do was get home, get a hot shower, and sink into her bed for what felt like a week's worth of sleep. She was exceptionally tired after her very early start this morning and hours of driving.

'I think we said all that we needed to say back in London, don't you?' she managed instead, proud of herself when her voice didn't shake or otherwise betray her.

Then told herself that she didn't feel anything somersaulting inside her when Ivan glowered at her like a winter storm ready to unleash itself.

'Not by a long way,' he growled, his voice low and dangerous.

A wiser woman might have taken heed but Ruby had never been wise where Ivan was concerned—clearly—and she wasn't about to back down. Especially now when heat prickled at the back of her eyes and emotions bubbled up in her, threatening to spill over at any moment.

'Well, I've said all I needed to say,' she bit out at length.

'Good, then it will make this conversation short and sweet,' Ivan growled. 'In answer to your earlier question, I'm here to bring you home.'

Whatever she'd been expecting him to say, it hadn't been that.

'I *am* home.' She frowned, confused.

'I think not.'

A prickle of unease crept down her spine, like long, thorny fingers walking their way over each and every vertebra.

'Ivan…'

'You are expecting my child, Ruby.' He didn't shout, didn't even raise his voice, yet the sound seemed to echo deafeningly, off every wall in the cottage. 'Did you really think I would just let you raise it without me?'

Ruby had no idea how she managed to face him down.

'After what you said a few hours ago,' she managed defiantly, 'I had thought that was exactly what had been decided.'

At least he had the decency to look guilty at that. If only for a fraction of a second. Then he caught himself.

'Decided?' he echoed incredulously. 'You came in, dropped your bombshell, and then walked out.'

Indignation, and something else that Ruby didn't care to name, coursed through her.

'That isn't what happened. I…told you so you could choose whether to be involved or not. You chose the latter—'

'I had no chance to choose anything,' Ivan cut her off harshly. 'So now your only choice will be to move in with me.'

Did the world speed up, or slow down? Ruby couldn't tell. Her mind was too busy racing to catch up with the sudden turn conversation.

'Move in…with you?' she echoed, her breath more ragged than she would have liked. But that couldn't be helped. 'You cannot be serious.'

'I assure you I am perfectly serious.'

'But…' She floundered, her brain still lagging embarrassingly behind. 'How would that even work? I live here. I work at City Hospital. You live in London and you have a private practice.'

'Which is why it makes more sense for you to move in with me.'

Ruby gasped—the air almost choking her as surely as if she was caught in the crushing grip of the fiercest storm. This wasn't how she'd imagined her future. And yet...

She shook any traitorous thoughts out of her head.

'No.' The word shot out of her mouth like a crack from a gun. 'My job is here. My friends. My family.'

'Your mother was your only family, was she not?' Ivan frowned, clearly not trying to hurt her—merely being factual. 'Vivian fostered you because when she passed, you had no one else.'

'Vivian *is* my family,' Ruby bit out. 'And Nell. And everyone at Little Meadwood.'

There was no mistaking the exasperation in his expression but that was likely to be expected. Ivan might care for Vivian, but he had never seen Little Meadwood as a home. Certainly not the way she or Nell had done.

Little wonder that he had set up a new life in London, where he could be anonymous. Her heart ached for him.

'You could take a leave of absence. Or you could easily transfer to a London hospital.'

'My whole *life* is here, Ivan. I'm not leaving.'

'Not even for this baby for whom you profess to want to do what is best?'

The cottage walls seemed to press in closer, as if peering in to witness such a moment, and Ruby's hand trembled slightly as she reached up to tuck a loose strand of her brown hair behind an ear, her hazel eyes darting away from Ivan's piercing gaze. The silence in the cottage was thick, punctuated only by the quiet ticking of the old grandfather clock in the corner.

'Look, Ivan,' she began, her voice steadier than she felt given how heavy the words were on her tongue. 'I understand what you're saying, but we don't need to live together to raise this child. We don't have to be a couple.'

No matter that a traitorous part of her had wanted him to do just that.

But because he *wanted* to, not because of duty. How naive was that?

The pain of her own upbringing echoed through her plea. Despite the unconditional love of her mother, the absence of a father figure growing up had left her longing for completeness. Was that why the sting of Ivan's initial rejection at the clinic remained fresh—a wound that no amount of goodwill could easily soothe?

'No, we don't need to be a couple,' he agreed, his voice a low rumble that seemed to fill the room. 'But if we want to provide a stable home for our child, then perhaps it is the best option.'

He stepped closer, and the air around them seemed to shift suddenly, becoming charged with an intensity that Ruby hadn't anticipated.

'I'm not sure that *stable* means throwing together two people who barely know each other,' she countered, trying to ignore the way her heart hammered against her ribcage. 'And contrary to what I said before, growing up as foster kids in the same house twenty years ago doesn't count.'

So why was it that whilst the rational part of her brain screamed for distance—for protection against further hurt— some irrational part craved the connection he offered?

'So, let me get this straight,' Ivan ground out. Furious sparks actually seemed to spit out from his coal-black eyes. 'You travelled to London expecting me to leap at the chance to get to know a baby that I didn't even know existed until a few hours ago. Then you ran away when I didn't do precisely that.

And now, when I say I will take responsibility, you claim we barely know each other.'

When he put it like that, it sounded nonsensical. But Ruby stood her ground.

'The fact is that you're only here now out of a sense of duty.'

'And you find that a problem?' he challenged, his voice edgier than she had ever heard him. 'What did you expect me to do, Ruby? Perhaps you thought I should throw a baby shower?'

'Obviously not,' she snapped again.

Which hardly helped to defuse the situation, but she found it impossible to do anything else.

'Then what?' His voice still echoed loudly in the small space.

Ruby wrinkled her nose but didn't answer. She didn't think he was looking for a response anyway. His eyes were too dark, and too intense, as they bored into her. The air was charged with electricity.

'Well?' he pushed, after a moment. 'I hurt you, I understand that. But you hardly gave me chance to do anything else.'

There was another beat of silence.

'I don't know what I expected.' She threw her hands up angrily. 'Just not…*that*.'

He glowered at her scornfully. 'Not what, Ruby? Shock? Apprehension?'

'Try horror and contempt,' she bit back, refusing to back down. Hurt still fired her up. 'Try suggesting I don't continue with the pregnancy.'

So much for that voice in her head trying to reason it through earlier.

'I never suggested any such thing.' Ivan's eyes blazed like an icy fire that somehow chilled her and burned her all at once. Yet there was no mistaking the hint of relief that rolled in behind his denial. All the same, Ruby wasn't about to let it go that easily.

'You said that me having this baby was unacceptable.'

'I said that having a baby *with me* was unacceptable,' he refuted instantly. 'But here you are, pregnant, and now we must deal with it.'

And what did it say that her heart didn't know whether to plummet or soar? She fought to keep her voice somewhat even.

'Then what are you doing here, Ivan?'

'I'm here to discuss what happens next.'

'Like me moving to London?' she demanded, forcing herself to stay calm despite every nerve ending jolting and sparking inside her. 'That isn't happening. So, what is there left to say? You made your position abundantly clear.'

'On the contrary, I believe you already decided how I should feel,' he countered, his voice so controlled now that it was almost more dangerous than the emotion he'd shown before. 'You decided how I should react. And when I didn't match the picture you'd built in your head, you simply left.'

She met his gaze, refusing to allow herself to be cowed.

'As you said, you were clear that a baby was unequivocally unacceptable to you.'

'You didn't even give enough time to process,' Ivan growled. 'When did you realize you were pregnant? Did you find out today and rush straight to London to tell me? Or have you been thinking about it for a week? A month?'

Ruby faltered, hating that he might have a point. She scowled at him but when it became clear that she wasn't going to get away without offering some kind of response, she lifted a heavy shoulder.

'About that, I suppose,' she agreed, deliberately not clarifying how long.

She might have known Ivan wouldn't allow that.

'Which one, Ruby? A week or a month?'

'Something between the two,' she admitted reluctantly.

'Yet you gave me an hour,' he pointed out harshly. 'Less.'

The indignation juddered to a halt inside her, and then something that felt a lot like a sliver of guilt slid alongside it.

Maybe he had a point but she was still too wound up, too hurt, too angry, to acknowledge it fully. Even so, she jutted out her chin defiantly as if that could stop the quiver inside.

'Your primal reaction was to have nothing to do with either of us, so I left. Would you have preferred me to stay and beg you to want us? To cry when you didn't? That isn't me.'

'I did not say I wanted you to beg or cry.' Ivan clenched his jaw, the veins in his neck pulsing with emotion. 'I said I deserved more than an hour to process such a weighty revelation.'

'And what would it have changed?' She threw her hands up. 'You weren't going to suddenly decide this whole situation was one you wanted.'

'Maybe not.' He reined himself in but his voice was still laced with frustration. The tension seemed to radiate off him in waves. 'But I would have handled it better.'

'You still wouldn't have suddenly, miraculously wanted a baby,' she accused.

Ivan cast her a pointed look.

'Do you expect me to believe this is the situation you would have chosen for yourself? An unplanned pregnancy was what you wanted?'

'This baby is wanted,' she reproached him instantly. 'Perhaps it wasn't planned or expected. But it is already loved and cherished. At least by me—and given how close you know I was with my own mother; you should know that is more than enough.'

And what did it say that Ivan instantly straightened, his expression almost softening for a moment? *Almost.*

'I'm sorry. I remember how close you and your mother were when you were younger.' His voice was oddly gravelly. 'I recall how you missed each other every time she was in hospital and you had to stay with us at Vivian's. And then, that last time when…she never came out.'

A hard lump lodged itself in Ruby's throat, and it took her several swallows to push past it.

'Thank you.'

The silence slid around them again, though Ruby was too lost in bittersweet memories to notice it.

She only knew that losing her beloved mother was why her baby *would* know how loved it was. Already.

Subconsciously, she gently cradled her bump, taking a moment to compose herself before lifting her head to Ivan. And then she was taken completely aback by the expression that had etched itself, without warning, into his uncompromising features.

It might have been unreadable to her, but there was no mistaking the fact that his gaze seemed fixed on the small swell that had previously been covered by her loose-fitting top. Slowly, unsure if she was doing the right thing or not, she let go so that the fabric flowed loosely over her stomach again, concealing it. After a moment, Ivan's gaze lifted back to meet hers—his eyes almost black as though he was veiling his very thoughts from her.

'Have you had your first scan yet?' he demanded at length, in a voice she barely recognized.

Ruby nodded, clutching her bag tighter as she wondered if she should retrieve the scan picture for him to see. She couldn't have explained why she decided against it. Her decision was reinforced by what he said next.

'I want to see for myself,' he announced abruptly. 'Now. There must be a private clinic nearby.'

'In the city.' Ruby pretended her heart wasn't hammering out of her very chest. 'I know the sonographer—she was a former colleague.'

And someone she had trusted with the secret. She hadn't wanted to risk the hospital grapevine before she'd had a chance to tell either her foster mother or her best friend. Though now that Ivan knew, she was finally free to tell them both.

'Good.' Ivan nodded his head, seeming more himself now that he had a goal. 'Then we'll go now. If I have to use every contact I have to get an appointment, then I will.'

And Ruby didn't doubt it though she pretended that it didn't make a difference to her either way.

CHAPTER FOUR

'THE LITTLE TYKE is definitely hiding their face from us.' The sonographer laughed softly with Ruby as she attempted to find another angle. 'Let's try this way.'

Ivan didn't join in. He couldn't. Not when every part of him was so consumed with the tiny life on the screen in front of them. A baby.

His baby.

It shouldn't be possible yet there it was. Despite every vow he'd ever made his entire life, he was going to be a father.

He couldn't mess this up.

Not like his own sorry excuse for a father had done.

But the thought filled him with absolute terror. Dread. Yet something else besides. Ivan shook his head as if that might make it clearer, but it didn't help. He couldn't quite grasp it.

It had been one thing to hear Ruby telling him that she was pregnant, another to spend hours in his car trying to process it as he'd raced up to Little Meadwood, and yet another to see the small swell when Ruby had cradled her bump back at the cottage. But it wasn't until the ultrasound earlier that Ivan thought he'd really started to understand what was happening.

The 4D scan they were doing now was an added bonus, but it was the small scan picture in his pocket that he kept clutching, tighter and tighter, as if every time he did so he could gain a little more clarity. *That* had been the moment when things had started to shift in his head—though he had yet to make sense of them.

This tiny nectarine-sized thing—almost nine centimetres long—had impacted him more than anything else had ever done in his life before. Growing perfectly, just as any parent might hope for. And that heartbeat...

Ivan had thought he might explode at that rapid, deafening sound that had cracked his formerly impenetrable chest. A tattoo that had seemed to slide and creep inside that black hole within him, and fuse with his own heartbeat. Making him feel...strange.

Changed...somehow.

And he feared he would never again be the person he had been only hours before.

No...not exactly feared, *more...something.*

He couldn't even begin to explain, and he was still struggling to understand how such a tiny thing could have upended his perfectly ordered, sanitized world when the appointment was suddenly over and Ruby was thanking the sonographer for fitting them in at the end of her packed evening of scans.

Somehow—he wasn't entirely sure how—Ivan managed to sound half-normal as he added his gratitude to the conversation. And then the woman was gone and his car was plunged into silence as he focused on driving Ruby—and their precious bundle—back to Little Meadwood.

His baby. *Their* baby. It had a placenta now. And it was swallowing amniotic fluid. It was weeing. It was a living being.

What was he even to begin to do with that knowledge?

Ruby spoke of family, but what would he know of that? For the second time today, Ivan found his brain sliding back to Maksim. To wonder what had happened all those years ago. Almost instantly, however, he slammed the brakes back on.

What was to be gained from going down such a road?

It was only when he had parked outside the darkened cottage and Ruby coughed awkwardly that he realized they still hadn't spoken a word.

'Are you coming in?' she managed, her voice throatier than usual. 'Or do you want to head straight back to London?'

He turned his head to look at her and it felt like a century or more before he could actually focus.

'This is our baby, and I will not be an absent father.'

He wasn't sure who he took by surprise more with the admission. But it was Ruby who broke the stunned silence.

'I'm glad you want to be a part of this baby's life. I truly am.' She licked her lips nervously. 'But I cannot leave Little Meadwood. It's my home, and it want it to be my baby's home, too.'

'I see that.' The words were out of Ivan's mouth before he even realized he was going to say them. 'We will have to find the right solution.'

'Yes, the right solution,' Ruby echoed, and despite her attempt at cheeriness he could hear the tightness in her voice. The uncertainty.

Wordlessly, he unbuckled his seat belt and exited the car, moving automatically around to open Ruby's door and help her out. Still, in silence, he followed as she let them into the cottage and then bustled quietly around turning lights on and closing curtains.

Then she turned to face him—back in the compact living room where their conversation had left off only a couple of hours earlier—and he finally began to speak again.

'I have a good practice in London, and financially I can ensure our child wants for nothing. But I cannot give this child love the way that you can. I know nothing of that kind of thing.'

A thousand words—explanations—slammed against his

brain. He ignored them. He had never voiced them to anyone before; it wasn't as though he was going to start now.

The only thing he ought to be focused on right now was that he was going to become a father—the one thing he'd always sworn to himself he would never be. Yet instead of a curse, it suddenly felt like a release.

It made no sense. He was lost, completely out of his depth, after a lifetime of ensuring that his life was *just so*, with nothing in it that could ever disturb the equilibrium. A baby was the very antithesis of that. But instead of loathing every moment of this unplanned revelation, it felt like an opportunity to change something he hadn't even known he would want to change. Like an unexpected freedom from a cage that he hadn't even known he'd been trapped inside.

An invisible cage of his own making—and he'd been oblivious to it.

And it was that particular realization that made Ivan feel unseated and toppled above all else.

Ruby watched the series of complex, unreadable emotions scud over Ivan's perfectly hewn features, wholly captivated despite herself.

The day had ended up so far from anything she had possibly imagined when she'd finally summoned the courage to slip behind the wheel of her car in the early hours of that morning and make that drive down to London—and to Ivan's clinic.

That note in his voice when he'd finally seen the scan and truly seemed to appreciate that she was carrying his baby had made her chest thud so loudly in her chest that she'd been shocked the entire clinic hadn't heard it.

But what did all that mean for her—for their baby—now?

'I'm glad you wanted the scan today,' she began. 'And I'm

glad you want to be a part of its life. But I still cannot move to London with you.'

Though it was an internal fight for her to ignore the part of her that was almost tempted.

'I will not be an absent father, Ruby,' he bit out. 'I will not settle for a part-time role in my child's life.'

'Then move to Little Meadwood,' she blurted out before fully knowing what she was about to say.

He stared at her incredulously.

'Why on earth would I want to do that? What can this place possibly offer?'

'Love,' Ruby answered simply. 'Family. Home.'

'And a draughty old cottage that you've shared with Nell since you were both students? I would have thought that you should welcome finally moving away.'

'Then you would have thought wrong.' Ruby folded her arms over her chest, furious and indignant all at once. 'I already told you that this is my home. I love it here, next door to Vivian, where we grew up. Or have you forgotten?'

'I have not forgotten anything,' Ivan snapped, but Ruby refused to hear the distaste in his tone. 'Vivian was the best thing about this place.'

'Then what could be better for my child than also growing up here?'

'Growing up anywhere but Little Meadwood,' he responded coldly. 'Let me clarify that Vivian was the *only* good thing about this place. This is no place to raise a baby.'

And Ruby's heart jolted right there, in her chest.

'This is *exactly* the place to raise a baby,' she managed through a mouth that suddenly felt full of marbles, or something equally unpalatable. 'For the last time, it's my home.'

'But it is not mine.' He began to move then, slowly but inexorably. 'My home is London, where my clinic is. My career. And where people do not stick their noses into other people's business.'

'Is that what this has all been about, Ivan?' she asked when she could stand the silence no longer. Tentatively. Guardedly. 'Your fear that people might see the scars you still carry from your childhood?'

'You have no idea,' Ivan answered flatly.

'Why wouldn't I? We were both Vivian's foster kids.'

'For very different reasons,' he shot back. 'You don't really know my story.'

'Because you've never talked about it,' she pointed out. 'Not when we were kids. And not in the couple of times we've met since.'

Certainly not that night they'd raced to their former foster mother's hospital bedside, only to end up seeking solace in each other's arms.

'Then it should come as no surprise that I have no intention of discussing the past now.'

But despite the harshly uttered words and the tautness in every line of his body, Ruby was sure she didn't just imagine that flicker of vulnerability in his usually black eyes.

It pulled her up sharply, like a douse of a fire extinguisher on the flames of her perceived injury. She'd known how damaged he had been as a teenager; she should have realized some wounds ran deeper than they first appeared.

As a kid, she had never really seen it. He'd been Ivan. Angry, rebellious, dissentient—the bad boy of so many teenage girls' dreams. But now, as an adult, she was suddenly beginning to see that mutiny for what it had truly been.

A kid who had never really known love. Vivian had only had a couple of years to undo the damage caused by a lifetime with a cruel father, or caught up in a terrifying system.

Why had she let him fool her into thinking that he was beyond that now?

Little wonder that Ivan's instinctive reaction was that the baby would be better off without someone like him as a father. Her heart ached for him despite her earlier anger.

'I'm sorry,' she forced herself to say. 'I know you have your demons.'

Ivan's gaze was like a silent storm, the pained expression clouding his features reaching inside of her and squeezing even harder than before. And then he clenched his jaw and shot her a look so jagged that it practically pinned her to the floor.

'There is nothing to be gained from dwelling on a long-gone past,' he growled. 'I am here to talk about the future. *My* child's future, to be more accurate. I will provide for this child in a way that neither of us ever had.'

'A few hours ago, you didn't even want to be a father.' She held her hands up. 'I got that. But I want to be a mother so—'

'What I want is neither here nor there,' he cut her off. 'I will be a father—I have seen that scan of my child. I will not turn my back on them.'

And his voice resonated with a sense of duty that both reassured and unnerved Ruby. She had always admired his sense of responsibility, even if it often bordered on self-imposed burdens. But right now, she had no wish to hear him talk about her baby as though it was nothing more than a duty.

For a moment, back there, she'd actually thought something had changed. That a part of him might just be starting to open up to wanting this. She silently begged him to give her a sign—any sign—that this would ever be more than just him doing the so-called right thing.

But he didn't.

It was enough to make her chest pull painfully, squeezing her heart tighter than any fist. As if it wanted to make her explode from the inside out. How she longed to turn on her heel, run up to her room, and just cry the frustrations of the day away.

Even though she never cried. And she still owed it to him to hear him out.

'That isn't necessary.' She shook her head back, thrusting away all the emotions that swirled around, threatening to choke her words. 'We didn't plan this baby, and having it is my choice, and my choice alone.'

'That isn't how it works, Ruby,' he ground out.

'Well, it can be how *this* works.'

'No.' His jaw tightened, his tone offering no room for argument. 'It cannot.'

The tension cracked through the air between them, a palpable force that seemed to push at the very walls of the small cottage.

'Ivan...'

'This child will have the family that neither of us ever had,' he continued as if she hadn't spoken. As if he *needed* to get his words out somehow.

A surge of conflicting emotions cascaded through Ruby. His intentions might be coming from a place of responsibility, and even a twisted sense of honour, but she couldn't shake the feeling that this decision was being forced upon him. The weight of expectations—her expectations as much as anybody else's—was pressing down on Ivan.

Her fault.

'Ivan, listen to me.' Ruby ruthlessly steeled herself against showing any sign of vulnerability. 'I appreciate your desire to do right by this child—I do. But forcing yourself into a role you don't want will only lead to resentment and pain for all of us.'

'I rather think it's too late for what you or I want, don't you?' His eyes drilled into her, and she was sure she could see the invisible war he was waging against himself. 'This baby deserves a father who will protect it. And I must be that father.'

'But you don't *want* to be that father,' Ruby repeated, her voice cracking for a moment.

Still waiting.

Still hoping.

Ivan's jaw tightened, yet she was sure she didn't imagine that flicker of something unexpected in his eyes. *Regret?* Surely not—and then it was gone.

'But I will be a father,' he stated flatly. 'And this child will have a family. You will move in with me and we will be a family together. Before the month is out.'

Shock jolted through her. The words hung heavily between them, laden with implications Ruby wasn't sure she could immediately process.

'A month? That's what you're giving me?'

'It's thirty days more than you gave me,' he countered unsympathetically.

Her mind raced.

'I never expected you to uproot your life, though, did I?' she retorted.

He arched one dark eyebrow.

'Did you not? The thought hadn't even crossed your mind when you drove to my clinic this morning to drop your bombshell on me?'

'Of course not,' Ruby cried automatically.

But to her horror, her voice didn't hold the level of indignation she expected. In fact, if she wasn't mistaken, there was a hint of hesitation in it.

Ivan's gaze skewered her to the spot.

'I thought as much,' he noted evenly. Too evenly. 'One month, Ruby. To speak to who you need to speak to. To work your notice. But be warned, if you haven't come to London by then, I *will* come and get you. And you may not like the very public way that I might do it.'

Then he was past her, out the door, and gone. Before the surge of defiance had quite risen within her.

Which might well have been a good thing, given the sliver of doubt that lurked beneath everything, that tiny voice needling her, and asking what she truly *had* wanted, when she'd started out that morning.

What had she wanted to achieve when she'd decided it was finally time single-minded, never-a-foot-wrong Ivan Volkov knew that he was about to become a father?

Perhaps she ought to have been more careful about what she'd wished for.

CHAPTER FIVE

'THIS IS GAVIN, thirty-one. At approximately 22:15 this evening he was travelling on his motorbike at around fifty miles per hour when a car pulled out in front of him. He swerved to avoid it and ended up going into a telegraph pole. Accident was witnessed by a car travelling the other direction who stopped to call the ambulance and police.'

'Right,' the consultant running the show nodded to the ambulance crew to continue with the handover whilst Ruby was already getting to work doing their own preliminary observations and hooking their patient up to the hospital's monitors and drips.

She usually loved her job as a senior charge nurse in the Accident and Emergency Department of City Hospital, but the past couple of weeks—ever since Ivan had left her cottage with his ultimatum—had been more fraught than usual.

She still hadn't made her decision on what she was going to tell him—*if* he even showed up again—just as she hadn't managed to bring herself to tell either Vivian or Nell her news. What if she took Ivan at his word, and acted accordingly, only for him to decide that he preferred to stay away? To pretend that night had never happened?

On the other hand, if he had been serious about giving her only one month, then her time was running out. Fast. Already half of it was gone, and she was still paralysed with indecision.

It certainly didn't help that there was a traitorous part of her that actually *wanted* to do exactly as he'd suggested. Give up Little Meadwood and play house with the man who was father to her unborn baby.

As if playing at the fantasy of togetherness could ever really match the reality of a happy, loving family unit. She was a fool to think the two were the same thing. At least in the meantime she had her patients to focus on.

Lowering her head and throwing herself into her tasks, Ruby hurried around the department, almost thankful for the distraction. By the time the ambulance crew had completed the list of top-to-toe injuries, and treatment provided, her head was back in the game and the consultant was turning to her for her initial survey.

'Airway's clear,' Ruby confirmed. 'Trachea central, and ultrasound confirms some free fluid in the abdomen.'

She stepped back to offer a clear view of the monitor as one of her colleagues continued with blood pressure and heart rate, whilst two more colleagues confirmed the visible top-to-toe injuries—the most obvious of which was the wide, deep gash on his face which had been lucky to miss his eye by a scant millimetre. Clearly it was going to need significant surgery, but it was the least of the man's injuries at this moment.

'Okay, so we really need to get him up to CT as soon as possible,' the consultant confirmed with a nod. 'See what's going on inside his abdomen.'

Working quickly and efficiently, the team set out about their individual tasks to get their patient ready to move. They were a slick, well-oiled machine that had multiple moving parts all working as one. And, within good time, they were in the CT department with their patient in the scanner.

'Several facial injuries,' the consultant noted. 'Some spinal fractures, too.'

'I'll alert the plastics and neurosurgical teams,' Ruby confirmed.

'Please. Otherwise the volume of fluid in the abdomen isn't as much as I had feared. Possibly he has stopped bleeding, but we'll need to keep an eye on it. I'm concerned he took most of the impact of the collision to his face.'

'Understood.' Ruby nodded. 'I'll accompany the patient back to A&E and get that dealt with.'

For the next hour or so, Ruby worked between this patient and another patient who had been admitted with a punctured lung and broken leg following a fall from a second-floor balcony. Then Gavin's parents arrived, panicking when their son couldn't answer their questions.

'It isn't unusual,' Ruby reassured with a gentle smile. 'Gavin has been in quite a bit of pain, which we're managing. But it does mean he won't have taken in all the information at this point.'

'Okay.' The father nodded jerkily, one hand enveloping his son's hand, the other tightly gripping his wife's hand. 'So can you tell us anything?'

'Of course.' Placing her tablet down so that the parents felt comforted that they had her full attention, Ruby offered another reassuring smile. 'So the results of Gavin's CT were sent to our colleagues, and the neurosurgeon wants to take a conservative approach with regards to his spinal fractures.'

'What does that mean?' the father asked immediately.

'It means that there is nothing immediate that they want to do. Once the swelling goes down it will be easier to determine if your son's injuries will heal on their own, or if an intervention from us will be necessary. Does that make sense?'

'So it isn't serious?' the mother asked hopefully.

Ruby lifted her hand.

'It's more that we can't be sure at this stage. We don't want to go jumping in there if intervention isn't needed, but at the same time we need to keep monitoring Gavin in case surgery becomes necessary.'

'Okay,' the father confirmed as his wife offered a jerky nod.

'Gavin?' Ruby smiled encouragingly at her patient.

'Okay,' Gavin managed, the pained expression in his eyes almost gone now that the morphine was controlling much of the pain.

If it hadn't been for the degloving, he might have even looked peaceful. Inspecting the ugly wound, Ruby smiled encouragingly at him and carefully replaced the bandage.

'For now, we are more concerned with the impact to your face, Gavin. Our plastic surgeons have already had a look at the scans so we're just waiting for them to send someone down.'

'They are going to deal with it here?' his mother asked.

Ruby shook her head.

'They'll take Gavin upstairs to run their own checks,' she assured him. 'Then, when they are happy he's ready, they'll take him into theatre.'

'Oh. Right.'

'You're doing well.' She smiled at him.

But before she could say more, one of her colleagues popped her head around the cubicle to confirm the plastic surgeon had arrived.

'Great,' Ruby affirmed, moving back from the bedside to give them room.

Her colleague lifted one shoulder uncertainly.

'Actually, they wanted a word first.'

'Oh?' Surprised, she nonetheless turned to offer her patient yet another reassuring smile. 'Be back in a moment.'

Then, her mind racing—had she done something wrong?—
she ducked out of the curtain.

And straight into Ivan.

An unexpected jolt ran through her entire body, her hand
reaching out instinctively to steady herself against his chest,
which did the opposite of helping matters. Solid, familiar—
the heat from his body seeped through his scrubs and into her
skin. Into her very veins, it seemed.

Startled, she snatched her hand back again.

'Ivan? What are you even doing here?'

The moment of silence which enveloped her felt like a lifetime until, finally, he spoke.

'I understand that you have a patient for me.'

Her breath caught in her throat as she realized too many
people were around—too many interested ears—for him to
answer the question she was really asking.

But it didn't make her heart hammer any slower. Dimly—
shamefully dimly—she began to put two and two together.

'Wait, *you're* the plastic surgeon I'm waiting for?'

How could that even be?

He inclined his head but didn't answer. And interested ears
or not, she couldn't help herself from blurting more out.

'But…your clinic is London.' She wished she could have
made it sound less like an accusation.

'I might have been a little…heavy-handed the last time
we spoke.' He inclined his head, his voice as low as hers was
hushed as he ground out the apology that she doubted he
wanted to make. 'So I decided to take a temporary post here
to give us a chance to discuss our options properly.'

Ruby wasn't certain she'd heard clearly.

'You can't really mean you're working at City now.' She
was struggling to wrap her head around it. 'What about
your clinic?'

'My partners have taken on most of my clients in the short term, and the board here has agreed that I can head back to London when necessary to see my remaining few patients.'

She shouldn't be surprised. They'd no doubt bent over backwards to accommodate anything Ivan had wanted, just for the chance to have him at City. Even on a temporary basis.

Even so, if felt surreal. Was this really about trying to make compromises? Or was he just flexing his career muscles and taking control?

'How temporary?' she heard herself asking, as if that was one of the real questions jostling around her brain in that moment.

'That's down to me,' he confirmed with a nonchalance that only served to get her back up all the more. At least, that's what she told herself was rolling through her at that moment.

'And?' she snapped, not sure why she felt quite so edgy.

Perhaps it was because of this skittering thing that was now darting around inside her chest. Something she couldn't quite place, let alone name.

'I haven't decided yet.' Ivan flashed a smile. 'They were only too keen to accept my offer of working here.'

'Of course they were.'

They would have been fools not to. Ivan Volkov was a talented surgeon with a rapidly growing reputation in his field. It would have been quite a coup for City, even for a month or so.

Or longer?

'Why are you going to all this effort, Ivan?' she demanded after a moment.

Ivan shook his head. 'That's a conversation for later. Right now, I believe you have a patient for me to see.'

Surprise and annoyance surged through her. She never, *never* forgot a patient, but this damned man had quite the way of getting under her skin. *Effortlessly*, on his part. It was more than a little galling.

Not that she was about to let him know it.

'Yes, of course.' She pasted a cheerful smile of her own to her lips as she turned back to lead him into the cubicle. 'So, this is Gavin. Gavin was involved in a motorbike accident resulting in a facial impact and some spinal fracturing. The neurosurgical team are also monitoring the situation, but it seems his face took the brunt of the accident.'

'Hi, Gavin, I'm Ivan, a plastic surgeon.' Ivan approached the bed with his usual calm, confident demeanour, which Ruby could see instantly set the other man at ease. 'I hear you've been having an altercation with a telegraph pole. Do you mind if I have a look at your facial injuries?'

'Of course not, Doc,' Gavin replied, his voice slightly muffled due to the bandage.

'Great.'

As Ivan began his assessment, Ruby found herself stopping and watching. He moved skilfully, checking the area around the injury as much as the injury itself, all the while talking to his patient calmly.

Would he be so quietly unperturbed with their baby? Bringing it to her at 2:00 a.m. for night feeds? Changing its nappy at three in the morning? Inexplicably, she imagined so.

And then she berated herself for letting her mind wander to that. It felt oddly intimate. Inappropriate.

Shoving the thoughts away, Ruby galvanized her legs back into motion and stepped forward.

Never mind that she felt like she was spiralling downward, caught up in a potent combination of anticipation and apprehension. Dragging her eyes away, she gritted her teeth and forced herself to concentrate on her remaining tasks. Their patient deserved her complete focus, and that was what she would give him.

And Ivan Volkov be damned.

Ruby's heart pounded against her chest as she rounded the corner to her little cottage in Meadwood, her nurse's uniform slightly crumpled after her long shift.

As if that was what had unsettled her the most.

Practically on cue, the sight that greeted her was unexpected and perturbing: Ivan Volkov.

Again.

This time he was leaning against his sleek sports car, looking completely out of place amid the quaint homes with their blooming gardens.

'Twice in one day,' she managed cheerfully. 'Am I supposed to be flattered?'

'You asked me why I was going to such effort.'

'And you told me that was a conversation for later,' she replied, before darting a look around at the surrounding cottages. 'But you know the neighbours are probably already twitching their curtains, watching us together.'

'I do,' Ivan drawled. 'However, I had assumed you would prefer this conversation to be away from the usual hospital grapevine.'

'Well…yes,' Ruby agreed grudgingly. 'Even so…'

'As for the neighbours,' he continued, anticipating her objection, 'am I to assume no one saw me visit your cottage the other week? Or perhaps they simply assumed I was here for Vivian as I was four months ago, and you're just finding excuses to try to keep me away?'

Ruby bit her lip. He was right. Gallingly. No one had actually seen him the previous occasion, which had to be something of a miracle for a tight-knit community like Little Meadwood.

Though she suspected his mention of four months earlier—the time when they had been intimate—was deliberate, to knock her off guard. Well, she refused to allow him to.

'Must you have an answer for everything?' she asked. Tartly.

'Would you prefer me to flounder and flail like a dying fish in the Meadbrook?'

Despite herself, Ruby let out a snort of laughter. Not only because the idea of Ivan floundering in anything seemed quite preposterous, but also because it snagged up a long-forgotten memory of one of Little Meadwood's most skilled fishermen taking Vivian's raggle-taggle group of foster kids on a much-needed day out to the river.

And even though Ruby was fairly sure all of them had railed against going, each and every last one of them had ended up enjoying it. Her, Nell, Ivan, and some other kid whose name she couldn't quite remember now. The calm and quiet of their surroundings, learning to cast a line, and to reel it in, and then that sense of accomplishment when they had cooked their own catches and eaten them with the bread Vivian had taught them to bake the previous day.

'I'd forgotten about those weekends,' she admitted with a soft smile. 'I think it was the first time I'd eaten something of my own that hadn't come out of a microwave.'

'It was the first time I realized what it must be like to have a father who cared,' Ivan admitted gruffly.

For several moments they just stood there, watching each other. And remembering.

'Evening, Ruby.' The bright voice of Vivian's neighbour on the other side dragged them back to the present. 'Oh, Ivan... back to see Vivian again? She must be thrilled.'

'Thrilled,' Ruby echoed instantly, plastering a wide smile as she swung around.

'I think she might be asleep, though, love.' The neighbour frowned. 'She was in the garden all afternoon, trying to weed the back flower bed. I think she might have overdone it a bit.'

Ruby groaned through the wave of affection that flowed through her.

'Of course she did.' She shook her head. 'She can't take it easy, can she?'

'Never could,' the neighbour laughed, moving towards her own door. 'You might want to leave it a little longer before you go and disturb her.'

Beside her, she could feel Ivan tense and she knew him well enough to know that he was disliking every second of talking about his foster mother with a woman he barely remembered.

And wasn't that the difference between the two of them? To her, the suggestion was just long-term neighbours looking out for each other. People who cared about each other.

Ruby smiled. This was exactly why she wanted to stay in Little Meadwood. She couldn't imagine the same thing happening in London. In any case, it never had when she had been living there with her own mother. No one had cared when they hadn't seen Annabel or Ruby for days. It was only when her mother had needed to be transferred to a specialist centre for different treatment—a place about an hour from Little Meadwood—that Ruby had realized what it was like to have a community that looked out for a person.

It frustrated her that Ivan didn't see things the same way.

'Will do.' She nodded, flashing the older woman another smile. 'Then I'll tell her off for overdoing it.'

The neighbour laughed. 'For all the good it will do. Anyway, evening love.'

Then she was gone, leaving Ruby no choice but to invite Ivan back into her own cottage. The last place she wanted him to be.

And never mind that voice in her head taunting her otherwise.

So Ruby stepped into her home with the man who had haunted her dreams for longer than she could remember. And who would now, thanks to the unborn baby that they shared, forever haunt her future.

'Are you really going to give up your practice for City Hosptial?' Ruby began the moment the door was closed behind them.

Ivan didn't reply; he simply strode up the corridor to the tiny kitchen and began to put the kettle on, leaving Ruby with no choice but to follow.

'Are you going to answer?' she demanded after a while.

'Tea?'

'Coffee,' she corrected haughtily. 'As usual. Or are you suggesting I must have tea now that I'm pregnant?'

'I'm suggesting that you've run out of coffee,' Ivan replied dryly as he lifted up the empty coffee jar for her to inspect.

'Right,' she grumbled, hating that she felt wrong-footed.

'So, tea then?'

It had never been so difficult to utter a single syllable.

'Thanks.'

She waited as he set the mugs out and dropped a teabag neatly into each one.

'I appreciate that our conversations the other week went badly—'

'You could say that,' Ruby interrupted, apparently unable to stop herself.

'But this is going to be a lot easier if we could move past that,' Ivan continued smoothly.

If it hadn't been for the tic in his jaw, she might have actually believed his casual air.

Still, sniping wasn't going to help the situation. Drawing

in a steadying breath, Ruby resolved not to let her nerves get the better of her.

It was hard enough trying to rein in her inconvenient attraction to the man who happened to be the father of her unborn child. Not that she had any intention of letting Ivan know that she was still pining after him like the schoolgirl she'd once been.

'Apologies,' she managed. 'Go ahead.'

Despite eying her suspiciously, he duly continued. 'I've managed to agree to a short-term lease on a house in a village between City Hospital and Little Meadwood.'

And Ruby told herself that her heart didn't just stutter and race.

'How? They're like gold dust.'

Rarer, actually.

'Call it a well-placed agent, and good timing,' was all Ivan offered. 'It makes your commute to work a little shorter, whilst still being within a twenty-minute drive of here. Of Vivian.'

'Wait,' she said and shook her hair out down her back if only to cover for the thrill that darted inconveniently down her spine. 'You expect me to live there with you?'

Ivan's mouth pulled into a tight, straight line.

'Do I need to remind you that you are carrying my baby?'

'Is that so?' Her eyes widened in feigned surprise. Because it was either that or explode with the potent mix of emotions swirling inside her. 'I'm so glad you reminded me. I'd quite forgotten.'

'The amateur dramatics are beneath you,' Ivan replied dryly.

It was all she could do not to flush with embarrassment. She knew he was right, and she couldn't keep avoiding the conversation, but it was so difficult to begin when nothing she thought would stay in place instead of sliding around in her brain.

'Fine,' she conceded at length. 'But you don't need to remind me that I'm pregnant. Or that you are the father. I just don't understand, given your initial reaction, why you insist on this charade.'

'There is no charade, Ruby.' Ivan frowned, setting down the mugs to look straight at her. 'I apologized for my initial reaction but I see nothing to be gained in continuing to do so. For now, I am trying to move forward.'

'You're trying to do the *right* thing by moving us in together. But this is the twenty-first century, not the nineteenth.'

'Why do you insist on fighting me?' Ivan clenched his jaw, and shame rushed through Ruby.

It wasn't Ivan's fault that she seemed incapable of acting rationally around the man—turning back into a foolish, mooning teenager every time he was in the mere vicinity. It was hardly as though he was just going to suddenly kiss her again out of nowhere—not that any bit of her brain imagined that he might, of course—so perhaps if she started acting like the usually responsible adult that she was, then she might finally start to feel like it again.

'You're right.' She lifted her hands in placation. 'I'm sorry.'

He cast her a vaguely suspicious look but, to his credit, apparently decided to take her apology at face value.

'Good, then you will move in tonight.'

'I said I was sorry for fighting you on everything. Not that I would stop fighting you on things that are wrong.' She wrinkled her nose. 'I just don't think that moving in together is a good idea.'

'Despite the fact that you are carrying my baby?' Ivan gritted out. 'We are going around in circles.'

'Because you keep insisting on *doing the right thing*,' Ruby exclaimed, trying to pretend she didn't feel hurt or disappointed by his entirely-too-principled approach. 'But neither you nor I had perfect childhoods. We both know that fathers who don't want to be fathers are better to stay away.'

'For the last time, I will not be an absent father.' He narrowed his eyes at her and she wished—oh how she wished—that she didn't feel so piqued yet so compelled to answer.

'Yes, but moving in with someone should be about wanting to be with *them*. Not about doing the *right thing* for a baby who won't care where its parents live, so long as it is loved. Unconditionally.'

And she hated the heat that flooded her cheeks when Ivan turned his incredulous stare on her.

'I am trying to do the right thing, whilst you are talking about attraction? Lust?'

Heat suffused her cheeks at his tone, but at least he seemed shocked, as though he hadn't considered it before. As though her inability to get over her inconvenient attraction to him fortunately hadn't crossed his mind. Even now.

'Don't flatter yourself,' Ruby retorted, hoping to goodness that her face wasn't as scarlet as it felt. 'It isn't as though I'm dreaming of romantic fairy tales. I just…'

Ivan's eyebrows shot up, his gaze pinning her to the spot right through her weak facade. And that look in them suddenly caused her to turn molten. Right when she least wanted to do so.

'You think I don't feel the same attraction? The same pull?'

If she'd suddenly leaped out of her own skin, Ruby wouldn't have been surprised.

'There's no need to mock me,' she managed. Rather too breathlessly.

But it was only when he blinked that it occurred to her that Ivan hadn't even realized he'd made such an admission.

But did that make it better or worse?

'I should never have said that,' he bit out, abruptly taking a step back as if that could somehow erase the moment.

It didn't. It only intensified it. And now the cottage felt as though it was pulsing with unspoken words.

Ignored desires.

'Let's try to be logical,' Ruby managed desperately. 'We can co-parent without sharing a roof.'

'You're peeved,' he replied simply, as though he was actually...teasing her?

Flustered, she instead resorted to glowering at him in defiance.

'I'm not peeved. I am merely stating facts.'

And if her tone was laced with frustration and something else that she didn't even dare to name, then at least she was the only one who knew it.

Right?

Except that Ivan was studying her with an expression that might have been agonizingly inscrutable, but was also making the finest hairs on her body dance with a kind of excitement. She could feel something dangerously close to desire prickling at her fingertips. In her toes.

'I have no desire whatsoever to live with you, Ivan.' She uttered the words before she could stop herself.

Then despaired of herself at the way her body kicked at the wolfish gleam in his eyes. The one that she had thrillingly put there.

'Would you care to put that to the test?' he rasped.

And she knew that voice. It was the one that had started things off between them almost four months ago.

She should tell him no. She should stop this.

'Would you?' she countered instead. Far too huskily.

When had he rounded the countertop to stand in front of

her? So close to her? She could practically feel the heat from his body.

'What are you doing?' she managed, lifting her hands to push him away.

But she was appalled to see herself rest them instead on his chest. Almost tenderly.

'I believe you know exactly what I'm doing,' he muttered, lowering his head towards hers before stopping. 'But all you have to do is say no.'

'This is a terrible idea,' she argued, but her voice lacked any kind of conviction.

Worse, her fingers appeared to be trying to curl themselves around the lapels of his jacket.

'Dreadful,' he agreed, lowering his head further until his face was within an inch of hers. His hot breath tickled her skin deliciously, as though he couldn't help himself any more than she could. 'But the word is *no.*'

And she opened her mouth to say it; she really did. But as his lips hovered so temptingly close to hers—keeping them so close, yet just out of reach—she found herself reaching up onto tiptoe to close the gap herself.

The kiss exploded straight through her. Intense, electric, and white-hot. A kiss that seemed to crackle with the intensity of a hundred thousand unspoken desires. As though the weekend that they had shared had started something hotter and brighter than Ruby had even imagined, and it had been smouldering away ever since—just waiting for this moment to reignite it. And now it felt wild, and out of control, and Ruby never, *never* wanted it to stop.

It hummed in her body and roared in her ears. It seemed to fill up every possible inch of her, yet still leave her thirsty for more. She'd been reimagining this for the past four months yet somehow her memories didn't seem to have done it justice.

Not remotely. Not even that most heady sensation of Ivan's lips moving over hers, his wicked tongue invading her mouth in a way that sent shock waves through her core. To right *there*— between her legs.

And when he slid his hands to her waist and pulled her closer, tighter, her softness seemed to melt perfectly against his hardness, like they had their night together. Like they were meant to be.

Except they weren't meant to be, were they? That had been the most intense, erotic night she'd ever known in her life— but it had also been highly out of character. Of all the times for the rule-abiding Ruby to go crazy, surely getting pregnant with Ivan's baby had to be the most insane.

Somehow—she would never know how—she managed to pull herself back from the precipice and level a direct stare at Ivan.

'I don't know what we've just proved,' she made herself say, all the while telling herself that this wasn't as big a deal as it might seem.

At least Ivan blinked for a moment, looking stunned before he answered.

'We proved nothing,' he rasped. 'Aside from the fact that keeping things practical between us would be a better option.'

And then he moved back around the desk counter and put as much space between them as he could. If only she knew what he was really thinking.

All the same, Ruby feigned a cheerful smile.

'Practical, yes,' Ruby agreed, fighting with all she had to keep from lifting her fingers to her still-tingling lips.

Because she couldn't let Ivan know just how deeply he affected her. *Still.*

No, she couldn't let him know that at all.

CHAPTER SIX

'IS PLASTICS HERE YET?'

Ruby's stomach growled as she hurried through the busy A&E department and to the central station.

Probably not the best idea to skip meals when she was pregnant, but the department had been slammed all shift.

'Not yet,' her colleague answered and shook her head. 'But they said they were on their way.'

'One can only hope,' Ruby muttered, half to herself.

Her patient needed attention as soon as possible but it appeared that the entire hospital was swarming with cases tonight. It had been a particularly nonstop, challenging shift in her department alone, and she was so tired that she was uncharacteristically looking forward to getting through the next hour and to the end of her shift.

Yet in some ways Ruby had welcomed the unrelenting nature of the day. At least it had kept her mind from spinning over her previous encounter with Ivan, almost a week ago now.

And, of course, that kiss.

If she closed her eyes, she knew she would still feel his warm breath on her lips, sending such sinful ripples cascading through her body. Making her feel alive in that way of his which always seemed to go beyond anything she had ever felt before. With anyone.

Which only made it all the more imperative that she create more distance between the two of them.

As if it was that easy, she snorted to herself. He had this infernal ability to make her lose her head every time he was around. She seemed to go from competent nurse, friend, foster daughter, to silly schoolgirl in a matter of seconds whenever Ivan made an appearance.

At least she wasn't the charge nurse for the day, so hopefully, by keeping her head down, she could avoid bumping into the man until she had regained a little of her self-control. And dignity.

The last time she'd seen him he'd been in a neighbouring cubicle with a patient requiring immediate surgery, so with any luck she would be out of here before he returned for another patient.

'How's the young girl in bed six?' She peered over her colleague's shoulder at another of her patients. 'I could nip in and see her whilst I wait for Plastics.'

'Urology finally came down about five minutes ago and took her.'

'Oh, that's good.' Ruby nodded. 'What about bed three?'

'Yeah, you could look in there if you have a moment. Ah, too late, here's Plastics now.'

And Ruby didn't need to turn to know that it was Ivan coming through the door. She could sense it; every nerve ending in her body seemed to be firing up in response to his mere presence.

How pitiful was that?

Yet somehow—she couldn't have said how—she managed to paste a bright, professional smile on her lips as she made herself turn around.

'I thought you were in surgery already?'

'I swapped with a colleague.'

'Why?' She hadn't meant to ask, but the question had just popped out.

'They hadn't worked on that kind of injury for a while so particularly wanted the case.'

It was a reasonable explanation yet Ruby couldn't help wondering if she'd imagined that fraction of hesitation before he'd answered. Still there wasn't a lot she could say.

'Right.' She cranked up her smile. 'So then are you here for my patient?'

'A serious dog bite?'

If he was as thrown as her, then he didn't show it. If anything, Ivan looked as though she could have been any one of her colleagues.

Which should please her far more than it actually seemed to be doing.

'Yes,' she said and nodded jerkily. 'This way. Patient is Dennis…' She stopped abruptly as she realized he wasn't walking with her. 'Ivan?'

'When did you last eat?'

Turning quickly, she hurried back to him.

'A while ago,' she admitted, hesitancy morphing to surprise when he lifted a sandwich, a bottle of energy drink, and a banana from out of a bag she hadn't noticed before. 'You got them for me?'

'It's unwise to skip meals when you're pregnant.' He frowned. 'It can cause increased risk of gestational diabetes, low birth weight, fetal growth restriction…'

'Decreased cognitive and physical function in the fetus, I know.' She nodded, pulling a face. 'I've tried to get away multiple times but the place is hectic today.'

'You're pregnant,' he countered flatly. 'They need to ensure your medical well-being.'

'But they don't know I'm pregnant yet. I still haven't had

a chance to tell Vivian or Nell and I didn't want them to find out from anyone else.' She stopped guiltily.

It might be more accurate to say that with all the uncertainty with Ivan, she hadn't wanted to say anything until it was all decided. But she didn't want to sound as though she was blaming him.

'You have to tell them,' he insisted, though not unkindly. 'In fact, given the circumstances, we should tell them together.'

She wanted to tell him no, that she would do it herself. But actually, it would be nice to have him there—he was the father, after all. And at least they all knew each other.

Would that make it better, or worse?

'Okay,' she agreed and nodded slowly. 'That might be a good idea.'

Ivan dipped his head in concession.

'I was planning on visiting Vivian tonight, so we can do it then.'

'Great.' She pasted a smile on her face, trying to look enthusiastic.

What if they weren't excited for her, given the circumstances? They were her family, the people she loved the most. She couldn't bear for them to ask her if she was going to keep it. Her hand dropped instinctively to cradle her small bump.

Well, she'd have to deal with it if it happened. Feigning confidence, she lifted her head to Ivan.

'Now, let me take you to the patient.'

'Not until you've eaten something.' He was unmoved. 'At least the banana. And you must eat the rest the moment you've handed the patient over.'

'Fine.' Ruby picked up the banana hungrily and began peeling it as she spoke, actually grateful to be able to set her own personal concerns to the back of her mind for the moment. 'So, Dennis is a forty-seven-year-old father, playing football in the park after school with his son when he was attacked by a dog. Lacerations to the glabella of the nose, the left cheek, and down to the carotid.'

'Facial nerve?'

'He can still smile, so we believe it has avoided laceration.'

'Okay. You finish eating that whilst I go and introduce myself.'

Before she could reply, Ivan dipped his head once just as he rounded the curtain, and she heard him chatting on the other side of the fabric.

'Evening, Dennis. I'm Ivan, one of the plastic surgeons here. How are you feeling?'

Ruby bit a grateful mouthful of food, her belly grumbling at the extra wait.

'Better now that you're here, Doc,' the father tried to joke.

'That's always good to hear.' She could actually hear Ivan's cheerful smile. 'And you're smiling, which I like to see. Mind if I just inspect the wounds a little closer?'

Another mouthful of the much-needed fruit, and she could imagine Ivan slipping on a fresh set of gloves and selecting his equipment from the tray that she had set up. By the time she had finished the banana and taken a drink before ducking into the cubicle, Ivan had already begun carefully lifting the flaps of damaged skin across the patient's face, working methodically from right to left. Despite everything, Ruby found herself mesmerized by his characteristic skill and focus.

'Can I just ask you to raise your left eyebrow for me?' Ivan asked after a minute.

Ruby watched as the man moved his face, but the eyebrow didn't really lift.

'And again,' Ivan encouraged, keeping his expression neutral when again nothing changed. 'And the right one again? Okay, that's good.'

Wordlessly Ruby prepared to update the patient's notes.

'Zygomatic nerve appears fine. However, frontalis branch on the left-hand side appears to have some contusion,' Ivan stated evenly. 'So, we'll look at that once in surgery.'

'Will you take him now?'

'Yes, the sooner I start, the better the healing should be.'

Calling in a couple of colleagues and working together, it wasn't long before their patient was ready to be wheeled out to the operating rooms, with her colleagues moving first, leaving her and Ivan momentarily in the patient bay together.

And Ruby couldn't explain why her heart was pounding so loudly in her chest like some distant drumbeat. She'd been half expecting it when Ivan stopped and turned back to her, leaving her helpless to deny the flutter in her stomach.

'And after we've got the conversation out of the way with the others tonight,' he gritted out unexpectedly, 'we should start again. You and I.'

Opening her mouth to answer, Ruby was horrified to realize she'd somehow been robbed of the ability to speak. She bobbed her head instead.

'A chance to *reset*, if you will,' Ivan continued.

'That would be…welcome.'

'Good. Then when are you off duty next?'

Her mind raced with conflicting thoughts but she finally managed to find her voice. 'Once I finish this shift, I have a couple of days off.'

'Ah, I have to return to see a private patient the day after tomorrow.' It was nice that he actually looked disappointed, before appearing to have a thought. 'How do you fancy a trip to London?'

London? Her stomach flipped over and she automatically opened her mouth to say no, but something stopped her. 'With you?'

'Like I said, I have to see a patient the day after tomorrow. But I think getting out of this place might help to press the reset button.'

The noise in Ruby's head cranked up, but she had to admit that it made sense.

'So...we would stay overnight?'

Together?

'My apartment in London is two-bedroomed,' he answered simply. As though reading her thoughts.

Lord, she hoped that wasn't true.

Particularly when heat pooled between her legs at the mere discussion of bedrooms.

She pretended not to notice. This was Ivan, the father of her unborn baby, not some... Well, whatever. Her brain floundered for a moment, searching for the neatest way out of the situation. But none came.

In fact, all she could hear was the little voice in her head whispering that maybe getting away from anyone she knew wouldn't be a bad idea. To maybe help clear her head. Especially if she was going to finally tell Vivian and Nell tonight.

She loved them both dearly, but they would each have their opinions on what she should do for the best—with the baby, and with Ivan—and Ruby wanted the space to make her own decisions, uninfluenced by anyone else.

And also, how could she expect Ivan to consider returning to Little Meadwood if she refused to even consider a short overnight trip back to London?

Hastily, Ruby summoned as cheery a smile as she could manage.

'Okay, we said this was a reset, so why not?'

His mouth quirked in a half smile of delight.

'Good. I'll finalize the timings tonight, when I've had the chance to make a few calls.' He tapped his screen with his pen. 'Now, before we see this patient, you need to eat your sandwich.'

She glanced at the forgotten item.

'Of course.'

But Ivan was right; she had to take care of herself. For the baby even more than for herself.

'In fact, you eat it now before some other patient comes in, and I'll go and prep for Dennis.'

Ruby watched him walk away before beginning to unwrap the baguette sandwich he had so thoughtfully brought her.

The more she got to know Ivan—the adult Ivan—the more he surprised her, and she found it a thrill to discover these new layers to his personality that she had never seen before.

But did that mean she was ready to spend a night with him in London, even if his apartment *was* two-bedroomed? She wasn't so sure.

But then again, she was hardly calling him back to tell him she'd changed her mind, was she? So what did *that* tell her about herself?

In that moment, Ruby couldn't say she cared to analyse it.

It had been an interminably long half hour, with Ivan feeling caught between Ruby and Nell, in Vivian's living room, as they waited for their former foster mother to finally feel ready enough to come downstairs.

How many times had the three of them sat in this tiny room over the years? Hundreds of times? A thousand? Including four months ago. Only it had never been so difficult to try to make small talk.

The ease they normally shared was eluding him tonight, and he knew Nell suspected something was wrong. Neither of them could have missed the fact that Ruby had twisted her sleeve into knots, waiting for their former foster mother to finally wake up and head downstairs.

He didn't need her to say anything to know that Ruby was wondering if they should leave their baby revelation for another night. Part of her would no doubt have liked nothing better, whilst it was obvious to him that another part of her could feel the news bubbling inside her, threatening to spill out any moment to the curious Nell.

He actually thought she was on the verge of blurting it all out when the doorbell rang, interrupting the moment and having Nell launching to her feet like the proverbial scalded cat.

It wasn't lost on Ivan that apprehension had seized Ruby the moment her friend rushed out of the room and down the hall to answer it as she turned slowly to face him.

'I'm not sure this is the right time.'

'I don't think it's ever going to be the *right* time,' he countered. 'But don't you think we owe it to them to tell them before they find out by themselves?'

'I guess so,' Ruby agreed grudgingly. 'But this was about telling Vivian and Nell, not whoever that is, crashing the party.'

Then she stood up and smoothed out her trousers in a trait he was beginning to recognize only too well as she cast an anxious look at the door.

Waiting to see who came through it.

But no one did. If anything, it sounded as though Nell was having an oddly hushed conversation on the doorstep.

'Perhaps we should send out a search party,' Ruby grumbled after another few moments.

Ivan merely offered a half smile. He hated waiting, especially with something like Ruby's pregnancy, which felt as though it was burning a hole in his chest. Vivian had been so good to him over the years that he hated the idea of keeping anything from her.

But he had no idea how she was going to react to the news.

'Perhaps tonight isn't the best timing, after all.' He leaned forward to Ruby. But whatever else he might have been about to say was cut short as Nell could be heard heading back down the hall with the impromptu guest audibly in tow.

'I should introduce Ruby,' Nell announced, stepping through the door. 'And Ivan. Both were also former charges of Vivian.'

Ivan stood up out of habit, then stared in shock at the man who stepped through the door.

A face—albeit slightly older—that was instantly recognizable, even though he hadn't seen it in about twenty years.

The silence rippled around the room. And then, before he could swallow it down, a gruff, incredulous laugh escaped him. Just as the other man did precisely the same.

'Ivan?'

'Connor?'

It was the last person he'd expected to see after all these years. But oddly, it was the one person he would have wanted to see, if he'd ever thought about it.

Connor Mason was the first person he'd ever met in Little Meadwood, besides Vivian. A couple of years older than he had been, and the lifeline he had needed.

As if on autopilot, the two of them stepped towards each other. For a split second, Ivan almost extended his hand in greeting and then, before he realized it, the two of them were embracing each other in a wide bear hug.

It was as if the past two decades had simply fallen away. Just like that. If he'd ever wanted to tell anyone the news about Ruby and the baby, then it would have been Connor.

'How long has it been?' Ivan growled at last, not sure how he even managed to speak.

'Too long.' Connor's voice rumbled with emotion. 'Decades.'

Ivan shook his head, still trying to process as the shocked silence wound its way around the tiny cottage room.

He might have known it would be Nell who broke it. She had always loathed anything she found too tense, no doubt a result of her own experiences of coming into foster care.

'I'd forgotten that you two had known each other.' She offered a slightly shaky laugh. 'But I'd never realized that you'd been so close.'

Without meaning to, Ivan glanced at Connor only to find his old friend staring back at him. And in that moment a whole history seemed to pass between them. But how did he begin to put into words the bond they'd forged? The way they'd had each other's back against the animosity from a handful of born-and-bred Little Meadwooders who had insisted the two of them were nothing more than outsiders?

As stragglers from Vivian's new waifs-and-strays project, how many black eyes, bruised ribs, and fat lips had they endured, sticking up for each other when no one else would? Despite everything, Ivan found himself grinning at an equally amused Connor.

'You could call it that,' Connor finally confirmed to Nell gruffly.

And Ivan wasn't surprised when both she and Ruby chorused their curiosity.

'What does that mean?'

Ivan didn't answer. He would let Connor answer that one, since Connor had always had it worse than Ivan had, possibly because he'd been that little bit…wilder. Probably just because he'd been the first kid the incredible Vivian had taken on full-time.

'It means that if any of the local kids started beating on one of us, then the other would have his back…' Connor offered simply in the end.

'And that was good enough.' Ivan stepped in—his way of assuring his one-time buddy that their old secrets remained just that. *Old secrets*.

Nonetheless, both Ruby and Nell continued to eye them curiously for several more moments until they finally realized nothing more was going to be said.

'Right.' Nell dipped her head at last.

'Okay.' Ruby nodded, as if that was it.

But Ivan couldn't shake the feeling that she was holding on to the unexpected revelation. Or that the conversation would come back around one way or another, once they were alone.

And he wasn't sure how he felt about that.

It was more than a little bit of a relief to hear Vivian making her way downstairs, and Ivan couldn't keep a genuine smile to himself as all four of them leaped up instinctively to help her. It was only the fact that Nell was closest to the door that made the rest of them stand reluctantly back.

He could only imagine what their quiet conversation was that had Vivian chuckling cheerfully through her wheezes as she headed down the hallway, and then into the room.

Her illness was taking more of a toll on her with every passing week, yet Ivan wasn't surprised when their former foster mother defiantly batted away any attempts to get her to sit down, instead taking in every one of them in turn.

And the love that shone from her eyes had Ivan swallowing hard, despite everything.

'Well, if it isn't my favourite foster kids,' she rasped, her delight evident as she stepped forward to hug Ruby, then himself.

'You always say that to all of us,' he rumbled in amusement as he enveloped her in his arms.

And his chest kicked painfully at just how tiny and fragile she felt in his arms.

'Doesn't make it any less true,' Vivian chided with a smile he felt even through his T-shirt. 'Just means I am truly blessed.'

Wordlessly, Ivan released her and guided her to turn slowly to the figure behind the door. He could only imagine how touched she would be to see him again, after all these years. And when she breathed Connor's name, her voice rattling with intense emotion, Ivan felt it in his own heart.

How close had the three of them once been? A makeshift family of two damaged, lost, angry boys and Vivian, the anchor that had kept them all together in the tumultuous sea, helping them to weather the storm.

'Hey, Vivian.' Connor seemed to hesitate only for a moment before enveloping her in his arms. And Ivan wasn't certain which of them was lending support to which.

Either way, it felt like an age before he finally released her again.

'You look good, kid,' Vivian rasped, her voice filled with love that was so familiar that it caught Ivan by surprise.

But then, perhaps it was just the unexpectedness of the situation. Coming here tonight, he simply hadn't been prepared for Connor to appear. It was raking up memories that Ivan had thought long-buried. Memories that he didn't want to have to deal with right now, or perhaps ever.

The homes he'd had before the Vivian-Ivan-Connor years. The places and people he didn't care to think about.

Lost in his own thoughts, Ivan missed the conversation between Connor and their former foster mother, only tuning back in when he realized the other four were all beginning to settle back down in their seats.

What had he missed?

He dropped down quickly into his chair, trying to look…normal. But when he glanced up, Ruby was watching him curiously.

Shrewdly.

'Are you okay?'

Ruby's question was quiet enough, but still he jerked his head around the room to indicate the others.

'Connor and Vivian are intent on catching up.' Ruby shook her head, murmuring quietly. 'And Nell looks a world away. Perhaps tonight isn't the best time after all.'

He hated to agree, but what choice was there?

'Perhaps not,' he managed to grit out, frustration surging through him.

There was a brief beat before she spoke to him again. 'We could try again tomorrow?'

He eyed her sharply. 'Second thoughts about London?'

She had the grace to flush. 'I did wonder if it might be wise.'

'Are you worried about the conversation or staying overnight in my apartment?'

'It isn't that,' she began, before hastily lowering her voice. 'Okay, maybe it's a little of both.'

He could understand that. Curiously, he felt a little strange about the idea of spending the night in his apartment with Ruby. It wasn't that he didn't think he could control himself— he wasn't a neanderthal—so much as he didn't understand why the notion of being so close to her, without actually being with her, should fill him with such...regret.

'I promised separate bedrooms, and I meant it,' he told her with as much enthusiasm as he could fake. 'But let's be fair— what is the worst that could happen anyway? It isn't as though we would be worried about pregnancy.'

And he should be ashamed of himself for the little squeak of shock that slipped from her lips. He hadn't exactly set out to tease her—actually, it wasn't his usual serious style—but he had to confess to a punch of delight when she surreptitiously slapped his arm in silent rebuke, then smothered a giggle.

'So I'll send a car for you tomorrow at nineteen hundred,'

he confirmed quietly when they had both stopped trying not to chortle like naughty schoolkids.

She blinked at him in surprise.

'You'll send a car? I thought you'd be driving.'

He could have, but instead he'd planned something better. And he could pretend it was about practicality and saving time—deep down, he suspected it was more about wanting to impress the woman sitting across from him.

Ivan pushed the notion aside and tried to focus on the mundane.

'Nineteen hundred.'

Again she hesitated, and he fancied he could see how she was torn between what the sensible thing to do might be, and what that traitorous part of her longed for. And then her hazel eyes snagged his and for a moment he was lost—right up until she spoke again.

'Nineteen hundred,' she echoed at length. 'I'll be there.'

But strangely enough, he didn't feel any more orientated.

CHAPTER SEVEN

RUBY WASN'T ENTIRELY certain how she managed to keep walking steadily across the tarmac of the private airport where the chauffeur-driven car had deposited her and towards the sleek helicopter that awaited her.

She clutched her small overnight bag even tighter. It had taken all day to pack the thing, second-guessing, then third-guessing every choice she made when usually clothing decisions weren't something that particularly took up much of her time.

Except when it came to staying the night at Ivan's London apartment, apparently.

Little wonder that her heart was hammering so loudly against her ribcage that she feared it might drown out the rhythmic *thwop-thwop* of rotor blades slicing through the air, whilst the setting sun cast a golden hue over the powerful machine, making its fuselage glint in a way that Ruby couldn't decide was more like a promise or an intimidation.

Either way, she had to keep her eye on the goal. To press that reset button whilst also setting up boundaries for her and Ivan. This was their chance to come up with a solution that was both elegant and efficient.

So why, when Ivan leaped down out of the machine—with a casual confidence that held no trace of that odd tension of the previous evening—did her legs almost stop working altogether?

'This is yours?' she managed in disbelief, shouting over the noise.

'Shared between a couple of clinics.' He shook his head. 'Some of our patients who value their privacy the most prefer us to visit them away from London. Helicopter is the fastest way to reach them.'

'And you get to use it at night. For…well…not a date, but…'

'Not as a rule,' he supplied with a smile. 'But as I mentioned, I'm meeting with a private client tomorrow, so this counts as a work flight. Ever been on one before?'

'Never.' She shook her head, her voice a mixture of excitement and trepidation though she doubted he could hear her.

'You'll be fine,' Ivan shouted again, his smile warm as the corners of his eyes crinkled in a way that made him appear less the daunting surgeon and more the boy from Little Meadwood who she remembered fondly.

Then, helping her into the helicopter and sliding in beside her, he adjusted her seat belt before signalling to the pilot that they were ready.

As the other man began to talk into his headset, Ivan adjusted Ruby's own kit, ensuring she could hear him properly. And then they were lifting off. The cityscape shrank below them, a miniature world retreating into the embrace of twilight. Ruby pressed her forehead against the cool window, her breath fogging the glass momentarily as she watched the sprawling lights of the city give way to the countryside.

She didn't know if this was meant to impress her, intimidate her, or something else entirely, but trying to work it out was just sending her head into a spin along with the deafening noise of the blades. In the end, she decided that the easiest thing to do would be to simply give in to the luxurious element of the evening and enjoy it.

When she did, she realized that, strangely, the loud roar of the helicopter seemed to be just what she needed to get out of her own head—if only for the fifty-minute-or-so flight—and Ruby found herself getting lost in the breathtaking scenery skimming past far below her. The twinkling lights of the city gave way to the deep black of the local reservoir, and the beetle-like cars were left behind by the hillside shadow of their aircraft itself.

There was something incredibly powerful about being up here, so high above her normal life. She couldn't put her finger on it, but it made her feel more in control than she had felt for quite some time. So for the better part of an hour Ruby found herself getting lost inside her own head, captivated by the world below her. Rolling hills, farms, the odd village which might look pretty but surely couldn't be as beautiful as her beloved Little Meadwood, which Ivan loathed so much, until at last the bright lights of London came into view.

Then, oddly, her insides did a little dance at the sight. From up here, it looked nothing like the London she remembered. From this distance, it looked like some hidden, sparkling gem far removed from their demanding lives at City Hospital. Almost magical—so very different from the London that she and her mother had experienced. Yet it wasn't this enchanted vista that Ivan loved about the place but rather the capital's anonymity.

Rather like Ivan himself. This was so...*him*, dropping in on the city by helicopter, enjoying selective elements of the place, but as though he wasn't really a part of it. Just as he did with Little Meadwood.

What was it about Ivan that made him so reluctant to actually call a place *home*?

A touch of sadness flitted through Ruby as she pondered such thoughts, unable to shake off the nagging question. It lingered in her mind even as the helicopter continued its descent towards a rooftop landing pad.

And what did it say about her that she was still drawn to Ivan's enigmatic aura even as he kept her at arm's length? How could they possibly raise a baby together when he wouldn't ever let her in?

By the time the helicopter landed, Ruby's mind felt like a dizzying whirlwind. She tried to focus on unbuckling her seat belt but her mind might as well have still been spiralling somewhere above her head, much like the whirl of rotor blades.

Allowing Ivan to help her down on the ground, she let the cool breeze rake over her skin before letting him lead her to the steps where a well-suited security guard waited for them. As they walked down the steps, Ruby couldn't help but steal glances at Ivan, his profile even more mysterious than usual, in the dimly lit evening.

Had she ever really known this man?

She was beginning to suspect not. Unconsciously, Ruby wrapped her arms around herself. The nervous flutter in her stomach hadn't subsided, but it was no longer due to the helicopter ride, and now it made her shiver.

'Are you cold?' Ivan asked instantly.

Then, before she could respond, his jacket was draped over her shoulders.

'Thank you,' she murmured, not wanting to explain what had really caused the shiver. Besides, the fabric was still warm from his body heat, and the gesture had been so instinctive, almost tender.

Or was that her imagination again?

'Shall we?' He extended his arm, and she slid hers through it, allowing him to lead her inside where the atmosphere enveloped her at once, then she gasped.

'Oh…'

She might have even stopped on the spot, had it not been for Ivan's solid, reassuring hold on her.

He leaned down to murmur softly in her ear, 'I remember you once told Vivian that when you and your mother lived in London, you used to pass this place and wonder what it would be like to eat here.'

Ruby stared at him incredulously.

She just about had a dim recollection of the conversation, though it felt about a thousand years ago. Maybe two. How had Ivan possibly remembered it?

A whole cocktail of emotions sloshed inside her, threatening to spill out if she wasn't careful.

Somehow, she made herself take one step. Then another. And each became mercifully easier, until they had finally reached their quiet, private table and Ivan was politely nudging aside the maître d' to pull out her chair for her himself.

'Thank you,' she managed, sitting down and struggling to take it in.

The place. And the company.

Fortunately, the cocoon of soft music and low, intimate conversations in the air around them helped to create a sense of warmth and privacy, aided further by the soft glow of artificial flickering candles which cast a romantic ambiance over the room.

'When you said we should press the reset button,' she ventured as Ivan settled down in the other seat at the table, 'this isn't exactly what I thought you meant. Have you ever been here before?'

'Do you mean, have I ever brought a date here before?' Ivan asked. 'If so, the answer is no. I just wanted to do something special for you after how badly I've handled things.'

'It wasn't just you.' Ruby pulled an apologetic face.

'You felt protective when you thought I didn't want this

baby. That's nothing to regret. And perhaps you were right when you said that I allow my own past to cloud *my* feelings.'

'I never really knew that much about your past,' Ruby began, sitting forward as she tried to find the right words to ask Ivan about his childhood.

She should have known that he would never allow that.

'Like you said—' he picked up the menu, his tone holding a clear note of finality '—it's all in the past. But this is about the future.'

And Ruby fought to quash the sense of disappointment which poured through her at that. Clearly there were things that Ivan would never share with her, and she had to stop hoping that he would.

The waiter arrived to take their order, interrupting the silence that had settled between them as they perused the menu. Ruby settled on the grilled sea bass with capers, confit potatoes, and tomatoes whilst Ivan chose smoked duck breast with a duck leg ragu.

And then the waiter left them alone again, and as Ruby searched for a way to continue the conversation, Ivan gestured discreetly around the elegant restaurant, at the exquisite artwork adorning the walls, and at the plinths.

'So, is this place everything you expected it to be?'

She cast a thoughtful glance around. 'I don't know,' she answered honestly. 'My mother and I used to concoct our own ideas of what it must be like in here, but as time went by, we allowed our imaginations to run wild. I never dreamed I would ever dine here, so I think I forgot long ago what I *actually* thought it would be like in reality.'

'You didn't promise yourself you would return one day, as an adult, and finally find out?'

Ruby lifted her eyes to the chandeliers overhead that cast such spectacular, shimmering patterns over the room—if only to keep back the tears which had unexpectedly pricked her eyes.

'I once promised my mother I would bring her back to London for one Mother's Day, or birthday but...after she died, I swore I would never return again. Ever. I think that was when Little Meadwood really became my home.'

'And you've never left.'

Ruby couldn't have said why she bristled at his tone. Or rather, she didn't care to.

'You make it sound like I'm scared to,' she said and scowled.

'I never said that.'

'But you implied it.'

Ivan eyed her for a moment. Perhaps too shrewdly.

'Or maybe it's something you feel deep down, but are too afraid to admit.'

There was no reason for her temper to flare at Ivan's words, and yet she could feel it puffing up inside her. And she never lost her temper. Another uncharacteristic effect this man seemed to have on her. His words cut through her as effectively as his surgeon's scalpel, and with every bit as much skill-exposing vulnerabilities she had thought long since healed.

He smiled then, though she could tell it was forced by the taut lines at the corners of his eyes.

'But we're at risk of derailing this evening before it has even started. How are you feeling?'

Back to the baby. Ruby tried to ignore the pang of disappointment at the abrupt shift in the conversation. Once again, Ivan was pushing her away whilst appearing like he wasn't—the way he always did.

All the same, she summoned a smile and tried to look unbothered. There would be nothing to gain from ruining the evening before it had even begun. Perhaps there was a way to get him to talk a little more about himself without the conversation going too personal.

'I feel fine.' She nodded, still trying to work out how to steer the conversation. 'No cravings. Sometimes I feel like I'm getting more tired than usual, but usually it's okay. What about you—how are you finding City? I realize it isn't the same as battlefield injuries but it must be different going back to traumas rather than the cosmetic procedures you've been specializing in these past few years.'

'Actually, I've quite enjoyed it.' Ivan looked thoughtful, taking her cue to discuss himself rather than the pregnancy with surprising ease.

As if he knew what she was doing and was obliging her. Even so, she was gratified when he launched into a couple of amusing anecdotes, and by the time the waiter brought their meals, the evening was mercifully back to an easier footing. She found herself fascinated by the subtle nuances in Ivan's expressions, like the way his eyes lightened when he laughed, or the imperceptible softening of his features when he spoke about his work.

Their conversation continued to ebb and flow throughout the meal, a delicate dance of pleasant conversation punctuated by occasional amusing memories of their time together at Little Meadwood, but nothing too deep.

For almost three hours they talked, ate, and enjoyed each other's company. Then, as the last notes of the piano's latest piece faded into the intimate hush of the restaurant, Ivan leaned back in his chair, his gaze drifting beyond the window, where the distant city lights glimmered like stars grounded to earth.

'This place has been a haven to me for the past couple of decades,' he announced, the soft confession surprising Ruby.

Almost as though the hours of uncomplicated conversation had brought them naturally back around to this.

'London has?' she prompted gently when he didn't continue. 'Why?'

'I don't know.' His fingers played idly with the stem of his glass, the motion betraying a rare moment of self-reflection. 'Perhaps I like the fact that no one really knows me in a place like London. No one looks on me as the kid who everyone abandoned.'

'Not everyone,' she reminded.

He drew in a deep breath. 'No, not everyone. Vivian was always there for me. But...'

'Other people made you feel like you weren't worthy?'

'No.' He frowned, then inclined his head to one side. 'Yes. Probably.'

Ruby reached out and laid her hand lightly on Ivan's. The weight of the words hanging between them was a reminder of the wounds he carried from his past.

'I'm sorry you had to go through that,' she said sincerely.

'Well, I wasn't the only one, was I?' Ivan met her gaze. 'You, Nell, all of Vivian's kids...we all had our battles.'

'No, but some were lonelier than others, I think. At least Nell and I had families who loved us before...they were taken from us. You didn't have that, did you?'

And she didn't miss the flicker of vulnerability that darted across his dark eyes before he shut it down.

'But we survived.' Ivan let the words roll off him, still refusing to let anything penetrate that armour of his. 'That isn't what defines us now.'

'Maybe not, but pretending it didn't happen doesn't mean we have dealt with it.'

She was pushing him, but she couldn't seem to help herself. Surely if they—if she and her baby—were to stand any chance of connecting, really connecting, with Ivan, then he was going to have to confront his past at some point.

Wasn't he?

Ivan fell silent, clearly not wanting to talk any further. His gaze locked on to some point beyond the hushed restaurant, beyond the clinking of cutlery and distant chatter, which seemed to fade into the background as Ruby held her breath hoping that any moment, he might knock down even just one of his walls and finally let her in.

The wiser part of her knew she should let it go. Give him his space. But how could she when it could be the difference between making him a father and making him a good father?

'So how is being back there after all these years?' Ruby began tentatively again.

She wanted to ask if that was why he had ended up with her that weekend he'd visited Vivian. Had she been a distraction for him? It would make sense.

'It's fine, though I never expected to see...' He tailed off, raking his hand through his hair as the casual mask finally slipped.

And though she tried not to, Ruby couldn't help but seize on the chance to exploit it. To maybe understand Ivan just that little bit better.

'Connor?' she supplied, struggling to keep her voice low. 'It must have been odd seeing him turn up like that last night.'

'I guess.'

Clearly Ivan wanted to change the topic but she couldn't let him. She was too desperate to know more. It felt like she kept getting tantalizing glimpses of who Ivan had become, but nothing clear. Certainly not enough to build a fuller picture—and she wanted to so very much.

For the baby's sake, of course, she assured herself quickly.

'Were you close?' she pressed carefully.

Perhaps losing him afterwards was too hard. Had Ivan finally felt like he'd had someone on his side at Little Meadwood, only to lose him when Connor had moved on?

'No.' Ivan shrugged, then relented. 'I guess so.'

'How close?' she pressed. 'Friends? Brothers, even? I know Nell has always been like the sister I never had.'

The expression that scudded across Ivan's face caught her completely off guard. His eyes darkened, like a squall whipping up without warning, and as his jaw tensed Ruby found herself holding her breath waiting for him to speak.

'We *were* like brothers,' he bit out harshly, as if every word was like glass in his mouth. 'But he wasn't the brother I never had.'

'Oh.' She tried to nod with sympathy, but Ivan was still speaking.

'Mainly because I already had a brother.'

CHAPTER EIGHT

IVAN WISHED HE could take the words back even as they left his mouth.

Why had he said that?

He never talked about Maksim. *Never.* It had always cut too deep, and the guilt had been almost crushing. But Ruby was right; Connor's unexpected appearance the night before had caught him off guard. Slicing open a cache of memories that Ivan hadn't been ready to see—especially when he was still reeling from that damned scan.

His fingers clutched the picture that was in his pocket, and had been in his pocket ever since the ultrasound—not that Ruby needed to know it.

He wasn't ignorant to the fact that Ruby's ploy to get him talking about himself—which hadn't fooled him for a second—had ended up working with surprising success.

The evening hadn't gone at all as he'd planned. But then, he'd noticed that every encounter he had with the woman seemed to veer off on a path of its own. Usually everything in his life was carefully arranged, planned out, yet Ruby Channing had an uncanny knack for turning things on their head.

He wanted to say he didn't like it. But even now, when her shock was evident and her hazel eyes were widening as she stared at him before setting her wine glass down, when she gave him her full attention, he found himself helpless to do anything but wait for her to answer.

He tried to take some comfort in the fact that she clearly hadn't known that much about his past, which meant that no one else at Little Meadwood was likely to have known, either.

The way gossip worked in the tiny village, a part of him had always wondered whether, at some point over the years, the truth had come out.

'I didn't know that.'

And he wondered if that changed what she thought about him.

'Does Vivian know?' she asked when he didn't elaborate.

'I have no idea,' he told her honestly. 'I always assumed she did though I never talked about him.'

And when he lifted his head to look at her, the empathy in her expression shook him to his core.

'Then she couldn't have known.' Ruby managed. 'She would never have taken one of you without the other, surely.'

The words hung on Ivan's lips but he couldn't bring himself to say them out loud. Instead, he found himself becoming lost in memories that Ruby wouldn't even begin to fathom. The weight of the world—the entire universe, even—seemed to hang in the air between them. And when he finally began to speak, each syllable was just a little bit too measured. Too loaded with long-suppressed emotion.

'We weren't both in foster care,' he gritted out. 'At least, not in the beginning.'

Yet despite best efforts to keep his tone level, he was certain Ruby could hear that faint ache beneath it, the one that would betray the depth of the wound that ran too close to the surface. The trauma that had festered, untreated over too many years.

But there was nothing he could to about that now. He was the one who had raised the subject of Maksim—he still couldn't have said *why*—so he couldn't realistically shoot down her questions now.

And, right on cue, she reached her hand across the table.

'What happened, Ivan?' she asked softly.

He stared at her long, elegant fingers, wishing he had the strength to lift his own hand and take them. Instead he simply drew in a deep breath, then another.

'I wouldn't even know where to start.'

'Then start with his name,' she suggested with a kindness that almost cracked his chest apart.

'His name was Maksim,' Ivan rasped at last, though it didn't feel like him talking. It felt odd, mechanical, as though his mouth was moving without his consent. And the name lingered in the room like a ghost long forgotten. The spectre that was always crouched there, deep in his chest, finally out in the wild for others to see.

'How old was he?' she encouraged.

'He was three years younger than me.'

And there was nothing to prepare him for the tsunami of pain that crashed over him when he summoned—possibly for the first time in over a decade—the laughing dark eyes of his impish little sibling.

Or worse, the agony and terror that had blackened them when their cruel father had got hold of him.

Ivan clenched his jaw so tightly that he was shocked it didn't shatter right there, at the table. The memories were too sharp, too raw. Even now.

'You were clearly very close, as brothers go,' she offered softly.

A statement rather than a question, though Ivan nodded once, tersely anyway.

'Once upon a time.' He wanted to shut the conversation down, but at the same time he could feel words gathering at the back of his mind, in his throat, as though finally waiting to be released. 'Though he was actually my half-brother. My mother died when I was around two and my father remarried. Maksim was my stepmother's son with my father, and she never let me forget it. Let's just say she was an extremely cruel woman.'

'Oh,' Ruby offered quietly.

Ivan hesitated another moment. 'Home life was the same for both of us, though, but I tried to protect him as well as I could.' He stopped abruptly as guilt sliced through him, sharp and unforgiving, causing him to choke out the final admission. 'Until I betrayed him.'

What wouldn't he have given to be able to say something—anything—other than that? Worse, the expression in Ruby's eyes suggested she didn't even believe him, and Ivan wasn't sure whether that was what tore him up the most.

'But there is nothing else to say,' he declared, shutting the conversation down coldly. 'It is in the past. Done with.'

Except that it wasn't, was it? He'd spent over a decade and a half pretending it was. Thrusting it to the back of his mind.

But then Ruby had told him she was pregnant, and just like that, all those old, unacknowledged feelings of guilt and shame had clawed their way out of the black pit of his soul. As if they had just been waiting for this moment to finally reassert themselves.

All he wanted to do was squash them back down again. He might have known that Ruby wouldn't let it go so easily.

'Tell me more, Ivan,' she pressed. As if she actually cared.

And though his head told him it was a bad idea, Ivan found himself obeying. The words tumbled over each other as he struggled to organize his thoughts into some kind of order.

'I don't know what to tell you... Maksim was smaller than me, and not just because he was three years younger. He was always thinner, weaker, probably because at least I'd had the love of my own mother for the first two years—not that I remembered her. But Maksim's mother was nothing like that. She met my father a couple of months after my mother died, and Maksim was conceived shortly after, though being pregnant is far from being a mother. She forgot to feed me, or wash me—or couldn't be bothered to—and it was no different for Maksim from the moment he was born.'

Ivan stopped; the jumble of thoughts were still tangled up his head. But Ruby didn't rush him. She just sat quietly, watchfully, waiting for him to continue in his own time. And that somehow made it easier.

'Anyway, Maksim's physical deficiencies only seemed to make our father despise him all the more. I tried to protect him from them—taking the beatings so that he didn't have to. And I learned to steal food from wherever I could. Shops, neighbours, anywhere.'

'My god, Ivan. How old were you?'

Ivan faltered. How old had he been when it had started? He couldn't remember. There had been a time when his father hadn't beaten him—when his mother had been alive, apparently—but he didn't remember it. As far as he could remember, his entire childhood had been centred around avoiding the raging beast that had drunk, and gambled, and snored in his TV chair.

What else had there been to remember about the man?

'I don't know. But the last time it happened, our old man had discovered I'd stolen his beer money. I should have known better, it was a stupid error of judgement, but Maksim was hungry and I was desperate.'

'Your father must have been livid.'

'He was.' The truth was that he'd been so crazed that Ivan had been convinced the old man was going to kill him.

As it was, a tornado was whipping up inside him with every word he uttered, and Ruby was watching him so intently with an expression that encompassed both compassion and concern. But that only made him feel all the more wretched.

'And no one knew? No one helped?'

'They knew,' he managed bitterly. 'We lived in a small village like Little Meadwood. Everyone knew everyone else's business. But no one helped. No one ever stepped in.'

'Oh.' One short syllable, but it held a wealth of understanding.

'I wish you'd told me all this before.'

'What good would it have done?'

'What good?' She peered at him in amazement. 'It helps explain your career choice in London, your reluctance to return to Little Meadwood, your adamance that this child should be brought up in the city.'

'It doesn't because I don't give it the real estate in my head,' he refuted.

Though he wasn't entirely sure he believed that himself.

For the second time that evening, Ruby reached across the table, her hand hovering but not touching, torn between the urge to comfort and the respect for his boundaries. Ivan couldn't decide whether he appreciated it or not.

'Where is Maksim now?' she asked softly, as if she wasn't certain she wanted to know the answer.

This was the question he'd been dreading, but he forced himself to answer all the same.

'I have no idea. I never saw him after that night.'

'You never tried to track him down?'

There was no accusation in her tone, but Ivan felt it anyway. Like a belt across his cheeks—just as he deserved.

'I tried,' he admitted flatly, hating the fact that he was lying by omission. 'But I never found out.'

'You could try again. There are lots of tracing services out there to find long-lost relatives. We deal with this more than you might think at the hospital.'

'I'm aware.' He had to shut the conversation down.

The room had already seemed to shrink with the enormity of his admission. And his guilt. The things he hadn't said slammed loudly into the walls of his brain, roaring the truth.

He concentrated on running his fingers over the rim of his wine glass, tracing the smooth curve before coming to rest. The soft clink of glass against wood cut through the silence that had settled over them like a thick fog.

'What are you afraid of?' Ruby ventured, her gentle voice pushing against his sense of culpability.

He flickered his eyes up to meet hers. 'It isn't about being afraid.'

She clearly didn't believe him.

'You can't feel guilty over something that you must know was beyond your control.' She spoke gently, her hazel eyes reflecting the light and illuminating her face with hope. He thought that might have been what clawed at him the worst.

'I don't,' he lied again.

It was a deflection, but it was the best he could manage. He might have known Ruby wouldn't be so easily evaded.

'If you don't want the tracing services, there are ways, Ivan—agencies, databases, social media...'

'No.'

One word. A command wrapped in layers of pain, and bound so tightly that it seemed to constrict his very breath.

And he hated that Ruby seemed to physically recoil as though he'd actually hurt her. But then she came back at him, her gaze holding his again.

'You were a kid, Ivan. You shouldn't take it all on as your responsibility.'

'You don't know what you're talking about,' he bit out coldly.

'Don't I?' she asked softly.

He hated that she might be right.

'I don't need you to psychoanalyse me, Ruby.' Ivan pushed back from the table, his chair scraping across the floor with an agonizing screech, and it was all he could do to cast an apologetic look around the room as though it was unintentional. 'I only told you so that you would know who I am, but not everything can be fixed, Ruby. Some things are better left in the past.'

Then, walking around the table to help pull her chair out, he gave her no option but to leave the restaurant with him. Instead of bringing them together, every conversation seemed to push them that little bit further apart.

'Ivan…' As she stood up, she reached out, but he sidestepped her touch, retreating behind an invisible wall that felt miles high.

It was the same armour he always donned, shielding himself from the emotional entanglement of their patients' lives. Only now, Ruby would know that he used it just as much to guard against the turmoil roiling within himself.

'Okay, Ivan,' she murmured as she fell into step alongside him, and they weaved their way through the tables, looking all the world like a normal couple having a normal conversation. 'We don't have to talk about this any more tonight.'

'Indeed.' He offered a curt nod that seemed to push them apart all the further. 'We will call it a night and head to my apartment. I'll see my patient as soon as I can and then we'll fly you back to Little Meadwood.'

He couldn't explain what it meant that part of him wanted nothing more than to bridge the gap between them and pull her into an embrace that promised her the kind of life he knew she wanted—deep down. That kind of undamaged family unit he could never offer her.

Setting one leaden step after another, he somehow managed to navigate them out of the restaurant. No, the evening definitely hadn't gone as planned, and he still didn't know what had possessed him to tell her about Maksim. But at least whatever ridiculous compulsion had overtaken him, it hadn't made him spill the whole truth.

If it had, he didn't think he could have borne the disdain in which she would surely have held him. Or that she might have then passed on to their baby in the years to come.

However much he feared he deserved it.

Ruby surged awake with a jolt, her eyes snapping open to the inky darkness of the bedroom. *Ivan's* bedroom, though he'd claimed never to have used it in all the five years that he'd lived in the apartment.

The place was a revelation. The whole evening had been, really. Ivan had opened up to her in a way that she doubted he had ever managed before, and her heart thudded against her ribcage as she tried to work out what to make of it.

She warned herself against reading too much into it, but it was hard not to—especially when her perfidious heart clearly wanted to take it as a sign. And Ruby was getting tired of the fight. Tired of battling her own desires, and tired of telling herself that Ivan Volkov was nothing more to her than the father of her unborn baby.

The truth was that she'd had a crush on him since she'd been a kid, and no matter how much she tried to pretend that she'd grown up since then, it was becoming obvious to her that her fondness had only matured as she had.

But it didn't mean she had to give in to it—even if him

kissing her the other night had only served to complicate the situation further.

And she wasn't naive. Evidently there was far more to his story—parts of his past that he had deliberately skirted—but that wasn't the point. The point was that he had opened that door, if only a crack, to finally let her in. Which was more than he'd ever done before.

It made her feel vulnerable and exhilarated all at once. Like she was walking a tightrope between two lives: her old one in Little Meadwood, with Vivian and Nell as her family, and a life that seemed to be unfolding before her, with her baby and with Ivan.

But was that really even a possibility?

Tossing and turning again, Ruby swivelled her head to look at the clock on the bedside table, the digits glowing 2:17 in the morning—each one a silent sentry in the deafening quiet of the night.

She lay there for another moment, still vainly trying to catch the last tendrils of her dream. The recollection of Ivan's shocking revelation, so raw and unexpected, and the words he'd used had left her feeling as if he'd finally permitted her a coveted glimpse at a hidden chamber in his heart. Something she'd begun to fear would never happen.

All she could hear was the pain in every syllable of each of his words, and the curve of his usually broad shoulders betraying just how much the secret must have been weighing on him. And all she could picture was that long moment when he'd just stared at her, jaw set like granite and eyes hard as flint. He'd been so distant and almost impenetrable, yet the lines on his face hinted at something more—a pain he had never shared with…anyone, it seemed.

But now he'd shared it with her, however limited.

Unable to sleep, Ruby swung her legs over the side of the

bed, the cool touch of the wooden floorboards grounding her as she padded out of the bedroom and down the wide, polished-wood staircase.

The apartment was quiet and still, save for the softest of hums of the refrigerator as she made her way towards the kitchen. And everywhere around her seemed charged with ion particles—the fallout from Ivan's confession.

She reached for a glass, filling it with cold filtered water from his fridge, when her ears tuned into a sound that didn't quite seem to fit. Unlike the quiet symphony of nocturnal creaks and sighs of Ivan's luxury home, this sound was more rhythmic, sharper, and unmistakably deliberate. The noise was coming from where Ivan should be sleeping. Her curiosity piqued, Ruby put the glass down and silently moved toward the source, her nurse's instincts melding with something more…personal.

Edging down the hall, she listened closer as she tried to work out the sound coming from Ivan's suite of rooms. There was no light under the heavy oak door, no hint of movement save for the sound that grew clearer with each step closer, and the sound didn't suggest anyone in distress, yet Ruby couldn't seem to make herself turn around and leave. Reaching the door, she lifted her hand, paused, and then knocked softly. The noise inside didn't falter, and there was no responding invitation to enter. With a deep breath Ruby's fingers curled around the door handle, turned it slowly, and pushed the door open with an almost silent *swish*, and she was on to the next, slightly ajar door.

Her breath stilled instantly in her chest, her body immobilized, as she gazed at the scene in front of her. Ivan, stripped to the waist, his sinfully lean muscles illuminated by the moonlight which filtered through the window, was moving around a punchball—dancing really—and knocking it so fast that the movements were almost a blur. Each jab was a masterful combination of speed and accuracy, whilst his focus was absolute and the speed of the beat was almost like an incredible music all of its own.

His short, dark hair was damp with exertion, and the intensity in his blue-black eyes so fierce that she wondered who he was imagining that punchball to be—himself perhaps? His guilt had been unmistakable when he'd talked to her tonight, though she still couldn't understand it. Either way, he was so engrossed in his solitary battle that he didn't notice her standing there until she was nearly upon him.

'Can't sleep either?' she ventured tentatively, her voice steady despite the thunderous beat of her heart.

Ivan's knuckles stilled against the leather of the punchball, his gaze snapping towards her. For a fleeting second, surprise flitted across his features before his usual mask slotted neatly back into place. But it was too late; she knew she'd caught him off guard, and in that brief half a second she had seen a flicker of the vulnerability he so rarely showed.

'Ruby,' he bit out in a neutral tone. 'What are you doing up?'

'I could ask you the same thing,' she replied and shrugged.

His chest heaved with his exertion.

'I'm just getting in a little exercise.' His clipped tone did little to conceal his irritation. She suspected that was intentional. 'I don't need an audience.'

Ruby remained unfazed, recognizing the defensiveness for what it was—a shield against the world. She moved closer, her gaze soft and unthreatening.

'Maybe not, but everyone needs a little company at times.'

'This is not one of those times.' A muscle ticked in Ivan's jaw, the only sign of his internal struggle.

'Perhaps I meant me,' she pointed out, 'rather than you.'

CHAPTER NINE

IVAN DIDN'T ANSWER, but eyed her sharply for a moment. Then, rolling his shoulders to release some tension, he turned away from the punchball to face her fully as the air began to palpably thicken.

She turned away, and he told himself that he was glad. Even so, as she made her way around the room step by step, he couldn't seem to bring himself to drag his gaze away and return to his workout.

Right up until the moment she reached his bookcase.

His breath caught in his chest as she slid her eyes over the items on display. Books, of course, but also some travel pieces, some trophies, and a handful of photos. He watched with mounting agitation as she noted the army photos, the medical pictures, and then that one nugget of history that no one else had ever seen.

Slowly, painfully slowly, he moved towards her as if he could distract her from the inevitable.

Her hands reached out to the old, dog-eared photo even before he was halfway across the space.

'This is you,' she breathed in surprise. 'You're a lot younger than when I first met you but I recognize you all the same.'

'Yes,' he managed, his mouth suddenly dry.

'And the smaller boy next to you?' She lifted her head abruptly. 'Is that him? Is that Maksim?'

Ivan opened his mouth to reply but the confirmation caught obstinately in his throat. It took him several rough swallows to get past it.

'Yes, that's Maksim. It was when a travelling fairground had visited the area and our parents were too boozed up to notice that we'd gone. We sneaked in, and sneaked on some of the rides until the guy taking the photos noticed us.'

'And he threw you out?' Ruby guessed, wrinkling her nose as she examined the photo a little more.

He and his brother were on the wooden horses of a merry-go-round, grinning inanely with little Maksim squinting into the sun. They'd had a lot of fun that day—and none of it le-gitimately.

'Yeah, he threw us out. But not before he gave us a photo each and told us to use it to remind us that if we wanted to be able to do fun things for real, then we were going to have to work harder than most people, because we were starting off further down the ladder.'

'Oh.' Ruby was careful to keep her expression neutral, though he was fairly sure she wasn't impressed.

In truth, it might have been the best bit of advice he'd ever been given—until he'd been fostered with Vivian. But her lack of understanding only seemed to underscore the differ-ence in their home lives. He couldn't have said why that irked him suddenly.

'Seen enough?' He crossed back to his exercise mat and the punchball.

'I'm here if you want to talk about it,' Ruby ventured, clos-ing the gap between them with a few cautious steps.

Her hand reached out tentatively, hovering just shy of his sweat-dampened arm before making contact. The touch sent a jolt through her and, by the looks of Ivan, it had done the same for him. He moved away, making her feel suddenly cold. Rejected.

'I think I did enough of that earlier tonight,' he ground out. 'And talking doesn't change anything.'

'I don't believe that.' She pulled a rueful expression. 'Maybe I'm wrong but I think you feel differently just for finally letting go of some of the things you've kept pent-up for so long. I think that's why you're here now, unable to sleep, because there's more you want to say. You just can't allow yourself to, can you?'

For a long moment, they simply stood there, the rhythm of their breaths in perfect sync in the quiet room. Close enough that Ruby could feel the heat radiating from Ivan's body, a result of his exertion, and something more besides.

'The thing is,' she began hesitantly when it became clear that he wasn't going to speak. 'We talked about demons earlier, but you aren't the only one who is battling them.'

'I told you, I'm not battling any demons,' Ivan refuted.

But she noticed that he didn't move away from her.

'You say that, but I see the shadow in your eyes,' Ruby told him softly. 'I recognize them from when I look at my own reflection in the mirror. The thought of raising this baby without my mother…without even Vivian—'

She stopped abruptly, biting her lip.

Carrying those fears had been bad enough, but actually uttering them aloud…? It made them that much more real, all of a sudden. Made the situation that much more real.

And still, Ivan didn't answer.

'My mother would have been the greatest grandmother that I could have wanted for any child—just as she'd been the greatest mother I could have ever hoped for.' A lump lodged painfully in Ruby's throat. 'Do you realize that by the time this baby is born, I will have spent more time on this earth without my mother alive, than I had ever enjoyed with her?'

And it stung.

More than stung.

Even so, it was only when Ivan suddenly enveloped her in his arms that she realized how desperately she needed to be comforted. She was only too ready to collapse against him. To draw strength from him. And surely they were going to need each other more than ever now that they were expecting this baby together.

Suddenly, she needed to know more than ever before just how much Ivan was acting out of a sense of duty, and how much he genuinely cared for her. Had it just been that one weekend together? She didn't think so, but she needed to know for sure.

No matter the circumstance, this child *would* be surrounded by people. It would have her, it would have the fun and talented auntie that her best friend, Nell, would surely be, and it would have the loving community that was Little Meadwood.

And even if cruel fate meant that her baby would miss out on knowing how it felt to never know what it was like to have Vivian, then Ruby was determined that she would share as many happy memories as possible.

But, most significantly, this child had a chance to have the father that Ruby herself had never known. A father who wanted to be a part of their life—whether he was doing it out of duty or desire, did it really matter so long as he was actually doing it?

Without warning, Ruby felt herself at a precipice. To retreat would be to return to the safety of solitude, but to move forward could mean embracing something that might be just as real, and true. It was time to let go of the foolish, childlike notions of Ivan falling in love with the idea of a baby, or a life as a family—or indeed her.

Because, whether she'd wanted to admit it or not, Ruby was finding it harder and harder to pretend that a part of her wasn't in love with Ivan.

It had been the case when she was a kid, and it still was now. And she could fight against it all she wanted, but it wouldn't make it any less true.

But that didn't mean that Ivan had to know that. She wasn't a mooning kid anymore. She was a grown woman, mature enough to set aside those unrequited feelings and simply accept what Ivan *was* offering her.

A different kind of life for her baby. Two parents who were working together for their child. Something neither of them had ever experienced for themselves.

'Thank you,' she murmured softly, carefully detaching herself from Ivan's comforting embrace and ignoring the voice in her head that railed at doing so. 'I'm okay now. I think being back here in London, and visiting that restaurant, just reminded me of my mother. It caught me off guard for a moment.'

'You never have to apologize for missing her,' Ivan rasped. 'I know you were her world. I can't even imagine what that would have been like.'

'But we can offer that to our own child.' Ruby lifted her head. 'If I move in with you, then we can create a family unit that may not be like another person's but that works for us.'

'One that has two people both wanting to do the best thing by the child,' Ivan agreed hoarsely.

And she tried not to let her heart race away with her when he gazed down at her, a flicker of surprise and something else she couldn't quite decipher in his eyes.

'It will still be more than either of us ever got to experience,' he continued. 'A chance to break the cycle. For me, at least.'

'Yes. Exactly.'

It was meant to be a moment of clarity; Ruby knew that. But as their eyes locked, she felt something shift between them. Ivan's usually guarded expression softened, if only for a moment, and she caught a glimpse of that well-hidden vulnerability that made her heart ache.

Almost as though he didn't realize what he was doing, he slid his hands to her shoulders, moving her back slightly so he could look straight into her eyes. Before she knew it, Ruby found her own hand lifting to rest against his chest, over his heart as it beat out a rapid tattoo against her palm.

The moments ticked by, unheeded as they allowed the sliver of unexpected intimacy to carry them away. There was a suspended moment where he no longer seemed to be a formidable surgeon, or a haunted former foster kid, or the father of her unborn child.

In this instant he was just a man, raw and open, standing in front of her and stripping her soul bare. And the world outside—with its demands and demons—fell away, leaving only the connection that they'd allowed themselves to explore once before.

So this time, what more consequences could there be?

Their breaths mingled in the small space between them, the air crackling with a palpable energy, and Ruby couldn't have said whether Ivan ducked his head to her, or she reached up to him, but at last—*at last*—their lips were brushing and they were kissing.

And what a kiss.

He claimed her with fire, and fever, and everything in between. Like the headiest liquor that rolled through her with the most indulgent laziness, and she was already punch-drunk on the taste.

His hand cupped the nape of neck, turning her head this way and that as he tasted her. He toyed with her, and he teased, kissing her so thoroughly, so comprehensively, that Ruby's lips began to tingle under the wickedness of the assault. And still, she was only too happy to revel in every single second of it. Every minute.

And then he shifted.

The small moan escaped her lips before she could catch it—but how could it not when his thigh was suddenly right *there*? Between her legs the hardness of his thigh was pressed so deliciously against the softness of her core. Where that greedy heat bloomed so instantly for him.

Had she moaned his name? She thought maybe she had, but then perhaps it was simply that it flowed through her veins, like an imprint all of its own. Stamping her as his whether he had wanted to or not.

She was ruined for any other man—that much was clear to Ruby. She had been ever since that night several months ago. And likely before that, when she'd first met him as a teenager and fallen head over heels in love.

And as Ivan began to peel her thin nightclothes off—almost reverently as he took the time to explore her changing body, with the curves and swells that bore witness to the life she was now carrying—she could feel that familiar tremble starting low in her belly and slowly moving out of her in waves.

She moved against him, trying to press herself closer. She wanted more—so much more—his hands all over her body. His skin sliding over hers.

'Patience, Ruby,' Ivan muttered as she shifted against him again.

And she took some gratification from the fact that his voice sounded much, much thicker than usual.

Then, without warning, he hauled the last of her clothing smoothly over her head, offered a low growl of approval as he drank in the sight of her, and then bent his head to take one proud, hard nipple directly into his mouth and sucked. Hard.

Ruby almost toppled from the gloriously dizzying sensations right there and then. Instinctively, she threw her head back and arched her back, as if trying to offer him even more of herself.

Ivan seemed only too happy to take it. With one hand splayed over the bump of her abdomen, and the other holding her backside, he appeared to take inordinate pleasure in swirling around the pink bud with his tongue. Sucking her in until he was *just about* grazing the very edges of his teeth in a way that felt wholly sinful, and then releasing her to the cool night air so that her nipple puckered up immediately in response.

Over and over, he teased her. And when she thought he was finally done, he turned his head and repeated the entire delectable process on her other breast. This time when he sucked, it sent such a kick of frenetic desire straight from her nipple to her aching core that she thought she might die from need if she didn't have him sliding inside her.

Now.

'This is wholly unfair,' Ruby gurgled dully when her brain had finally remembered how to make words.

But Ivan only laughed, a dark, intimate sound that sent fresh thrills cascading through her, and carried on. Glutting himself on her as though she was the most desirable creature he had ever known.

Even more than he had last time, she registered dimly. Though she had no idea what to make of the realization. And even less desire to bother trying—not when every lick, and suck, and swirl of his tongue was sending her closer and closer to the edge.

Then, before she had fully registered what he was doing, she found herself lifted up into his arms. Swept through the air like she weighed nothing—bump and all—and then he was carrying her back through his suite.

Ruby had a vague recollection of him shouldering his way through the heavier oak door of his bedroom, and then she was being deposited on a huge, wooden carved bed in a room that felt masculine, yet not too dark. And then she didn't care to notice anything else, because Ivan was pulling off his own clothes and crawling up the bed between her legs—his skin sliding feverishly over hers and his shoulders gently nudging her a little wider apart.

And then, when he was happy where he was, Ivan lowered his head between her legs, and licked her *right there*.

Where she ached for him most.

Ruby almost came apart there and then. Waves of pleasure were assailing her from every angle, but then Ivan slid his hands under her backside and lifted her up to meet him and it all got so much worse. Or better.

Certainly hotter.

She heard herself cry out his name but it all seemed somehow distant. Muffled. As though she was outside her own skin and he was the one who was twisting her inside out. Over and over, he used his wickedly clever tongue to tease her, driving her closer to the precipice than ever.

And then with one last slide of his tongue, one last graze of his teeth, she lost it. She came apart right there against his mouth and his hands, arching her back and crying out his name. All the while he held her. As though she was infinitely precious, and to be cherished—always.

If only that were true.

But there was no time to dwell, because now Ivan was propping himself up between her legs and her hands were already reaching down for more of a touch. If she wasn't pinned so delightfully down beneath him, she might well have taken her tongue and licked all along his hardest ridge. Slipping him into her mouth, tasting him, and enjoying the sight of him losing control exactly as he had just made her do.

And then, the thought was gone the moment the velvet-smooth tip of him nudged at her heat. Automatically, Ruby slipped her hands around his body, over the swell of his biceps and down the ridges of his back muscles. Finally, her name on his lips like some kind of prayer, he slid inside her.

Ruby cried out softly, his sheer maleness sliding into her molten heat—tentatively at first—as though it had been waiting a lifetime. As though they were finally home. Slowly, slowly, he moved in and out, his pace leisurely at first, building up the heat, and sending those waves lapping through her again. Until Ruby slid her legs around his waist and pulled him in harder, meeting each thrust with a faster, harder rhythm. Making Ivan fracture and splinter the way he had done with her.

And when she lifted her hips and dug her fingers into his back, Ruby was finally rewarded as a low, guttural moan was ripped from Ivan's lips and he sank himself fully into her, tossing her straight back over the edge—and following her besides.

Ruby had no memory of falling asleep, but when she woke several hours later to find herself still in Ivan's bed—his body fresh from the shower—she was more than gratified when he hauled her back to him, rolled over, and began the explorations all over again.

If this was what living with Ivan would also be like, then Ruby was beginning to think that the first thing she would do when she got back to her cottage in Little Meadwood would be to pack.

CHAPTER TEN

'OKAY, MIKEY.' Ivan smiled at the fourteen-year-old patient in front of him. 'So Ruby has explained what's happening? You know that although it's quite a clean cut, the wound on your face does go down to the cartilage, so I'm going to have to do it under a general anaesthetic.'

'Right here?' The boy grinned, whipping his phone out now that the examination was over, so that he could take some delightfully gruesome selfies to send to his mates. 'Cool.'

'No, not here.' Ivan shook his head. 'We'll get an operating room prepped for you and get you down there.'

'Sick. Can I video it for my mates?'

Across the room, where she was dealing with the equipment trays, Ruby tried not to look too much at Ivan, but there was no stopping the thudding that started in her chest every time he was near.

After their night together—and Ivan's subsequent patient review—it had been a strange flight back home. They hadn't discussed what had happened, but every brush of their hands had felt deliciously contrived, every glance had felt intensely protracted.

If it hadn't been for the unexpected call just as they had landed, urgently requesting him to attend an emergency at City Hospital, Ruby still wasn't sure where they would have ended up going next. By the time she'd hurried in to cover a shift herself, her head had been a jumbled mess of excited uncertainty.

It still was—though this wasn't the time to delve into her thoughts. It was almost a relief when young Mikey cut into the moment, lowering his mobile phone from his face.

'Hang on. You say general anaesthetic, Doc, but I'll still be able to get back to rugby training soon, right? We've got a match coming up against Rock Bay Rousters and they're, like, our arch-nemesis. I *gotta* be back in time for it.'

Despite her nervous tension, Ruby smothered another smile. She'd been dealing with the young patient for the previous hour, and she knew what was about to come.

'Not unless your idea of *soon* is several months,' Ivan answered firmly, turning back to focus on his patient. But they both suspected it would go in one of Mikey's ears then promptly out the other. 'This is a traumatic soft tissue injury. Early management has given us our best possible chance of good healing with minimal scarring, but further damage risks additional bleeding, possible airway obstruction...'

'Yeah, but it's the *Rock Bay Rousters*,' the boy exclaimed, slipping the phone away. 'I can't miss that match.'

If young Mikey had made that point to her once, he'd made it ten times already. If nothing else, she had to admire the kid's sense of invincibility as well as his dedication to his team. All she could hope was that he would listen to the advice if it came from a man like Ivan, rather than her.

'Sorry bud.' Ivan sounded sympathetic, yet immovable. 'We can't risk any complications by rushing back, even for the Rousters. Your health and recovery have to come first.'

'Yeah, but I'm a really good healer, you know? I bet you've never seen anyone heal as fast as I do.'

'You'd be surprised.' Ivan plastered another smile to his lips.

And Ruby watched as he patiently explained the risks to

Mikey in greater detail. His authoritative yet caring attitude calmed the boy despite the disappointing news. She couldn't help admiring how Ivan handled the situation and clearly the boy appreciated the man-to-man talk—which was fortunate given that the boy's mother was still outside in the waiting room, refusing to come in to speak to her son presurgery as she couldn't bear to see his injuries.

Not that she couldn't do it alone, but it would certainly make it easier to talk to both Vivian and Nell if Ivan was there with her. Hopefully it would make them worry about the situation less.

'I'm going to explain it to your mother now,' Ivan told Mikey as he finished up with his patient. 'Then I'll get set up for you.'

'Cool.'

Mikey nodded happily, his phone already coming back out of his pocket, and Ivan took the opportunity to briefly indicate to Ruby to join him outside.

She told herself that she wasn't all too eager to oblige. Her heart was thudding in her chest.

'We should talk about the other night,' he noted quietly, after ensuring no one was around to overhear them.

The thuds grew louder but she forced herself to answer.

'Yes. We should.'

'You will move in with me tonight.'

As *talking* went, it was more of an instruction, but Ruby didn't point that out. She was too focused on the detail of what Ivan had just said.

He *did* still want her to move in; the relief was almost dizzying, given a part of her had feared he might have changed his mind after their recent shared night together.

She couldn't have stood it if she'd robbed her unborn baby of its chance of a family—quasi family—simply because she couldn't seem to control herself whenever she was around Ivan.

Not that she had any intention of saying any of that to him.

'Tonight,' she confirmed, wishing her voice hadn't sounded quite so husky. So sultry.

A flicker of emotion chased across Ivan's face before he smoothed it into blankness. Ruby tried not to feel so hurt. Plainly he still wasn't prepared to let her in fully, but she could only hope that he'd be less guarded with their baby, when it finally arrived.

'Have you time for a break after this?' he asked. 'Grab a snack? Make sure you're still eating.'

'Here?'

In the hospital?

Was it really wise to meet Ivan here, where the hospital grapevine would be swinging into action before the two of them even took their first sips? Okay, slight exaggeration, but not far off.

Then again, people were going to have to find out about her pregnancy soon, and if she was going to be moving in with Ivan—*if*—then it wouldn't take them long to fit the puzzle together. Perhaps it was better to get it out in the open and the gossip over with?

'It's just a snack, Ruby,' Ivan's mouth tugged up at the corners as if he could read her mind. 'How about meeting me once I'm out of surgery? Shall we say *Re-cup-eration*?'

'In the downstairs atrium where everyone can see?'

'Well, I don't fancy a vending machine drink. Whatever those things spew out, it isn't coffee.'

'You know that isn't what I meant.' She tried to pull a face, but her insides felt too fluttery to carry it off.

'You meant because everyone will see us? And because of what happened the other night at Vivian's, you still haven't had the chance to tell her about the baby?' he half teased for a moment before turning serious. 'But time is passing by, Ruby, and at this rate it will be born and I still won't be able to be a proper father.'

Which, she couldn't help noticing, was a complete change from that first day she'd told him the news. Wisely, she kept the observation to herself. She doubted Ivan would welcome the reminder.

'I know,' she conceded seriously. 'I don't want to keep putting it off, but I would prefer them to know about the baby first. Maybe it will even give Vivian a bit of a boost.'

To her relief, Ivan bowed his head in acknowledgement. It was a delicate balance that she was trying to find right now, but if anyone understood why her foster family was so important to her, then it would be Ivan.

On the other hand, it should concern her more that she was increasingly turning to him to provide the support she had initially anticipated Vivian and Nell would show. Despite their shaky start, Ivan had proved to be more of a rock than she could have imagined.

So why couldn't she shake the foreboding feeling that, unless he finally did something to confront his demons—like finally summoning the courage to sign up to a tracing site for his younger half-brother—then they were missing the very foundations for this fragile world they were beginning to build together?

And her fear was that the slightest storm could easily bring it all crashing down.

Mill Cottage turned out to be less of a small, low-ceilinged dwelling and more of a sleek-lined, dizzyingly vaulted open space.

Ruby stood in the hallway; her neck craned right back as she gazed up at the glorious, honey-coloured beams at least eight metres above her head.

'This is what you managed to rent at short notice?' she breathed, struggling to take it all in.

'Like I said before, lucky timing.' Ivan shrugged dismissively. 'And a good contact.'

'One who you now owe a case of wine or something?'

'Probably.' He grinned, leaning against the door jamb and fixing her with a too-direct stare. 'So do you want the full tour, or would you prefer to find your way around in your own time?'

'The tour, definitely.'

Surely she shouldn't be so giggly about the move? It was supposed to be about practicality. Instead, she felt like her insides were fizzing and popping with delight. And it definitely wasn't the baby.'

Thinking about which...

'What about the nursery?' she blurted out excitedly. 'Do you have a room in mind for that?'

Belatedly it occurred to her that Ivan might not be planning that far ahead. With a rush, she considered that maybe he thought they would be out of Mill Cottage and in London by then.

It was a relief when he returned her smile with a wide, apparently genuine one of his own, and lifted his arm to gesture to the upstairs.

'You have three choices of bedroom. Take your pick.'

'Really?'

'And if you want to put your stamp on them, choose some swatches or I can bring in a decorator to help.'

Ruby paused, glancing at him in surprise. 'I can paint?'

'Sure.' He didn't look bothered. 'It's in the contract. As long as we revert everything to its original state when we hand it back, we have free reign. So if we end up staying here a little longer, say after the birth...then at least it can feel like ours.'

That certainly hadn't been what Ruby had expected from him. With each passing day, Ruby was finding it harder and harder to remember that they weren't a proper couple. And that would inevitably be a problem.

She stilled without warning, her mind suddenly opening itself up to the uncertainties that she had been trying to keep at bay. The buzzing was faint at first, but it grew louder the longer she stood still. She felt torn between the joy of planning her baby's nursery and the unspoken doubts that lingered in her mind every time she caught that sad expression of Ivan's that she didn't know he had. Or the way he pulled back from her sometimes without even noticing.

And, her chest heavy, Ruby realized that she couldn't quash it any longer. She couldn't pretend everything was okay. She *had* to say something before she talked herself out of it.

'Ivan…'

But as he turned, swivelling on his heel as he moved to face her, Ruby felt the flutterings she'd been feeling for the past few days—only suddenly, she knew what it was.

She lifted her head to his in shock.

'The baby is kicking,' she managed, grabbing the wall with one hand and her own belly with the other. 'Oh, Ivan. You need to feel it.'

Ivan's expression turned to one of surprise as he immediately stepped closer to her, his hands lifting to hover uncertainly over her abdomen. Ruby couldn't help laughing, her mounting misgivings scattered and lost in the moment. Ivan had likely operated on thousands of patients as a doctor, seen thousands more as patients, but faced with the energetic kicks of his own unborn baby, he looked as startled as any lay father might be.

Carefully, solicitously, she took his hands in hers and placed them gently on her belly. The baby didn't take long to show off its prowess.

'That can't be… It's incredible,' Ivan breathed, a mixture of emotions scudding across his face.

Suddenly all Ruby could do was nod and laugh and cry all at once—and nothing else seemed as important anymore.

So what if Ivan had his fears—didn't everyone? And did it matter if he didn't want to search for his brother to find out what really happened? Perhaps Maksim had been part of Ivan's old family, but she and their baby were his family now. They could take care of each other—*love each other*—more than anyone else ever could.

And in that moment, Ruby vowed to do just that. She would forget any notion of looking for Ivan's family, and she would concentrate on her own.

Starting now.

So, for the next few hours, Ruby explored her new home with Ivan. She followed him eagerly from room to room, sharing her initial thoughts as each one boasted its own unique charm. One had a large picture window that let in lashings of light, another had beams that snagged the eye and captured the imagination, and yet another had the prettiest built-in shelves that she soon learned housed a hidden door which led to a secret room behind.

When they finally stopped to feel for more baby kicks, Ivan's hand lifting to catch a stray tendril of her hair behind her ear, she gave in to the desire to be intimate with him again. Their bodies were moving together with familiarity but still that same electric thrill. And that connection between them was feeling stronger and more unbreakable by the day.

But Ruby might have known the outside world would come rushing back in sooner or later. And when it did, it would crash over them with an icy reminder of all the questions she'd allowed to go unanswered.

CHAPTER ELEVEN

THE FOLLOWING FEW days bled into the following few weeks for Ivan, with days often spent with Ruby, whether at the hospital or baby shopping; and nights spent with Ruby, whether under him, over him, or in his arms.

It ought to have been hell—this little sliver of unplanned domesticity. But inexplicably, it wasn't.

Not by a long way.

Which might have explained why Ruby was always at the edge of his thoughts. Her sharp wit and killer smile invaded his brain at the most inappropriate of times. And all too often he found himself wondering where she was and what she was up to—wanting to share in her life far more than he felt was appropriate given the circumstances.

Which was ironic, really, Ivan snorted as he vaulted out of his car and into the house that had become far more of a home than he cared to admit.

He found Ruby standing in the room he had earmarked as his office, a patchwork of pastel-hued tester colours dotted on the walls and her head tilted back as she considered each one in turn. And when she didn't see him, Ivan found himself stepping back and indulging in several moments of admiring her without disturbing her.

And no matter that he had no business doing either.

It was only when she began to turn around that he stepped forward as though he had just arrived at the doorway.

'Are we going for a circus theme?'

'Very funny.' She pulled a face. 'But for the record, babies can see brighter colours much better than pastels, especially early on.'

'I'm aware.' He smiled, watching as she dipped her brush into a palette of colours and added another one to the wall with careful, deliberate strokes.

'But this is just for a backdrop to the room. I can introduce high-contrast blacks, whites, reds with accessories like the baby mobile, or bedding.'

'Right.' Ivan leaned in the doorway, watching her despite himself. 'Looks like the beginnings of a masterpiece.'

Ruby glanced over her shoulder in surprise, returning his smile with a bright one of her own that seemed to sneak inside his chest and coil itself around him, her hazel eyes catching the fading light.

'It's got to be perfect,' she replied, her voice light but underscored with the weight of her dreams. She brushed a strand of brown hair from her face, leaving a smudge of lavender on her forehead.

'Any favourites?' she invited him to join in, but he shook his head.

He was terribly afraid that if he pushed off the door jamb and headed over there, he might do something stupid, like try to clear away that blob of mint green on the tip of her nose which—rather than making her look like a clown—only seemed to make her look all the more adorable.

'Whatever you choose will be fine.' he assured her. 'But I will paint it—don't tire yourself out. I only came in to see if you were ready for the restaurant tonight.'

In a moment of romantic madness, he'd booked a table at

the most upscale restaurant in the city, a gesture that he still wasn't entirely sure why he'd made.

But right now, he had the distinct impression that Ruby would far rather stay in, order a local takeaway, and chat at the dining table over a glass of elderflower cordial.

He couldn't say the idea didn't appeal.

'Unless you'd prefer I cancel?'

She pulled an apologetic face, and her tiredness showed for a moment.

'Would you be awfully disappointed?'

'Devastated,' he drawled, loving the way her eyes crinkled up in delight.

Well, not *loving*, he amended hastily as he called the restaurant. But…*appreciating*.

'You might want to get a shower anyway, though,' he teased after he'd finished the brief call. 'You appear to have mistaken your skin for the wall a couple of times.'

How he loved how her cheeks flushed a soft pink at his mention of the shower, and how endearing the colour looked on her warm skin—like a delicate rose blooming in the early-morning sun.

And he tried not to think about stepping into the large shower enclosure with her as he had the previous night, and making her scream his name even louder. And his body reacted, as it always seemed to do, like an adolescent, at the mere memory.

'Go,' he muttered hoarsely, before his baser instincts got the better of him. 'I'll clean up and get us a takeaway. Any requests?'

Ruby paused for a moment, thinking, a mischievous glint crossing those hazel depths.

'Let's surprise each other. You take care of the dinner, and I'll handle dessert.'

He chuckled at her playful suggestion, feeling a warmth slide through him at the easy banter they shared. It was moments like this that reassured him that family life *could* be different from the one he'd known in his childhood. That he wouldn't perpetuate the cycle of his cruel father.

With Ruby's help.

Watching her move through things with such passion and purpose was like a breath of fresh air in his too-structured life, and he couldn't shake the feeling of contentment that washed through him, especially when he wasn't looking.

He couldn't remember the last time he had felt this level of peace and contentment with another person and it was a peculiar sensation.

He ought to have known that it couldn't last.

'Ivan, wait. Don't go.'

Ruby halted Ivan as he was heading out of the Resus Department a week later. Tonight he had been home rather than working and still, just as she'd begun to realize that the shift was already half-over and she still hadn't had chance to eat, he had appeared with a home-cooked meal and an instruction to take a break.

Now, moving around to the same side of the desk as her, Ivan lowered his head to her ear and followed the direction that she was watching.

'What is it?'

Ruby pulled a face.

'I don't know. I can't say exactly.' Only there was something in the way a boy in the opposite cubicle—in for a fractured arm following a fall down some steps, as she recalled from her colleague—flinched when his father approached his bedside.

It had been fleeting, no more than half a second, something and nothing that could so easily have been missed given how normal the family had been acting moments earlier, when her colleague had been in the room.

Yet Ruby couldn't shake the feeling of apprehension that had settled in her stomach.

'Do you see anything?' she ventured, wondering if it was just her imagination.

'Yes.' Ivan's low, unhesitating response caught her off guard. 'Whose patient is it?'

Her food once again forgotten, she glanced around for the colleague in question, not surprised to see them caught up with another case. Clearly, they were tied up for a while so did she let it play out, or follow her gut?

Her gut won out.

'I want to head in. You'll observe from here?'

She didn't wait for Ivan to respond before she was hurrying across the floor to the bay, her eyes hastily taking in every-thing from the way the boy refused to meet his father's eye, to the way he held his good arm across his stomach in an overly protective manner. And another boy—a younger brother, pos-sibly—was perched on a hard plastic chair, swinging his leg whilst apparently not engaging with anyone.

'Are you injured somewhere else, sweetheart?' she asked brightly, ensuring her smile was open and approachable, and not the least bit threatening.

The boys' father was by her side within a matter of a second.

'That's nothing.' He moved his arm as though to form a barrier between Ruby and his son.

Ruby nodded, cranking her smile up further.

'Thank you, but I should like to examine your son for myself.'

'Your colleague didn't need to.' The man didn't move, but his smile set Ruby on edge. 'He ain't complained of no pain other than his arm.'

'No problem,' Ruby said brightly. 'But I *would* like to just check so that we can ensure you aren't stuck here any longer than necessary.'

The father seemed to take a moment to weigh up her words, though he still refused to step out of the way. His attitude was doing little to ease the tension Ruby felt.

'Is there any reason my colleague shouldn't check your son for other injuries?'

At the sound of Ivan's casual tone, Ruby exhaled the breath she hadn't realized she'd been holding.

The father scowled at Ivan, but Ruby noticed that he moved back an inch. Still, his jaw jutted out pugnaciously.

''e didn't complain of nothing else. 'e just needs his arm sortin' and we'll be outta here.'

'Absolutely.' Ivan moved towards the man in as nonthreatening a way as possible. 'But perhaps, with the obvious fracture of the arm to contend with, your son didn't realize he'd sustained another injury at the same time.'

'At the same time?' the father echoed, the wheels clearly beginning to turn in the man's head, and Ruby couldn't help think he was grasping at plausible explanations for what he knew they would find. 'Yeah, it's possible. Likely, really, now you mention it.'

Ruby watched Ivan handle the tense situation, engaging the man in a calm conversation whilst giving Ruby the opportunity to move around to the other side of the boy's bed. The younger brother was no longer swinging his leg but watching her intently—right up until the moment when she glanced his way and he bowed his head as if he wanted to disappear into the floor.

She turned her attention back to the patient.

'Hey there, I'm Ruby. Mind if I take a quick look at your stomach?'

It tugged at her heart the way the boy refused to meet her

eyes; his eyes fixed on a spot on the floor. Keeping her voice gentle and reassuring, she managed to prise the T-shirt from out of the boy's tiny, tight grip and lift it.

Bruises peppered the boy's stomach and chest. Small bruises. And lots of them. Yellow, black, purple, green, all revealing different lengths of time. Not injuries that he could have sustained in the recent apparent fall, but she couldn't afford to jump to conclusions. They could have been sustained from the two brothers having kids' blaster-gun fights, firing foam darts at each other, or…?

But coupled with the boys' demeanour, both terrified and flicking glances at their father and away again, it didn't quite seem to sit right. Her gut was warning her not to let it go. She'd been here before as a nurse. Too many times for comfort.

Ruby tilted her head to Ivan, careful to keep her expression neutral.

'More injuries,' she confirmed in as light a voice as she could. She was still acting as though she believed the injuries had been sustained in the recent fall.

No need to alert the father yet.

Still, the micro-expression that slid over Ivan's features caught her off guard.

She couldn't shake the feeling that this was more familiar to him than he would ever have cared to admit. And though she told herself not to, it was impossible not to watch as he skilfully managed to manoeuvre the resistant father out of the cubicle, still playing along with the idea that the injuries had been sustained that day.

Finally, she hit the bell to summon the colleagues dealing with the case, voicing her misgivings so that they could start their usual procedures.

And this time when she watched Ivan head out of the door, confident that the matter was being handled appropriately,

Ruby sucked in a steadying breath and thrust aside her guilt over having filled out the form to enable Ivan to trace the younger brother he claimed not to have seen in almost two decades. After all, what did they say—*it was better to ask for forgiveness than permission*?

Especially when she was pretty much ninety-nine percent convinced that he would *never* give the latter.

Ivan should have taken a bet on Ruby resurrecting the subject of Maksim after the incident with the father and his boys.

He could even have taken a bet that she would raise it that night, as they settled down in Mill Cottage kitchen for their meal. Not that he was enjoying it. Despite the glorious ingredients and skilful cookery, everything tasted bland to him today. He'd be better when he could get to bed and escape into sleep.

Tomorrow would almost certainly be a better day.

'Are you sure you're okay?' Ruby asked for the third time in as many hours. 'I'm here if you want to talk.'

'I don't,' he bit back, before trying to soften it. 'Thanks all the same.'

Still her persistent gaze—so full of concern—threatened to send a crack through the dam of his memories. Abruptly, she pushed her half-finished plate to the side.

'Ivan, I can't just sit back and say nothing,' she burst out. 'I saw your expression with those boys today. I know it cost you to be in that room.'

'You're mistaken.' He tried to shut her down but he might have known his Ruby wouldn't be so easily deterred.

His Ruby? Where had that even come from?

'I don't think I am.' Ruby leaned forward urgently. 'Why don't you contact him, Ivan? It's obvious you want to. Your brother clearly meant a lot to you.'

Her words crashed over him like a huge stormy wave slamming into a tiny fishing vessel—like the ones his hated father had once taken them on, forced them on, really. The kind of boats that had always made Maksim so violently sick—and their father laugh and sneer at his youngest son's lack of fortitude.

Wherever his brother was now, Ivan could only hope he was far away from their old life.

'You are mistaken,' he ground out, his eyes finally swivelling to meet Ruby's. 'Tracking down Maksim is the last thing I would ever want to do.'

'Why?'

Exasperated, Ivan dropped his fork onto his plate with a loud clatter. Frustration, fear, and—mostly—guilt all slammed into him at once and made him utter the words he hadn't ever wanted to tell her.

'Because I don't even know that he is alive.'

And in that instant, he knew that even though he wanted to take them back, he never could. Just as he also knew that Ruby wouldn't rest now until she knew the truth.

Standing up as steadily as he could, Ivan gathered their plates together and began heading back to the kitchen—more to take the opportunity to regroup than anything else. But by the time he started to speak again, he had his thoughts more organized in his head.

'I told you what happened the last time I saw Maksim,' he began. 'When I'd stolen the beer money to buy some food and, actually, to pay the meter.'

'You told me your father was angrier than you'd ever seen him before,' Ruby concurred.

'Well, I thought he was going to kill me. So I decided to leave that night and go for help. Get the authorities. Anyone who would listen. I raced out of the house—I banked on the fact that as bad as Maksim's mother was, she would never have let my father actually hurt Maksim—and I ran.'

'And you found help?'

'After a fashion.' Ivan shrugged, trying not to let the injustice of it all permeate his soul, even now. 'I sent them to the house but our parents were ready. They had a story all concocted, about how I was a troublemaker and had been ever since my mother died. They told the authorities that I was a danger to my half-brother, and they even had a couple of neighbours there to lie and back them up.'

'That's horrendous,' Ruby muttered, the fierce expression on her lovely face almost making the unpleasant trip down memory lane seem bearable.

'I was taken into care and they got to keep Maksim. I delivered him right into their hands.'

The guilt and unfairness of it burned inside him even now. Too bright. Too hot. He pushed it aside and tried to focus on Ruby.

'So that was the last time you saw Maksim?' she asked, her brow furrowed as if she actually cared.

'The last time,' he gritted the words out. 'I tried to get back to him that first week. I ran away from the home. But I got caught. The second time I ran was about two weeks after that, but when I got home both Maksim and his mother were gone.'

'Gone?' Ruby cried automatically. 'Gone where?'

And he gave a bitter laugh at the expression on her face.

'I don't know. I asked around. I asked scores of neighbours, but they all said the same thing. That they'd been there one day that first week, but by the time people had woken the next morning, there had been no sign of them.'

Ruby stared at him aghast.

'You don't think…?' She caught herself, shaking her head. 'No, of course you don't.'

'I don't think that my father did anything to them?' Ivan offered a hollow, bitter laugh. 'The thought has crossed my mind.'

'And?' she prompted, clearly unsettled by the idea.

And he liked his Ruby all the more for it.

'I don't know,' he told her honestly. 'There was one neighbour—old lady Craven—who finally told me that she had helped them. She claimed to have kept hold of whatever his mother gathered together to pack, and then helped them out of the village that first night.'

'Well…that's good news, isn't it?'

'It is.' He dipped his head once. 'If she was to be believed—she was never exactly kind to us. But I prefer to think that was what happened.'

'Right.' Ruby nodded slowly. Uncertainly.

And she looked so bereft that Ivan felt responsible.

It was his past, his story, that had cast a shadow over Ruby. This pregnancy should be a happy time for her but his history was tainting it. Just as he'd feared from the start.

Just as it had been for that family in the hospital today.

'And if I agreed to leave it,' Ruby began again, more hesitantly this time, 'do you think it would help? Would you want to move on? Would you feel more inclined to try to see what might have happened with Maksim?'

'It would not,' Ivan clipped out, frustrated that his own shortcomings were making Ruby second-guess her own choices like this.

Maksim was in his past; he didn't want to revisit that. But neither did he want to brush it under the carpet any longer, as if the little boy had never existed.

So where did that leave things?

As much as he was loathe to admit it, perhaps it was time to stop being selfish, and instead to consider whether Ruby and his unborn child were actually benefiting from having him in their lives.

Or whether it would actually be better for anyone if he returned to his distant, isolated life.

'I've missed this.' Nell linked arms with her as they strolled through the park opposite the hospital. 'This morning was mayhem.'

'Tell me about it.' Ruby smiled, squeezing her friend's arm in return and rubbing her other hand over her eyes, grateful to finally have time with her best friend.

From their time as foster kids together, it had been their weekly ritual to take a walk around Little Meadwood and share any worries or concerns, and offer advice—a habit that had continued until recently.

Until Ivan.

Dimly, it occurred to Ruby to wonder what might be going on in her friend's life right now such that Nell had seemed equally distracted of late—enough that she'd accepted Ruby's absence as a result of crazy overlapping night duties. But her mind was already racing too much with her own worries to really give it more thought.

The unexpected phone call from Maksim had caught her completely by surprise. And now she was supposed to be meeting the man in two days' time—in a city halfway between Little Meadwood and London, where she could be anonymous—so that she could determine for herself whether seeing his brother after all this time might help Ivan or alienate him further.

Right now, she needed a neutral pair of eyes more than ever. But how did she even begin to explain it all to her friend?

'I'm used to Resus being slammed but that was insane.' Ruby tried to keep the small talk going when Nell didn't speak.

Tried to sound normal, and in control of her careening emotions—if only to buy herself more time. 'I think there are still roadworks in the city so it has been quicker and easier to get all the emergencies here. And for the record, I've missed this, too. I'm sorry if I've been a bit distant recently.'

'Want to share?' Nell asked, her voice full of empathy and something else that Ruby couldn't quite identify. Suddenly it occurred to Ruby that she might not have been the only one caught up in their own life recently; now she thought about it, recently Nell hadn't been around as much as usual, either— or her friend would certainly have dragged the truth out of her by now.

Ruby opened her mouth, then closed it before rubbing her hand over her eyes again, torn between wanting to blurt out about her and Ivan and the baby. Torn also between the fact that Ivan had a brother, and not wanting to spread a secret that he had clearly kept hidden for a reason.

'It's crazy. And complicated.'

But then, if anyone could offer sage advice, it would be Nell.

'You don't have to feel obligated.'

'I know,' Ruby sighed. 'But… I want to. I just don't know where to start.'

And why did she feel that Nell's nod was that little bit too heartfelt?

'Start wherever feels comfortable.'

Ruby almost laughed. She had no idea where that would even be. Everything was just so…jumbled.

'It's just I've been…wondering about what it would be like to live somewhere else.'

It sounded so much worse, out there in the open. As though she was abandoning the place that had offered her haven after her mother's death. Or was that just her emotions talking?

'Oh.'

It was hardly the response that Ruby had been wanting. Which, in itself should probably tell her more than she'd been prepared to admit.

'Haven't you ever thought about leaving Meadwood?' she asked, trying not to sound too hopeful.

At least if Nell had had the same thoughts, she wouldn't feel so ungrateful.

'Not really.' Nell shrugged.

And Ruby couldn't have said why she didn't believe her. Possibly because her heart was already aching.

All these years and she had never known the truth about Ivan's childhood. She could have been kinder. More empathetic. Maybe she could have even helped—though she wasn't sure how.

But she could help now, if only he would let her.

Deep down, she knew it wasn't her place to push Ivan. Nor was it her place to decide whether his own childhood was affecting his current decisions more than she had realized. The form that she'd filled out on his behalf still weighed heavily on Ruby.

How many times had she tried to find the words to tell him what she had done almost a week ago now, only to lose her courage at the last moment?

The weight of some of Ivan's words still lingered in her mind. That determination not to let their unborn baby grow up the way either of them had—without a proper family. The shocking admission that he hadn't really known anything of love for the first fourteen or so years of his life.

She could still hear that steely note to his voice. The one that told her he'd hated how trapped he'd felt. How helpless. But she also knew what had happened with the boys from the hospital that night—against all protocol, she hadn't been able to stop herself from finding out—and it gave her a small sense of victory to know that they were no longer under their father's control where he could hurt them, but were instead now ensconced with a set of grandparents who loved them and wanted to keep them safe.

If only the same could have been done for Ivan and his brother.

Without warning, her mind slid back to the photo in Ivan's London apartment. He and Maksim with their devilish smiles, having a ball at the fairground and clearly as close as two brothers could be.

And Ruby couldn't ignore the gnawing feeling that until she understood Ivan's past better, she would never fully be able to understand the man who was the father of her unborn child.

Which was why she would be doing the right thing if she met Maksim in London on her day off the next day—however much her conscience needled her that if she did so then she would be acting behind Ivan's back.

Betraying him—which was just about the last thing she would ever want to do.

Shaking her head, Ruby stared across the park, missing half of what her best friend was saying. She needed to tell her about Maksim, and about the past they'd never known about Ivan—if anyone could offer her some much-needed advice, then it would be her former foster sister.

But the words wouldn't come, and Ruby couldn't find a way to express to her friend all the things she really wanted to say. And even though they talked, Ruby wasn't sure she would re-member a single word of it afterwards.

But perhaps that was for the best. After all, filling out those forms had been her decision—so it should equally be her de-cision to meet with the man behind the back of the father of her baby.

And it certainly wasn't fair to now start dragging an oblivious Nell into it all, but Ruby couldn't seem to help herself. She pushed on with the conversation anyway, even though she still had no idea how to articulate her worries.

As if it might somehow reveal answers to the questions she hadn't yet had the courage to ask.

CHAPTER TWELVE

RUBY WALKED IN through the door, throwing her keys on the table with exhaustion.

It had been a revelation of a day, but now she was shattered—drained—and not just because her baby had been kicking wildly at her all afternoon.

Meeting Maksim had been an eye-opener. Half-brother or not, the man was exactly like Ivan, and yet nothing like him. They might look like carbon copies of each other, but there was a softness to Maksim that Ruby had always known existed in Ivan—but that Ivan had long since learned to harden.

A softness that she had been glimpsing more and more often—however fleetingly—in the time she had been living in Mill Cottage.

Maksim had enjoyed a decent life—a far more stable one than Ivan—in the end. But it had been gratifying to hear the other man acknowledge just what his big brother had sacrificed for him.

Now all she had to do was convince Ivan to hear Maksim out, and she was sure—*certain*—that it would be the push Ivan needed to finally break free of his chains and embrace his future.

With her and their baby.

'You're back then?'

She swung around guiltily as Ivan's rich voice sounded behind her. Covered in paint but looking mildly satisfied with himself, he began to advance on her.

'Did you have a successful day?'

For a moment, she floundered. 'Successful?'

'You were looking for some things for the baby, were you not?' His smile was almost indulgent this time.

And as he stepped closer, she found herself leaning in, drawing a kind of strength from the warmth that was radiating from his body. His familiar scent enveloped her, and filled her senses with need and longing.

But she couldn't. She mustn't.

Ivan closed the space between them, his hands sneaking around to her shoulders to pull her back to his comforting, muscular chest.

'You know you are breathtaking when you're flustered?' he teased, his lips grazing her ear.

And she knew she should step away, but she couldn't seem to make her legs move.

'Am I?' she whispered, leaning closer still.

His presence was intoxicating, and Ruby found herself drawn by the magnetic pull of him, despite the voice screaming in her head that this was not the time.

She just wanted this one last moment. This one last, guilty pleasure. After all, what harm could it do?

Their lips met, and the world seemed to fade away, leaving only the sensation of warmth spreading through her veins. And as Ruby clung to him, her fingers tangling in the short strands of his dark hair, his arms wrapped around her and he held her close, as if he were afraid she might slip away.

He was wrong. She had no intention of going anywhere—*ever*. Not when every fibre of her being responded to his touch, affirming that her feelings for Ivan ran to her very core.

They parted, breathless, foreheads resting against each other's. The doubts that had clouded her mind seemed less formidable now, overshadowed by the raw emotion that resonated through her entire body. The way he claimed her as his without even saying a word. What words were needed, especially when his mouth, the way his hand held the nape of her neck, the way his arms had her sprawled against him, said it all?

He kissed her again, and again, and again taking his time, being thorough. Each time more perfectly delirious than the last, and every time that kiss swept over her mouth, demanding more, the fire only seemed to burn brighter in her very being.

'These really do have to go,' he teased, lifting his hands to unhook her top and ease down her jeans.

The clothes fell with a *swish* to her feet, gathering in a little denim puddle that she stepped so neatly out of. And then she heard Ivan's sharp intake of breath, and she felt the tiny grin tug at the corners of her mouth. For there, under the clothes, she was wearing the tiniest scraps of lace briefs, and a lacy bra.

He pulled back from her for all of a second, shedding her of the rest of her clothing with ruthless efficiency.

And then she was standing there naked, in front of him, and not feeling the least self-conscious. If anything, Ruby decided feverishly, she felt wanton, womanly, and wholly desired—especially when he slid his hands down to her gently swelling belly to cradle it with a kind of reverence.

But she was all too hot, too needy, to bear it for long.

'I feel that one of us is wearing entirely too much clothing, and the other too little,' she managed after a few moments, reaching down with trembling fingers to try to remove his paint-splattered shirt.

'That can be remedied,' Ivan growled, shedding the garment in an instant before hauling his shirt over his head.

And her throat went immediately dry at the sight of the

man, naked to the waist, standing in front of her with a devilish gleam in his eyes.

Suddenly, before she realized what he was doing, he had hauled her into his arms and was carrying her across the room to the soft couch in the corner only to lay her out like his own personal feast. His gaze slammed into hers with so much desire stamped in their black depths that, for a moment, she thought it might have stolen her breath clean away.

And then he dropped his head and took one proud nipple deep into his mouth—and she knew her breath *had* been stolen.

Need rolled through her like a rumbling thunderstorm, making her judder and shake with every wicked sweep of his tongue. He drew whorls on her skin, hot and wet, then let his teeth graze oh so gently against her—and Ruby thought she might well be burning up from the inside out. And once he had satisfied himself with one nipple, he simply swapped sides and started on the other.

She almost shattered from that alone. But Ivan had other plans. He built her up, higher, and higher, and higher still. Tracing patterns with his tongue whilst letting his hands explore the rest of her. Her waist, her back, and suddenly, her bottom. Too late, she realized what he was doing as he lifted his head, drew a long line with his tongue over the swell of her abdomen, and settled, without warning, between her thighs.

Ruby wanted to come apart right there and then.

His tongue slid over her. Everywhere all at once. From the inside of her thighs to the place where she ached for him most, he was there. Teasing her, taunting her, making her groan with need. Just like he had last time. Just like he was the only man who ever had.

And when she wriggled that little bit too much, he slid his hands beneath her backside, slipping around her bottom and holding her in place whilst he licked into her, hot and deep. He took his time, discovering exactly what made her jolt, what made her moan, and then he set about pleasuring her until she was crying out his name, her hands raking through his hair, not knowing where else to put them.

He learned every inch of her. And then he learned it all over again, making her writhe against him, making her buck her hips, making her arch her back. And just when she thought she couldn't take it anymore, he lowered his mouth and sucked on the very core of her need, sending her spinning off from one burning fire into the next. And each one hotter than the last.

By the time she came back down to earth again, Ivan was naked. As big and thick and perfect as ever, and fresh need juddered through Ruby as she remembered their last time, when she had tasted him. Everywhere. Making him groan in a way that had rumbled right through her entire body. Making her feel more powerful than she had ever felt before—especially in bed.

But this time, it seemed, he had no intention of letting her take charge. Flipping himself onto his back, Ivan hauled her body onto his—giving her the illusion of control though she had no intention of being foolish enough to fall for it. He was like a storm moving over her, through her, and when he used one knee to nudge her legs apart so that he could nestle in between, it was all she could do to obey.

Then, at last, *at last*, he was sliding inside her. Filling her up until she felt utterly possessed. Utterly *his*. And this time there was no stopping herself from screaming his name. Over and over as he hurtled her into space—so high she didn't think she would ever come back down. All she could do was slide her hands around to grab his backside, to pull him into her deeper. Firing them both to the same white-hot finish, and hoping he would catch her when she plummeted back to earth.

And afterwards, Ruby felt happier than she had done in so long—perhaps ever. Everything was a haze of happiness. Euphoria. A surge of emotion welled up within her. Pure, unguarded, almost deliciously overwhelming.

'I love you.'

She didn't realize she'd said the words aloud until she felt Ivan freeze in her arms. Then pull sharply away.

Her hazy brain whirled, trying to replay the last few moments. Had she really said those words out loud?

'That—' Ivan's voice cracked out like thunder '—cannot be.'

'Ivan…'

'I don't do love.' Ivan stood up abruptly, putting physical distance between them, as if that could somehow insulate him from her declaration.

But she refused to apologize for her feelings. Hadn't she been doing altogether too much of that recently?

'And yet, I love you—' she repeated. Firmer this time.

'I won't allow it,' he said to cut her off, his sharp tone as cold and biting as a blade slicing straight through her.

The precision of a scalpel cut to the heart, wielded with all the skill of a surgeon like Ivan. Ruby fought to brace against the pain, but it was impossible. The warmth that had enveloped her only moments before had turned in an instant into an icy chill.

Worse, the man she had just opened her heart up to was now standing apart from her—perhaps only a few feet literally speaking—but he would clearly wish himself entire worlds away if he could. He was a complete stranger to her.

She pulled the sheet up around herself, feeling suddenly, horribly, shamefully exposed. And not just by the fact that she was naked.

'Ivan—' she tried again, only to be cut off. Again.

'I suggest you think very, *very* carefully about what you say next.'

Sorrow poured through her like heavy, wet concrete. His walls were clearly back up, higher and thicker than ever. Any sign of vulnerability was wholly, irrefutably gone.

'Please, Ivan.' It was a fight with herself not to allow her voice to sound even half as panicked as she felt inside. 'I shouldn't have said that.'

'You are going to tell me that you didn't mean it?' he demanded harshly.

But she couldn't lie. 'No, but I was going to say that you don't need to say it back. Not if you aren't ready yet.'

'Yet?' He stared at her incredulously. 'You think this is something that will change? You're wrong. It won't. And you cannot love me. I will not permit it.'

A lesser woman might have been cowed by the commanding tone.

'This isn't something you can, or cannot, permit,' she pointed out softly. 'Much as you may wish to.'

Ivan fixed her with a look that should have been enough to send chills down her spine. But it didn't. She saw that anger and frustration in his eyes, but there was something else, too. Something deeper. And Ruby thought—hoped—that she knew what it was.

'Then it must end. Right now.'

She eyed him for a moment longer, tilting her head ever so slightly to one side.

'Why?' she asked him softly.

His hands balled into fists at his sides, as if he was fighting some internal battle. No doubt against himself. But his stern expression didn't slip, even for a second.

'You know why,' he rasped. 'This…whatever it is between us…is not real. It never was. It is nothing more than an agreeable extension of our convenient family for the baby that you are carrying. *My* baby.'

The tension in the room thickened, almost suffocating her with its intensity as Ivan's words demanded an answer. Acquiescence.

But she couldn't oblige. She wouldn't capitulate. Not when she was so certain that he loved her even if he couldn't admit it. Not even to himself. And not when she suspected that Ivan's guilt over his brother was the reason he'd locked away his heart. Refusing to allow himself to be vulnerable.

'It might have started that way.' Her voice sounded louder and clearer than she could have hoped. 'But you and I both know that there is more than that between us. Perhaps there has been from the start.'

'No. I do not accept that.'

'And still, the signs have been there for both of us to see,' she continued gently.

Because the more moments that passed, the more certain she was becoming that his reaction was born more of fear than anything else. That he was trying to shield himself—and possibly her, too—from potential pain.

But it didn't erase the truth in her heart. If anything, it only gave her the courage to continue.

'I love you, Ivan. And I think you love me, too.'

Ivan's jaw clenched visibly, but he didn't move so neither did she. Instead, she watched, waiting and hoping that his cold facade might begin to fissure and crack under the weight of her gaze. A battle of wills between them as they each determined to stand firm to their own truth. Neither of them willing to yield despite the tumultuous emotions patently swirling between them. She could see the conflict raging within him. Surely one of them would have to break eventually.

She might have known, though, that Ivan would never be the one to do so.

'You are mistaken,' Ivan ground out ultimately, when the silence between them had grown so thick she had thought it might crush them both. 'I do not believe in love. I never have. I'm incapable of it.'

'No.' She shook her head, raising herself up onto her knees on the bed, the sheet still wrapped around her. 'I've seen the way you care for your patients. The depth of feeling you have for Vivian. The way your brother knows you loved him.'

'You have no idea what my brother would or would not have felt about me.' Ivan spun away, picking up his discarded jeans first, then his shirt.

'Actually, I do.' The words were tumbling out of her mouth before she could stop them. 'Because he told me.'

The room stilled completely. A vacuum of sound and space. And it might have lasted a second, or it might have lasted entire aeons, until finally, *finally*, Ivan began to turn around.

'What did you say?' he demanded slowly, as if he had trouble articulating every single word.

Ruby swallowed, but forced herself to continue. 'He's alive, Ivan. That neighbour you spoke to *had* helped them to get away. I met with Maksim today.'

That she had made a mistake was instantly evident.

Ivan's reaction was so immediate, so intense, that it sent a chill creeping right down her spine. If the room had felt cold before, it was nothing compared to the subzero chill that filled it now. Ivan's eyes hardened, darkening to the blackest onyx. His jaw so tight that she was afraid it might actually shatter.

'My brother is alive?' he bit out, as if every syllable was glass in his mouth. 'And he was here?'

'No… I thought it best to meet away from here so when I said I was in town, I drove a couple of hours south.' She paused for a moment, trying to gauge his reaction. 'I thought it was best until I knew what Maksim thought.'

'*You* thought it was best?' Ivan asked far too quietly for Ruby's liking.

'Yes, I...' Ruby's voice petered out.

All she'd wanted to do was help Ivan, but it was patently obvious just how seriously she had misjudged the situation.

Yet still, she couldn't bring herself to feign ignorance. There was too much pain in Ivan, and until he dealt with it, she was terribly afraid that there could be no real future for them as a family. She owed him this much. And, Ruby thought as she cradled her belly, she owed it to their unborn child.

'Ivan, just because you lock the past away in a box and bury it, it doesn't mean it's gone. It only means you're denying its existence.'

'It's gone for me,' he bit out harshly. 'Over. Done with.'

His words were a shield against the truth that seemed to haunt the room, and Ruby's heart clenched painfully at the sound of them. He looked so distant, so guarded—a man so utterly besieged by ghosts that she couldn't even begin to see.

'Except that it isn't,' she whispered. 'Not when I know you keep that old fairground photograph in your apartment. And not when you can't even hear me tell you I love you.'

'Stop saying that,' he barked, and her chest cracked open at the expressions of pain that snatched at his impossibly handsome features.

'Why?' she pressed quietly. 'Because it might make you feel something?'

The growl he emitted was almost animalistic.

'No,' he snapped and gritted his teeth. 'Because I don't want to hear it. I don't believe in it. Love isn't real—it's nothing more than a dangerous lie. It gets people hurt.'

Yet the words seemed to cost him more than he was prepared to pay. Turning abruptly away, Ivan moved away from her and into the shadows that danced at the edges of the soft night light. Like Hades moving towards the darker underworld.

Ruby watched the rigid line of Ivan's back, the bare muscles of his back taut with an anguish he refused to let her see as he stared out the window into the night.

'Don't you even want to know what he said?' she ventured, after what felt like an eternity.

'I do not.'

Except that he didn't try to shut her down. He didn't even move.

'He has had a good life, Ivan,' she told him simply. 'Not straight away, but pretty quickly.'

'I do not wish to hear,' Ivan growled—possibly at her but more likely at his own reflection.

'His mother fled the night the old woman said. Maksim said she dragged him from one village to another, begging, borrowing, stealing, but never staying in the same place for long.'

'I do not care,' he bit out when she paused for breath.

But Ruby ignored him. 'This story is Maksim's to tell rather than mine, but whilst you're too scared to face him, I'll have to give you the bare bones.'

'Do not bother.'

'Too late.' Ruby feigned nonchalance. 'So, for the first month or so, she actually managed to look after him better than might have been expected, but after that she fell back into old habits. This time, however, a neighbour saw and they stepped in. Maksim ended up in a home, but he got lucky and the long-term foster placement he was given turned out to be a perfect fit. They fostered him for five years, and then adopted him as soon as they were able.'

'Sounds like a fairy-tale ending,' he drawled, his tone suggesting different.

And anyone else might have been fooled, but Ruby wasn't. This was classic Ivan, concealing his hurt, his scars, with indifference and distance.

'They loved Maksim, and he loved them. A *fairy-tale ending* doesn't sound like it's too far off the mark,' she agreed brightly. 'And you did that, Ivan.'

She'd hoped Ivan would be relieved. Proud. Even happy. But Ruby quickly realized that she'd underestimated that, too.

'Don't you see, Ivan?' she prompted softly when he still didn't answer. 'You saved Maksim. Just as you'd set out to do.'

'I seriously doubt that,' Ivan spat out, making her blink in surprise.

Her heart picked up its pace. Clearly, he hadn't heard what she'd said. He hadn't had the chance to process it.

'What isn't in doubt, however,' he continued furiously as he finally spun back around, 'is that you crossed a line by tracking down my brother. Worse, by contacting him.'

'I wanted to help you,' she cried. 'You must see that.'

'I've kept my past buried for a reason.' Ivan ignored her cry, his frustration and fury growing by the second. 'You had absolutely no right to go digging it all up.'

And all she wanted to do was hurry over to him and throw her arms around him, the way she knew he needed her to do. The way he was so desperate for someone to do.

But deep down, she knew he wouldn't thank her for it. Not now. He still wasn't ready to let go of the past and move on. Yet the more she tried to gently nudge him forward, the more she was clearly pushing him away.

And still, she had to keep trying.

'A past that you've buried because not knowing was too horrifying,' she pointed out. It was not an accusation so much as a plea for him to consider alternative outcomes. 'And that's stopping you from really opening your heart to love.'

'Perhaps so,' Ivan managed harshly, his control slipping as his voice rose. 'But love doesn't erase fear, Ruby. Nor does it fix broken families or mend years of torment.'

'What if love gives us strength to face those fears? To start to heal what has been damaged? You could just try, Ivan. Just meet your brother. Hear whatever he has to say. At least you'll know.'

'No, I cannot.' Ivan shook his head, a maelstrom of emotion swirling behind his eyes. 'I won't. It's too much of a risk. It's over and done, Ruby. If what you say is true, then Maksim and I have our own lives now and they are completely separate from each other. That's how they need to stay.'

And she could let it go right there and then. But how could she when her heart grieved so dreadfully for him? Just as Ivan mourned the brother he'd lost in trying to save him.

'Whatever you think, Maksim is a part of you, whether you want to admit it or not.' She desperately scanned his face for any sign that she was reaching him. 'He's a vital part of your past, and I'm terribly afraid that until you make him a part of your future—or at least your present—then you can never put the past to rest.'

'You have no idea,' Ivan spat out, no longer able to contain his anger. 'And you had no damned right to contact him.'

'I just thought…'

'No, you didn't.' He stalked across the room, buttoning up his paint-soiled shirt with such force that it was amazing it didn't shred right in his hands. 'You didn't think at all. You knew I had chosen not to search for Maksim, but you did it anyway.'

'To help,' she pleaded, but his face was as hard and implacable as his icy tone.

'I trusted you, and you betrayed me,' he told her. 'And I can never forgive you for that.'

'Ivan…'

'I'll support my child, and this house is yours as long as you want it. But this…' He gestured between them, a gulf that suddenly seemed impossible to bridge. '*Us*. It was a mistake. We cannot be a part of each other's lives.'

Her heart splintered at his words, so violently that she half expected the room to be showered in its fractured shards.

'You don't mean that,' she gasped, scarcely able to breathe.

'Believe whatever you want to,' he clipped out. 'I no longer care.'

And then, as she sat on the bed scrambling for something—anything—to say to stop him, he yanked open the door so that it swung violently on its hinges, and strode out.

Leaving Ruby alone in a room that felt like it was closing in on her with every passing second. The sound of her ragged breathing reached her ears but she was helpless to silence herself. The future that she had begun to imagine—full of hope, and promise, and *love*—now lay shattered at her feet.

In so many tattered pieces that there was no hope of ever patching it back together again.

CHAPTER THIRTEEN

FINISHING METICULOUSLY SCRUBBING IN, Ivan carefully fitted his mask over his face and inhaled with relief as he stepped through the doors of his operating room in his private London clinic.

This place had been his sanctuary these past couple of weeks. Sixteen painful days, to be exact. He knew it down to the hour, and the operating room had been his haven in all that time, his escape from the turmoil that had been chasing through him every moment since Ruby had no longer been a part of his life.

Out there, in the real world, he couldn't seem to push back down the strange mix of emotions that she had brought bubbling to the surface with her efforts to get him to reconnect with his estranged brother. And the unfamiliar, unwanted, and most of all deeply unsettling emotions churned through him, over and over, whether he was working in his office, cooking a meal, or pounding the parklands for mile after mile after mile.

But his OR was his fortress of concentration. In here, it was all about the patient, the surgery; there was no room for any other thoughts. And somehow, that offered him much-needed peace. Four simple walls which somehow created a powerful haven from the jumble of sentiments. The place where his years of dedication, and honing his skills, were all that mattered. Where his surgical precision and instinct were all that counted. No self-recriminations. No second-guessing. Every second in here was carved into the fabric of fate, yet it all felt second nature to him.

Unlike the complexities of sharing his life with Ruby.

Thrusting the unwanted thoughts from his head, Ivan focused on the imminent surgery—an abraded punch graft procedure.

Carefully, he dermabraded the area before correcting the pitted facial scars. It was a slow and meticulous task which demanded his concentration and left no room for any other, unwanted thoughts.

Of anyone.

Though it seemed all too ironic that the marks on his patient's face were nothing to the scars he knew Ruby carried in her heart. Something he wouldn't have been so sensitive to a matter of months ago.

Now she almost reminded him of himself, and he wielded his scalpel like a sword against the memories and doubts that would threaten to slay him. And he wouldn't ever admit to anyone that there was a secret part of him that wondered as he carefully punched, abraded, and sutured—healing the damaged skin and making it appear whole again—if perhaps one day, he could find a way to also heal the fragments of his own fractured world.

As he worked, slowly and methodically, the edges of Ivan's vision tunnelled, the bright overhead lights casting an unforgiving glare on the exposed tissues before him whilst the rhythmic beeping of the heart monitor kept a low, monotonous beat as they counted the seconds, then the minutes, and finally the hours.

At last the surgery was complete and his focus was over—and even before he had finished scrubbing out, the real world started to instantly press on the edges of Ivan's mind.

Like wondering how Ruby and the baby were doing, given that Ruby was officially approaching her third trimester.

And then he told himself that the frisson that just rippled through him at the realization was nothing more than medical curiosity rather than a surge of unexpected emotion.

At twenty-one weeks their baby would be developing essential skills like sucking and breathing, it would be evolving its sense of taste, and it would be establishing its waking patterns, which could well be when Ruby was trying to sleep.

He hoped she wasn't feeling overwhelmed with the changes her body had to be going through.

Was she taking care of herself? Getting enough sleep?

Ivan berated himself. It was not his business to tell her what to do, yet he couldn't shake the feeling of concern for her well-being, and as he changed out of his surgical scrubs and into his daily clothes, the weight of his thoughts about Ruby and the baby settled heavier on his shoulders.

With each step he took back to his office—away from his operating room sanctuary—the more he felt the pull of his personal life growing stronger, tugging at the edges of his carefully compartmentalized mind.

His footsteps grew heavier as he made his way back to his office and thought of the cold emptiness of it. What wouldn't he give for a coffee at *Re-cup-eration,* or to hear Ruby's gentle laugh that whatever the vending machines at City Hospital spewed out, it wasn't *coffee*?

Throwing open his office door, Ivan thrust the memories from his thoughts and faced the stack of paperwork on his desk and the flashing lights on his phone that indicated a couple of messages. With a sigh, he sank down heavily into his chair and played the first one. He was about to move onto the second when it lit up with an interruption from his receptionist.

He answered it quickly, and there was a nervous clearing of the throat on the other end.

'There's a visitor for you in reception, Dr Volkov.'

Ruby?

He schooled himself not to react. To quash that flash of hope that he suspected had been about to penetrate his chest. Because what good would it do for them to speak again? What had changed in the past couple of weeks?

Was it only that long? It felt like an eternity, perhaps two.

And the simple truth was that nothing had changed. *Nothing.*

Because she had still betrayed him, contacting Maksim— *meeting* him. And Ivan had nothing more to offer her than he had two weeks ago. He was still the same broken, wrecked man he had been then. Being a surgeon was his only saving grace— it was the only thing he should be focused on from now on.

'Advise her that I will be indisposed until late into the evening.'

And no matter that he hated the sound of each word that came out of his mouth. Almost as much as he hated himself for saying it.

The line crackled and Ivan braced himself for his instruction to be acknowledged. He certainly wasn't expecting his receptionist to counter him.

'It isn't a *she*.' The hesitation in the voice was unmistakable. 'It's a man and he says he's your brother.'

Something jagged and exacting shot through Ivan in that instant.

'Maksim?' Ivan wasn't aware he'd uttered the name aloud until it was confirmed by the voice over the intercom.

'He says he'll wait as long as it takes.'

Time seemed to freeze. His mind first went utterly blank, then was filled with so many half-finished thoughts that Ivan didn't know where to start. And all of it happened within a fraction of a second.

Conflicting emotions charged around his brain as he gritted his teeth so tightly that he was half-afraid his jaw might shatter. It took Ivan longer than it should have to push aside the doubts that momentarily haunted the edges of his mind at the revelation that the unexpected visitor was Maksim of all people. But there was something else, too. Something Ivan hadn't been able to eject even though he tried.

That traitorous hint of hope. And the realization that Ruby had been right to contact his brother after all. No matter everything he'd told himself about keeping his distance and letting the past lie buried, the realization that Maksim was here, *now*, filled Ivan with an undeniably fierce need to hasten down the corridor and look at his baby brother with his own eyes.

To understand what had happened.

And suddenly, it became too clear to Ivan that it was the *not knowing* that had chewed him up inside, far more than anything Maksim could have to tell him. However his little brother judged him for that fateful decision two decades ago, whatever kind of life Maksim had endured—it was better to know than to fear the worst.

Before he knew what he was doing, Ivan found himself out of his seat and halfway out of the room, marching briskly as he navigated the warren of corridors with renewed purpose. Because even if Maksim hated him for his choices, Ruby was right to have pushed him to confront them. She hadn't been wrong when she'd urged him that it was better to face his demons than to hide from them any longer.

She hadn't been betraying him; she'd been trying to set him free. So why the hell had it taken this long to see it?

Ruby. She'd understood the weight of his past choices bearing down on him, threatening to crush him, far better than he ever had. She'd cared enough to want to help him find a way out from under it. And he'd thanked her by accusing her of betraying him—by leaving her to deal with the pregnancy all alone.

He'd let her down the way he'd let Maksim down—precisely the opposite of the very man he'd wanted to be.

Right there he made a vow that the moment he had spoken with his brother—no matter if Maksim hated him, or had come to terms with what he'd done back then—he would return directly to Little Meadwood and find Ruby. Perhaps not to make things right, since it was too late for that, but to apologize for what he'd said and to thank her for the courage and wisdom that she'd clearly shown.

But first, he had to get through this—and even as he approached the reception area, Ivan couldn't prevent his pulse from speeding up. From anxiety settling in every bone of his body. What would his brother say to him? What was he even to begin to say to Maksim? Would they even know each other?

For a moment, he wished Ruby was with him. One look in those warm, hazel eyes that always seemed such a balm to the tempest within him—even when she was mad with him. Her mouth that could curve up in a way that her smile was as glorious as the dawn breaking through the darkness. Her touch that seemed so gentle yet fired him up in a way no woman had ever done before.

Ivan felt a smile play on his lips at the memory as he paused, temporarily frozen, on the other side of the reception doors. Ruby was the only person who had made him feel everything—and nothing—all at once. So alive, yet burden free. And he had pushed her away. What kind of a pathetic man did that make him?

The kind who knew he couldn't give her what she needed,

a voice needled inside his head, reminding him of facts he would do well not to forget again.

Ruby deserved better than he could ever offer her.

So, wiping the foolish smile away, Ivan thrust out his hands to the heavy oak and strode across the threshold.

Then stopped dead.

Maksim.

Even if he hadn't known his estranged brother was waiting in that room, he would have recognized the man who rose instantly to his feet from the waiting room couch. Gone was the scrawny kid that Ivan remembered, and in his place a man who felt so familiar that it was almost like looking in the mirror.

Yet somehow there was an easiness about Maksim that Ivan didn't recognize. A softer side, as though he hadn't been worn down by life's harshest strokes, the way that he himself had been. Or was that just his subconscious, wanting to believe what Ruby had said about Maksim's childhood having turned out far better than much of his own?

The unfamiliar sensation of uncertainty threaded its way through Ivan much like his shared history with his brother—a tapestry woven with pain, resilience, and the violence they'd never spoken about even as kids. Not until he'd shared a glimpse of it with Ruby. Did Maksim have someone in his life like that?

Ivan had no idea how long he stood there, rooted in place and staring at the familiar stranger who wasn't moving or speaking, either. Did he, too, sense the past that loomed between them, tangible and disquieting?

'Maksim,' Ivan uttered at length, his usually commanding voice faltering and betraying his surprise.

The other man's tentative smile did little to mask the apprehension in his dark eyes—eyes so like Ivan's own but with flecks that were lacking when Ivan looked in a mirror. How had he forgotten that detail about his little brother?

Yet he wasn't convinced it was merely the almost-identical colour which was so unsettling. Ivan couldn't shake the sense that this other man's eyes reflected a world he had fought hard to leave behind. A world that he had convinced himself he actually *had* left behind.

But now the memories were creeping back. Unkind and unwelcome, leaving Ivan struggling to suck in a breath and feeling winded—as though his father was right there in front of him, ready to beat him as he always had. It was only Maksim's voice which dragged Ivan back into the present.

'Hello, brother,' Maksim spoke with a careful neutrality. 'It has been a long time.'

For a second, Ivan wasn't certain he would be able to reply. He moved his vocal cords up and down, as if unsure his mouth would cooperate.

'It has,' Ivan managed a reply at last, though the words felt foreign on his lips.

'Yes.'

Another long silence, and Ivan resisted the sudden urge to move his weight from one foot to the other, the polished granite floor suddenly felt like shifting sands beneath him. If that wasn't enough, the charged silence jolted through his body, shaking Ivan to his core and awakening even more ghosts of memories that now demanded to be heard.

Everything suddenly felt too bright, too sharp, too stark. But it was too late to slam the lid back on that proverbial box. Too late to walk away. Especially when—the longer they stood there—the more the stream of unwanted memories became a deluge, threatening to break through the dam that was his composure.

Not just memories of beatings, but memories of a cold so

biting that it might as well have taken their fingers off; a hunger so excruciating that he could happily have hollowed out his own stomach with the bluntest of knives.

But abruptly—unexpectedly—among those painful memories, Ivan caught a few surprise snatched moments of happiness. That forgotten closeness that he and Maksim had once shared. The weeks they had been okay, just the two of them, when their father had been away from home on some bender or other, and Maksim's mother had been too out of it to help. The vow he'd made to protect little Maksim against their father's wrath, and the pride he'd felt at succeeding.

Which only made it all the more painful to reflect on how they had ended up here. No longer boys, but men—no longer brothers, but strangers. Bound by blood yet separated by a chasm filled with years and unsaid truths. But none of them to be voiced here in reception, in front of too many sets of prying ears.

'Come through,' Ivan clipped out curtly, pulling himself together at last. 'We can speak in my office.'

As his younger brother offered a terse dip of his head, Ivan spun around and led the way back down the high-gloss corridors and to the door marked with his name. His brother was keeping pace with him, yet neither of them closing the gap at all on the other.

Even when Ivan pushed open the door, he walked in first, leaving Maksim to follow at a considered distance. Then, as if by unspoken agreement, the two men claimed chairs on opposite sides of the desk, as though each was taking comfort from the physical distance. Then, once again, the quiet pressed in on them.

'I can't believe that you are here, Maksim.' Ivan forced himself to break the silence, though he feared the wariness that laced his voice also belied his attempt to show that he was in control of his emotions.

Although if his brother noticed then he didn't show it.

'Ruby found me.' Maksim fixed Ivan's gaze with a direct stare of his own. 'She related to me the story you'd told her. I realized it was time we spoke.'

'Up until a few minutes ago I would have said that she should not have done that,' Ivan growled. 'I had no intention of intruding on your life.'

'That was made clear to me.'

And though Ivan scrutinised the words for what Maksim wasn't saying, the tension in the room seemed to be thickening with every passing second yet he felt powerless to prevent it. His brother's expression remained frustratingly neutral, a mask that revealed none of his true feelings.

Ivan pressed on anyway.

'However the moment my receptionist told me you were here, I realized that it has been the not-knowing that has bound me all these years. Even if you hate me, I am grateful that Ruby did what she did.'

'Ruby does not seem like the kind of woman who seeks permission for things she believes to be right,' a soft smile played around Maksim's lips, startling Ivan momentarily. 'Or am I wrong, brother?'

Any further disapproval Ivan might have been ready to make evaporated in an instant. All he could focus on was how the word 'brother' hung in the air between them. A relic from a past Ivan had never thought he'd hear again. A name he'd long-since compartmentalized and sealed away.

Brother.

He wanted to leap up and clasp Maksim in the embrace he once used to do, and never let go. Ivan's fists grasped the arms of his chair as he kept himself absolutely still.

'How is she?' his brother asked suddenly. 'And the baby?'

'Ruby and I are no longer together,' Ivan admitted, not realizing he'd been about to utter the words until he heard them spilling from his mouth.

Too much information. But it was too late to swallow them back now.

Maksim, however, narrowed his eyes shrewdly.

'Oh?' There was that irritatingly calm demeanour again. 'That is a shame. Not everyone finds that person who will fight for them the way she did for you. The way that you did for me.'

Ivan tried to stop his jaw from clenching, but he couldn't. That ache around his chest tightened further as he stared at his brother. What was he to say? Or think? There were too many emotions crowding inside him, pulling him in different directions, threatening to rip him apart.

'I'm ashamed to say it took me far too long to realize that,' Ivan manged simply. 'But now I have, I intend to remedy it as soon as possible.'

How was it he was confessing things to his brother that he would never have confessed to anyone else? As if they had never been apart?

It had to be Ruby's influence—another thing to be grateful to her for.

'I'm glad,' Maksim noted after a pause. 'She seemed like quite a remarkable woman. But I did not come here to lecture you on your life. I did come here to talk about you and I. About our past.'

Despite the neutrality of his tone, his younger brother leaned forward as though psychologically wanting to bridge some of the distance between them. But though Ivan realized he wanted to do the same, he found it impossible to move.

It only made it all the clearer to Ivan that although Ruby had already helped him to soften so much, he still had a long way to go. But for the first time, he knew that he wanted to. He had spent years crafting his environment, his world, to ensure that nothing reached him, but he no longer wanted to be so remote, so detached, so isolated.

And that was all thanks to Ruby.

'I would like that,' he managed to answer his brother at last.

And for a moment they merely sat in silence. But far from being an awkward one, it gave them both chance to regroup.

'The truth is,' Maksim began, and this time Ivan was gratified to hear the crack in his brother's voice which suggested the younger man wasn't as in control as he appeared, 'I owe you more than you know. You shielded me from the worst of what happened in that house. You fed me, washed me, clothed me. How many nights did you go hungry just so that I wouldn't have to?'

'I was the older brother.'

'You were my brother, my father, my mother, all rolled into one,' Maksim countered. 'I don't think I would have survived if not for you.'

'It was my job to protect you.'

'And whose job was it to protect *you*?'

As his brother's words found their mark, Ivan felt his breath catching in his chest. His defences, so carefully constructed, began to erode.

He suspected Ruby had already played her part in softening them, too.

'That isn't how it works...' he choked out, unable to bear looking at his brother.

How could he, when the image reflected back at him was not one of a hardened survivor, scarred and bitter, but rather a guardian whose love had been fierce and unwavering? It wasn't right. It wasn't accurate. It wasn't who he'd been.

Yet his brother seemed to disagree.

'You were there for me every single day,' Maksim ground out. 'You saved me and I let you down.'

'Stop.' Ivan barked out the single-word command like a reflex honed from years in the operating room. 'You make me out to be something I was not. I was trying to survive, but I didn't save you. If I had, then I never would have left you.'

'If you hadn't got out, he would have killed you,' Maksim spoke quietly but there was no denying the thickness in his voice. 'We both know that.'

'But in doing so, I left you there with him,' Ivan choked out as he thrust back his chair and stood, too pent-up to stay seated any longer.

'You had no choice.' Maksim shrugged. 'And you did what you said. The authorities got there that night.'

Fury spread through Ivan. 'And they did nothing. They ignored your bruises, they believed his lies, and they left. I let you down.'

'You frightened them,' his brother pointed out. 'Enough that he didn't come near us for a week. By then, my mother had planned her escape. We left in the middle of the night.'

'Because I failed you.'

'You didn't fail me,' Maksim refuted, pulling something out of his pocket. 'You were my hero, Ivan. Always.'

'I ripped our family apart,' Ivan growled, and though he fought not to, his voice broke as his self-control crumbled. 'I *left* you with them. I should never have done that.'

He turned his back to his brother, caught off guard when Maksim slid something across his desk. An old photo, much like the one he himself had kept, except with slightly different poses.

'Do you remember this, Ivan? Do you remember the pact we made to always protect each other?'

His hands shaking uncharacteristically, Ivan placed his fin-

gers on the photo and pulled it to him. His eyes raked over
the fairground picture slowly, absorbing every familiar detail.

But whilst in his photo the two of them were on a horse
merry-go-round, in Maksim's they'd been dunking for apples
and were both soaked.

'I remember,' he rasped, his voice cracking.

'Well, you did that, Ivan. You saved my life,' Maksim said
quietly. 'Many times, but especially that night. You risked everything and I let you.'

His brother's words echoed in the room, louder than the
most deafening of silences. The words were swirling in the
air around them, settling on him, threatening to exploit any
crack they could find in the high walls Ivan had spent years
building for himself.

Walls that he suspected Ruby had already begun to weaken
from their very foundations.

'I looked for you, you know,' he admitted at last. 'I returned
to that house, but you weren't there.'

'Ruby told me.'

Ivan took a breath. 'I didn't know if he'd done something
to you. No one would tell me.'

'Most didn't know. Only old lady Craven—she took our
bags and hid them until we were ready to go.'

'I asked her, too,' Ivan ground out. 'She eventually told
me you both left in the middle of one night. But I never knew
whether to believe her or whether that was just what my father had told her.'

'You did everything you could possibly have done,' Maksim
confirmed. 'You were there for me, but I should have been
there for you, too. I should have told someone—anyone—what
was happening. I should have protected you, too.'

A swell of emotions threatened to undo Ivan. Pride, regret,
and an ache for the bond they once shared—all intertwined.

'How could you have protected me? You were a kid.' Ivan shook his head, the very idea being too much for him.

But it seemed that was his brother's point.

'I could have looked for you the way you looked for me. I could have told my adopted family that I had a brother. I left you alone, Ivan. And I'm more sorry than you will ever know.'

'That isn't necessary,' Ivan murmured, but a fissure was forming in the walls around his heart, and if he wasn't careful, he was rather afraid it might blow those walls out.

'Maybe not for you,' Maxim insisted gently. 'But for me, it is.'

Ivan shook his head, struggling to take it all in. And as the two brothers sat there, their shared dark history finally beginning to dissipate now that it had finally been aired in the bright light of day, something cracked deep inside Ivan and everything simply...*shifted*.

'I never expected to see you again, Maksim,' he confessed, his voice low and sincere. 'Let alone for you to forgive me.'

For a moment, the younger man merely stared at him before replying, 'You misunderstand, big brother. There is nothing to forgive.'

And that simply, that easily, the crushing weight of years of self-recrimination, loathing, and guilt seemed to just seep out of Ivan's chest. With it, he could feel the weight of his childhood lighten ever so slightly—the acknowledgement from Maxim acting as a balm to old wounds that he had never even known he needed.

But Ruby had known. And she had done the one thing that he himself could never have managed. If not for her conviction that meeting Maksim was the closure he needed on his past—the turning point for him to finally move on with his future, and with their child that she was carrying—he would still be caged up inside that prison of his own making.

She had known what he needed when he himself had railed against it. And she had fought for him in spite of his ire.

No matter how much he tried to tell himself that he didn't care about this crazy, funny, unique woman, Ivan knew it was a lie. Perhaps it had always been a lie. And now these feelings, this...*tenderness* pushed inside him—tentative but growing all the same, like the first hopeful sprouts pushing through the cracks of a long-frozen earth.

A fondness—more than fondness—for Ruby, a woman whose kindness was innate and who saw beyond his guarded exterior to the vulnerability he had never dared to expose. And he should loathe her for doing so. But he didn't. He couldn't. He loved her.

He loved her.

For the first time in his life, Ivan felt the floodgates of his heart begin to buckle. A tentative drip at first, and then a trickle. Before long, it would be a river and then a torrent of emotions that he had kept tightly sealed for far, far too long.

He was in love with Ruby, and though he and Maksim had more—so much more—to discuss, once that was done, he knew the first thing he needed to do would be to find Ruby. And to tell her how she'd also been right about the way he felt about her.

He loved her. And he loved their unborn baby.

It was finally time to stop hiding from himself, and to claim his family.

CHAPTER FOURTEEN

RUBY WAS SMOOTHING down her favourite steampunk outfit at Nell's stall for the village fête—waiting for her friend to finish talking to an eager couple who were clearly trying to decide which costumes to choose—when she sensed Ivan behind her, moments before he spoke.

'Ruby.'

Uncertain if she'd imagined it, she turned. Slowly. As though she was afraid that if she spun around too fast it would cause him to disappear.

But when she finished her agonizing pivot, he was still there. In the flesh.

'Ivan,' she began, hating herself for the way she seemed to just drink him in—head to toe—unable to help herself.

But something hitched inside as she realized something was…*different. He* was different. And she didn't need him to tell her that he'd finally spoken with his brother. It was etched into every ridge on his impossibly handsome face. Given away by that sudden…*lightness* to him, as if a huge burden had been lifted from his shoulders. Even the darkness of his eyes somehow held a glint that showed he was… *happier.*

And even though she knew he would never forgive her for betraying his trust, it brought her relief to know that what she'd done hadn't been a total loss. Even so, she was shocked when he started to speak.

'You were right,' he stated, his voice raspier than she had expected.

Ruby blinked, unsure what she was supposed to say. 'Okay,' she managed weakly, at last.

'About Maksim. About me.' He took another step towards her, then stopped. 'About everything.'

He was breathing as hard as if he'd just run a race, though it was clear he had done no such thing, and whatever she'd hoped for in those secret dreams in the darkest hours of the night, it hadn't been this. Ivan Volkov, the Prince of Guarded Emotions, standing in front of her, vulnerable and open. The heady rush of emotions almost left her breathless.

The words hung in the air between them, his raw honesty taking her utterly by surprise. After all that had been said between them—or hadn't—this might have been enough for her. But it seemed Ivan had more to say.

'Can we talk?'

His voice was low but sure. Determined. Not that she had any desire to refuse him. Not when she'd spent so long willing him to open up to her. Even a little bit. All the same, Ruby had no idea how she managed to keep her tone so calm and even.

'Of course.'

With a brief glance over her shoulder to see Nell still absorbed in conversation with the young couple, Ruby gave Ivan a slight nod and followed him out of the stall and across the bustling village green.

'You were right about Maksim having had a good life,' Ivan told her once they'd walked the length of the cricket pitch.

Again Ruby nodded, but it was the sheer relief in Ivan's tone that tugged at something deep within her. The release from the blame that he'd placed on himself all these years. And as she walked beside him on the quiet path that ran down from the green to the abandoned railway line, she couldn't help noticing the subtle changes in him. Even his gait seemed somehow less…laden with duty.

Was it just her imagination, or was she sensing that familiar connection building between them—only better? As though Ivan was no longer fighting to keep his distance? To shut her out?

Ruby fought to control the flare of hope that went off inside her chest.

As they reached a secluded bench under a canopy of trees next to the abandoned Victorian railway line—its tracks long gone with only the cinder path the remaining witness to the line's heyday—Ivan sank down almost gratefully and stared off into the distance before retrieving something from his pocket which he placed in Ruby's palms. And his hands, usually so rock-steady when wielding a scalpel, trembled faintly as he traced the outline of the old fairground photograph that Maksim had handed him.

The edges were worn, and the colours were faded, but there was no mistaking the image of two young boys with tentative smiles—a bond that had been both a lifeline and a source of infinite pain.

'Maksim kept this,' Ivan murmured, his voice barely above a whisper, the sound swallowed by the hum of the village fête around them. 'He said it reminded him of our promise, our pact to always look out for each other.'

He handed it to her and she took it carefully.

'That's like the photograph in your London apartment,' Ruby murmured, love blooming all the brighter inside her.

Except that Ivan didn't want her love. He didn't want anything from her at all.

Then why is he here?

The voice whispered in her head before she could silence it, so instead she pretended not to hear it. She focused on the unmistakable battle in Ivan's eyes—evidence of a war waged within his own head, between regret and acceptance.

'I was wrong to say you had betrayed me,' Ivan continued, lifting his gaze to meet Ruby's. 'I was wrong to blame you. All those years, I carried the guilt of my separation from Maksim, and I didn't want to face it. It was easier to be angry at you for raising the past than it was for me to actually confront my own missteps.

'Maksim never blamed you, did he?' Ruby couldn't help herself from asking. Gently, without condemnation. A feather-light touch that urged Ivan to finally unfurl the truth that was clenched so tightly in his fist.

He exhaled heavily, a breath that seemed to carry years of misgivings with it.

'No, he never blamed me. How brave he had to have been, left alone with them.'

'Bravery doesn't always wear a medal, Ivan.' She shook her head gently, reaching out to return the photo to him so that he could look at it again. 'Sometimes it's in the choices we make, the ones that change the course of our lives. You and your brother made a pact to protect each other, and that was what you did—just perhaps not in the way you had expected to. Your courage wasn't in fists or force. It was in your voice, your willingness to shatter the silence that traps so many others.'

'He told me that he forgave me,' he rasped at length. 'Actually, that isn't true—he told me that there was nothing to forgive.'

'From the conversation I had with your brother,' Ruby offered tentatively, 'I think he's right.'

'He isn't.' Without warning, Ivan reached his hand out; his

long fingers stroked her cheek just once, but it was enough to make her almost feverish.

'I need to know if you can forgive me,' he rasped. 'I treated you badly, telling you that you had betrayed me—even *believing* that you would have done so. I was scared, and racked with guilt, and I took it out on you.'

'You didn't trust me,' Ruby managed, her throat thick with emotion. 'You wouldn't even hear me out.'

'And that was my mistake. But one, I swear to you, that I will never make again. I should have believed in you, Ruby, the way you always believed in me.'

She almost forgot how to breathe.

'Yes,' she choked out.

'Why did you believe in me?'

She hesitated. The answer was so complex yet simultaneously so straightforward.

'Because the teenage boy I knew all those years ago, back at Vivian's, was kind and compassionate. I could never stand to see the way you seemed to hate yourself. I thought you were worth far more.'

She stopped as the words hung in the hot summer air. The quiet rustle of the leaves and distant murmur of the village fête stopped the silence from becoming too heavy.

'I was broken, Ruby.' His voice was low, but no less charged with emotion. 'I was terrified of becoming *him*, my father, and passing on that cruel streak. And his selfishness.'

Ruby's hand tentatively found its way to his, her touch light but anchoring.

'You are not your father, Ivan. You have a kind heart. I see it every day in how you care for your patients, for me, for our unborn baby.'

'I want to believe that.' Ivan swallowed hard, the muscles in his jaw tightening. 'I've been so afraid of the darkness in me, of the legacy I might pass on…but my brother showed me another side to myself that I had never allowed myself to see before. The side that you've been trying to show me all this time. I'm sorry I didn't listen to you.'

'I understand why you needed Maksim to be the one to make you see it,' Ruby assured him. As though her chest wasn't swelling with all the emotions she was trying to keep in.

'I want to be a father, Ruby,' Ivan announced suddenly. 'Not like him—never like him—but someone who is present, caring…loving. Someone our child can depend on.'

'I know that. I've always known it.'

'Well, I want to do that with you.' Ivan's eyes were earnest, reflecting the clear blue sky above them. 'I want us to build a life that's ours, filled with love and not the shadows of either of our pasts.'

Ruby's breath caught in her throat as she absorbed his words. Could it really be that her own dreams of a real family were finally coming to life right in front of her? But this was no fantasy, dreamed of in the middle of night when her mother was in hospital and her foster mother was asleep. This was potentially real, with all the complexities and scars they both carried.

'I want that, too,' she managed, barely recognizing her own voice.

'But do you really believe we could have a future together that is untainted by the past? Pure?'

'I do,' she assured him solemnly. 'Love is not a force to be wielded, Ivan, but a gift to be offered without strings.'

'Then I am offering my love to you.'

'Before you do, you should know that I have a confession of my own to make,' Ruby began, licking her lips as she searched for the right words. 'These past few weeks have made me wonder if that picture-perfect vision I had of a future family—of a life together—might not be quite realistic.'

'Oh?'

She could practically see the shutters begin to drop in his expression and before she could stop herself, Ruby shot her hand out to touch his chest.

The contact was electric. Her hand splayed, palm down as if drawing energy from the contact.

'And I think that's a good thing,' she stumbled on, still searching for the right words. 'I think I needed to let go of those naive, childlike expectations. The perfect life that I used to pretend I had when I was a kid. Like being a princess and living in a castle.'

'I'm not a prince,' Ivan told her gravely. 'And I don't have a castle.'

'That's my point.' She lifted her eyes to meet his. 'It might have taken me a while to grow out of that fantasy—my comfort blanket from being in and out of foster care—but I'm finally realizing that I don't need either. I just need someone who will stand with me through life's storms. No matter how fierce they may get.'

And it was true. Gone were those girlish daydreams of white picket fences and storybook endings. Life wasn't like that. It was messier, more complicated, and filled with give and take. Just as Vivian had always tried to teach her.

Life with someone you loved meant finding a balance. And Ruby wanted that balance with Ivan Volkov, more than she ever could have imagined.

'And what if sometimes *I* am the storm?' Ivan rasped, a tormented expression momentarily clouding his eyes.

'Then I'll be your anchor,' she declared and pressed her hand harder to his chest. 'Besides, sometimes a storm is exactly what is needed to bring a new, brighter dawn.'

'I believe you will.' Ivan's eyes softened as he gazed at her. 'And I vow to spend every second of every day loving you for it. And making sure you never regret that decision.'

And the smile that touched Ruby's lips flooded up from deep inside her. The weight of his words and depth of his commitment to her washed over like the softest of embraces on a hot summer day.

It was only when he slid off the wooden bench and onto one knee on the grass before her that she realized what he really meant.

'Ruby, there's something I need to ask you.'

As her breath hitched, exhilaration pulsed through her and her gaze dropped of its own volition to Ivan's upturned palm. A sapphire-and-diamond ring sat nestled on the most velvety blue cushion.

'Be my wife, Ruby?' Ivan's voice cracked with vulnerability she didn't think she'd ever heard before. 'Not out of duty, and not because of the precious baby that you are carrying, but because we love each other. Because together, we can overcome any challenge that comes our way.'

And Ruby wasn't sure it was only her holding her breath, or if the entire world around them was doing the same. For a moment, the breeze seemed to still in the trees, the sounds of the fête growing suddenly silent. She blinked rapidly, her eyes hot and prickling as she slowly edged to the front of the bench, her hands reaching out to cradle Ivan's face.

'Yes,' she whispered, her voice thick with emotion. 'A thousand times yes.'

As his face cracked into the widest smile, he slid the ring on her finger and pulled her close, his mouth claiming hers in a way she knew she would never in a dozen lifetimes grow weary of. And as he held her to him, she felt her chest rise and fall against his, her body fitting his as though they were handcrafted for each other.

'I love you,' he murmured, his breath tickling her ear and sending shivers down his spine. 'And I believe in us—in the family we will become.'

'I love you,' she echoed softly. Reverently.

Three simple words that held myriad promises.

'Whatever life looks like in the future,' he told her solemnly, taking her face in his hands and staring deep into her eyes as though he could see through to her very soul, 'we'll face it together, won't we?'

'Together,' she agreed, a sincere vow that held every bit of promise she would ever have. 'Now and forever.'

And as his arms enveloped Ruby in an embrace that felt like the closing of a circle, the final suturing of a wound that had been open and aching for years, her response was every bit as fervent. Winding her arms around his neck, she allowed him to pull her close, then moved herself closer still. The village fête was still going on in the distance—its laughter, its music, its clattering games—fading into a distant hum as their focus narrowed to each other.

'Ruby,' Ivan murmured, his voice a low rumble against her ear.

She tilted her head back, gazing into his eyes, those deep pools of blue that had once seemed inscrutable but now overflowed with emotion until finally, *finally*, his lips met hers in a kiss that was more than just a mere meeting of lips. It was a promise. A vow. A pledge of shared tomorrows. Passionate and tender all at once, it was a kiss that spoke of battles fought and won, of fears overcome, and of a future ripe with possibility.

He might have kissed her for a lifetime—he might have kissed for two—all Ruby knew was she lost in a moment that she never wanted to end. And when they did reluctantly pull

apart, their faces remaining close, and their breath still min-
gling, Ivan tenderly brushed a lock of hair behind Ruby's ear,
his touch reverent.

'Thank you, Ivan,' she breathed at last.

'What for?'

'For finally having the courage to let yourself love me.'

'You are easy to love, Ruby Channing,' he assured her. 'But
it is me who should thank you for being my beacon, and my
hope. You guided me to the light when I didn't even realize I
was lost in the darkness.'

And as they stood there, on the periphery of the village yet
still a part of it, Ruby knew that together they would build not
just a family, but a sanctuary—a haven of love, understanding, and unwavering support.

Their journey was just beginning, and Ruby knew she
couldn't wait to find out where it would lead them. Because
as long as Ivan was by her side, she was no longer living in a
bubble, too afraid to enter the world outside Little Meadwood.

In fact, she was finally ready to face anything.

* * * * *

If you enjoyed this story,
check out these other great reads from
Charlotte Hawkes

Trauma Doc to Redeem the Rebel
Neurosurgeon, Single Dad… Husband?
His Cinderella Houseguest
Shock Baby for the Doctor

All available now!

THE SINGLE DAD'S SECRET

SECRET

ZOEY GOMEZ

MILLS & BOON

To Mum. For a lifetime of encouragement,
love and support.

And, based on all our years of watching *ER*
and *Casualty* together,

I know you would love this book as much as I do. x

CHAPTER ONE

THIS WAS THE worst Zoom interview of Dean's life. He'd dashed to the kitchen at the last minute, to grab a glass of water, and returned to his desk a moment after the three-person interview panel connected to the meeting. Just in time for them to watch him spill half the water down his arm, and to notice that he was wearing jeans with his suit jacket, because he'd been convinced they wouldn't see him below the waist.

On top of all that, they could probably tell Dean was sitting in his bedroom. He quickly shifted the laptop, so the edge of his unmade bed wasn't in view any more. This was a nightmare. He didn't usually get flustered, but this was no ordinary meeting. The outcome of this interview would affect his entire life.

He took a deep, calming breath, and subtly wiped his wet sleeve on his jeans, as the woman in the centre of the panel introduced herself as Helen, the practice manager. Then a shot of adrenaline rushed through him when she introduced the man on her left as Dr Lucien Benedict. Lucien nodded and said hello as Dean tried to control his surprise.

Lucien's voice was so deep and gravelly Dean swore he felt his own chest vibrate. He didn't look anything like Dean had imagined. His profile on the practice's website had been brief, with no photo. So, as Dean got his first look at Lucien, his gaze ran over the man's features quickly, trying to take him in without being too obvious about it.

Lucien's dark grey eyes were heartbreakingly familiar, but they were paired with sharp cheekbones, a strong jaw and messy, just-got-out-of-bed hair. It was hard to believe he was finally seeing Lucien's face after all these years. It almost felt as if he was seeing a celebrity.

Dean took a sip of water and tried to concentrate on the interview.

'So, first question...' Helen smiled warmly. 'What do you know about our practice?'

Dean smiled back. 'I know it's very different to my current practice, which is located in a pretty chaotic area of South London. But your practice is very similar to the one in which I trained. It's compact, but still busy, with three GPs and a small staff, located in the centre of a small market town with a population of about four thousand people.'

Helen nodded along, smiling, and the last of Dean's nerves disappeared. Things improved further as Dean answered all their questions with ease. He was comfortable talking to people he didn't know, and his charm and bad jokes seemed to be winning two of the interview panel over. Not so much Lucien, who spent most of the interview staring down at his notepad or looking blankly in the general vicinity of the camera, his eyes glazed over, as if he was thinking about something else.

Helen asked her next question. 'Do you predict any challenges in keeping a healthy work-life balance?'

Before Dean could answer, his bedroom door swung open. Dean froze. A six-year-old boy with a shock of messy black hair yawned and stretched his arms above his head.

'Please can you make my breakfast now?'

He stepped closer and punctuated his request by casually lowering one arm and shooting Dean in the head with a suction dart from his plastic gun.

Dean's cheeks flushed as he closed his eyes, sighed, and pulled the dart off his forehead with a pop. Two of the panel laughed kindly, and when Dean's face finally returned to its normal colour he took it as a sign that they would be fun to work with. Lucien, however, simply frowned, and Dean's smile faded. It looked as if Lucien wasn't a fan of kids.

'I guess that answers the work-life balance question!' said Helen.

Dean took Rafael's hand and pulled him on to his knee, hugging him close. 'As you can see, I come with an assistant. So I'll need to balance working with taking care of this monster.' Rafael giggled quietly. 'I'm a single parent,' Dean continued.

It still felt strange to say that. Rafael was the son of his best friend Charlotte, no blood relation to Dean at all. Dean had always been the fun uncle, just like he was everyone's fun friend. He generally avoided responsibility, and had no long-term relationships other than with his job. He'd moved to London for work, and he and Charlotte had all but lost touch. Then, one night about six months ago, he'd got a call to inform him that Charlotte had died in a road traffic accident. And that was when Dean had heard the news that would change his life for ever.

In the event of her death, Charlotte had appointed Dean as Rafael's legal guardian.

That had been one hell of a midnight phone call.

Helen nodded and smiled. 'Accommodation is provided with the GP position. It's been that way here for decades. Where possible, the staff live right by the practice. It's a lovely old brick building, with plenty of room for both of you.'

Lucien looked sharply at Helen, but didn't say anything.

For Dean, an apartment being included in the job was almost too good to be true. It would be a huge relief not to have to search for a place to live on top of moving himself and a kid and starting a new job. That was if he got it.

'We only have one more question,' said Helen, looking down at her notes. 'What draws you to practise medicine here, in Little Champney?'

'That's partly to do with this guy too.' Dean squeezed Rafael's shoulders. 'After he lost his mother, he came to live with me. And, as nice as my flat is, and as professionally fulfilled as I've been working in London, this immediate area isn't somewhere I would ideally want to raise him. We need a new start. Somewhere quieter…a little more child-friendly. Somewhere safe, where we can be part of a community.'

Everything Dean said was true. Especially the part about living in London. He might have some lingering nerves about how he and countryside living would get along, but he'd heard numerous parents discussing incidents of knife crime and drugs outside the local primary school. Enough stories that he couldn't bear the thought of keeping Rafael there.

But there was one other reason he wanted to come to Little Champney, and to their practice in particular. Something he couldn't possibly let anyone know yet. Not even Rafael.

'Well, you'd certainly get that from Little Champney.' Helen put down her pen. 'We know you're a busy man, and we don't want to leave you in suspense. So if you're in agreement, and you could wait for a few moments while we mute the meeting, we can have a discussion and get back to you with a decision right now?'

'Sure, that would be great.'

Dean was surprised, but grateful. If it was bad news he'd rather get it over with as soon as possible.

He waited nervously, his knee bouncing up and down, as Helen muted the meeting. Dean promised to make Rafael some food as soon as the call was over, and with one last plastic dart, this time shot at the mirror, Rafael marched out of the room.

Dean turned back to the screen and his eyes were drawn immediately towards Lucien. Dean took advantage of the fact that the panel wouldn't be able to tell who he was looking at to outright stare at Lucien. The man's lips moved and the other two panellists turned to him. Lucien was talking more now than he had during the whole interview. His eyes flashed when Helen shook her head at him but, try as Dean might, he couldn't lip-read anything they were saying.

A muscle in Lucien's neck flexed as he chewed on his lower lip, and his thick black hair looked even messier now, as if he'd been running his hands through it. Dean was no expert in body language, but it seemed Lucien might not be his biggest fan.

Dean wasn't sure what he'd expected from Lucien, but it wasn't what he saw on the screen in front of him. With his wide shoulders and thick, muscular arms, barely contained by navy short sleeves, Lucien looked like a Hollywood actor playing a doctor—not a real GP in a country town. Very handsome. Despite the fact that he came across as semi-hostile and monosyllabic.

'Dean?'

Dean snapped out of his reverie.

'We'd love to offer you the position.'

Lucien threw his notebook and pen on to the desk and collapsed into his squeaking office chair. His colleagues had completely ignored his reservations and given Dr Dean Vasquez the job. Outvoted two to one. He was used to them ganging up on him, but that was usually regarding which of the two sandwich places in the town to get lunch from, or whether to get a new coffee machine for the kitchen. He'd erroneously thought they might actually listen to him over something important, like deciding with whom he had to share a workplace and, much more importantly, a house.

Lucien had enjoyed having the house all to himself for several months. Helen had six kids and a huge mansion near the surgery, so she didn't need a room, and the GP Dr Vasquez would be replacing had been over seventy, quiet as a mouse, and had relocated some time ago, leaving them with locums and some very beautiful antique furniture.

Furniture not compatible with a boisterous child.

Lucien put his head in his hands. He couldn't live with a six-year-old!

Lucien didn't hate children, exactly. He had to deal with them at work almost every day. But he couldn't pretend they didn't make him uncomfortable. He never knew what to say to them—and, to be honest, most children started crying the second they met him. The feeling was mutual.

But he could leave them at work and go home. He worked so hard… He threw everything into being the best doctor he could be. He had no social life and almost no hobbies because being around other people drained him. And being a GP meant interacting with dozens of people every single day. Home was his one relief. The only place he could be alone, relax in peace, and get the recharge he needed in order to cope with the next day of work. And, yes, that might mean he got a little lonely now and again. But who had time for friends when you had as demanding a job as he did?

Dr Vasquez didn't seem the type to understand what Lucien needed. Judging from the interview, he was the polar opposite to Lucien. A chatty, charming extrovert who drew energy from being around lots of people. Lucien, contrary to what other people might think, was happy with his quiet, well-ordered life. Everything was just how he wanted it, at work and at home. He didn't need excitement, chaos or attractive new doctors in his life.

That thought stopped him in his tracks. *Did* he find Dr Vasquez attractive? He shook his head. It was unlikely.

'Stop sulking, Lucien. Dean was by far the best candidate we interviewed, and you know it.'

Helen strode past his desk—where he was not sulking at all, thank you—and patted him on the head.

The panel had interviewed several potential doctors that week, and admittedly none of the others had seemed right to Lucien. But still… He waved her hand away and prepared to meet his first patient.

She turned out to be a woman in her twenties who was sure she was suffering from appendicitis. After a brief examination and a couple of questions, Lucien was able to inform her it was merely trapped wind. Embarrassed, but laughing with relief, she moved forward for a tearful hug. Lucien held out a firm hand for her to shake instead.

It didn't pay to get too familiar with the patients. Before she died, his mother had been Little Champney's GP, and everyone's best friend. She'd given huge swathes of patients her home number and had been available to them at all times.

That stress had made her ill in the end—Lucien was sure of it. A cool, professional distance was what kept him afloat and sane. A safe distance between himself and his patients, and between himself and his fellow doctors. The last time Lucien had got close to someone everything had ended in disaster.

There had been a man once. A man who had put up with his quirks although he hadn't exactly encouraged them. Lucien had succumbed to the constant pressure from his mother to find someone. And that someone had been John. John had been Lucien's neighbour for over a year before Lucien had felt comfortable accepting one of his regular offers of a date. Lucien had been flattered by his attention...maybe he'd convinced himself he could be happy with someone like John. He was well regarded, had a stable job at a local museum... They had interests in common, he was handsome, and Lucien had supposed that might be enough.

He had mistakenly thought John could be someone special, and they'd become so close that Lucien had allowed himself to be consumed by their relationship. Unfortunately he'd been so preoccupied with it that he'd missed spotting dangerous symptoms in his mother's health. She'd died of a heart attack, which he was sure would have been avoidable if only he'd been paying attention. And evidently Lucien had not been enough for John anyway. He'd left him shortly after Lucien's mother had died.

Never again. He couldn't risk that happening a second time—to a family member or a patient. When it came to Lucien, work was incompatible with a love life. And that was just the way it was.

Eight patients later, it was lunchtime, and Lucien was still seething over Dr Dean Vasquez. He couldn't get the man out of his head.

He couldn't for the life of him think why. Yes, he was very handsome, and his eyes were a particularly stunning shade of green, but Lucien very rarely found anyone attractive. He barely noticed the way most people looked and almost never got distracted by a handsome face. He usually had to really get to know someone before he could find himself attracted to them. But here he was, unable to get a near-stranger out of his head. Or the freckles on Dr Vasquez's nose, which were so clear they'd been visible on-screen. Not to mention the dimple that showed in his cheek when he smiled...

It was ridiculous. So what if Dr Vasquez had looked adorably happy hugging his son? The last thing Lucien needed was to have any kind of feelings for a new colleague. Especially a likely straight one who had recently lost the mother of his child.

Helen seemed to have some superhuman ability to tell when Lucien was seething, and she approached him at the coffee machine—only to hop back into her defence of their decision to hire Dean, as though there had been no pause in their earlier conversation.

'I know you're not a people person. But Dean seems personable enough for both of you. I bet he'll be super-easy to live with. And being around both him and his son might just help you with that little bedside manner problem you've been having.'

Lucien glared at Helen. He was an exemplary doctor. He'd got the highest marks all through his training, always top of the class. He just happened to have one small blind spot. His bedside manner wasn't all it could be. Especially with children. It had been mentioned in every piece of feedback at medical school and things had never improved. Apparently people found him 'blunt' and 'grumpy'.

But if Helen thought being woken up at five a.m. by a child watching cartoons every morning would fix that she was sorely mistaken.

Lucien downed his coffee and made a second cup. There

was nothing he could do now about Dr Vasquez getting the job. And he certainly couldn't move out of the shared house, so he was stuck with them there too. But the house was big. He could keep his distance from both of them. Dr Vasquez might well be the most extraordinary-looking man Lucien had ever seen, but that didn't change the fact that he was going to make Lucien's life hell if he stuck around.

Besides, Lucien's reservations about giving Dr Vasquez the job weren't entirely selfish. What could an inner-city doctor like him find appealing in a place like Little Champney? He was probably all about bright lights and exciting shifts…crowds and bars and clubs. He'd only applied to work here under some misguided belief that children shouldn't be raised in an urban environment. Soon he'd be bored to tears, realise his mistake, and go running back to the city. And then everyone would be inconvenienced.

Maybe Lucien could save everyone some time and trouble.

He was resolute. He would keep his new houseguests at arm's length and discourage any offers of friendship. Maybe giving them the cold shoulder would help Dr Vasquez realise he'd be better off somewhere else and give Lucien his life back.

With Rafael dropped off for his induction day at Little Champney Primary, Dean headed to the surgery to meet Helen. She would give him the keys to his apartment, and he would unpack the few boxes and bags he'd managed to cram into the back seat and boot of his car. He'd left his furniture and most of his belongings in storage in London. His first day at work wasn't until tomorrow, and maybe after school, when he'd finished unpacking, he and Rafael would have time to take a walk around the town and see what it had to offer.

He drove slowly, wondering if he'd just moved into a storybook. A babbling brook ran all the way through it, parallel to the road. There were green spaces and lush trees everywhere he looked. Colourful flowers grew from pots and troughs along every pavement. People even waved to each other as they strolled along.

He bumped over a cobbled road, creeping past an ancient pub with ivy around the door and a line of little stone cottages with hanging baskets, until he saw an ornate hand-painted sign that read *Doctors' Surgery*, with an arrow pointing to the right.

He'd done some research on Little Champney. It had won Best-Kept Market Town eleven times, it boasted a very exclusive private school on the outskirts of town, and the surrounding acreage seemed to be a top pick among Hollywood actors once they decided to buy a mansion and retire to the sticks.

Dean stood outside the GP practice's reception door for a full minute, surrounded by an alarming number of terracotta pots bursting with red and yellow tulips. He was breathing as if he'd just run a marathon. This was ridiculous. He'd already met everyone on Zoom. There was no need to feel nervous.

He took a deep breath, regulated his facial expression and pushed the door open.

Lucien was standing right on the other side of it.

'Finally figured out how to use the door, Dr Vasquez?' Lucien asked dryly.

The Zoom call hadn't done Lucien justice. In the flesh, the man was breathtaking. An effect which was strangely intensified by the way he glared at Dean.

Dean suddenly realised he hadn't yet said a word, let alone answered Lucien's question. What had it been again?

He wet his lips and tried to think of something sensible to say. 'Dean!' he exclaimed, embarrassingly. 'Call me Dean.'

A white cat appeared as Dean stepped inside and rubbed against his legs, leaving fur on his black jeans and purring loudly.

He bent down and stroked its soft, warm fur. 'Hello, there.' Dean scratched it behind the ears and its purring intensified. 'Aren't you beautiful?' Dean looked up at Lucien. 'I've never heard of a GP surgery with a cat before. Libraries and bookshops maybe, but not a surgery.'

'You still haven't,' responded Lucien flatly. 'That's my cat, and she's supposed to be at home.' Lucien frowned down at the cat, then turned his frown on Dean. 'She doesn't like new people. Normally.' Lucien picked up the cat and gently dragged her away from rubbing her face all over Dean's hands. 'Come on, Binxie. Let's get you home.'

Lucien made for the door, glancing back to throw Dean one last disapproving stare. Dean shrugged and walked towards Reception. It wasn't his fault the cat had loved him on sight. He couldn't help feeling rather smug about it. Lucien looked somehow even more intriguing when he was put out.

Helen arrived at Reception with a smile and gestured for him to follow her outside. Dean trotted to keep up with her as she headed straight to his car. He supposed the car park was small enough that she could guess which was his—the fact it was visibly full to bursting with his belongings might have helped too.

'There's a little lane just beside the surgery, almost hidden by weeping willows. Just drive through there and it'll lead you right to the accommodation. I'll meet you there in two minutes!'

The building was just as beautiful as the rest of the town. Red brick, with thick white windowsills, and walls covered in pink climbing roses. It consisted of three floors and held, Dean assumed, three separate flats.

Helen unlocked the front door and ushered him into the ground-floor flat, just as her phone beeped loudly. She grabbed it and read the message.

'Oh, fudge. I have to pop back to the surgery for a minute. Have a look around, and I'll be back to give you the grand tour in a minute!'

With that she was off, and Dean ventured further into the flat alone.

But he wasn't alone for long. Dean stepped into the large flagstone floored kitchen and his hand flew to his chest when he found Lucien crouched over by a double fridge.

'What are you doing in my flat?'

Lucien jumped up and that muscle in his neck twitched again. 'This isn't your flat, Dr Vasquez.'

'No?'

'There aren't any flats—there is one house. And we're sharing it. Apparently.'

'No way.'

A small white blur dashed into the room, and Binxie started eating from the bowl on the floor which Lucien had clearly been filling.

'Yes. Sorry to disappoint.'

'No, I didn't mean— It's fine that you live here.'

'Glad to hear it.'

Dean took a breath. 'Can we start again?'

Lucien waited, giving him nothing, and Dean took that as a sign that the starting again was up to him.

'My name's Dean. I'm your new GP and apparently your new housemate. It's lovely to meet you.'

Lucien looked at Dean's offered hand and then gave it a firm shake. His hand was large and warm, and a thrill ran through Dean as they touched. But by the bored look on Lucien's face he clearly felt absolutely nothing. Which was good. The last thing this situation needed was more complications. Dean was definitely relieved.

'Nice to meet you too,' Lucien murmured.

'So, you and Binxie don't mind two complete strangers moving in?' Dean asked, more as a joke than anything, but by the look on Lucien's face he minded very much.

'I'm sure it will be fine.'

'Rafael's great with animals, so you don't have to worry about him upsetting the cat.'

Lucien nodded wordlessly.

'Well… We'll keep out of your way as much as possible.'

Dean refused to apologise for Rafael's existence, but at the same time he could see how suddenly having a child in the house might be a bit of an adjustment. In fact he knew that better than anyone.

'Helen said she'd be back in a minute, to show me around.'

'Did she get a text from the surgery?'

Dean nodded.

'Then she won't be back for ages—if at all. You'd better come with me.'

Lucien led Dean out of the kitchen and past a living room to a wide staircase. Dean followed Lucien up two flights of stairs, through intermittent splashes of blue, red and yellow light cast by the stained glass windows on the landings. It was a tall house, but each floor wasn't all that big. When they reached the top storey Lucien opened a door. 'This will be your room.'

It was a big space, with arched windows and a sloping

ceiling because they were up in the roof. There was a double bed on one side of the room and a single on the other, plus a sofa, desk and a matching wardrobe and dresser.

'I'm glad there's furniture. Did all this belong to the last GP?'

Lucien seemed a little awkward all of a sudden. 'No, this was my room. Dr Haywood couldn't manage all these stairs. I swapped rooms with him after he left.

'Ah. So you're one floor down?'

'Yes. The floor below holds my bedroom and my office. Then the kitchen and living room are on the ground floor. Perhaps—perhaps your son should take my office.'

Dean could tell Lucien had to force that suggestion out. The guy was clearly uncomfortable that they were in the house at all—Dean couldn't sweep his office out from under him as well.

'No, it's fine. Rafael and I can share a room. That's probably more practical anyway.'

Lucien's shoulders visibly relaxed. 'I'll leave you to it, then. I have to get back to work.'

'Thanks for showing me around. By the way, Rafael will probably be here when you finish work…just so you know.'

'Right.'

Lucien looked so sad at the prospect Dean almost felt sorry for him.

Dean started bringing in his and Rafael's belongings from the car. The little courtyard was completely private, and surrounded by tall leafy trees, so he was very brave and left the car boot up between journeys. His city-boy heart was telling him not to, but he was determined to ignore it. He was in the countryside now, and this was how they did things.

He gave the driveway one more furtive look before carrying two boxes and a bag upstairs, walking a lot faster than usual.

Most of the car was taken up with Rafael's toys and books. Dean marvelled at what his life had become. He had a long history of one-night stands and short flings. People often wanted to date him, or go to him for a good time, but they found him very easy to leave. No one ever saw him as a long-term prospect. Since Rafael, he'd found himself utterly uninterested in sex or romance. Right now he had to concentrate on his son. Theirs was the only long-term relationship that mattered.

God, if any of his exes could see him now... They wouldn't recognise him at all. Rafael had changed Dean's life in a heartbeat.

Dean stacked Rafael's books on to the shelf by his bed, and tried to make the room look welcoming and cosy for Rafael's first impression. Dean didn't have much to unpack in the kitchen, aside from a few bits Rafael apparently couldn't live without, Dean's favourite glass mugs and his beloved coffee machine, which had cost close to a month's wages. Lucien didn't seem to have one of his own, so hopefully he wouldn't mind if Dean set it up.

On his last visit to the car, Dean grabbed a few flowers from a plant by the front door that had dozens of blooms to spare. Then he searched the kitchen cupboards for a vase. He left the flowers on the kitchen counter stuffed into a clean bottle from the recycling box with some water inside. Hopefully it would make Rafael smile.

Dean had never even considered having kids. And then, out of the blue, he'd become the one person totally responsible for a small, vulnerable human. As stated in Charlotte's will, his responsibilities were to keep Rafael healthy, make sure he got a good education and give him somewhere safe to live.

Dean had no family to turn to for help—only a brother who was currently in law school and could only provide supposedly encouraging monthly phone calls, earnestly telling Dean he could do anything he put his mind to. And most of the time, Dean was confident he *could* raise Rafael alone. But Rafael deserved more than just him. He deserved as much family in his life as possible. And after a lot of thinking Dean had come to the conclusion that there was only one person who could help with that.

Rafael's biological father.

There had been the small matter of finding him. And then working out if the man was trustworthy. Or even interested. Dean had known he would have to vet him first. Check him out. Make sure he was a good person. Charlotte hadn't talked about Rafael's father much. Dean could only remember her mentioning a first name and a town. And the fact that Rafael had been the result of a casual one-night stand with a fellow medical student at the end of training.

So a few weeks ago Dean had flexed his Google-fu and searched online, not really expecting to find anything. But he'd discovered the man was still exactly where he'd been seven years ago, when Charlotte had last seen him, still doing the same thing. That was a mark in his favour, right? Dependable, solid, boring... Those were good traits for a father. Dean would have loved a boring dad. Rather than an irresponsible drunk, which was what he'd got.

At that point Dean had almost had second thoughts about the whole endeavour. When Dean was a child, his own mother had let him get attached to several of her partners and he'd lost all of them, which had left him feeling abandoned and unlovable. He wanted something better for Rafael. He couldn't let him get attached to someone who wouldn't stick around. The poor kid had been through enough already. But Dean knew Rafael would have questions one day, and he deserved to have the opportunity to know his biological dad.

After finding the father online, Dean had discovered this surgery's website, and after reading his bio, and trying fruitlessly to tell what kind of man he was from barely thirty words, he'd found a job listing on the site. The practice was looking for a new GP. Dean had already decided he and Rafael needed to start again somewhere new, and this discovery had felt as if the universe was trying to tell him something.

And now here they were.

All of a sudden Dean was about to start living in the same house as the man who had unknowingly fathered Rafael. Lucien had never been told his son existed, and somehow Dean had to keep that a secret until he figured out whether he could trust Lucien with the truth. Whether he could trust Lucien with Rafael's heart.

Exhausted, Dean took a rest on the sofa. It was possibly the softest, comfiest one he'd ever sat on—or maybe he was just the most tired he'd ever been.

From his vantage point he could see the whole living room. There were a few nice pieces of art, but no family photographs. Much of the wall space was taken up by bookshelves. Lucien seemed to be a particular fan of medical textbooks and horror novels. And there was a plethora of healthy-looking pot plants crammed on to the window sill and occasional tables. It was a very homey living room. Dean felt comfortable there already.

Binxie appeared from nowhere and climbed carefully on to Dean's lap. He froze, not wanting to scare her off while she made herself comfortable, kneading his leg with her sharp claws. Dean winced, but didn't move a muscle until she stopped kneading and drifted off to sleep. Binxie's purrs made Dean sleepy and he leaned his head back. The cushions smelled familiar. Where had he smelled that nice clean, woody scent recently? Oh, it smelled like Lucien. That made sense...

He'd come to check Lucien out from afar—or from as far as two colleagues could get in a GP practice. He certainly hadn't expected to be living in Lucien's pocket. Rafael was about to share a house with his biological father. And neither of them knew it. This had the potential to get very complicated, very fast.

It was all up to Lucien, if only he knew it. If Dean found Lucien to be a good, kind man, then Dean would introduce him to his son and let him into Rafael's life. If Dean found him wanting, then he and Rafael would skip town, forget this new life, and no one would ever have to know why they'd come.

CHAPTER TWO

ON THEIR FIRST morning sharing a house Dean and Lucien barely saw each other. Dean and Rafael had their own bathroom on the top floor, where Dean showered, then got Rafael ready for school in the familiar morning routine that they had perfected back in London. The only difference was it took a little longer, as Rafael was behaving ten times more chaotically than usual due to his excitement about finally joining Miss Havery's class. He'd taken to her on the induction visit, and apparently she was Rafael's new favourite person.

Dean had decided not to take it personally.

Rafael's footsteps pounded across the landing. 'Walk—don't run!' Dean yelled.

The thought of Rafael toppling down three flights of stairs made his blood run cold for a moment. These semi-irrational fears had started hitting him about ten times a day since Rafael had appeared in his life, and were one of his least favourite parts of suddenly becoming a dad.

By the time Dean made it to the kitchen Rafael had already started looking for the cereal by himself. Half the cupboard doors were open, but he'd finally located the right one—judging from the four boxes of cereal stacked haphazardly on the kitchen floor.

Dean picked up Rafael's favourite and put the rest away. 'Climb up on the stool and I'll pour you a bowl.'

Rafael placed his packed school bag by the front door and then started putting his shoes on.

'Don't get ahead of yourself, buddy. We're not ready for shoes yet.'

Dean busied himself pouring Frosty Stars into Rafael's favourite yellow bowl. He got out the milk, and dropped some bread into the toaster for himself. He barely noticed Lucien come into the room, his mind occupied with all the tasks they had to complete before he could walk Rafael to school.

'Careful!' Lucien shouted, and Dean whipped around.

Rafael held a huge four-pint milk carton awkwardly in his tiny arms, while a large pool of milk spread over the counter and dripped on to the floor. Binxie appeared out of nowhere to help clean up the milk on the floor, and Rafael giggled.

'Oh, God.' Dean grabbed the carton out of Rafael's hands and reached for a cloth. 'Not really a laughing matter, Raf. You knew that was too big for you.'

'I did not!'

'Cats aren't supposed to drink cow's milk,' Lucien muttered.

That was news to Dean.

'They're lactose intolerant,' Lucien continued.

He picked up Binxie with one hand and deposited her by her bowl of water in the corner.

Dean spent a couple of minutes wiping up all the milk and wringing out the cloth into the sink. The room was silent, but Dean could see Lucien out of the corner of his eye, sitting as far away from Rafael as possible and eating toast and coffee while reading a medical journal. Rafael hadn't eaten a bite. He sat, legs dangling off the stool, one shoe on and one shoe off, staring at the bowl.

'Eat up! We don't have long before we have to leave.'

'I don't want it.'

'You have to eat breakfast. It'll keep you strong all day.'

'Don't want to.'

'You wanted cereal two minutes ago.'

Rafael stared at the bowl. 'It's too milky.'

'And why's that?'

'It was an accident!' Rafael shouted.

Lucien glared at them over the top of his medical journal.

Rafael was usually so good and quiet in the mornings. This was not making the first impression on Lucien that Dean would have liked.

'I know it was an accident, Raf. We all have them. How about you eat my toast instead?'

Rafael crossed his arms and glared at the table. 'I'm not going to school, so I don't need toast.'

Dean heaved a sigh. Where was this suddenly coming from?

He sat down on the stool next to Rafael and talked to him quietly and calmly. 'I know you're probably a bit overwhelmed with all the new things going on today, but I could really use your help. I need you to eat one piece of toast before you can leave the table.'

'No!' Rafael shouted, and kicked out in frustration.

Unfortunately he hit Dean with the foot wearing a shoe.

Dean cursed under his breath and jumped up, rubbing his shin furiously. Rafael looked just as shocked as Dean felt.

Lucien rose from his chair in the corner, grabbed his stuff and strode towards the front door without a word, half a slice of toast still gripped between his teeth.

'Sorry, Dean! I didn't mean to get you.' Rafael's eyes were big and watery.

'I know, buddy. It's okay, it didn't hurt,' Dean lied.

The kid had a hell of a left foot on him.

The front door slammed and Dean sighed. Lucien leaving in disgust at the first sign of a little morning chaos wasn't the best sign. But Dean couldn't worry about that now.

He wiped Rafael's face gently with the soft sleeve of his sweater until his tears were all gone. 'Are you nervous about your new school? Is that why you're all out of sorts?'

Rafael turned his big grey eyes up at Dean and gazed at him for a moment. 'You're meant to use a tissue, not your sleeve.' he said, parroting back Dean's oft-used admonishment to Rafael.

'That's for your nose. Tears are okay—they're only water.' Dean squeezed Rafael's shoulder.

'I'm not nervous. I just want to stay with you.'

'You'll have much more fun at school than you would with me. And I'll see you right after. You'll forget all about me once you start having fun.' Dean smoothed Rafael's hair back into place.

'I miss Mummy.'

It felt as if a bucket of ice-cold water had been thrown over Dean's head.

'Of course you do, sweetheart.'

Dean took a deep breath as Rafael flung his arms around Dean's neck. He wrapped the boy in a hug and tried to think of something that would cheer Rafael up.

'It's your birthday next week. Think of all the cake and presents you're going to get.'

You probably weren't supposed to cheer children up with

material things, but by God Dean was planning to buy him a lot of presents.

'Mummy won't be here.'

And that was Dean done for.

He wiped his own eyes on his sleeve, sniffed, and took a steadying breath.

'I miss her too.' He pulled back and caught Rafael's gaze. 'I'm sorry, but I'm all you've got now. You're all I've got, too. It's just you and me, Raf. And I promise that we're going to be fine.'

Rafael gave him a watery smile and Dean exhaled, relieved that he seemed to be cheering up. He smiled conspiratorially at Rafael. 'I don't think we've made a very good first impression on Lucien.'

'I like him,' answered Rafael.

'Same here.'

Dean just hoped he could like them too.

'Can I have your toast now?'

Dean laughed and handed it over.

Finally at the practice, after dropping Rafael at school, Dean checked the time. He still had ten minutes free before eight-thirty, so he pulled out his phone and started filming a video.

'Hi, everyone. Dr Dean here. I promised to show you my brand-spanking-new practice, so here it is.' He switched to main camera and stepped through the practice entrance. 'I won't say where it is, because I don't want any of you lot stalking me, but we have gone through the looking glass, guys. We are not in London any more. Imagine the opposite of London and that's where we are. Thatched roofs, roses around every door, fields full of buttercups—all that good stuff.'

He walked through the empty reception area and waiting room. Helen greeted him from the break room and he panned left to leave her out of the video.

'Morning! You want to be on Instagram live?'

'Sure, why not?'

She laughed and waved at the camera as he pointed it at her. 'This is my wonderful new boss...'

'Oh, I'm hardly your boss.'

'But you *are* wonderful?'

'Of course!'

He spoke from behind the camera a little more as he continued through the corridors. The place was bigger than he remembered it being. When he arrived at his consulting room he was pleased to find that someone had already put a sign on his door reading *Dr Vasquez*. He made sure to get a good shot of that on the video, then opened the door.

Only to find Lucien inside.

'Oh, hey.' Dean twisted his hand so that the camera pointed to his desk instead. 'Sorry guys, tour's over. I have to get to work now.'

'What on earth are you doing?' asked Lucien.

'Shouldn't I be the one asking you that?'

Lucien frowned, as if confused, and Dean looked back over his shoulder to check that his name was indeed on the door, as he'd thought.

'I was just getting some latex gloves,' said Lucien as he turned away to shuffle some boxes around on the shelf. 'You have three spare boxes in here for some reason.'

'It's fine,' said Dean, with a smile. 'You're welcome in my consulting room any time.'

Dean shoved his phone in his pocket.

'Why do you make everything sound suggestive?' Lucien mumbled.

Dean hadn't meant to, but he was glad to hear that Lucien thought so. He hesitated. Should he take this opportunity to apologise for Rafael's difficult morning? It might be best not to bring it up. After all, Rafael hadn't really done anything wrong. He'd been understandably upset and nervous. Dean's shin was the only real victim.

'I was just updating my Instagram,' Dean said in answer to Lucien's initial question.

'Who were you talking to?'

'My followers.'

Lucien rolled his eyes. 'Who on earth would be interested in seeing this?'

'Over a million people say they find my content pretty interesting.'

'*How* many?' Lucien gaped at him.

Dean grinned. 'I have one point two million followers.'

'How?' Lucien sounded absolutely gobsmacked.

'I'll try not to take offence at your tone, Dr Benedict,' Dean joked. 'I use my account to educate people about what GPs do. There's a lot of misinformation out there. I like to present a "warts and all" view of the reality.'

'Well, I hope you don't include anyone's personal information.'

'Of course not. I'm completely discreet.'

'And I hope I wasn't in that video. I didn't give my permission for you to film me.'

'It's fine. I missed you out.'

Dean hoped he had—he'd already posted the video. He'd check it in a minute.

'Be more careful in future. There's a reason I don't bother

with all that social media nonsense. I have no interest in being put online.'

'Oh, that's right…you don't even have a picture on your profile.'

'What?'

'On the practice website. Your profile is just a bio.'

Lucien's cheeks coloured a bit and he picked up his box of gloves. 'I'm a very private person.'

'Nothing wrong with that.'

Lucien grunted and left, saying, 'You should be working—not filming.'

Dean soon forgot all about the video when he sat down to run through some of the admin already piled up on his desk, and to check his schedule for the day. He signed in to his computer and tried to find his way around the system. It was almost the same as the one they'd used at his last practice. Just a few slight differences.

What were his old colleagues back in London doing now? he wondered. With any luck it wouldn't be long before his new colleagues here became his friends, but that didn't stop him missing his old ones. They'd all worked hard at the London practice, but they'd still made the effort to socialise when they could—even if it was just going for a wind-down drink on a Friday evening when they were all exhausted from a week at work.

Around this time of year was normally when his old practice started doing their educational school visits, teaching kids first aid and telling them what to do in an emergency. He loved meeting new people, and those visits always fulfilled that tiny part of him that had always secretly wanted to perform in front of an audience. Or maybe his ego just liked him being the centre of attention now and again. Hence his Instagram account, he supposed.

He fought off a wave of homesickness. He'd have to make sure to find time later on to text his old friends and see how they were doing without him.

Dean welcomed the first patient of his morning surgery into his consulting room at ten past nine. It felt somehow momentous, his first ever patient here, but he decided not to say anything. No need to make it weird.

He looped his pink stethoscope around his neck and sat down at his desk, twisting the chair to face his patient, who was a man of around fifty, wearing jeans and a plaid jacket caked in mud.

'What can I help you with today?'

'You the new one, then?' his patient asked.

Dean grinned. 'I am. And you're my first ever patient.'

'Ever? I didn't volunteer to be anyone's guinea pig.'

'Sorry, I meant my first one here,' Dean explained. 'I've been a GP elsewhere for several years.'

And now he'd made it weird.

'I'm only joking, son. I don't mind being a guinea pig—everyone's got to start somewhere.'

'Quite right. So, what brings you in today?'

'My stomach's giving me a heck of a problem.'

'In what way?'

'It hurts when I move. I can't stand up without feeling like I'm being stabbed.'

'Have you experienced any nausea or problems eating?'

'No, Doc.'

Dean took a full history of the patient's symptoms, then pushed his chair back. 'Okay, if you'd like to lie on your back on the examination table and pull up your shirt, I'll take a quick look.'

The patient lay back, getting mud from his jeans all over the white paper cover, and groaned as he pulled his muddy boots on to the foot of the bed. He yanked up his T-shirt to reveal a large red patch of skin, turning blue in the centre.

'That's a nasty bruise,' said Dean. 'Any idea what caused that?'

'Not sure, Doc. Although, now you ask, the pains did start after Maisy kicked me in the stomach.'

'Who's that?' Dean frowned. 'Your wife? Or—'

'My cow.'

Dean drew back. 'Your cow?'

'She was about to drop a calf and I tried to check how far along she was. She rather took against it.'

'Oh, you were trying to…?' Dean gestured with one arm.

Using his very limited knowledge of what farmers did to help cows give birth, he wasn't surprised she'd kicked him. Dean had been kicked himself doing much less invasive procedures during a patient's childbirth. His current patient nodded, wincing as Dean used both hands to gently press over the area. He didn't think any ribs had been fractured, but he couldn't be sure.

'I think we might have to get you an X-ray. Make sure she hasn't knocked anything out of whack.'

'Very technical, Doc.'

'I do try.'

Dean wrote up the patient's notes and ordered the X-ray, then whistled happily as he cleaned the mud off the examination table. He thought he'd seen everything back in London, but he was thrilled to learn there were still new experiences to be had in his new practice.

'Someone's happy.' Helen knocked briskly on the door as she opened it, and sniffed the air suspiciously. 'Which is unusual in a room that smells like manure.'

'Yeah, I think I might need a bucket and a mop rather than antiseptic wipes.'

'Well, it will have to wait. I've got a patient on the line for you.'

She pointed at the phone on Dean's desk. He dropped the wipes in the wastebasket and sat down on his chair, picking up the phone and just managing to press the right button as he spun from the momentum.

'This is Dr Vasquez. How can I help?'

He was met with the heavy breath of someone in a panic. 'I wanted Dr Benedict, but they said he's busy.'

'I'm sure I can help you. Tell me what you need.'

'My wife's pregnant, but she's not due for another week. I think she's having it now. What do I do? Her contractions are only six minutes apart!'

Trying to assess the situation, Dean asked a simple question. 'Is this her first child?'

'No, you idiot, this is her husband.'

Dean tried to hold in a laugh. 'I'm sorry, I wasn't clear. Is this your wife's first pregnancy?'

'Yes.'

'Okay. Keep calm…everything's going to be fine.' Dean heard someone groaning in the background. 'How's she doing?'

The man mumbled something away from the phone. 'I asked her, but she swore at me. A lot.'

Dean smiled. If he was going through labour he'd be swearing too. At the very least. 'What's in your birth plan? Is it a home birth or in the hospital?

The man's breathing calmed slowly. 'Hospital. I was supposed to drive us, but my car is at the garage. I thought I had another week… I've called an ambulance.'

'Okay, that's wonderful.'

'But what if the baby comes now? I need someone on the line to help me. Dr Benedict told me to call him if I was worried about anything. Well, I'm worried.'

Dean's door swung open and Lucien stood there, looking handsomely dishevelled.

'Speak of the devil.' Dean gestured questioningly between Lucien and the phone and Lucien nodded, holding his hand out for the receiver. 'Dr Benedict's just arrived—I'm passing you over.'

Lucien leaned against Dean's desk and Dean sat back in his chair, looking at his computer monitor but listening to Lucien's side of the conversation.

'Six minutes? The ambulance should have plenty of time to get to the hospital. There's really no need to panic.'

Dean could smell Lucien's woodsy scent again. Was it his aftershave or his shampoo? It was intoxicating... Dean tried not to take in any obvious deep breaths. Lucien's hip was only an inch away from Dean's arm, and Dean could feel the man's body heat. Lucien shifted as he answered a question and his hip pushed against Dean's elbow. Lucien was staring out of the window as he spoke, not paying Dean any attention at all. He probably thought he was pressed against Dean's chair.

Dean held his breath and didn't move a muscle. His elbow tingled where it was pressed against Lucien's warm, solid form. He hadn't felt this ridiculously affected by something since he was a teenager.

Lucien talked calmly to the patient for a few more minutes, until the ambulance arrived, then said his goodbyes and handed Dean back the phone, finally pulling away from his arm. Dean saw Lucien look down at their point of contact in surprise. So he really hadn't known it was happening.

Dean smiled and spoke quickly. 'Things are very different here.'

'What do you mean?' asked Lucien.

'I've never heard of a patient calling their GP for help during childbirth. They usually contact their midwife or the hospital.'

'He's my grandmother's gardener. He's been very nervous about things all through the pregnancy. I've been trying to help.'

That was very sweet. And it went above and beyond Lucien's job description. Maybe he wasn't as closed off as he seemed.

During a short lull between patients, Dean stepped into the break room to grab a drink.

'Helen! Just the person I wanted to see.'

'This sounds ominous. What do you need?' Helen looked up from her tea.

'Do we do any school visits? You know...teaching the kids basic CPR or first aid?'

'As it happens, I've organised for Lucien to do something just like that next week.' She paused. 'I haven't told him yet...'

'Great! It worked really well at my last practice. We visited workplaces too. The more people who know CPR the better.'

'Absolutely. You should join him—it would be the perfect opportunity for you to get to know your new community.'

Lucien appeared from his consulting room and Dean smiled. 'You up for that, Lucien?'

'Sorry, what?'

Lucien looked confused and sleepy, which seemed to be his default expression. Admittedly, it wasn't an unattractive one.

'You and I are going to find some spare time and impart wisdom and confidence to the kids of the local community.'

What could be a better test for someone's dad potential than seeing him interact with a classroom full of kids?

'Spare time? What's that?' Lucien asked grumpily. He narrowed his eyes at Dean. 'Are you just trying to find endearing things to put on Instagram and gain you more followers?'

Dean tutted. 'No. You can't film strangers' kids and put them online. Not everything I do is for content. Sometimes I actually do wonderful, selfless things out of the goodness of my own heart.'

Helen chuckled. 'Come on, Lucien,' she encouraged. 'This'll be good for you. And it'd help you with you know what,' she said more quietly.

What the heck was 'you know what'? Dean wondered.

'It'll be fun. I promise.' Dean did his best to give Lucien the puppy-eyed look that he was reliably informed was irresistible.

Lucien just raised an eyebrow and looked at him in silence, reminding Dean of every disapproving teacher he'd ever had.

'Fine,' said Lucien, turning on his heel and disappearing back into his room.

Dean smiled. He knew he still had it.

At lunchtime, Lucien made himself a coffee in the break room and leaned against the counter drinking it. The mug warmed his hands, and the delicious scent calmed his nerves. Dean and Helen sat at the table on the other side of the room, eating. Lucien was reluctant to join them in case they roped him into something else ridiculous.

This morning at home had been tense. Lucien didn't

know much about children, but even he'd been able to surmise that the child might be having trouble settling into his new environment. So he had decided to leave, in case his presence was making things worse. Dean looked much happier now, so Lucien hoped the child had cheered up once he'd made himself scarce.

Nice to know his terrible success rate with kids had not improved one iota. If he was in the room, kids cried.

He'd heard Rafael call Dean by his name, just before the door had shut behind him. Not Daddy—just Dean. Not that it was any of Lucien's business, but he couldn't help but ponder over it. Perhaps the child had lived with his mother and hadn't seen Dean very much…or maybe he'd called someone else Daddy.

Lucien sat down and pulled out his phone. The only apps he had were news sites and medical databases. Did you have to join Instagram to look up someone's account?

His eyes met Dean's across the room and Lucien shoved his phone back in his pocket.

Even eating, Dean looked attractive. It was unfair. Dean's gaze slid to Lucien again, even as he chatted with Helen, and a hot flush ran through Lucien's body. Lucien studiously avoided making eye contact again, unwilling to feel so thoroughly undone at work, and he soon zoned out, sipping his coffee and thinking about a patient.

'What's on your mind?'

Lucien jumped. He hadn't known Dean was still in the room, let alone paying him any attention. 'Why should anything be on my mind?'

'You've been glaring at that window for five minutes straight. What did it do to you?'

'It's nothing. I'm just contemplating a patient.'

Dean slid on to the seat beside him. 'Tell me.'

Lucien sighed. If Dean must insist on pressing his warm body up against him, and smelling so distractingly good, he could hardly be blamed for doing exactly as the man asked.

'I haven't seen her in the consulting room for quite some time, but she used to suffer badly from auditory and visual hallucinations. I prescribed her antipsychotic meds and CBT. And she hasn't been back in since.'

'That's promising,' said Dean.

'I hoped so. But an aunt of hers cornered me in the shop yesterday. She thinks the patient's mental health may have recently declined.'

'That's not good,' said Dean. 'So what are you going to do?'

'What can I do? I'll wait for her to make an appointment. And if she does, I'll provide her with the appropriate treatment.'

'Is that it?'

'What would you have me do? Visit her at home out of the blue and ask how she is?'

Which, he realised as he said it, was exactly what his mother would have done.

Back when Lucien's mother had been the village GP her door was never closed. She'd pick up a call from a patient day or night. Even if it meant being pulled away from Lucien's bedtime story, or missing his big line in a school play. And her endless, ceaseless generosity had killed her in the end. Run her into the ground. She'd never had a day off in her life.

Lucien never wanted to be like that. When he closed the door to his home, it was closed. That didn't mean he wouldn't do whatever it took to care for his patients. But he never crossed that line into taking his emotions home or getting personally involved.

'That would be inappropriate,' he said. 'I suggested that her aunt encourage her to make an appointment with me if she feels she needs help. That's all I can do.'

'We need a doctor out here!'

The desperate shout from outside broke the calm. Dean dropped his sandwich and jumped up to look out of the open window.

'We're on our way!' Dean called out of the window, then turned back. 'Someone's collapsed in the car park. Looks to be a male in his sixties.'

Dean and Lucien ran outside to find a man on the ground. His head had only missed the kerb by inches, and most of his body was crammed into the small space between two cars.

A woman stood over him. 'Look at all the commotion you've caused, Harold.'

'No commotion. It's what we're here for,' Dean reassured her smoothly.

Lucien knelt awkwardly by the man's shoulders, unable to get any closer, and felt for a pulse in his neck. 'Can you hear me, sir?'

Harold groaned.

'My husband does have an appointment, but we're a bit early.'

'It's okay. We won't make you wait until the allotted time,' said Dean.

Typical Dean, thought Lucien, joking at this of all times.

'What was he coming in for? Do you know?' he asked Harold's wife.

'Oh, he's been having terrible headaches. He refused to make an appointment, but today he couldn't see for a few seconds. I should have made him come in sooner.'

'Don't worry,' said Dean.

'I don't like his pulse,' said Lucien. 'Let's get him inside and call an ambulance.'

Dean nodded and called to Helen, who was watching from the doorway. 'We need the stretcher, and an ambulance here as soon as possible.' He turned back to Harold's wife. 'Just a precaution.'

'Whose are these cars?' shouted Lucien. 'We need to get at least one moved.'

Helen ran inside. She returned quickly carrying the light-weight stretcher, a blanket and a resuscitation kit. 'The ambulance should arrive in ten. I've checked inside and the cars don't belong to anyone here.'

Thoughtless shoppers were always parking their cars in the practice's small car park. Not only was it a pain, it was also technically illegal. This time Lucien was going to take their number plates and damn well report them to the police.

Dean situated the stretcher as close as possible to the man on the pavement, then he and Lucien got into position to transfer their patient. But Harold's face was dangerously pale, so before they moved him Lucien checked his pulse again. He couldn't find one.

'Damn, I've lost the pulse.'

Lucien gently tipped Harold's head back, then leaned his head down close to his face to check for breath. Nothing. Lucien felt the carotid artery with his fingers, but still couldn't find a pulse. He was going to have to try CPR in this ridiculously enclosed space.

He stood, swung his leg over the man's body and strad-dled him, then started compressions on the patient's chest using both hands. 'Dr Vasquez,' he barked. 'I need your help. Sit by his head.'

Dean jumped to follow his instructions, and they took it in turns, Lucien compressing, then giving his aching shoulders a welcome rest for a few seconds while Dean squeezed the bag valve mask Helen had brought out with the stretcher. They worked together in perfect unison, keeping Harold alive until the ambulance siren indicated that help was almost there.

When the paramedics reached them, Lucien climbed off the patient and jumped out of their way, letting them work. The paramedics, more practised in manoeuvring patients out of tricky places, got Harold on to a stretcher in seconds and continued to perform CPR as they swept him off to the ambulance.

Adrenaline rushed through Lucien's entire body, and he breathed hard as he shook out his burning muscles. He wiped his sweaty forehead on the bottom of his shirt, unwittingly flashing his stomach to all and sundry in the process. He noticed Dean staring and tucked his shirt back in carefully, embarrassed.

Dean was helping the patient's wife over to the back of the ambulance, one arm around her shoulders, talking to her quietly. He held her hand as she climbed the steps, and gently shut the door behind her.

Everything seemed very quiet after all the excitement. Luckily it was a slow afternoon and there wasn't a waiting room full of patients clamouring to be seen. Dr Vasquez insisted on taking the only waiting patient, and Lucien downed an entire bottle of water, then took the opportunity to talk to Helen while Dean was out of the way.

'Helen? Do you have Instagram?'

'Yes?'

'I suppose Dr Vasquez has convinced you to follow him already?'

'As a matter of fact, I followed him a while ago—just after his interview.'

Lucien nodded, not sure how to ask what he wanted to ask.

'Do you want his handle so you can follow him?'

'God, no. But…' Lucien paused. 'He was filming inside the practice earlier. I would like to check if he was being suitably discreet. Medical records. Privacy. All that.'

'Wouldn't it be easier to just talk to him?'

'If you don't want to help me, that's absolutely fine.'

'Of course I do. Here.' Helen held out her phone, already open to Dean's profile, and Lucien took it.

The newest post was a video.

'Have you watched this yet?' Lucien asked.

'Hmm?' Helen was already captivated by whatever work she was doing on her computer screen.

'Never mind. Thank you.' Lucien moved across the room to the window and pressed play on the video.

It began outside the surgery, focused on Dean's face, his eyes squinting shut against the morning sunlight, which flashed off his bright green eyes when he blinked. He rubbed a hand quickly through his hair, perhaps to tidy it for the camera. With the birds chirping happily in the background it sounded idyllic.

'Hi, everyone…'

His voice sounded deeper on the recording.

'I promised to show you my brand-spanking-new practice, so here it is.'

He smiled shyly at the camera, and Lucien spotted the dimple in his cheek. He could practically hear Dean's followers sighing in adoration.

Dean switched the view from front-facing to back and continued into the practice. He didn't show any of the signage or posters outside that viewers might use to identify the location, which was smart, Lucien grudgingly admitted. Dean made a joke about avoiding stalkers and Lucien couldn't help but smile. After he'd entered the practice and greeted Helen, he continued alone through the corridor.

The background noise receded and Dean talked quietly. It suddenly felt more intimate, like one of those ASMR videos Helen watched to help her meditate at lunchtimes. Dean's deep, gentle tones sent a little shiver down Lucien's spine. He was starting to understand how Dean might have amassed a million followers.

Lucien glanced over at Helen, but she was still ignoring him. He moved slightly, so he was hidden by the break room fridge, then carried on watching.

'I'm a little bit nervous, actually,' Dean was saying. 'It's always scary starting somewhere new, trying to fit in with a group of people who've known each other for years.'

It hadn't occurred to Lucien that Dean would be nervous. Or that he was even capable of the emotion. He seemed so confident and laid-back about everything.

'Hopefully I won't annoy them too much. I know exactly how annoying I can be from all of your comments,' he said, the smile audible in his voice. 'Oh, I got myself a new stethoscope to celebrate the move.' Dean flashed the end of a hot pink stethoscope in front of the camera. 'They all seem really nice so far. Especially my fellow GP. He's pretty cool.'

Lucien's heart stuttered. He was stunned to be mentioned.

'Oh, hey, here's my room.'

The camera zoomed in on Dean's nameplate. Dean swung his door open wide, and Lucien flinched as he saw his own back on the video. He'd almost forgotten why he was watching it in the first place. He saw himself turn around, holding the box of latex gloves like an idiot.

He could see the moment Dean thought he'd turned the

camera away, but he hadn't turned it far enough, and Lucien remained clearly visible on the far right-hand side of the shot. Was that really what his hair looked like? He looked as if he'd been freshly dragged through a field. Lucien didn't normally worry about his appearance, but he didn't like to look sloppy. What on earth had he been doing to look so dishevelled?

On the video, after Lucien had asked Dean what he was doing, and Dean had turned to look at the name on the door, the camera stayed on Lucien and showed him very clearly looking Dean up and down, blatantly checking him out before he could turn back around.

Lucien cursed under his breath. Unable to find any way of rewinding the video only a little way, he impatiently watched the whole thing again, his heart racing until he got to the part he really wanted to rewatch. It was impossible to miss. His eyes swept over Dean's body from top to bottom then up again. On the screen Dean said something else, and ended the video, but Lucien wasn't paying much attention.

His cheeks were hot with embarrassment. Up to a million random strangers would now have seen him clearly checking Dean out. He didn't even remember doing it—it must have been instinctual. But it was so obvious. No one would miss it. Dean must have seen it too. And Helen. Everyone would think he was interested in Dean. And he most certainly was not.

Lucien closed down everything on Helen's phone and leaned his forehead heavily on the fridge. This was exactly why he hated social media.

He handed Helen back her phone and ignored her curious look. If Dean hadn't been so careless this would never have happened. Maybe he'd done it on purpose? A boost for his ego and a laugh for his fans all in one?

Lucien stormed through the open door of Dean's consulting room to find him sitting on the edge of his desk, texting and laughing to himself. He looked up and smiled.

'Talking to your adoring fans again?' Lucien asked scathingly.

Dean didn't seem to notice his tone and smiled warmly. 'No. I'm still part of my old practice's WhatsApp group and they're asking me what we did today. They're getting a real kick out of all the crazy countryside shenanigans.'

Lucien could just imagine what that conversation was like. Dean telling his sophisticated city friends about the country bumpkins.

'Well, I don't know what cases you were used to in London. Shootings and terminal rudeness, I don't doubt. But the patients here are just as important and deserving of respect.'

'Oh, no, I wasn't—'

'And I thought I asked you not to put me online. I suppose you thought it would be funny to just do it anyway?'

Dean frowned, looking genuinely confused. Then his expression changed to one of horror and he started tapping away on his phone. 'Oh, God, I forgot to check the video. Were you on there? I really thought I'd moved the camera away.'

Dean paused as he watched the video he'd posted earlier—evidently for the first time, unless he was a skilled actor on top of all his other annoying talents.

Dean swore quietly. 'I'm so sorry. I never would have done that on purpose. I know I didn't have your permission. I'll delete it.'

Lucien's shoulders dropped, his anger deflated. Dean clearly hadn't done it on purpose. After all, it wasn't his fault Lucien found him physically attractive and was stupid enough to have checked him out on camera. Part of him wanted to tell Dean not to delete it—it had been a nice video aside from Lucien's bit part ruining it. But at the same time he couldn't bear his secret attraction being up there for eternity for all to see.

Unless… Maybe it wasn't obvious to anyone else? Maybe he was just being paranoid?

'Were you checking me out?' Dean was staring at his phone.

Lucien stopped dead, closed his eyes and pinched the top of his nose. 'This is mortifying.'

Maybe if he left now he could pretend none of this had ever happened.

Dean chuckled softly. 'I'm gonna delete it…it's okay.'

Lucien forced himself to make eye contact, then watched as Dean's gaze returned to his phone and ran across his screen for a moment.

'You didn't read any of the comments, did you?' Dean asked.

'No. Why?'

'No reason.'

Oh, this couldn't be good.

Lucien crossed the room and leaned closer to Dean, trying to get a look at the comments.

I assume that's the other GP you mentioned? The one you like? I can see why!

Hashtag hot doctors! Is everyone who works there gorgeous?

Oh, my God, the sexual tension. I can see the fanfic being written as we speak!

'Fanfic?' said Lucien.

'Don't ask.' Dean scrolled some more.

'I can't believe how many comments there are,' said Lucien, watching as hundreds of comments flashed across the screen.

'Yeah, and they're mostly about you.'

Lucien decided to ignore that. 'Do you always get this many?'

Dean shrugged. 'I always get interaction for videos.' He paused. 'Have you finished reading? I'm gonna delete it now.'

'Can you delete something even after it gets…' Lucien checked the number by the heart symbol '…forty-two thousand hearts?'

Dean smiled. 'They're called "likes". But I like hearts better. And, sure, you can delete stuff any time you want.'

Lucien suddenly felt a small and ridiculous sense of loss at the thought of the one video of them together being erased.

He shook his head to force the thought away. 'I'm finished reading.'

But Dean must have sensed something, because he looked searchingly up at Lucien for a moment. Being in such close proximity to Dean's green eyes was quite breathtaking, and Lucien's pulse quickened. He swallowed dryly.

'I can archive it,' said Dean. 'That will make it invisible to the public, but it will still be there.'

Lucien found himself nodding. 'Yes. Do that.'

CHAPTER THREE

LUCIEN SIGHED HEAVILY and shifted in his uncomfortable chair. Helen had been organising furiously behind the scenes and had arranged their first visit to the local primary school. Lucien had experienced easier mornings. Like the home visit during which he had treated a family of eight suffering from gastroesophageal reflux disease and uncontrollable projectile vomiting. He had enough trouble getting along with one child, and now he found himself sitting in a school filled with the little creatures.

He and Dean were perched on plastic chairs at the front of the hall, between a piano and an inexplicably large papier-mâché palm tree. The children all sat in rows on a shiny wooden floor marked out for various games, their legs crossed and their fingers on their lips after their teacher had ordered it.

Rafael waved excitedly at Lucien from the third row, and Lucien couldn't help but smile back. He glanced over at Dean, who he was surprised to find was already looking at him.

The teacher introduced them as Dr Dean and Dr Lucien with what seemed like unnecessarily enthusiastic vigour, as though they were famous rock stars rather than just local GPs. But the kids ate it up and let out an excited noise en masse. To be fair, Dean didn't look completely unlike a rock star. He jumped up and greeted the kids in the same manner as the teacher, but on him the enthusiasm seemed authentic. Dean explained to the children what he and Lucien were there to do, and made some jokes, and by the time he'd finished talking the kids were practically vibrating with excitement.

How did he do that?

Dean came over and stood near Lucien, before continuing to talk to the children. 'Accidents happen, and at some point everyone gets a little bit hurt. It's never fun, but we can help it feel better by acting quickly and calmly to help! That's called first aid. Has anyone heard of that before?'

A chorus of several dozen kids chanted, 'Yes, Dr Dean!' and Lucien smiled to himself.

He hadn't set foot in a school since he was small enough to fit into one of those tiny chairs. But not much had changed. The faint smell of school dinners and the walls covered with children's paintings and alphabet charts were giving him a serious nostalgia rush. And he was rather enjoying it. He supposed you missed out on this kind of thing when you didn't have kids...

'If someone gets hurt or feels ill,' Dean continued, 'there are a few simple things to remember. First, try to find a trusted adult and get help, and then, if you can't find one, always call 999. Then you'll get someone a bit like me to come and help you.'

A little girl put her hand up.

'Yes?'

'If I call 999, will you answer?'

Dean laughed kindly. 'Sadly not. But you'll always find someone very nice and helpful on the other end. Okay—second thing: only help if it's safe for you to do so. Keep yourself safe first.'

Lucien saw a few confused faces, and it seemed that Dean noticed the same.

'That means,' Dean continued, 'if someone gets into trouble in a pond, don't jump in to help. That would just make two people in trouble instead of one.'

There were a few nods.

Dean walked back and forth across the hall in front of the kids as he spoke, making eye contact with them. They all watched him, enraptured.

'Okay, what are some common injuries that you can think of? Hands up.'

Twenty kids' hands shot up at once, some children wriggling in place desperately. Dean laughed and pointed at the kids one by one until they'd all had a go. Some suggestions were sensible, like cuts, burns and nose bleeds. And some were akin to the ramblings of a tiny psychopath, like accidentally eating a poisonous lizard, being swallowed by a Venus flytrap and drowning in quicksand.

Dean beckoned to Lucien and he stiffened, expecting Dean to introduce him to the kids or invite him to talk to them as a group like he had. But Dean didn't—he just split the children into small groups and started to demonstrate how to use a bandage.

After a moment of watching Dean, Lucien took his own group of children and did the same. Over the next hour they covered how to clean and bandage small cuts and grazes, how to cool burns and scalds, and how to deal with nose bleeds. It all went surprisingly smoothly. And, frankly, it was a wonder they'd never done this before. Lucien had to concede that Dean's London surgery might not have been so bad after all.

After the demonstration the children were told it was break time, but most of them stayed in the hall. Dean was immediately surrounded by dozens of kids, some practically trying to climb him. Lucien stepped back, emotionally exhausted after having spoken to so many people, and folded himself down on to a long bench that sat against the wall, much too low for his tall frame.

One little girl approached Lucien by herself and sat down next to him, eating her lunch quietly. After a moment she held out her open crisp packet to Lucien, offering him a crisp. He took one wordlessly, and gave her a smile before eating it.

Then Rafael barrelled up to Lucien and stopped himself at the last second, his hands braced against Lucien's knees. 'Hi, Mia,' he panted, addressing the girl next to Lucien. Then, 'Lucien, come and see my friends.'

'I can see them all from here.'

'Okay...' Rafael turned around to look at everyone and used Lucien's leg as a leaning post.

'Your dad's good at this, isn't he?' said Lucien.

'At what?'

'Teaching people how to do things.'

'He's not a teacher! He's a doctor!'

Lucien couldn't really argue with that, so he dropped the subject.

'My favourite bit of today was when you taught us how to tie a sling,' Rafael said.

'It was?'

He'd thought Dean's groups had certainly seemed to have much more fun than Lucien's. And he couldn't blame them.

'Yeah. I like the way you explain stuff. And you don't make embarrassing dad jokes.'

Lucien huffed a laugh. 'Don't tell Dean they're embarrassing.'

'He knows. That's why he does it!'

Rafael looked disgusted, which made Lucien laugh again.

Dean looked over, perhaps hearing Lucien laughing. Lucien's gaze met his for a moment, and they shared a shy smile.

Dean threw his work clothes into his bedroom hamper and showered quickly, then pulled on some soft grey sweatpants and a comfy T-shirt. He wanted to get started on cooking early, so all three of them could eat together and perhaps get rid of the residual tension that was hanging between the two of them.

They'd been sharing the house for several days now, but still kept mostly to their own rooms. The atmosphere between them was much less frosty than it had been, but there was still an awkwardness that Dean wasn't sure would ever disappear.

Dean's heart had been warmed by seeing Lucien at the school. He'd been reluctant with the children at first, but they'd loved him. It was probably the way he spoke to them like adults—he didn't temper his language or talk down to them.

Dean was planning to make his special spaghetti Bolognese. Rafael loved it, and so did everyone he made it for. Although it suddenly occurred to him that Lucien could be a vegan for all he knew. He tried to remember what was in the fridge downstairs, and if he'd seen any meat in there.

Lucien hadn't showed up at home yet, even though they'd both finished work at about the same time. Hopefully he hadn't arranged to go out and eat somewhere else.

'You okay in there?' Dean called as he passed the half-open bathroom door.

'I can manage to use the bathroom by myself, thank you.'

Dean smiled. Rafael was adorable when he got all prim

and self-righteous. 'Good work, buddy. Are you okay if I go down to the kitchen?'

'Yes!'

'See you down there in a minute.'

Dean heard Rafael grumbling to himself as he headed off to the stairs. And just as Dean reached the ground floor Lucien arrived home. He shook off his umbrella over the doormat.

'When did it start raining?' asked Dean.

'About five seconds after I left the opticians. And about five minutes before I remembered I had an umbrella.'

'You should call me next time. I'll come and pick you up in the car...save you getting wet.'

Lucien's hair was soaked, and tiny rivulets of water ran down into his eyes as he ruffled it dry with a hand.

'So that's why you're late? You had an eye test?'

'No.' Lucien looked at Dean with a puzzled expression. 'I was just picking up my new frames. Did I arrange to meet you here or something?'

'No, no. Nothing like that. I just thought it would be cool if I cooked for us all.'

Lucien put down his bag and shrugged off his coat. 'You cook?'

'If there's one thing you should know about me, it's that I'm an excellent cook.'

'And so modest.'

'Is there anything you don't eat?'

'No, I'll eat whatever anyone makes for me. I can't cook at all.'

Dean waited for Lucien to hang up his coat, then took his arm and directed him into the kitchen. He loved a challenge.

'You can be my sous chef.'

'Didn't you hear me? I burn water.'

Dean sat Lucien down on one of the stools. 'I can teach anyone. You'll be great.'

Dean got the spaghetti out, then a pack of minced beef and a bottle of red wine, and set them on the table. Then he collected chopped tomatoes, onions, carrots, tomato puree and olive oil from various cupboards.

Lucien looked at all the ingredients in consternation. 'I didn't know we had any of that.'

'I got it all at lunchtime.' Dean grabbed a wedge of Parmesan from the fridge. 'Your first job is to grate this.' He paused. 'Do we even have a cheese grater?'

'I think so...' Lucien got up and pulled open the wide drawer next to the sink. 'My grandmother gave me a box of kitchen stuff years ago. I've never really used any of it.'

Dean joined him and looked into the drawer. He gasped at the array of delights like a kid at Christmas.

'Look at all this cool stuff! There's a box of professional kitchen knives in here. Do you know how much they cost?' Dean had been pining for a set like that for months, but couldn't justify the expense. He lifted them out. 'This is awesome. Can I use them?'

Lucien shrugged. 'Go for your life.'

Dean, way more thrilled than he should be over kitchen utensils, unpacked a couple of the knives, rinsed them under the tap, then dried them carefully. He got down his thick wooden chopping board and tried one of the knives out on the onion, groaning happily at how clean the cut was.

'Oh, my God...'

Lucien gave him a funny look. 'It can't be *that* stimulating.'

'You don't know.'

Lucien shook his head indulgently, and sat down with the cheese grater.

Dean pushed a plate over to him. 'Grate about half of it on there. I like a lot of cheese.'

'Noted.'

Lucien did as he was told. He was a much easier student than Rafael, who found it necessary to ask about fifteen questions before completing any task. Dean wouldn't have him any other way, though. And he was proud of him. The kid had mastered a lot of basic cooking skills in just the few months they'd been living together.

Thinking of Rafael seemed to conjure him into the room. He wandered into the kitchen dragging his battered cuddly dinosaur along the floor with one hand, clutching an action figure in the other.

'Hi, Lucien.'

'What am I, chopped liver?' asked Dean.

'I said hi to you already.'

Rafael dropped the dinosaur, pulled himself up on to the stool, then gazed expectantly at Lucien.

Lucien turned to Dean, confused.

'He wants his colouring pens—they're up on the shelf. Could you get them? My hands are all oniony.'

Dean went back to his chopping, but kept one eye on them to see how Lucien would respond. Lucien paused, wiped his hands on a tea towel, then stood and gathered the neat stack of paper and coloured pens that Dean had tidied away the night before. He deposited them gently on to the table by Rafael, then looked back at Dean questioningly, as if to ask if he'd done it right.

Dean smiled.

Yes, it was a small thing, but sometimes you had to start small.

Rafael reached for the pens and started scribbling. 'Is dinner ready yet?' he asked.

'As you can see, we're just cooking it. It'll be a while, but it's your favourite,' answered Dean.

'Lasagne?' Rafael asked excitedly.

'Okay, your second favourite.'

'Cool, I like all my favourites.'

'Why did you decide to cook for me today?' Lucien asked Dean. 'Any special reason?'

'It's an apology dinner.'

'Why?' Lucien looked up suspiciously. 'What did you do?'

'The accidental videoing.'

'Oh, that.'

'And roping you into the school visit. I know it's not normally your kind of thing.'

'No apology necessary.'

'Why? Because you secretly loved it?'

Dean winked at Lucien, and he swore Lucien's cheeks went pink.

'I wouldn't go that far.'

'But you didn't hate it?'

Suddenly Dean was worried. Maybe Lucien wanted to be alone…maybe Dean should stop teasing him and give him some space. Although surely Lucien would go up to his office if he really didn't want to be talked to.

Lucien smiled, although he seemed to be trying to hide it, and Dean's tension settled.

'It made a nice change, I suppose.'

'I'm glad,' said Dean.

Lucien finished grating and shook the last flakes off the grater on to the plate. 'Some of those children were very unusual.'

Dean shrugged. 'Kids are.'

'Half the things they said were completely illogical. And the Venus flytrap obsession…?'

Dean laughed. 'You say illogical—I say imaginative. Don't you remember being a kid and thinking the greatest dangers you would face in adult life would be killer plants, giant whirlpools and quicksand?'

'I can't say I do.'

Dean smiled. He couldn't imagine Lucien as a kid. Just as a tiny version of himself, with suede elbows on a tiny jacket, carrying a mini brown leather briefcase.

'I thought you said you were bad with kids,' said Dean, tipping the chopped onion into a large pan and adding some crushed garlic.

'I am.'

'Didn't look that way to me… Looked like you connected with them pretty well.'

Lucien shrugged shyly. 'What should I prepare next?'

Dean handed him a carrot. 'Maybe you've had some practice with a relative's kids? Or a girlfriend's?'

Lucien raised an eyebrow at Dean. 'I don't have girl-friends, Dean.'

Dean nodded. 'Gotcha.'

'And there are no children in my family—at least none that I spend time around.' Lucien looked at Rafael, who was now colouring in what looked like an elephant with a green pen. 'They are a totally alien species to me.'

'Hear that, Raf?' said Dean. 'He called you an alien.'

Rafael looked up indignantly. 'I'm not an alien!'

'Dean,' Lucien admonished sternly, raising an eyebrow, and making Dean's heart rate quicken. 'Stop getting me in trouble.'

Dean swallowed hard. Lucien being authoritative should not be that sexy.

'Raf? Why don't you go and watch TV on the sofa in the living room? Then you can spread out your stuff on the coffee table.'

'Okay!' Rafael gathered up all his pens and paper and hurried off to watch the big screen TV.

'He loves your TV,' Dean told Lucien.

Lucien smiled. 'Glad someone does. I hardly ever use it.'

Their hands touched accidentally as they both reached for the vegetable peeler. Dean flushed and busied himself stirring the onions. Lucien glared at his carrot as he awkwardly peeled it.

'Didn't your girlfriend mind you moving out of London?' he asked.

Dean side-eyed him. 'What girlfriend?'

'I just thought… I mean… I've gathered that you and Rafael's mother were apart for a long time? So you might be in a new relationship now?'

Dean nodded, unsure of how to respond. 'I've been single for a while.'

That was the second part of Lucien's question covered. Now for the first part. Maybe he could just gloss over it? He was such an idiot… He hadn't thought to prepare in advance what he would tell Lucien about himself and Rafael's mother. What was safe to share without revealing his secret? How should he handle this? He'd rather tell Lucien as much of the truth as possible, considering the big lie that was at the centre of all this.

'I was never really with Rafael's mother at all.'

Dean glanced into the living room at Rafael, but he was happily watching the television, pen in hand, about to get ink all over his knee if he didn't start paying attention to it. Regardless, he was well out of earshot and wouldn't hear whatever Dean was about to say, or not say.

Lucien frowned. 'You weren't?' His face cleared after a moment and he continued quietly, 'So Rafael was the result of a one-night stand?'

Dean paused. 'Yes, that's true.'

'And after his mother passed away Rafael came to you?'

'Yes.'

'I'm sorry for your loss,' Lucien murmured. 'I don't think I've said that yet.'

'Thank you. She was my best friend.'

Lucien seemed to make a move to reach for Dean's hand, but he aborted it at the last moment and put his hands in his lap.

Even now, talking about Charlotte made Dean's eyes sting. And the sweet, genuine look on Lucien's face wasn't helping. Dean felt so guilty for concealing the truth. Part of him wanted to shout it out there and then: *You're Rafael's father!* But he couldn't. It was imperative that he put Rafael's safety first. He had to keep quiet about it just a little longer.

'Can I ask something else?' said Lucien.

'Sure.'

Dean gave himself a metaphorical shake and made himself smile. He took the peeled carrot from Lucien and chopped it, still marvelling at the sharpness of the knife.

'Not that it's any of my business,' Lucien continued. 'Actually, forget it.'

Dean laughed. 'Lucien, you can ask me anything. I'm an open book, buddy.'

'Well… I've noticed that Rafael calls you Dean. I must admit, I did wonder why. But, as I say, it's absolutely none of my business.'

Oh.

Dean's stomach swirled with sudden nerves. How could Dean not have realised that would raise questions? He was so used to Rafael calling him Dean that it hadn't occurred to him that it might sound strange to other people. It looked as if he'd have to come clean about a little more than he had planned.

Dean took a deep breath. 'Technically, I'm his legal guardian—not a blood relation.'

'Oh,' said Lucien, gazing at him thoughtfully.

Dean steeled himself for judgement, or more difficult questions. Or even some anger that he'd bent the truth a few moments ago.

'I'm surprised. He looks just like you.'

'He does?' Dean's heart soared at that, and he wasn't sure why.

'He has your freckles! And that dimple. And the ability to be infuriatingly cheeky and endearing at the same time.'

'Oh, really?'

Lucien avoided Dean's gaze and bit his lip.

Dean chuckled softly. 'I was around him a lot when he was born,' Dean said. 'His mother and I knew each other for years. She was amazing. You know, she could—' Dean cut himself off. If he gave too many details Lucien might somehow recognise Charlotte from his description.

He'd been about to explain how Charlotte could play any song you wanted on the piano by ear, without sheet music. But if he told Lucien that he might also tell him about how she could somehow bake anything, with no recipe and no measuring, just by instinct. And how she could make up the best bedtime story you'd ever heard off the top of her head.

Despite all that, she'd never thought she was anything special. Dean had never met anyone quite like her, and he never would again. He didn't mean to romanticise her perfection now she was gone, or forget all her flaws, but with Charlotte there weren't many to forget. She truly was the kindest, funniest person he'd ever known, and it broke his heart that Rafael wouldn't get all those years he deserved to spend with her.

Rafael had indeed been the result of an impulsive one-night stand at the end of Charlotte's medical training. It had always been a running joke between them that the one solitary time in her life that she'd ever slept with a man she'd managed to get pregnant. Charlotte had already arranged to move hundreds of miles away from the southern town where she and the father had trained for her first position in medicine, and she hadn't thought he would be interested. Besides, she'd been perfectly happy to raise her child alone.

She'd never really talked about the father much. And Dean hadn't given the man a second thought until a few months ago.

Lucien was still waiting for Dean to continue, his gaze soft and encouraging.

'One night I went to bed and everything was perfectly normal. Then I was woken up by a phone call and my whole world changed. My friend was dead and apparently she'd mentioned me in her will. I was thinking she'd left me a book or a letter. But it wasn't.'

'It was Rafael?'

Dean nodded. 'It was a huge shock at the time, but I'm so glad she did. I love him so much…'

Lucien smiled, and Dean found himself continuing. Even though he'd never really felt comfortable talking about this to anyone else.

'When someone has a baby they always say that when they hold it for the first time this unfathomable tidal wave of primal love rushes through them, and they know they would die for them immediately.'

Lucien nodded.

'I didn't know that could happen to me. With a kid who wasn't even mine. But the first time I held him—' Dean shook his head. 'I knew that I'd die for him, kill for him, raze cities to the ground… All that good stuff.'

'I can see that.'

Lucien's gaze ran over Dean's face and stopped on his mouth for a second. Dean swallowed and looked away. He hadn't meant to open up quite that much, but something about Lucien made him want to be honest. Maybe it was Lucien's quiet manner…the way he gazed at Dean, just listening, waiting for him to say more. Not trying to jump in with his own words, never just talking for the sake of it. And when he did speak it meant something.

The sauce was nearly done, so Dean threw some fresh spaghetti into a pan of boiling water. It would only take a few minutes to cook.

'So anyway… To double back to your initial question. There's no partner back in London.'

'I see. I suppose having a child must make dating harder.'

'Oh, I'm not even thinking about dating any more.'

'Why not?' asked Lucien. 'Is it hard to find the time? Or babysitters?'

Lucien side-eyed Dean quickly, and Dean smiled. Lucien's face was so easy to read. Dean would bet money that he was very much hoping not to be asked to babysit.

'It's not that,' he said. 'I just think my dating years are over.'

Lucien shocked him by laughing.

'What?' asked Dean.

'Oh, I didn't mean to laugh at you. It's just you said that like an eighty-year-old who's just become a widower. I think you have a few years left in you yet, Dean.'

Dean shook his head, amused at Lucien's laughter. 'Nah.

I'm just not into casual dating any more. You can't really do that with a kid in tow. And I'm clearly not husband material. So that leaves me nowhere.'

'Who says you're not husband material?'

Dean shrugged. 'Everyone.'

He'd never really thought about it before. It was just something he accepted about himself. Ever since he was a child, people had found it easy to leave him. He was likeable, but not loveable. People wanted to date him once or twice, but rarely anything more.

'People don't see me as a long-term prospect,' he said now. 'My longest relationship was six months. She dumped me to get back with her ex. And the longest before that was only four. He left me when he met someone better. I'm just not the sort of person people think of in terms of for ever.'

Lucien frowned at him for a long moment. 'Well, you have a son now. That's for ever.'

Dean smiled. 'He's the only long-term relationship I need.'

'He's a great kid.'

'You think? You like him?'

Lucien nodded. 'Of course. He's very…surprising.'

Dean called Rafael and they sat down to eat together around the kitchen counter. Lucien set out a knife, fork and plate neatly for Rafael without Dean even having to ask.

Dean served up the food, giving Lucien the biggest plateful. Then he eyed Rafael trying to twist spaghetti on to his fork and placed a large pile of napkins near his plate.

Dean had practically told Lucien his entire life story. How had that ended up happening? He was just so easy to talk to. But maybe it was time to change the subject.

'So, everyone at work today was talking about a charity auction?'

'What?' said Lucien. He coughed and grabbed a napkin to wipe his mouth. 'Oh, no, that's not a thing.'

'Seemed an awful lot like a thing to me.'

'Well, I wouldn't know, because I don't get involved with it.'

'So they said.'

'Oh, I bet they did. What exactly did they say?'

'That you're a big Scrooge and that the charity would probably make double the money if only you joined in.'

'I don't see how.'

Dean smiled. Lucien really was endearing when he was grumpy or evasive. 'So what do they mean? What is this auction about?'

Lucien shook his head. 'It's so ridiculous…'

'Tell me.'

'It's practically medieval. I assume they were trying to get you involved?'

Dean nodded. 'I asked what I could do to help, and they told me to get you on board.'

Lucien rolled his eyes so hard they almost fell out of his head.

'But I still don't really know what they want us to do,' Dean finished.

'I'll tell you what they want us to do…'

Lucien was getting more animated by the second, fuelled apparently by indignation. He reached into his back pocket and got out his glasses, slipping them on before he continued.

'They want to parade us around on stage and get rich local women to bid on us like cattle.'

Dean wasn't prepared for how attractive Lucien would be wearing glasses. He stared a little before he remembered how to speak. 'Like cattle, huh?'

'Exactly. A meat market.'

'Start from the beginning—I'm not following.'

Lucien sighed. 'It's this big charity event that takes place every year. It's been going on for decades. My grandmother runs it. *But*—' Lucien held up one finger resolutely '—that does not make it my responsibility to take part.'

'No, buddy.' Dean nodded along. 'Of course not.'

Lucien looked at Dean in surprise. 'Well, you're the only person that agrees with me. Anyway, they ask me every year to be involved, and every year I say no and write a very nice cheque to assuage my guilt.'

'But what do they want you to do?'

'They make people line up on stage and then they go along the line one by one as members of the public bid on them for dates.'

That all sounded very innocuous to Dean, but Lucien obviously found the idea utterly horrific.

'Oh, God,' said Lucien, 'it's probably your idea of fun.'

Dean smiled. 'I mean, it doesn't sound so terrible to me. People bid, everyone has a good laugh, the charity gets some money. And then you spend a couple of hours on a faux date with someone you don't know...probably have an okay time and maybe make a new friend. That's not so bad, is it?'

Lucien had a look of shocked disgust on his face. 'How are we even the same species?'

'Okay, describe it to me from your point of view.'

'First of all, what if no one bids on you? That would be mortifying.'

Lucien's gaze ran over Dean's face, possibly lingering on his lips again for a nano second, but Dean couldn't be sure.

'Obviously that wouldn't happen to you, but try to imagine the concept in the far reaches of your imagination.'

Dean laughed. Lucien was funny when he was sarcastic.

'Okay, yes, that would be embarrassing,' Dean admitted. 'But you can't think that would happen to you?'

'Of course it would.' Lucien looked at him as if he was crazy. 'Second of all, hundreds of people are staring at you, expecting you to perform for them or something. Hideous. Plus you could trip or fall at any moment.'

'Not if you're careful.'

Lucien had never said so much at once, and Dean was delighted.

'And, worst of all, the second you're on stage in front of a crowd you're being judged,' Lucien continued. *That's the outfit he chose for this? He thinks his hair looks good like that? He thinks this is appropriate behaviour for a doctor?* No, as a matter of fact, I don't—' He suddenly seemed to remember Dean was there listening to him and finished his passionate rant rather quietly. 'Yeah, so that's why I always say no.'

'Have you ever actually been to the charity auction? Maybe it's not as bad as you think.'

'I haven't been for a few years, but I used to go when I was younger. Now I stay at home, with a locked door between me and anyone who might think it wise to try and drag me into it at the last minute.'

'Like who?'

'Have you met Helen? Plus my grandmother isn't great at understanding the word *no* when it comes to these sorts of things. I'm amazed I've managed to argue her down all these years, to be honest.'

Dean pushed some dislodged spaghetti back on to Rafael's plate with his fork. 'Now, don't get cross with me, Lucien. But, speaking of Helen, I did promise her I'd try to convince you to take part this year.'

'Dean!'

Dean stopped. 'You've finally called me Dean, instead of Dr Vasquez.'

'Sorry, I—'

'Don't be an idiot. I *want* you to call me Dean. We do live together, after all.'

Lucien nodded and looked down at his plate.

Rafael's plate was mostly clean, so Dean wiped Rafael's face with a wet cloth and sent him upstairs to get ready for bed. He knew that in ten minutes he'd go upstairs to check on him and find that he'd been reading or playing Nintendo Switch the whole time, but that was their routine, and they both liked it that way.

'So, now Raf's gone, do you want some adult dessert?' asked Dean.

'I dread to think what makes it "adult".'

Dean laughed. 'It just has rum in it.'

He pulled open the fridge and took out two glass bowls of dessert and a bar of seventy percent cocoa cooking chocolate.

'They're premade. We just have to add chocolate flakes on top.'

Dean grabbed one of Lucien's new knives and unwrapped the chocolate.

Lucien watched. 'Can I do it?'

Dean hesitated, he wasn't sure about Lucien's knife skills, and the blade was insanely sharp, but Lucien looked so eager to help that he couldn't say no.

Dean handed over the knife. 'Okay. But be careful.' Dean placed the dark chocolate on to the wooden chopping board. 'Just slice it thinly into chunks. We don't need all that much. Unless you particularly love chocolate?'

Lucien looked up. 'What kind of man do you take me for? Of course I particularly love chocolate.'

'Then go at it.'

He did. And within seconds cursed under his breath and dropped the knife, letting it clatter to the table.

Damn it, Dean should have listened to his instincts. Since having a son, he'd found his sixth sense for danger had sharpened considerably, and was rarely inaccurate.

'What have you done?'

'I cut myself.' Lucien examined his finger. 'But it's fine.'

Blood dripped down Lucien's hand on to the chopping board.

'Come here.'

Dean took Lucien's wrist and led him around the table to the sink. Lucien followed without question and let Dean push his hand under the cold tap. He held it firmly under the water for a moment.

'It's not too deep. Shouldn't need stitches.' Dean wrapped some paper towel around Lucien's finger and pressed it firmly. 'Wait here.'

Dean ran to the bathroom and returned to Lucien with a red and blue Spiderman plaster. 'Sorry, it's all I have.'

Lucien let him wrap it around his finger. 'This is ironic,' he said.

'How?'

'The very same day we lecture children on how to bandage cuts…'

'True. Oh, Raf's gonna be gutted he missed out on putting your arm in a sling.'

'Maybe tomorrow.' Lucien smiled.

Dean realised it was probably time to stop patting Lucien's arm and let him have his hand back.

'What if they did something different this year?' he asked.

Lucien gazed at him questioningly.

'At the auction. Maybe they could take the dating aspect out of it. They could offer other things.'

'Like what?'

'Like if the person being auctioned didn't want a date, they could offer some other prize instead.'

'I don't have the first clue what prize I could give anyone. Free GP consultations for a month?'

'They're free already.'

'A box of latex gloves? A stethoscope? A special chair in the waiting room?'

'Lucien! Think outside the box.'

'I don't know what that means.'

'Something that's not related to the practice.'

'Oh.'

'There's a concept!' Dean teased. 'What do you do outside of work?'

'Absolutely nothing.'

'There must be something,' Dean encouraged.

Lucien adjusted his glasses. 'I read books. I study bees. And I go rock climbing.'

'You climb rocks?' Dean asked.

'Yes.'

'As in cliff faces, ropes, abseiling, crampons?'

'That about covers it.'

'Oh.' Dean stared at him hard, then looked him up and down slowly.

'You seem confused?' said Lucien.

'No. No, I just… I didn't know you did anything like that. You're full of surprises, aren't you?' he murmured quietly. 'So, if I clear it with Helen, instead of a date, maybe you could give someone a climbing lesson?'

Lucien frowned. 'I suppose I could do that, yes.'

'Sounds good to me!' Dean wrote a note in his phone. 'We're coming back to that bee thing later, too.'

CHAPTER FOUR

DEAN BURST INTO Lucien's home office just after seven p.m. 'Rafael's out of Frosty Stars. If he doesn't have them in the morning he'll be unbearable. I have half an hour before the shop shuts, so I'm running out to get some. God, I hope they have it. Can you watch him? He's downstairs in front of the TV.'

Lucien barely had time to process Dean's garbled monologue before Dean had whirled off down the stairs, pulling on his jacket.

'Okay,' Lucien shouted. 'But don't be long!'

'I'll only be ten minutes!'

'This is most unsatisfactory,' Lucien said to the cat, who until then had been sleeping quite comfortably on Lucien's lap.

Binxie leapt down to the floor and stood in the doorway, looking after Dean. The front door slammed, and Binxie turned back to Lucien to chirrup.

After last night, Lucien felt a lot closer to Dean. He'd even been given answers to some of the questions that had been floating around his mind for days. But now he had new questions. Dean wasn't related to Rafael by blood, but he'd been tasked with raising him. He could only assume that perhaps the biological father was deceased, or a horribly unsuitable person.

But he'd already pushed Dean to answer enough personal questions—he certainly didn't want to push further. So he'd just have to wonder.

Dean had not stopped surprising him. First he'd learned that Dean wasn't the over-confident egotist that Lucien had first assumed. He had the capability to be shy and to doubt himself. And it had stunned Lucien to learn that Dean had such a low opinion of himself and his attractiveness as a partner.

Admittedly, Lucien had only known him a few days. But when he had so stupidly cut himself chopping chocolate, Dean hadn't mocked him or left him to take care of himself. That was probably the father in him. He seemed to thrive on looking after other people. Not an uncommon trait in a doctor, but Lucien had known a lot of doctors, and few were as warm and caring as Dean seemed to be.

Binxie put her front paws on Lucien's knee and licked his hand.

'You like him, huh?' Lucien put his book away and Binxie mewed. 'Yes, I'm sure he's very nice. But I'm the one who feeds you. Remember that.'

Not having had younger siblings, or nieces and nephews, Lucien wasn't exactly sure what watching Rafael meant. Was he simply required to be an available adult in the house that Rafael could come to for help were it needed? Or was he supposed to literally watch him? And how had he got to this age without knowing this sort of thing?

Lucien gave Binxie a head-rub, the furry little traitor, then rearranged a pile of papers on his desk. 'Okay, Binx, you're right. Now I'm simply hiding from the child. Let's go down. How bad can it be?'

It was probably best to err on the side of caution and keep an actual eye on him.

Lucien felt half panicked and half flattered that Dean trusted him to look after his child. Maybe not half and half...perhaps more of a sixty-forty split on the side of panic. Or ninety-ten.

Lucien headed down, followed by Binxie. Which in cat terms meant weaving between Lucien's legs all the way down, cutting him off at every corner and generally trying to trip him at every opportunity. Which made no evolutionary sense. For if Lucien lay dead in a crumpled heap at the foot of the stairs Binxie would have no one to open her bags of gourmet cat food or scratch her under the chin. But Binxie's strengths didn't lie in logic.

Lucien found Rafael curled up on the sofa, watching what looked like a horrifically violent superhero film on television. Had he switched over to this the second Dean left? Or was this sanctioned viewing?

Lucien hesitated at the door, then sidled in and sank on to the other end of the sofa. 'What are you watching?'

'It's the best bit of *Iron Man*. Loki throws him out of a window, but his exoskeleton armour jumps out too and saves him.'

'Ah...' Lucien nodded, not having a clue what half those words meant.

'Do you like Iron Man?' asked Rafael.

'I don't really know much about him, to be honest.'

'Really?' Rafael looked gobsmacked. 'Who's your favourite superhero?'

Lucien cast his mind back to the last time he'd cared about superheroes. He'd probably been the same age as Rafael. 'I guess I like Superman?'

Rafael nodded. 'Yeah, that makes sense. You kind of look like him.'

Lucien decided to take that puzzling comment as a compliment. 'What superhero do you look like?'

'Hmm...' Rafael grabbed a cushion and hugged it as he thought. 'There aren't many kid heroes. But maybe Wiccan? He's in Marvel. He's cool.'

'And which is Dean like?'

'Oh, he's Captain America. Cause he's so strong and smart and stuff.'

Lucien nodded, and wondered what to say next.

Rafael stared around the room. 'You have a lot of books.'

'Yes, I suppose I do. But I'm not the only one. I saw your dad unpacking a lot of books when you moved in.'

All the boxes he'd walked past on the stairs that first day had seemed to be stacked full of things for Rafael. Dean didn't seem to have brought many of his own belongings in comparison.

'You have like a whole library.'

The child sounded a little in awe. And Lucien couldn't believe he was about to say this, but... 'If you're careful, you can read anything you want.'

'I can?' Rafael stared at him open-mouthed. 'Dean said I wasn't allowed to touch anything.'

'Oh, well, he wasn't to know. Books are made to be read, you know? And shared.'

'Wow.'

Rafael jumped down off the sofa, TV forgotten for a moment, and started looking through the lower shelves. And Lucien was strangely okay with it. No one had ever shown an interest in his books. He had a lot of non-fiction filled with big glossy pictures. Books about palaeontology, bugs, butterflies, space and maps.

With some difficulty, Rafael pulled out a large, heavy book about the beetles of Asia, and was soon marvelling over the gigantic close-up photographs of iridescent gold beetles and bright purple-horned stags.

This wasn't going so badly. It was easier to hold a conversation with Rafael than he'd thought it would be. Usually Lucien felt as if people were judging what he said, but Rafael just went with the flow unquestioningly, and Lucien felt he could say anything, however silly or pointless, and Rafael wouldn't think he was odd. The boy seemed remarkably well adjusted for having been through such a trauma at an early age. He was fortunate to have a dad like Dean.

'This beetle is the best one.' Rafael pointed at a glossy blue and green beetle with a ferocious horn and spiny legs, and grinned up at Lucien.

Lucien smiled. 'Great choice. That's the Asiatic Rhinoceros beetle.'

It was one of Lucien's favourites too. He was proud of Rafael for noticing how special it was. Suddenly Lucien wanted to impart every bit of knowledge he had that Rafael might find interesting. He shifted closer to Rafael and turned a couple of pages in the book. There was one specimen he remembered being obsessed with when he was Rafael's age.

'You'll love this one...'

Rafael read out the name of the beetle Lucien pointed to and cackled. Then he moved the book on to both their laps and hugged Lucien's arm tightly. 'You're funny.'

Lucien had never been so disarmed in all his life. He cuddled Binxie all the time, but she never hugged back. He never really let anyone else close enough for hugs. The last person to hug him must have been his grandmother, at his mother's funeral, and even that had been under duress.

Lucien sighed as he identified the emotion he was currently feeling. It was fondness. He'd allowed himself to become fond of Rafael, and even Dean. This was literally the opposite of everything he'd planned. But he knew there was no turning back now. You couldn't flick a switch and stop feeling affection. If he could do that he never would have kept Binxie after she'd shown up tiny, mewling and soaking wet one stormy night. He could have given her to a shelter any time in the first week or two after he'd let her into the house. But he'd fed her, and talked to her, and she'd purred on his lap and he'd become fond.

But a cat was very different from two human beings. If he opened his heart and his life to them things would get very complicated. As adorable as Rafael was, and as attracted to Dean as he might be becoming, that didn't change the fact that people got hurt when Lucien allowed himself to get distracted by his personal life. His ex and his mother were proof of that. And the only solution for that was simply not to have one.

He'd allowed Rafael and Dean in too much already.

Dean wandered up and down the small cereal aisle at the local mini supermarket. Luckily, they did have Rafael's Frosty Stars. Dean grabbed a box off the shelf and carried it under his arm. Of course there had been plenty left for Rafael to eat in the morning until Dean himself had polished them off. But he'd needed plausible deniability. And a reason to duck out of the house for ten minutes.

How else could he gently test out Lucien's progress with Rafael? It wasn't a big test—he just wanted to see how they got on without him there as a buffer. Would Dean get home to find Lucien had stayed upstairs in his room? Would he have forgotten he was supposed to be watching Rafael altogether? Dean didn't think so, but he didn't know for sure. He trusted Lucien not to go out and abandon Rafael, of course, or he would never have left Rafael with him.

The shop was small and bright. The fluorescent strip light above flashed on and off minutely, and made Dean feel faintly nauseous. The tinny music playing through the speakers wasn't great, but at least it was quiet.

'Hello, Doctor!'

Of course, having left the house for only a few minutes, he would have to run in to one of his patients. Such was the beauty of a small town. Dean plastered a smile on his face and turned around.

It was the man who'd been kicked by the angry cow.

'Fancy seeing you here,' the man said, grinning.

'Well, it is the only shop in town.'

Dean took the offered hand and shook it warmly.

'Fair point. Run out of cereal, did you?'

Dean laughed politely.

'Not a very healthy choice for a doctor.'

'It's my son's favourite. Apparently he can't live without it.'

As Dean had learned from some rather distressing tantrums early on in their relationship. He grabbed a chocolate bar for Rafael too, feeling a bit guilty for using his son as a Lucien test.

In his short wait in the queue, he managed to be spotted by a second patient from that day's surgery, and then smoothly deflected a request to look at a rash on the checkout lady's neck. After encouraging the poor woman to make an appointment with him at the surgery, Dean finally got away.

Those interactions might have made him feel frustrated back in London. He had always been trying desperately to get home, or get to work. Wherever he was, he'd always been supposed to be somewhere else. But here he felt he had time for these people. This was what his job was all about.

And, as out of place as he had felt at first, and as dangerous as it was to let himself want this, maybe this was exactly where he was supposed to be…

Dean stepped out into the fresh, warm breeze and glanced at his watch. With the two-minute walk back home, it was time to get going. His stomach churned on the walk back, and he felt weirdly anxious as he turned the key in the lock and let himself into the kitchen. He left the cereal and chocolate on the counter and found Rafael and Lucien in the living room.

What he saw dissolved all his worries and warmed his heart.

Lucien and Rafael sat closely on the sofa, a huge book open over both their laps. Rafael was giggling at something Lucien had said. After a minute, Lucien looked over his shoulder and noticed Dean watching them. His face seemed to go through a number of emotions, then he sighed and stood, taking the book with him.

'Did you get the cereal?'

Dean nodded. 'You look like you're having fun.'

Lucien looked down at Rafael and gently passed him the book. 'I've got work I really need to get back to.'

Lucien strode past Dean and disappeared up the stairs.

Dean took his place on the sofa, feeling deflated, and put an arm around Rafael. 'What have you got there, buddy?'

'It's about bugs. It has really cool pictures.'

Rafael seemed quiet. 'What were you two laughing at before?' asked Dean.

'Lucien was telling me about the dung beetle.' Rafael paused. 'Did I do something wrong to make him go?'

'No, of course not. I think Lucien has some important work to do.'

Dean distracted Rafael with the chocolate and felt awful. Lucien's hot and cold routine was fine when it was directed at Dean, but not acceptable when it hurt Rafael. Was Dean right to worry after all? Was Lucien not dad material? It would be heartbreaking to have to leave now, so soon after he'd allowed himself to feel he might belong.

At work the next day, Helen slammed her clipboard on to Dean's desk, almost making him choke on his lunchtime baguette.

'I've added you two to the official auction schedule. So there's no backing out now.'

Dean nodded, coughing. 'No problem. We're both happy to help.'

'You'll have to tell me how you convinced Lucien to do it. That ability could prove very helpful to me in future.'

Dean laughed. 'We just talked about it and I found a way to make it less of a nightmare for him. Like I told you, shifting the focus off winning a date and on to winning a prize.'

Helen nodded. 'That was a pretty good idea—thank you for that. The auction board loved it. And even Lucien's grandmother thinks it'll give the whole event a bit of a rejuvenation.'

Helen quickly reapplied her lipstick in the small mirror hanging on the wall over Dean's printer.

'You don't fancy being auctioned off yourself?' Dean asked.

'If I was on stage, I wouldn't be able to look after Rafael for you, would I? And, not to give you a big head, but I think you'll pull a bigger audience than me.'

'Hey, no negative self-talk. Mr Helen is a lucky guy.'

Helen put her lipstick away and blotted her lips with a tissue. 'Quite right.'

Then she turned her focus on to Dean, and he could tell he wouldn't like what was coming.

'So, what about you?'

'What about me?' Dean responded.

'I might be wrong, but I don't believe there is a current Mr or Mrs Dean?'

'Correct.'

'Have you ever been involved with someone serious?'

Dean shrugged. 'Not really.'

Everyone Dean had loved had left him. His father. His mother, who'd tried her best but failed. Every one of his mother's boyfriends, who had paid him attention to impress her, but bailed on him eventually. As an adult, he'd never been short of dates, but that was all people thought he was good for or interested in. No one ever wanted to stay.

After so many years, he'd learned that the fewer people he allowed to get close to him, the less he could be hurt. He hid it with bravado, but he felt broken inside.

'Does that bother you?' asked Helen.

Normally Dean would laugh off a question like that and change the subject, but something made him pause. 'It never used to. But lately—I don't know. It might be nice to find the right one.'

Helen patted his arm. 'They're out there somewhere. Or maybe you've found them already?'

Lucien's face popped up in his mind and he blinked it away. 'I don't know about that. Sounds too good to be true.'

It really was time to change the subject now.

'Fancy a coffee?'

Helen tutted, but acquiesced, and Dean got her a cup from the machine, and himself a glass of cold tap water.

'So how long have you known Lucien?' Dean asked, once back at his desk.

Helen smiled wryly, and Dean realised he might not have changed the subject quite as smoothly as he'd hoped.

'For ever,' she answered. 'He had his first placement here.'

'Oh, wow—so you knew him back when he was a baby doctor?'

'I had to hold his hand through his first mid-consultation fainter, his first burst catheter and his first projectile vomiting baby.'

'I've been there...'

Dean smiled. It was strange to imagine Lucien as new and inexperienced.

'I still remember in his first few months on the job,' Helen continued, 'when my daughter was eleven, she broke her wrist and came to Lucien for a check-up. At the end of the consultation she asked him to her middle school prom.'

'No!'

'He was mortified, but a total gentleman. He let her down very gently.'

Dean laughed. That was adorable.

'So, you seem to be settling in very well. How are you finding country life, really?'

'Surprisingly good. I was nervous about it. About whether people would accept me or think I was out of my depth.'

'Or whether you'd find the place boring as all get out.'

'Not boring. Just different. And it is. But I kind of love it. And it's so much better for Raf. He already loves it here. Acts like he's never lived anywhere else.'

'I must say you are doing remarkably well at this dad thing.'

'Well, I'm getting there. Doing my best.'

Dean always felt self-conscious when people gave him compliments about being a father. He didn't feel he'd earned them yet. Or that he even knew what he was doing, half the time.

Helen grinned. 'You're doing better than you think you are. Now, get back to work.'

CHAPTER FIVE

On AUCTION DAY, Helen dropped around to collect Rafael.

'You remember Helen?' said Dean. 'The lady I work with?' Rafael nodded shyly as Helen waved down at him. 'She's going to take you to play on the bouncy castle outside the town hall, then after that she'll go with you to the auction, and we'll meet you there later.'

'After our ritual humiliation,' Lucien cut in.

As soon as Dean said 'bouncy castle' Rafael's eyes lit up, and he pulled on Helen's sleeve, propelling her towards the hall.

'Okay, take it easy,' Dean called. 'You be good for Helen, like we talked about, and do everything she asks.'

'Okay!' Rafael answered, still running.

'Raf!' Dean yelled, stopping Rafael in his tracks by the front door. Dean knelt down and pointed to his cheek. 'Don't I get a kiss goodbye?'

Rafael rushed at him, gave him a quick hug, then ran back to the front door and a grinning Helen. 'Bye, Daddy!'

Rafael was gone before Dean could fully process what Rafael had said. He remained kneeling on the floor and stared at the closed door in silence, his lips parted.

Lucien stepped closer. 'Was that the first time he's ever called you that?'

Dean nodded. His blood rushed in his ears and he felt as

if he might explode. How could Rafael bless him with that gift and then just leave? What was he supposed to do with this rush of emotion? He felt as if he'd just jumped out of a plane at ten thousand feet. Who could he hug?

He turned to Lucien, a huge smile on his face, only to find a matching one on Lucien's. Which suddenly brought Dean smack back down to earth. Lucien was Rafael's father too. He deserved to hear that word from Rafael just as much as Dean—maybe even more.

Needing to hug Lucien now more than ever, he reached out, and Lucien let Dean pull him into his arms, holding him tight as Dean squeezed a silent apology into his shoulders.

'It felt that good, huh?' Lucien murmured, right by Dean's ear.

'You have no idea.'

The morning of the auction had dawned bright and terrifying. The dread had been heavy in Lucien's chest even before he was fully awake, but he'd sighed and dragged himself out of bed. He'd successfully avoided this auction for over a decade, but the second Dean came along he had managed to let himself get roped in.

What an idiot.

But now, standing in the hall with an armful of elated Dean, the day didn't seem so bad after all.

Lucien had intended to avoid Dean for a couple of days, embarrassed about the way he'd acted, and convinced they were getting too close. Dean had seemed a little standoffish himself—which was hardly surprising when Lucien had been so abrupt. But everything had changed after lunch the following day.

While Dean had been busy changing the oil in his car, Rafael had asked Lucien to make him pancakes. Now, when people said they could burn water, they were usually exaggerating, but with Lucien it was accurate. He could barely make toast without setting off the smoke alarm, and he normally stuck to eating ready meals from the mini supermarket or wolfing down a quick piece of toast.

But Rafael had gazed up at him with his big charcoal-grey eyes and a strange determination had come over Lucien. He would make this poor child pancakes if it killed him. And it very well might.

Anyway, cut to an hour later, and Lucien had had two of Dean's cookbooks open on the counter, trying to combine two pancake recipes because he couldn't find all the ingredients for either one. He'd used every bowl and spoon in the house, and the table had been covered in spilled flour and broken eggs when Dean had finally found them. He'd stared at the mess, and at Rafael giggling, and at the flour Lucien had suspected he had on his cheek, with a small smile, before gently taking over. Within ten minutes they'd had a clean kitchen and a pile of pancakes each. Dean hadn't even needed to use a recipe.

He made everything look so easy.

Since then Dean had seemed to be on some kind of mission. Over the last twenty-four hours he'd been much more attentive to Lucien, spent more time around him, and kept trying to feed him. Lucien wasn't sure what that meant, but it was certainly nice to have someone who cared enough to make him eat better food than microwave meals and toast.

So now, when Dean found Lucien lacing up his boots, Lucien wasn't surprised when he asked him where he was off to.

'I just thought I'd go for a quiet walk to centre myself before the auction.'

Dean paused. 'Can I make you some food to take?'

Lucien couldn't help but smile. 'I won't be gone that long.'

'You want company?'

How to say no without being rude? Lucien couldn't think of a way, and before he knew it Dean had taken advantage of his silence and was pulling on his own boots and grabbing his jacket. He even took a scarf off the hook and looped it over Lucien's shoulders, then reached up to secure it gently around his neck, leaving Lucien flustered and warm.

Lucien's introvert nature meant that being around people drained all his energy—and by God he was going to be around a lot of people later today. He needed to well and truly fill up that well of energy. And that was why he was heading out. There was a place he went to when he needed to recharge.

Dean followed Lucien along the pavement towards the woods at the end of the road, kicking through orange leaves. Lucien kept extra-quiet as he passed the wrought-iron gate that formed the entrance to his grandmother's property. She was often out walking in the grounds, bothering the gardener, and he didn't want her to sense his presence with her ultra-focused grandmother powers like she normally did.

'So, where are we going?' asked Dean loudly, just as they passed her gate.

Lucien sighed and tried hard not to shush him. 'You'll find out when we get there.'

Dean shrugged happily and carried on striding beside Lucien. 'Anyone ever tell you that you walk too fast?'

Lucien slowed his pace slightly. Now that Dean mentioned it, Lucien could hear the man was panting to keep up. Lucien did walk too fast for most people, but it wasn't his fault he had long legs.

They climbed over a stile and walked along the grassy edge of a ploughed field, before taking a left turn and crossing a tiny brook on a short, slippery bridge made from a stone slab covered in moss.

Lucien led the way across an overgrown graveyard towards an old stone church topped with a crooked spire. Every time Lucien came here he was reminded that one day he should come back and tidy the place up. Someone needed to weed around all the headstones, pull the brambles down from the church walls, rake the leaves, perhaps even mow the grass. But, to be honest, he rather liked the ramshackle feel of the place. And the last thing he wanted was for other people to feel welcome there. He liked it hidden—his own overgrown secret. So he'd never quite got around to it.

'Someone should come and neaten this place up,' said Dean, reading Lucien's mind.

Close to the church, the grass was almost crowded out by moss, soft and spongy beneath their boots. Lucien pushed hard on the wooden door of the church until it burst open, its hinges squealing.

'Should we be doing this?' asked Dean. He glanced behind them, as if checking for an angry priest about to yell at them for breaking into his church.

'It's fine—it's deconsecrated. No one uses it any more. In fact, I think I'm the only person who's been here in the last ten years.'

The church had been abandoned years ago. At the time, a handful of people had relocated their loved ones' remains elsewhere, wanting to continue to pay their respects at a place with a priest and a groundskeeper, but most of the graves still held people who'd been gone for hundreds of years. One of the oldest headstones Lucien had seen was for a man named Albie Merrieweather, dated 1699-1728. No one was coming to see him.

Inside it was as quiet as ever. The only noise disrupting the cool, calm air was their echoing footsteps. They walked between the pews to the centre aisle, where stained glass threw red shadows across the wooden floor.

'Now what?' asked Dean.

'We go up.'

Dean followed Lucien to the narrow spiral staircase and they climbed up stone steps built hundreds of years previously. Their middles were worn down and made shiny by centuries of priests' footsteps.

'Be careful, it's pretty uneven.'

Not a moment after Lucien spoke Dean tripped and grabbed the back of Lucien's shirt, cursing quietly as he righted himself.

'I did say…'

'Shut up, Lucien.'

Lucien reached the top, pushed open another stiff wooden door and stepped out on to the bright, breezy tower. He looked out over the chest-high ledge surrounding it and gestured for Dean to join him. The tower was only about ten feet square, and open to the elements, so Lucien's hair was immediately blown into his eyes.

The spire loomed above them, supported by four thick pillars of stone, one on each corner. This left wide spaces on each side of the tower through which to admire the beautiful views.

'Wow, this is a lot higher than I expected.'

Dean stayed in the doorway, biting his lip and holding on with both hands to the doorframe.

Lucien frowned. 'I didn't know you were scared of heights.'

If he'd known he wouldn't have brought him up here.

'I'm not scared, just… How safe is this tower?'

'It's very sturdy. It's been here hundreds of years, and it's made of solid stone.'

Dean peered over the ledge from his place by the door.

'It's safe, I promise,' said Lucien.

Dean reluctantly let go of the doorframe and ventured towards the middle of the platform. Lucien tried not to find it adorable that brave, capable Dean was nervous about being higher than the first floor.

Lucien leaned his arms against the ledge and rested his chin on them. All he could see was green, and it was infinitely calming.

Dean joined him.

'Wow...' Dean turned slowly in place, taking in the three-hundred-and-sixty-degree view. 'I can't see a single building!'

'The trees hide everything,' Lucien answered.

Even though they could see all the way to the horizon in several spots, by coincidence—or somehow by design—all the surrounding villages and farmhouses were hidden from view behind the trees.

He breathed in the smell of woodsmoke and shut his eyes as a cool breeze rustled through trees that would soon overtake the height of the tower. 'I sometimes come here when I get overwhelmed with work. Or family. Or anything.'

'How long have you been coming?'

'Since I was at school. My mother's ashes are scattered here.'

Lucien frowned. He wasn't sure why he had shared that.

Dean stepped closer until their shoulders were touching. 'Where is she?'

Lucien pointed down at one corner of the graveyard, where the grass was lush and thick and covered in a burst of roses and wildflowers in yellow, pink and blue.

Dean nodded. 'Great place to choose.'

'Sometimes I come and talk things over with the flowers when I need help figuring stuff out. It's stupid, but often while I'm here I ask her to give me a sign. You know…that she approves of my decisions.'

Apparently, his mouth could not stop sharing private information with Dean today.

'That's not stupid. What kind of sign?'

Lucien shrugged. 'You can make anything a sign if you want it badly enough. A leaf falling from a tree on to your lap. A bird leaving a feather as it flies away.' Lucien suddenly felt self-conscious. 'Anyway… It's a great place to come and get centred.'

'I can see why you came today, then.' Dean laughed. 'We must be pretty overwhelming.'

Lucien was taken aback. That wasn't why he'd needed to come here at all. In the days since Dean had entered his life not once had he felt the pull to come here because of him and Rafael.

'No. It's not you. It's the auction.'

A wood pigeon fluttered from a tree on to the church roof, and settled down, cooing softly.

'I can see why you like it here,' Dean murmured. 'My blood pressure's lowered already. Could have used a place like this in the city.'

'Where did you go to escape things?'

'I don't know… The gym?'

'You find exercising with a group of strangers relaxing?'

'It felt relaxing in comparison to work, but… Maybe I was kidding myself. To be honest, it feels like coming to Little Champney is the first time I've taken a breath in years.'

'You can come here too if you want. When you need a

minute. I don't mind. If you can brave the mountainous heights, that is,' he added as an afterthought.

Dean slapped his arm lightly with the back of his hand. 'Thank you. I just might.' He paused. 'You know, despite being a graveyard, it has quite the romantic vibe.' Dean nudged him playfully with his elbow. 'Do you bring all your dates here?'

Lucien laughed dryly. 'I've never brought anyone here before.'

'Wow. Then I'm touched.'

'You invited yourself, if you remember.'

'Oh, God. I did. Sorry.'

Lucien smiled. 'It's fine. I'm happy to have you.'

It was stimulating to be in Dean's company. And yet he'd found his visit to the church just as relaxing and recharging as he would have had he been alone. The strangeness of that did not escape him.

Dean moved closer, his arm pressing against Lucien's. Lucien tried to suppress the shiver that ran down his spine at the contact. Dean closed his eyes and tilted his face up to the sky, and Lucien took the opportunity to watch how beautifully the breeze caressed Dean's hair and the sun lit his features. His gaze slid slowly down Dean's throat and across his wide, muscular shoulders.

'It's nice being here with you, Lucien,' Dean whispered.

Lucien flinched. While he'd been distracted, Dean had caught him watching. But he didn't seem to mind. In fact, unless Lucien was mistaken, Dean seemed to be rather preoccupied with Lucien's mouth.

Lucien licked his lips briefly and Dean's eyes followed the movement.

Lucien's name sounded wonderful whispered by Dean,

and suddenly he couldn't think of anything he wanted more than to hear him say it again.

'Dean?' Lucien murmured, shifting closer.

Dean turned to face him fully. Their fingers collided on the cool stone wall and Lucien held his breath. He swallowed hard, and forced himself not to pull his hand away from Dean's heat. The blood rushed in his ears, and he could barely think straight. Dean moved closer, trailing a hand slowly up Lucien's arm, and he found himself leaning in, drawn like a magnet to Dean's irresistible pull.

A twig cracked loudly in the graveyard below them and they both turned towards the noise. Between the trees, an elderly, very-well-put-together woman appeared, clutching a leather handbag. She smoothly navigated the bridge and mossy grass, despite her sleek high heels.

Lucien stood up straight as soon as he spotted her, and withdrew from Dean. 'Oh, no.'

'What?' asked Dean.

Lucien tried to pull himself together and brushed his clothes off, finding grit from the wall on his sweaty palms. He took a few deep breaths to recover his poise. 'Gird your loins.'

'What? Why are we girding? Who is she?'

The woman looked up at them and saluted. 'Hello, fellas.'

'Hello, Grandmother,' answered Lucien reluctantly.

Dean stared at him for a moment, mouth open, then grinned.

'Who's your young man?' Lucien's grandmother called to them, holding her hand up to shield her eyes from the bright sky.

Lucien rolled his eyes. 'She knows exactly who you are—she just trying to get a reaction. We'll have to go down. But please promise me you'll ignore anything she says. She's an extremely acquired taste.'

They convened between a grave and a small stone angel under the cool shade of an enormous oak tree. Lucien's grandmother looked at him expectantly. And Lucien acquiesced.

'Even though you know perfectly well who he is, let me officially introduce you to Dr Dean Vasquez. Dean, this is Nancy Benedict, my grandmother.'

Dean and Nancy shook hands.

'It's very sweet of you to accompany my grandson here on this difficult day.'

'It is?' asked Dean, looking bewildered.

'Grandmother—' Lucien tried to interrupt.

Nancy touched Lucien's arm briefly. 'I know this day is hard for you, dear.'

Lucien sighed. 'Shall we just go and see her?'

Nancy nodded, and Lucien gestured for her to go first. Then they followed her around the corner of the church towards the wildflower bed.

Lucien spoke quietly as he walked close to Dean. 'It's my mother's birthday today.'

'Oh.' Dean nodded, then looked awkward. 'I'm really sorry I invited myself, man.'

'Don't be. I'm glad you're here.'

Lucien was rewarded with one of Dean's bright smiles, and he nearly stumbled over a tree root.

'Is everything all right?' Lucien asked his grandmother. 'You don't normally come to see Mother on her birthday.'

Lucien couldn't help but be slightly suspicious that Nancy had appeared so suddenly.

'I remember her in other ways,' Nancy said.

'I know, Grandmother.'

'I mainly came here to find you. Do you have a light, darling?' Nancy pulled a silver cigarette case from her handbag and took out a cigarette.

Lucien rolled his eyes. She knew he always carried a lighter on him, exclusively to light her slim French cigarettes, because she insisted that carrying a lighter of her own was undignified.

'So,' she said, as he held the flame up to light the end of her cigarette. 'I hear you've finally been convinced to join us in the auction?'

'I can always change my mind again,' answered Lucien, feeling himself inching ever closer to doing just that.

Nancy turned to Dean. 'My beloved grandson is not one of life's joiners.'

'Grandmother—'

'No. And we love you despite that...' Nancy spoke over Lucien's protesting '...but every now and again you just have to suck it up. Do you think I enjoy being the chair at every neighbourhood watch and local council meeting?'

'Yes, I do,' answered Lucien.

She paused. 'Well, you're right. But do you really think I enjoy having to attend every church jumble sale and the opening of a new café?'

'Yes. You're usually the one at the centre of any official opening ceremony.'

'It's not my fault I look good with a ribbon and a huge pair of scissors.' Nancy brushed him off. 'Regardless... Can we thank Dean, here, for his good work?' Nancy turned to Dean. 'God knows, I've tried to convince Lucien to take part in the auction for years. But despite decades of my efforts he's refused point blank. Then, strangely, *you* enter the field and he's there in a flash.'

Lucien hoped he could blame his flushed cheeks on the chill in the air.

Dean knocked him gently with his shoulder. 'He'll do a great job, Ms. Benedict. Maybe it's like opening a jar…you loosened the lid and I opened him.'

Lucien's grandmother actually giggled, 'Oh, you are going to be fun. Call me Nancy, please.'

Lucien made a face and looked over at her to check he'd heard correctly. Nancy never giggled. Honestly, Dean needed to be studied by the government—because whatever pheromones he was giving off should be weaponised.

Nancy took Dean's arm as they stood by Lucien's mother's resting place. Since Dean didn't have much of a family himself, he hadn't envisaged bumping into any more of Rafael's. It was blowing Dean's mind that Rafael had a great-grandmother—especially as, sadly, his grandmother had already passed. The fact that she was now gripping Dean's arm, only moments after he was pretty sure he'd almost kissed Lucien, was almost too much to handle.

Had he almost kissed Lucien? Or had Lucien almost kissed him? He wasn't sure, but his mind felt scrambled.

After a few moments of silence, when all Dean could hear were the bees bumping lazily from flower to flower and birds singing from the tall trees, Nancy gently cleared her throat.

'I hear you have a young son?'

Dean nodded.

'I must apologise on Lucien's behalf—he has a terrible effect on children.'

'No, Rafael likes Lucien very much.'

Dean glanced over to find Lucien's mouth open and his eyebrows raised, as though Dean had said something surprising.

'And I him,' Lucien said. 'You're both a pleasure to live with.'

It was Nancy's turn to look surprised. She gazed at Lucien for a moment, before addressing Dean. 'He must be a very special child.'

'Thank you—he is.'

'It's so nice of you to provide your family with a child to dote upon. They must be so happy to have him.' She looked back pointedly at Lucien.

Dean rubbed the back of his neck. He hadn't signed up for this. Keeping the truth from Lucien was bad enough, but now he was lying to one more of Rafael's blood relatives, and neither of them knew about it but him. It reminded Dean how closely he was flirting with danger. There was so much riding on this situation that he'd got them all into. And if it all went wrong there were so many people who would be affected.

'I'm not in contact with most of my family,' he said. Which was why it would mean so much if these people welcomed Rafael into theirs.

Dean tried to imagine Nancy interacting with Rafael. He wasn't sure she was the type to bake him cookies or knit him a winter hat…

'Oh. I'm sorry, dear. You know, I've always found Little Champney to be very welcoming to people in need of a new start.' Nancy patted Dean's arm, then briefly squeezed his hand before letting go.

Dean felt a burst of affection. She might not be a bad great-grandmother at all.

Which was why he could never risk a relationship with Lucien.

Dean's heart plummeted at the realisation.

Lying to Lucien was so much harder than he'd expected

it to be. And when Dean finally told Lucien his secret there was no knowing how Lucien would react. Dean still believed in his reasons for hiding the truth—Rafael had to come first. But that was exactly why Dean must never complicate things by falling for Lucien. If things went wrong... if they ended badly... Dean would be forced to rip Rafael away from the only blood family he had.

Thank God Dean hadn't kissed Lucien.

He had narrowly avoided a complete disaster, and he couldn't risk doing the same thing again.

All the Zen Lucien had built up at his beloved tumbledown church was obliterated as he and Dean approached the town hall together.

They passed the bouncy castle on the green, and stopped for a minute to wave hello to Helen and Rafael. Dean grabbed Rafael and gave him a quick hug, before sending him back to the castle, and then they made their way towards the town hall entrance.

Lucien had kept so far away from this event for the last decade that he hadn't even seen the hall decorated for it before. When he'd last attended they'd never bothered to decorate the outside. But today there were countless banners of brightly coloured fabric—probably handmade by the Women's Institute—and the trees on the cobblestone forecourt were strung with warm white fairy lights. He hadn't known it was possible for a building to be covered in quite that much bunting...

'Looks like Christmas,' said Dean.

Lucien was too nervous to speak, and just grunted in reply. Then he saw something truly horrendous, and stopped walking just outside the entrance. Dean bumped hard into his back, but it didn't move Lucien one inch. Before Dean could say anything, Lucien grabbed his arm and pointed at the door with his other hand.

When Dean saw what he was pointing at he burst out laughing, but Lucien did not see the funny side. Covering one half of the door was a large poster advertising the auction. Underneath the time and day of the event was a list of the people who would be going up for auction. And right in the middle, clear as day, in jaunty purple Comic Sans lettering, were the words *Sexy GPs Dr Lucien Benedict and Dr Dean Vasquez!*

'"Sexy GPs"?' Lucien eventually spluttered out.

When Dean finally took a look at Lucien's face he grimaced sympathetically. 'They're just having a bit of fun, I'm sure they don't mean anything bad by it.'

Lucien massaged his temples with both hands, feeling the beginnings of a headache. 'I trained as a doctor for ten years—how has it resulted in this? We both did. Doesn't this bother you?'

Dean shrugged. 'The use of Comic Sans does.' He rubbed Lucien's arm and glanced back at the poster. 'It's okay. It'll be okay. Look—they've called the vicar "handsome".'

Lucien checked. They had.

'And they've called Mayor Jean "enchanting".'

Lucien nodded, feeling his heart rate come down slowly. He was not sure if it was Dean's words, or the fact that he was still rubbing Lucien's arm comfortingly.

'We can do this.' Dean made eye contact with Lucien, and smiled. 'Or, if you really don't want to, we can go back home right now.'

They stared at each other for a long moment. Dean's eyes really were a wonderful shade of green...

'Lucien?'

Oh. Yes. 'Let's go in and get this over with.'

Dean winked, patted his arm once more, and they walked inside.

They crossed the small reception area and peeked into the hall. The room was cavernous, and brimming with people on his grandmother's organisational team. The stage at the far end made Lucien feel sick with nerves when he looked at it. There were maybe two hundred chairs set up in rows, pointed at the stage, and behind those sat a large wooden dance floor, with speakers and DJ equipment set up in one corner. To the side of that was a dining area, with several circular tables covered with white tablecloths, and long tables laden with buffet food.

The hall was often used for big weddings, plays and dances, and it had plenty of room for everything. High windows cast shafts of bright light on to the chaos beneath. Two people were on tall ladders, still stringing the last few lengths of bunting, and others rushed around beneath them, getting the chairs into neater lines and adding cutlery to tables. The doors were due to open to the public in half an hour, so anything they didn't get done soon would have to go undone.

Still hesitating at the entrance, Lucien and Dean were grabbed by Betty, Nancy's personal assistant—a woman Lucien had known his whole life. She dragged them through the hall to a back room, surprisingly strong for someone so small, and Lucien wouldn't have been surprised if her tiny hand had left a bruise after gripping his forearm so tightly.

'Dean—meet Betty,' he forced out through gritted teeth.

Dean laughed. 'Lovely to meet you.'

Betty hadn't yet said a word to either of them. She pushed them up a narrow, creaking staircase and deposited them both on a threadbare old couch by a window.

'This is the green room. You have half an hour before

the auction starts. Do *not* go missing.' She punctuated her order by pointing directly at Lucien.

'I'll keep my eye on him, Betty,' said Dean.

Betty gave a rare warm smile. 'I'm sure you will, dear.'

And with that she was gone, in a whirlwind of pleated skirt and lavender.

'How come she likes *you*?' Lucien asked. 'You've only known her thirty seconds—she's known me thirty years.'

'Just my natural charm, I guess.'

There were already two other people in the green room, chatting in the corner by a decrepit-looking coffee machine—probably another two victims for the auction. One looked vaguely familiar, but Lucien couldn't quite muster up the concentration to place him.

'How are you holding up?' asked Dean.

And with that, Lucien's nerves came rushing back.

He stood up. 'I'm fine. Stop fussing.'

If he didn't talk about it he could pretend it wasn't happening—at least for a while. He leaned his forehead on the cool glass of the window. There were already small groups of people on the forecourt, waiting for the doors to open. Panic flooded his chest and he took a deep breath.

Maybe making an awful cup of coffee would take his mind off things.

Lucien left Dean over by the window and grabbed two paper cups from a stack behind the coffee machine.

'I wouldn't drink that, if I were you.'

Lucien looked up to find the friendly brown eyes and messy blond hair of the village vet, Nika. So that was who the vaguely familiar man was.

'You're not being sold off too?' asked Lucien.

'Your grandmother's a very persuasive woman.'

'Tell me about it…'

'I noticed you and your fellow "sexy GP" advertised outside.'

Lucien's face grew warm again, and he glanced back at Dean, who smiled, openly listening to their conversation.

'Sadly I didn't make it on to the poster,' Nika continued. 'But I like to think my descriptor would have been "adorable local vet".'

Nika and Lucien had been out for dinner once, about five years ago. Nika had asked him out, and Lucien hadn't been able to figure out a polite way to decline, so had found himself saying yes to avoid the awkwardness of the moment. The evening had been typically disastrous, and they'd turned out to share not a hint of sexual chemistry, despite how handsome and charismatic Nika clearly was.

'Well, it certainly wouldn't be modest,' Lucien replied.

Nika laughed good-naturedly. 'I can't believe you're doing this. I didn't think it was your sort of thing. You know there'll be hundreds of people watching?'

Suddenly the enormity of what he was about to do hit Lucien all over again, and he found it hard to catch his breath. He fumbled with the paper cups, but before he knew it a strong hand had taken his shoulder and gently led him back over to the sofa by the window.

Dean pushed him on to the seat, then knelt on the floor in front of him.

Nika grimaced an apology, then backed off and resumed his previous conversation.

When Lucien was sure they'd both stopped watching him, he was able to tune in to what Dean was saying.

'Lucien? Look at me.'

Dean spoke quietly and calmly. And when he told Lucien to breathe, Lucien did. Big, deep, calming breaths, just like Dean said. He focused on Dean's face, his eyes glowing green in the golden hour light from the window, his jawline strong and faintly stubbled. This close, he could see the flecks of brown in just one eye, and the freckles scattered adorably over his nose.

Lucien felt guilty for putting that worried look on his beautiful face.

'Are you okay?' asked Dean.

Lucien wanted to say yes. He wasn't used to being open about his anxieties. His life had been full of bad experiences when people had made him feel foolish for sharing them.

In the past, when he'd felt nervous about doing something, the people closest to him had either forced him to do it, or suggested he was being lazy or stupid and tried to shame him into doing it. He knew by now that it came from a place of love, however misguided and ignorant, at least where his grandmother was concerned. And he had ended up as a successful doctor, hadn't he? So his grandmother was convinced she'd helped his mother raise him the right way. As if any success he'd found was down to her, rather than despite her.

She would never change. But he knew she truly loved him and meant well. She was simply from a different time. He'd learned to humour her and not take what she said to heart.

But, either way, he'd learned to hide his anxieties from other people. No one wanted their doctor to show vulnerability. He had become excellent at pretending and masking and covering when he needed to. He wasn't stupid enough to think that was the healthiest way to deal with his anxiety, but it was all he could do right now. Maybe when he retired, in thirty years, he'd have time to find a therapist and become happy and well adjusted.

'Lucien?' Dean said, and Lucien got the feeling Dean might have said his name more than once. 'Are you okay?'

Lucien nodded and tried to carry off a casual smile, brushing the whole thing off. But the way Dean rubbed one thumb over his shoulder so gently made his smile wobble and he gave up trying to pretend.

'Dean, I don't think I can do this. I can't wait here for my name to be announced and then parade across the stage with everyone looking at me. I just can't.'

Dean stared at him for a second. 'Is that the part you're most scared of?'

Lucien frowned. He didn't quite understand why he was being asked that question, but he thought about it anyway. 'Yes, I think so.'

'Wait here. I'll be back in a minute.'

Dean left.

Suddenly alone, Lucien leaned his head back against the cool wall and tried to continue the deep breathing. He wiped the sweat from his temples and upper lip on his sleeve, then spent the next few minutes battling with the ancient window, trying to open it enough to let a bit of air in.

Dean returned five minutes later, red-faced and breathing heavily, his shirt untucked.

'What on earth have you been up to?'

'I've sorted it. Betty wasn't happy with me at first, but I asked her to change a few things last minute. When the curtain comes up all the auctionees will already be seated onstage behind a line of tables. The MC will stand by each of us in turn to auction us off. No big entrance. You'll just have to sit there. And a table will be in between you and the audience. How's that?'

Lucien was amazed by how much better he felt. The relief washed over him, and he took his first easy breath in what felt like ages. Then he took another look at Dean, trying to tuck his shirt back in and straighten himself up using the window as a makeshift mirror.

'Thank you, Dean.'

Dean shrugged his gratitude off. 'I'm here to serve.'

'I mean it. But I have to ask… How did you become so unkempt in the space of five minutes?'

'I had to move all the tables.'

Lucien laughed. 'I'm sorry.'

'Why?'

'I'm sorry I'm like this.'

Dean looked puzzled. 'Like what?'

Lucien shrugged. 'Making a fuss about nothing.'

'It's not nothing if it makes you anxious.'

Lucien shook his head. Dean didn't understand. 'I'm a grown man. I shouldn't mind being in front of a crowd. And it's not just here. I didn't exactly pull my weight at the school event either. I'm sorry I left you to do all the work.'

Dean shook his head. 'Don't say that. Different people have different strengths, and it's okay to play to them. I love doing the talking, so you don't have to.'

'Then what do *I* bring to the table?'

'You look pretty!' Dean joked.

That surprised a laugh out of Lucien.

'You connected with those kids one on one,' Dean continued. 'They loved you. Stop worrying about it. You're exactly who you're supposed to be. Our differences make us work better as a team. Think of the chaos if everyone loved being the centre of attention. Two of me would be a nightmare.'

'That's true,' Lucien said, lying through his teeth.

To him, two Deans sounded amazing.

Dean was the first person he'd ever known who didn't want him to put on a mask. Dean never made him feel small. He listened to his worries, then found a way he could help him. It was what Lucien had always wanted but hadn't thought was possible, or maybe deserved. He was used to doing everything the hard way. Now he had a friend who would help him… It seemed unlikely, but okay…

'Thanks for helping me,' he said.

'It's nothing—forget it.'

Lucien nodded, and almost did as Dean asked. But something welled up in his chest and he started talking without even meaning to.

'It's not nothing. Everyone's always told me I'm too quiet, or too introverted. It's made me feel like my personality is wrong, somehow. That I'd be a better person if I would just be more extroverted. It started in school and it'd carried on through college, university, the workplace. *Join in more…speak up more…socialise more…date more…* Their demands may come from a well-meaning place, but it's relentless. And, as much as I try to block it out, sometimes it still hurts.' He paused. 'As sad as it might seem, you're the first person who seems to accept me as I am.'

Dean looked embarrassed as hell by Lucien's little speech. He scratched at a loose thread on the sofa between them and stared down at his hand.

'Of course I accept you, man. You're awesome. All I want to do is try to help make the difficult things easier for you. You deserve to have someone around who can do that.'

Lucien didn't know what to say.

Betty chose that moment to march them backstage. Two doctors, along with a vicar, a vet and a mayor. The thought that it sounded like the set-up for a joke flashed through Lucien's mind in a moment of deranged panic.

As they stood quietly in the wings Dean slung an arm over Lucien's shoulder and squeezed him tight for a second.

Lucien hoped Dean couldn't feel him shaking. Whether that was nerves, or surprise at being suddenly crushed into Dean's warm, hard chest, he wasn't entirely sure.

'We're gonna be fine,' whispered Dean, directly into Lucien's ear, just for him to hear.

And, God help him, Lucien almost believed it.

Dean clearly couldn't wait for his time in the limelight. His eyes were bright and excited, and it seemed he couldn't wipe the grin off his face.

Lucien marvelled over Dean's enthusiasm. 'You're actually looking forward to being out there, aren't you?'

'You can't keep a good show-off down.'

Never had Lucien felt more that he and Dean were two different species. But Dean looked beautiful like this. Confident, excited, happy. He was truly in his element. If they weren't surrounded by people he might be tempted to take a second try at that almost-kiss they hadn't talked about…

The curtain still down, Betty dragged Lucien and Dean by their elbows to two seats behind the long row of tables Dean must have moved earlier. The tables were now covered in plain white tablecloths and had name cards by each chair. Lucien's knee jigged up and down as he wiped his palms on his trousers and tried to find a way to sit comfortably in the wooden chair. The legs screeched on the stage as he moved it closer to Dean.

'Stop fidgeting!' Betty whispered furiously.

The crowd on the other side of the curtain were invisible, but audible. A constant hum of chatter, laughs and coughs. Lucien thought his heart might beat out of his chest—until he felt a nudge in his side. He turned to find Dean smiling at him. He winked, and Lucien calmed down slightly.

'You good?' Dean whispered.

'I still don't like the thought of having all that attention on me, but I can do this.'

'Don't worry. I'll make sure their attention is elsewhere.'

As the curtain swept back to reveal the cheering hordes Lucien just had time to fully regret his life choices before his heart started racing at such a speed he genuinely started to calculate how long it would take an ambulance to travel from the hospital to get here and treat him for a stroke. But then Dean squeezed his knee under the table with one large hand, and Lucien took a breath. He noticed that everyone in the audience was smiling and clapping. He wasn't dying… he was okay.

The evening's MC was enthusiasm personified, and while his manner made Lucien cringe a little, he was actually very good at his job, and had the audience whipped into an excitable frenzy within minutes. He announced each of their names in turn, with the crowd going increasingly crazy with each one.

When he got to Dean, Dean jumped up on to his chair and extended his arms, playing to the audience and whipping them up even more. Half the WI screamed as if they were at a rock concert.

And when the MC announced Lucien's name next, he felt secure in the knowledge that not a single soul in that hall was looking at him.

Dean gazed down from his chair and grinned at Lucien.

Except one, perhaps. And it felt wonderful.

The MC continued with his patter, explaining each of the prizes. Lucien had settled on giving a two-hour climbing lesson on the climbing wall in the nearest large town. While Dean had kept it simple, just offering to go out to dinner with the highest bidder. The MC somehow managed to make each offer sound exciting, and had the crowd responding enthusiastically to all of them. Nika the vet's prize was him painting a portrait of the winner's pet, and the mayor's was a tour of the council buildings and trying on the mayor's robe and chains.

Which didn't sound like much compared to a date with Dean, if Lucien was honest.

'Are you sure about this date thing?' Lucien murmured to Dean from the corner of his mouth.

'I don't have any hidden talents in art or climbing mountains. In fact I have no skills to offer the Little Champney public at all other than being a thoroughly charming date.'

Lucien laughed. He almost found himself relaxing—until the bidding started.

Dean was second up, and he stood as his name was announced. He did a slow, confident spin, displaying himself for the audience and making them laugh.

'I'll start us off at fifty pounds,' the MC said into his microphone.

About six different hands went up and the crowd tittered. Within what seemed like seconds, and after much shouting and catcalling, they were up to five hundred pounds.

Lucien smiled at how keen everyone was—and quite rightly too. He craned his neck to see who was bidding so high on Dean. But the stage lights shone into his eyes and made him squint. He had assumed some nice, retired lady might bid on Dean and take him for afternoon tea, but from what little he could hear and see there was actually a furious bidding war taking place between various men and women way too young and attractive for Lucien's liking.

Dean was clearly being spurred on by the crowd's energy. He jumped up and punched the air when his total was declared at six hundred and fifty pounds, and waved at the winner before sitting back down. Lucien couldn't help but laugh at Dean's smug look.

But then it was Lucien's turn to be bid on. He exhaled heavily and made sure not to make eye contact with anybody. If he steeled himself, this would all be over soon. No one would bid on him, it would be humiliating, and then it would be over.

He was shocked and flattered to find that he received what might almost be considered a flurry of bids. Again, he couldn't see who was bidding, but the MC ended Lucien's auction on a total only just less than Dean's. Evidently someone out there really wanted to learn how to climb...

The rest of the auction seemed to fly by in seconds, and before Lucien knew it they were climbing down from the stage. He felt light as a feather, and even a little drunk, although he hadn't touched a drop of alcohol.

Dean nudged him as they reached the bottom step. 'You did great!'

'Thank you! I think I'm experiencing some kind of adrenaline high.'

'That'll do it.'

Villagers came at him from all sides, with smiles and handshakes and congratulations—as if he'd just got married or won the lottery.

'They're just happy to see you here,' said Dean, in response to his quizzical look.

Lucien hadn't felt this good in years. He even felt the stirrings of an unfamiliar emotion. If he wasn't mistaken, he was actually feeling quite proud of himself for having taken the leap. It hadn't been as horrific as he'd feared, but without Dean's help he never would have found that out.

'Best auction in years, Dr Benedict.'

A patient he knew from the clinic took his hand and

shook it vehemently. When Lucien finally got his hand back he thanked her, and moved on to the next waiting congratulator.

Everyone was being so nice. He knew it was Dean's charismatic contribution that had made it the best auction in years, but he was quite pleased to have been a part of it nonetheless. It was nice to feel so much goodwill poured his way. Maybe he was more liked than he'd thought. Maybe he was a part of the village too—not just a useful cog people tolerated because of his mother and his grandmother.

He certainly wasn't going to become some social butterfly, but maybe once in a while it would be safe to step out of his box…just for a second. Dean had come to Little Champney and everything had changed. Lucien's life was busier, the village was brighter, and the practice was more involved with the community. People Lucien had kept at a safe distance for the last decade were suddenly becoming a part of his life.

Helen appeared, carrying Rafael on her hip, even though he was really getting too big to be held. One of her teenage daughters walked alongside and fed him sweets one by one, straight out of the packet.

'You were both amazing!' said Helen. 'I would have bid, but I had my eye on the vet.'

Dean grabbed Rafael's face and kissed him loudly, ignoring his mortified squirming. 'I see you're being well served by your minions.'

'He's been such a good boy.'

'Did you see us on stage, Raf?'

Rafael nodded. 'Helen gave me a chocolate cupcake.'

'Fair enough—that *is* the bigger news of the evening,' answered Dean.

They mingled a little longer, then Nancy pulled Lucien

away to introduce him to some local councillors she'd been trying to get him to meet for years. Lucien soon found himself close to reaching the maximum on his social meter. He'd just had time to wonder where Dean had got to, when the man himself appeared at Lucien's shoulder.

'There you are!' said Dean. 'Have you met your winner yet?'

'She's gone home already. Apparently she wanted the session for her teenage son.'

A beautiful woman appeared at Dean's side.

'Oh, this is Jenny—my winner.' Dean stepped back to give her some room. 'We're heading out now.'

'You are?' said Lucien.

'On our date,' she trilled, flashing her teeth and snaking a hand over Dean's forearm.

'No time like the present.' Dean smiled at Lucien and shrugged. 'Helen suggested we do it this evening. She offered—actually, more like begged—to look after Raf overnight for me. I've already run back home and packed him an overnight bag. So that means you can stay out...or go home and make the most of the peace and quiet.'

Lucien nodded. Jenny was very pretty. He could see why Dean would jump at the chance to spend the evening with her.

Dean punched Lucien's arm lightly. 'See you at home?'

Lucien nodded as Dean and Jenny made their way across the emptying dance floor. Peace and quiet sounded very good right now. But Lucien stayed where he was, hovering by the food tables, feeling strangely empty.

Next to the buffet was always a good place to stand if you wanted to avoid conversation by looking busy, and it also offered the added bonus of having something to do with your hands, so you didn't look like a spare part. He selected a breadstick that looked as if it probably hadn't been grabbed by the grubby hands of children, and nibbled on it as he watched Dean and Jenny leave the building, her arm still wrapped around his like a limpet.

A moment later, he watched Helen take Rafael home. He smiled fondly as Rafael grabbed her hand before stepping outdoors, just as Dean always told him to. Then, realising everyone he really cared to speak to had left, Lucien decided to go home too. His ordeal was over! He was free to escape, and escape he would. He had things to do at home, and this was the perfect chance to take advantage of an empty house.

'I'm so glad I won. Tessa from the bakery put up quite a fight, but I knew I could come out on top. She beat me last year when I bid for a date with the dentist. Have you met him yet? He's very good-looking, but he obviously didn't like Tessa at all. She ended up settling for her old school boyfriend…they're married now. If it had been me, I wouldn't have let a dentist slip through my fingers. I love a man in uniform, you know?'

Dean hadn't yet got a word in edgeways, and was swiftly regretting ever taking part in the auction at all. But at least he could get this date with Jenny over and done with in one night.

How early would it not be rude to leave?

'I'm a bit disappointed you're not wearing your white coat and stethoscope, actually.'

Dean laughed, but then slowly realised she wasn't joking.

'Can't really wear them out of the surgery. Anyway, don't you like what I'm wearing now?' he asked, mock insulted.

'Oh, yes.' She looked him up and down longingly. 'You look gorgeous. So, where are you taking me on our romantic date?'

'Uh… I just thought we'd grab a quick meal at the Horse and Hare?'

'Oh, okay.'

She looked disappointed for a moment. Then shrugged and shoved her arm through his as they walked.

Helen had told Dean that it was a nice place to eat. He hadn't wanted somewhere romantic, as he'd assumed the person who won wouldn't be treating it like an actual date— rather as a fun chat and an interesting way to donate to the charity. At least the food was supposed to be great there. He wanted to get something enjoyable out of the evening.

Dean racked his brain for something to say that wouldn't result in her flirting with him again. 'So, what do you do for a living, Jenny?'

'I love the way you say my name. Such a sexy accent.'

Dean tried subtly to pull his arm from her grip, but she just tightened her hold and he gave up.

'I don't think I really have an interesting accent…it's just London.'

'I wish I lived in London. It must be so exciting there.'

'Have you ever been?'

'Only once. We went on a school trip to see a musical in one of the theatres in the West End. I bet you went to the theatre every weekend when you lived there.'

'Oh, God no. I'm not that into plays. And certainly not musicals.'

'I love them. *Mamma Mia* is my favourite. Don't you just love Abba?'

Dean did not, but he hummed vaguely in response.

'Oh, silly me—I didn't answer your question! I'm a hair-dresser.'

She reached out, and before Dean could even blink she'd run a cold hand through his hair.

'Looks like you need a cut and style.' She magicked up a business card as if from nowhere and thrust it at him. 'Promise me you'll come to me soon?'

Dean took the card and grunted as noncommittally as he could. 'Curl Up and Dye,' he read out. 'Nice pun.'

'Thank you! I came up with it myself. I'm so glad you like it.' She paused. 'So, the most important question of the evening…'

Dean dreaded to think what that was going to be.

'Do you have a girlfriend? Or a wife, even?'

'No, I don't.'

Lucien's face suddenly popped into his mind for some reason. He wondered how he was doing at the auction, and if he'd left to go home yet.

'I heard you have a son?'

Dean tuned back in to the conversation. 'Yes, that's true.'

Jenny proceeded to gush about how great she was with kids and how she'd love to meet him. But Dean was not getting good vibes from her. He was getting *I want to spend time with you because you're a doctor who wears a white coat and I'll say anything to make you like me* vibes. She might be a very nice person, if she ever got real for one minute and stopped saying whatever she thought would impress him the most.

A plump pigeon landed on the pavement in front of them, chasing a stray chip. Jenny let out a little scream and kicked out her foot in its general direction. 'Horrible creatures,' she said with a shiver.

Then again, he might be giving her a little too much credit.

She might be some people's perfect cup of tea. But she certainly wasn't Dean's.

He yanked open the door to the pub, and warm air and

the smell of food smacked him in the face. He ushered her through with a flourish, wanting to get the evening over and done with.

After a couple of hours of polite but uninspiring conversation, Dean was thoroughly losing the will to live. He'd drunk two or three halves of bitter, by that point, and eaten one plate of chips and a delicious burger to soak it up, and now he was running out of things to talk about.

'So, what did you do today at work?' asked Jenny. 'Your job must be so exciting.'

Dean thought back to the abscess he'd drained in the morning, and the intimate rash he'd inspected last thing. 'I can't really discuss any patient details.'

'Oh, please… There must be something you can tell me?'

Dean took a long sip of his drink, and wondered again how early he could politely bail on this date. 'It was all very mundane, I promise.'

The only exciting moment of the day had been when Lucien had spilled lukewarm coffee all over himself and decided to change his shirt right in the middle of the staff room. As if that was a perfectly normal thing to do and wouldn't give any innocent passing colleagues heart palpitations.

But she probably didn't want to hear about that—and Dean didn't want to share it. That was a memory just for him.

'What are you smiling at?' she asked.

'Nothing.' He drained his glass.

Despite all the facts, Jenny obviously saw this as a real date, and Dean knew it was time to end the evening and stop wasting her time.

She'd find the right one eventually. But would Dean?

'It's getting late. I should see you home.'

Dean stood and passed Jenny her coat, then shrugged on his own.

'No need. I live literally two doors away. But how sweet! You're such a romantic. I knew you would be.'

Dean attempted a smile that he was sure turned out as more of a grimace. He held out his hand to shake hers, and she took it after a short hesitation.

'It was lovely to make a new friend,' he said.

She nodded, smiling. 'Message received.'

Dean was taken aback. He hadn't expected her to give up the chase so easily. Maybe they actually could be friends.

Dean sighed, feeling relaxed for the first time that evening. Finally he could get back to Lucien.

Ever since he'd found Lucien trying his hardest to make Rafael pancakes, even though he'd had no clue how, simply because Rafael had asked him to, something had shifted in his heart. Something had clicked into place and he wanted to be around Lucien all the time. He felt this strange need to take care of him, protect him—something he'd never felt before outside of his family. He wished Lucien were here with him now. He would have loved that burger...

Would kissing Lucien really be that much of a risk? What if things between them ended well? Wouldn't it be worth it?

Maybe Helen was right.

Maybe Dean had found the right one already.

CHAPTER SIX

LUCIEN WAS ALONE for what felt like the first time in weeks, and it was the perfect moment to finally finish the project he'd been working on.

Lucien pulled on an old sweatshirt and went to the garage, to grab a few bits and pieces from the cupboard behind his car. He hummed industriously as he carried them to the kitchen floor and sorted through them, evidently still coasting on a high from the auction, mixed with a huge dose of relief that it was over.

He was still in disbelief that he'd tried something that terrified him and that it had gone well. It probably would have been a disaster without Dean. But Lucien liked to think he might have had something to do with it himself too. He'd had a shot of self-confidence, and it was a hell of a drug.

He smiled and twirled a paintbrush in his hand, feeling quite pleased with himself.

His mood wasn't perfect, though. He couldn't say he was completely happy that Dean was out on his date. The woman had seemed altogether too interested in him for Lucien's liking. He'd only seen them together for a minute, but in that one minute she had touched Dean six times. Not that Lucien had been counting. And not that he was feeling territorial over his house mate. Dean could date whomever he wanted. He could go on dates every night of the week if that was what he was into.

Lucien took a breath.

She was just an auction winner. And it was none of his business anyway. Plus, he had other things to think about. He smiled as he gathered up a small tin of blue paint and a paint-spattered plastic tray and roller, then trotted upstairs with his arms full to the first floor.

He flung open the door to his office and deposited his things on the carpet, then looked around at the almost empty room. He'd been planning this for a week now, and there wasn't all that much left to do. He'd already sneaked a lot of his office equipment into his bedroom, while Dean had been working or out with Rafael. He'd been surprised to find there was plenty of room under his bedroom window to put his desk and chair. It would be perfectly fine to have a bedroom office. He'd also managed to move out all his books and boxes of files without anyone noticing.

He'd bought the paint from the independent hardware store near the surgery after asking Rafael what his favourite colour was—subtly, he hoped. He was only planning to paint one wall as an accent. The cream walls had only been repainted last year, and they were still in perfect shape— plus they were half covered in built-in shelves anyway. Which meant Rafael would have plenty of room for all his toys and books.

He spread out a plastic sheet over the carpet and popped open the paint tin with a screwdriver. When he realised he hadn't brought up a stick to stir the paint with, he shrugged and used the screwdriver. As long as he remembered to rinse it off before it dried it wouldn't be too much of a di-saster. He didn't have time to keep running up and down stairs. He wanted this done before Dean got home from his date. And there was no knowing when that might be.

Part of him hoped Dean was having a terrible time with Miss Grabby Hands, and that he escaped to come home early, but the other part of him needed him to be out for a couple more hours so he could get this finished.

He painted all the edges carefully with a paintbrush, and had the first coat rolled on and finished within thirty minutes. He rinsed off the screwdriver in the kitchen sink, washed out the roller, and made himself a coffee to keep his energy up. Then he started doing everything else.

He took down his thick charcoal-coloured curtains, and put up some blue ones with rocket ships on, then unrolled a small matching rug.

The biggest job left to do was building the flat-pack bunk bed he'd purchased, but he'd already managed to pre-make it into two pieces, and it was stashed in the unused shed in the garden. It had been locked in there for two days, since he'd popped back for a couple of lunch breaks to put it together. It had been worth going back to work a bit sweaty and out of breath. Although it had caused a few jokes at work about what on earth he'd been up to.

Dean seemed like the kind of guy who could build a bed from scratch with his own two hands, so he'd worked hard on making the bunk bed look at least passable.

Lucien jogged down to the shed and grabbed the first piece. It was pretty light, being for a small child, and he manoeuvred it up the stairs with no problem. When he came back for the second piece he had to have a little break while he caught his breath. He might have overestimated his fitness level… After a few deep breaths, he grabbed the second piece, locked the shed door, and hefted it up the stairs a little more slowly than the first one.

All the bed needed was a few extra screws drilled in to attach the two halves together. Once it was sturdy and safe, he grabbed the two little mattresses from where they'd been hidden under his own bed and the bunk bed was finished. It would need Rafael's quilt and pillow, but he'd let Dean and Rafael add those. He didn't feel comfortable going into their room by himself.

After all that, he touched the paint on the wall with his fingertips. Dry enough for the second coat.

When he'd finally finished painting, and cleaned up Rafael's new room as much as he could, he pulled on the bathroom light and looked in the mirror. What he saw made him tut in annoyance, and he wet a cloth, then tried to wipe off the dozens of tiny blue dots he'd spattered all over his face.

He checked the time. Eight o'clock. Dean and that woman had been having dinner for maybe two hours by now. So he must be having a decent time, then. Lucien tried to ignore the drop in his stomach that thought aroused. Dean was probably just being polite. She had bid a lot for the date, after all. It would be rude not to give her a decent chunk of time and a nice meal.

What would a date with Dean be like? He was ridiculously charming and harmlessly flirty with everyone at the best of times. Date Dean must be ten times more attractive and intimate and attentive. He'd probably pull the chair out for her at the table. Compliment her on her clothes. Listen to her closely as if she was the only person on Earth.

She was probably halfway in love with him by now, Lucien thought glumly. And he couldn't blame her. Who could resist Date Dean?

The house was so quiet without Dean and Rafael. Even when Dean returned it would still feel strange to be alone together, just the two of them, with no Rafael running around.

When Dean got back, would they sit together? Would Dean tell him all about the date? Would Lucien be able to talk about Dean's night like a grown man without sounding like a jealous idiot?

It was a shame nothing could ever happen between them...almost a waste of an empty house.

Lucien shook his head. He was being ridiculous.

The only thing left to do to Rafael's room was add the final finishing touch. He'd seen an embarrassingly large blue gift bow in the shop in town, and at the time he'd thought it might be a nice idea to stick it on the door of Rafael's new bedroom. But now he was looking at it in the stark light of home he felt like an idiot.

This wasn't him. He wasn't demonstrative. It was just a stupid piece of decorative ribbon.

But somehow it seemed to mean more than that. Much more.

Ugh, this was mortifying.

He ripped the backing off the ribbon and slammed it on to the outside of the door, then stalked off before he could change his mind.

At nine o'clock Dean still wasn't back.

Lucien had put all his painting equipment and tools back in the garage. He'd hoovered the carpet after he'd noticed some sawdust from drilling the bunk bed. He'd slightly rearranged everything in the bedroom, drawn the curtains, brought up a lamp from the living room to make the room feel cosier, and left it on, so that when Dean saw the room it would look its best. He'd even grabbed a few of Rafael's toys that were lying around the kitchen and sofa and brought them up to arrange on the empty shelves, to make it look a bit more like a kid's room.

He'd finally decided there wasn't anything else he could

do, and he was now just fiddling, so he closed the door, adjusted the bow, considered for the tenth time taking it off and throwing it in the bin, decided not to, and then left it alone.

His body ached from all the traipsing up and down stairs, but he was too hyped up to rest. He tried reading a book, but attempted to read the same paragraph fifteen times before he gave up in frustration. He sighed and grabbed the TV remote. There must be something he could watch.

At ten o'clock, with still not a hint of Dean, he suddenly had a horrible thought. What if Dean didn't come home at all? What if he'd had such a great time that they'd decided to have drinks after the meal, and then they'd kissed, and then Dean had gone to her house for the night?

The more he sat with that thought, the more likely it seemed. They were both adults, they were both confident, probably sexually active single people, he assumed. Otherwise why would she have bid for a date with Dean?

Of course they were going to sleep together. That was what normal people did. Just because Lucien had become a person who couldn't even consider sleeping with someone unless he'd known them for months and felt completely comfortable with them, it didn't mean that most people felt that way. A lot of people were perfectly comfortable sleeping with someone they'd just met. And, as long as everything was consensual and safe, there was absolutely nothing wrong with that.

Lucien just wasn't built that way. At least not any more. The only time he'd ever been with someone he hadn't had serious feelings for was when he'd slept with that girl at medical school. What was her name? Cheryl…? Carla…? Charlie. That was it.

She'd been an amazing friend. But he'd known perfectly

well he wasn't attracted to her—not in any real way. She'd been beautiful, and funny, and a way cooler person than he'd had any right to be friends with. But she'd been the kind of person who was kind to everybody—even the biggest dork at medical school. Which was how Lucien had thought of himself, despite how many people told him he was wrong.

They'd only slept together because they'd both been drunk and silly and it had been the last day of university. She'd said she wanted to do something that she'd never done before. One last social experiment before she left university and had to be a proper adult. And, as she was mostly attracted to women, sleeping with a man was one thing she'd never done before. Lucien had found himself perfectly happy to oblige. Drinking had always made him a little horny, and very bad at decision-making.

The next morning he'd expected to regret it, but it had been the perfect morning-after. She'd made him banana pancakes, he'd made her a caramel iced coffee—from a packet—and then they'd bade each other farewell for ever, smiling, happy and perfectly at ease with their silly, rebellious last night as students. They'd promised to keep in touch, but he'd known they probably wouldn't. Like so many other people he'd felt close to in medical school, they were all too soon consumed with their own lives.

Lucien sank down further on to the sofa and swung his legs up onto the cushions. He reached behind him to the shelf that held his alcohol collection and tumbler glasses. This had suddenly turned into an evening that required whisky.

Of course Dean wasn't coming home. The date had gone well, and Dean, for one rare night, was free from any responsibility. Maybe even free for the first time since he'd had Rafael. Of course he was going to stay over and spend the night with a beautiful, willing woman.

Lucien felt naive and so, so stupid for not realising that hours ago. He was such an idiot. Of *course* Dean would prefer her to him. She was probably fun and sociable. They must have so much in common. Why would Dean ever want Lucien when he could have someone like that?

Lucien knew he was spiralling spectacularly when he started picturing her as Rafael's future mother. What if Dean married her? What if Dean wanted to move her in here? What if Dean was falling in love with her right now?

The whisky burned his throat, and he slid the bottle back on its shelf. He didn't want to get drunk. He wanted to watch sad old films on TV and feel sorry for himself.

He browsed through the movies, selected one, then snuggled down into the cushions.

Lucien rarely understood people at the best of times, but he had been sure that Dean was attracted to him. There had been too many moments between them. Moments that had meant something. When the air between them had felt hot and charged and laden with possibility. But, as open a person as Dean was, Lucien had the feeling there was something Dean was holding back. Something Dean hadn't told him, or maybe even something Dean didn't know himself.

Whatever it was, it was stopping Dean from letting Lucien all the way in. And, try as he might, Lucien couldn't fully ignore that tiny voice inside him telling him that Dean might be holding back because Lucien wasn't good enough for him. Or for Rafael.

Lucien finally fell asleep, exhausted, hugging a cushion and unable to deny to himself that he was nursing an enormous crush on his house mate.

* * *

Dean and Jenny left together, stepping out into the cool, refreshing air. Dean waited at the pub as Jenny walked the few steps to her house and unlocked the front door. She tripped up the step slightly, then giggled and waved at him, before disappearing inside.

Dean smiled, then checked his phone and cursed under his breath. He'd had no idea it was so late.

Dean sobered up completely on the cold walk home. His breath made clouds in front of his face, and he shoved his hands in his pockets to try to stave off the cold. On the way through the streets, following the quietly babbling brook, he thought about what Lucien had said. About how Dean was the only one who accepted the real him. He couldn't imagine why anyone would want to change a thing about Lucien. He was perfect.

He suddenly couldn't wait to see him. They'd had this one solitary evening. They could have spent it alone together, without any little voices asking to be played with or refusing to go to bed, and he'd spent it with a stranger. There was only one person he wanted to be with, and only one place where he could finally finish that kiss they'd started. He hoped he hadn't missed his chance.

Dean broke out into a jog.

His body tingled with a rush of pleasant heat when he finally stepped inside the front door. He hung up his jacket and as soon as he reached the living room spotted Lucien lying on the sofa. Damn it, he was too late. Lucien was fast asleep.

Dean crossed the room and reached out to shake Lucien's shoulder, but then thought better of it. He looked so peaceful lying there, his face completely relaxed and his thick hair even messier than usual.

Lucien would get a bad back if he spent much longer lying in that position… Dean made a decision. He would shoot upstairs to get changed, then come back down, gently wake Lucien and make them both some hot chocolate before bed. They could at least enjoy a conversation, or sit and watch TV together on the sofa for a little while on this, their one and only night without Dean's mini-me.

As he ran up the stairs he noticed something blue out of the corner of his eye, but ignored it, keen to get out of his cold denim jeans and into something more comfy, so he could go back downstairs with Lucien. He looked so warm and soft on the sofa, and something inside Dean just wanted to snuggle up next to him and nest.

He threw his clothes in the hamper and pulled on his comfiest sweatpants and an old, faded hoodie over his T-shirt. On his way back downstairs, he actually focused on what the blue thing was and stopped dead. Why the hell was there a huge gift bow on Lucien's office door? Was someone else here? Did Lucien have someone over who'd got him a gift and put it in his office? Was it Lucien's birthday?

Dean tilted his head, staring at the incongruous bow. He should probably just go and ask Lucien, but something drew him over to the door. He'd just take a little peek to see what was up…

When he opened the door, he knew immediately what was up. It couldn't be anything else. Lucien had made Rafael a bedroom.

A lamp threw warm, cosy light over the whole room, there was a new bed, new curtains and a matching rug, and the wall was Rafael's favourite shade of blue, for God's sake. How had Lucien even done this? *When* had he done this? It was like a tiny miracle. It must have taken so much time and planning and effort.

Dean felt his heart expand, too big to fit in his chest, and he turned to run down the stairs. But then he stopped.

Lucien had done all this tonight. Alone.

That was why Lucien had fallen asleep on the sofa—partly from exhaustion, and partly because he must have been waiting up excitedly for Dean, so he could show him what he'd done. Lucien had put a bow on the door and everything. And Dean had ruined it all by being late home.

He felt the heart that had just that moment expanded break. He felt terrible. But touched beyond words.

Binxie jumped out of the shadows and rubbed against his ankles, so Dean reached down and grabbed her on his way to Lucien. Maybe things would go better if he brought a beloved gift.

He turned off the TV, tentatively deposited Binxie on Lucien's lap and knelt down by his side. He looked so sweet asleep, gently snoring… Dean whispered Lucien's name and gently touched his bare arm.

Lucien twitched and snuffled into his cushion, before slowly opening his eyes. 'Dean…' He gazed up at Dean for a moment, before blinking and sitting upright. 'You're home.' Lucien's eyes slid away. 'How was your date?'

'It wasn't a date.'

Why did everyone keep calling it that? And why wasn't Lucien maintaining eye contact?

Dean must have really made a misstep by not coming home sooner.

'How was your not-date?' Lucien mumbled.

'It was a nightmare, to be honest. And I'm glad it's over.'

Lucien gave a small smile, and Dean took that as a tentative win.

'I missed you.' Dean couldn't hold it in any longer.

Lucien's smile turned into a confused frown. 'You missed me?'

Dean nodded.

'Why?'

'I always miss you when you're not around,' Dean said quietly. 'Also, if I'd been home, instead of out, I could have helped you do what you've done upstairs.'

Lucien blushed right before Dean's eyes. They were so close that Dean saw the colour bloom over his cheeks and even up to his temples.

'You saw?'

Dean nodded. 'I don't know what to say, Lucien. I'm speechless.'

'Do you think he'll like it?'

'He'll love it.'

'He doesn't have to move in there if he doesn't want to. He probably likes being with you at night.'

'No, no he hates it. I snore.'

Lucien snorted out a laugh. 'Oh, that's unfortunate.'

'No one's ever done anything like this for me before. I mean for Rafael. You did it for Rafael, not me.'

Smooth, Dean. He tried not to roll his eyes at himself.

'I did it for both of you.' Lucien shrugged one shoulder. 'It's nothing, really.'

'It's everything. Stay right where you are. I'm making us hot chocolate.'

'I can do it.'

An image of the mess Lucien had managed to make with pancakes flashed through Dean's mind. And, as adorable as that would be to see again, he shook his head.

'You just DIYed your little heart out—the least I can do is make you a drink.'

'That's true,' said Lucien, grabbing another cushion and shoving it under his head.

He lay back on the couch and watched as Dean returned to the kitchen. He grabbed a pan, some milk and cream from the fridge, and some chocolate to melt. He was going to give Lucien the best hot chocolate he'd ever had.

'We have powdered stuff in the cupboard,' called Lucien.

Dean slapped his hand over his heart, mock-offended.

'Powdered? Wait till you taste this—it'll change your life.'

Ten minutes later, Dean poured smooth, steaming chocolate into two large mugs. He sprinkled pink and white marshmallows on top, then carried them through to Lucien.

Lucien sat up and accepted his mug with a shy smile, cupping his hands around it, warming them. 'Thank you. This looks so delicious. Would it be rude to down it in one?'

'It would require a visit to A&E. Blow on it for a while first. It's too hot—you'll burn your tongue.'

Dean made a face at himself. Way to sound like a dad.

Lucien obediently blew on his hot chocolate, and Dean put his mug on the coffee table so he could reach over and grab a blanket from the far end of the sofa. Deciding not to overthink it, he threw the blanket over both their laps and moved closer to Lucien. He put the TV on to create some background noise, but rather than face the screen he shifted to face Lucien, and watched as he tentatively sipped his drink.

'I can't believe you kept it all a secret,' said Dean. 'I didn't know you had it in you.'

'I'm quite sneaky.'

Dean laughed. 'Who knew?'

But then he was reminded of the secret he was keeping, and it didn't seem so funny any more. He wished so hard that he could tell Lucien the truth. If he knew then Dean could enjoy this closeness without being scared that it would be ripped away at any moment.

His heart raced as he realised it might be time to tell him everything. How could Dean be any more sure that Lucien was safe to be around Rafael? What was he still waiting for?

He took a long swallow of hot chocolate.

'The bed was hidden in the shed for days,' said Lucien. 'I was nervous one of you would find it.'

'I didn't even know we had a shed.'

'Then I guess I'm lucky you're so oblivious.'

Dean opened his mouth, not sure what he was going to say, but intending somehow to tell Lucien the truth. But before he could speak Lucien interrupted him.

'This is so nice. I haven't felt this relaxed in months.'

'You haven't?' Dean responded weakly.

'Normally I only fully relax when I'm alone. Being around people, however much I like them, usually makes me feel on edge. But you're different, somehow.' Lucien turned towards Dean, mirroring his position, and settled his head against the back of the sofa. 'You make me feel really calm.'

'Just call me Diazepam,' Dean joked.

Lucien smiled lazily, his eyes hooded, and continued to gaze up at Dean. 'I'm cold.'

Dean pulled the blanket further over Lucien, up to his waist, and tucked it around him. Then he took a breath and bravely snuggled closer, pressing their thighs together under the blanket. Dean's hand remained trapped underneath the warm fabric and he flexed it, itching to reach over and make contact with Lucien.

Lucien finished his drink, then eyed Dean's empty mug. He removed it gently from Dean's grip and placed them both on the coffee table. As he leaned forward Dean caught a faint trace of his shampoo, and sensed the solid weight of his body as he passed him. When Lucien settled back into position, he seemed even closer.

Dean swallowed, ultra-aware of Lucien's warmth, of their bodies, touching now all the way from shoulder to knee in a burning hot line of firm contact.

Dean pushed down his intention to tell Lucien everything. It could wait a few hours at least. He should give Lucien one last stress-free evening before he ruined it.

'Are you sure about losing your office?' Dean asked. 'It's one of your last private spaces—the only place you can hide from me.'

Lucien glanced up, and something in Dean's chest went a little askew when he looked into Lucien's eyes from so close a distance. Black eyelashes framed grey eyes the colour of storm clouds...clouds currently crackling with electricity. Heat emanated from Lucien's body and Dean couldn't help but lean in.

Lucien drew a breath as Dean got closer, and his eyes flicked down to Dean's lips. Did that mean what Dean thought it did? Dean licked his own lips quickly, and Lucien's pupils dilated.

'I don't want to hide from you any more,' Lucien whispered.

Dean had a moment of doubt. What was he thinking? He shouldn't be doing this. It was too risky. But Lucien was so close, and so warm and so soft. And so beautiful. It would be the easiest thing in the world for Dean to move a little closer and finally feel Lucien's lips on his.

So he did.

Lucien seemed frozen in shock—but only for a moment.

He soon kissed back, soothing Dean's nerves and eagerly kissing away his worry that he'd misinterpreted everything.

Lucien cradled Dean's face in his hands, his thumb stroking over the soft skin of his cheek until it made Dean shiver. It was crystal-clear that Lucien wasn't anywhere near the man Dean had thought he was when they met. Lucien would stop at nothing to help not only his patients, but also the people he cared about. His walls had just been protecting the vulnerable man underneath.

Lucien stroked his fingers lightly all the way up Dean's arm, giving him goosebumps, and then he gripped Dean's neck as they kissed. Dean moaned into Lucien's mouth. Lucien grasped Dean around the waist and heaved him closer. Dean found himself sprawled on Lucien's lap, his knees straddling Lucien's thighs.

'Hi,' Dean whispered, smiling against Lucien's lips.

Lucien gripped Dean's waist tighter. 'Should we take this upstairs?'

Those words sent a thrill up Dean's spine, and he nodded breathlessly. 'Yes, please.'

CHAPTER SEVEN

EVER SINCE DEAN had kissed him, everything had happened on pure instinct—almost without thought. When his brain finally kicked in Lucien tried to get as close to Dean as he could, and found himself with the exquisite weight of Dean's body in his lap.

He gazed into Dean's eyes and reached forward to kiss his beautiful soft mouth—because apparently he was allowed to do that now. Dean kissed him back—hard—and Lucien explored Dean's body, running his hands up Dean's thighs and over his solid, muscular chest, enjoying the broad expanse of his back and squeezing his thick upper arms. All the while Dean gripped Lucien's hair and kissed slowly up his neck towards his ear. Heat and pleasure flared through Lucien's body.

Upstairs. Yes. They needed to be there as soon as possible.

He shifted Dean into place, wrapped his arms firmly around his waist and stood up. Dean gasped and held on tighter, wrapping his long legs around Lucien's back.

'Oh, wow...' Dean whispered, almost too quietly for Lucien to hear.

They somehow made it up one flight of stairs, stumbling most of the way, unable to keep their hands off each other long enough to concentrate on walking. Lucien wondered for a moment whose room they should head to, but then Dean pulled him through a door, kicked it shut and slammed Lucien up against it, pressing him into the wood and kissing him with a surprising sweetness for someone so fired up.

It looked as if they were choosing Lucien's room.

Lucien got his hands caught up in Dean's shirt and tried to say something, but Dean's kisses made it indecipherable.

Dean pulled away. 'What?'

'I said, you're wearing too many clothes.'

Dean grinned and yanked his shirt off over his head, dropping it to the floor. Then he helped Lucien out of his.

Lucien couldn't wait any longer, and pushed Dean back on to his bed, immediately crawling after him and covering him with his body. When his knee slipped between Dean's thighs, pushing them apart, he could feel that Dean was just as excited as he was.

It struck him that he was living out in Technicolor all the things he had been scared Dean would be doing with some-one else that night. He felt thoroughly embarrassed over his earlier spiral into despair, but was pleasantly rescued from his thoughts when Dean sucked his lower lip into his mouth and bit it softly. It sent sparks shooting through his body and a hot jolt of lust.

'You taste so good,' Dean whispered.

Lucien wondered fleetingly if it was possible to die from pleasure, and he felt his cheeks blush pink.

'Look at you…' Dean breathed reverently.

All Lucien could do was look back.

Then Dean licked into his mouth and proceeded to take him apart.

* * *

Later, feeling sated, sweaty and completely boneless, Lucien wrapped his arms around Dean and tugged his warmth tight to him.

He held him close like a limpet and decided simply never to let go…

Dean woke up first, blinking in the early-morning sunlight. Only to find a sleeping Lucien facing him. Their fingers were entwined between them on the pillow.

He'd never held someone's hand in his sleep before.

He listened to Lucien's even breaths and smiled to himself when he felt the soft twitch of Lucien's fingers as he dreamed. Pretty adorable for a guy who could lift Dean up and carry him around as if he weighed nothing at all.

Christ, that had been hot.

Dean was so warm and comfy he drifted back to sleep, and when he awoke again he found it was Lucien's turn to stare at him. He reached out to cover Lucien's eyes, and Lucien pulled away, laughing.

'Let me look.'

'Why should I?'

'I was counting your freckles.'

'Oh.' Dean shyly hid his face in the pillow. 'I have too many.'

'I love them.' Lucien cleared his throat. 'Do you…regret anything about last night?'

'Yes…'

'Oh.'

Lucien's face fell. Dean could tell from the line that appeared between his eyebrows that he was worried, so he finished his sentence quickly. 'I regret you sitting alone all night when I could have been here with you.'

'Oh.' This time Lucien smiled.

'By the way, I think Helen knows about us.'

'What? How? It's only just happened. Even *she's* not that good.'

'She saw it before we did, I guess. We talked about you the other day at work. I also heard some very interesting stories about your early days as a GP,' Dean teased.

'Oh, God.' Lucien ducked under the covers for a moment. 'Maybe I don't hide my feelings as well as I thought I did.'

'I'm starting to think you're not the only one,' said Dean.

'I don't like people very often, you know.'

Dean nodded. 'I know. I don't know why the hell you like me. But I'm glad you do.'

Even if it probably wouldn't last long once he knew the truth.

'I can't imagine how anyone *couldn't* like you. How anyone could work with you every day, or pass you once in the street, and not fall irreversibly in lust with you for the rest of their lives.'

Dean's face grew hot and he squirmed away. 'Shut up.'

Lucien grabbed him around the waist and yanked him effortlessly back against him. Dean's back slammed against Lucien's chest and he lost his breath for a moment.

'Careful,' murmured Dean. 'Or we might need to have round two.'

'Don't threaten me with a good time,' Lucien whispered hotly into the back of Dean's neck.

Ten minutes after the best round two of Dean's life, Dean waited for Lucien to finish using the shower so he could have a turn. He could have climbed the stairs and used his own shower, but he didn't want to be a whole floor away from Lucien. How pathetic was that?

Dean sighed and ran a hand over his face. This had got very serious, very fast.

In the kitchen, Lucien kissed Dean's forehead as he passed him his coffee. Not for the first time, Dean's heart did a little flip at how adorable Lucien looked first thing in the morning, rubbing his sleepy eyes with one hand, then trying to tame hair that was even wilder than usual with the other.

As Dean cooked breakfast Lucien hugged him from behind and nuzzled his neck, while Dean talked him softly through how not to burn eggs and bacon.

Dean felt safe and special and cared for. But he couldn't enjoy the moment as much as he longed to.

Dean couldn't avoid it any longer. He knew it was finally time to tell Lucien. But that realisation didn't stop his chest tightening with nerves when he considered what Lucien's reaction might be to the truth.

Now that he had developed feelings for Lucien he was terrified that he would reject Dean for keeping the secret for so long. And, worse, he might reject Rafael along with him—all because of Dean's actions. And why shouldn't he? Dean wasn't good enough for Lucien. After all, everyone in his life had left him—why would Lucien be any different? Sooner or later he'd realise that he deserved someone better than Dean.

But, regardless of that, it was time. Dean resolved to tell him the truth and take whatever consequences came his way. He would do it after Rafael's birthday party. He couldn't risk ruining his son's big day.

CHAPTER EIGHT

SINCE LUCIEN AND Dean had spent the night together things had been a little strange. They'd had that one wonderful night, and an even better morning-after, but since then nothing. Dean was still affectionate, and funny, and sweet—just like always. But there was something between them. As if Dean was holding something back.

Lucien tried not to worry about it, even though some traitorous part of him worried that Dean regretted sleeping with Lucien.

Maybe he was sick of country life and bored with being stuck with Lucien all the time. Maybe he wanted more space for Rafael. Or a family home without a random stranger in it.

Although Lucien hoped he wasn't a random stranger any more. To either of them.

Lucien smiled as he remembered Rafael's reaction to his new room.

'Daddy says some people don't like hugs so you have to ask first,' he'd said.

Lucien had smiled. 'That's exactly right.'

'Would you like a hug, please?'

Lucien had blinked down at Rafael and realised he would—very much. And when they'd hugged Lucien had felt something deep inside him click into place.

'It's the best room I've ever seen!' Rafael had told him. 'Blue is my favourite colour!'

'I heard it might be.'

'I'm heading into work. I'll see you later.'

Lucien just managed to put down his toast before he had an armful of Dean. Dean hugged him tightly around the middle and Lucien squeezed Dean's shoulders close to him, breathing in his scent.

Dean spoke into Lucien's neck. 'I'll start setting up for the party when I get home. Hopefully I'll have most of it done by the time you finish work.'

'You don't have to. I can help with it when I get back. Not that I know the first thing about children's parties.'

Dean leaned back to peck him on the lips, then stepped away. Lucien immediately missed his warmth.

Dean smiled. 'I'll teach you.'

With that, he grabbed his bag and left.

Almost at the end of a long shift, during which Dean spent all his breaks planning last-minute touches for Rafael's party, Dean's last patient of the day shuffled into his consulting room and sat down, clutching a backpack on her lap. Dean skimmed through her notes on his monitor. An eighteen-year-old named Lydia.

'What can I do for you today?' Dean asked, smiling warmly and trying in vain to make eye contact.

'I normally see Dr Benedict,' Lydia mumbled at the floor.

'I hear that a lot.' Dean smiled. 'But I'm afraid he's not in right now, so can I try to help?'

She sighed deeply, and Dean waited for her to speak.

'I've not been feeling very well lately.'

'Okay. Can you tell me more about that?'

'I didn't want to come here today,' said Lydia.

Dean waited patiently for her to continue.

'I just wanted to stay at home. It's safe there. But my dad was the same as me. He died because he didn't get treated, and I don't want to be like him.'

'That's very brave, Lydia. I'm sorry about your dad.' Dean glanced again at Lydia's records on his screen. 'When did he pass away?'

'Last year.'

'Sadly, it's still very common for men not to feel comfortable asking for help with their mental health.'

Lydia nodded and stared down at her hands.

'Anyway, you've done the right thing coming in. We're always here for you.'

'I don't want to bother you with something stupid.'

'If you've got symptoms you're concerned about, you shouldn't be struggling with that alone. That's exactly what we're here for.'

She shifted in her seat. 'I've been hearing things.'

'What kind of things?'

'Whispers. Constant whispering. Telling me things.'

Dean nodded. 'What kind of things are they telling you?'

'That you're a terrible doctor, and this is completely useless, and you won't be able to help me.' She finally made eye contact. 'And I bet they're right.'

Dean tilted his head.

'And I have a knife.'

Dean glanced at her hands. She wasn't holding anything.

He kept his voice calm. 'What are you saying, Lydia?'

'I'm not saying anything. I just have a knife.'

'Where is it?'

'In my bag.'

'What are you planning on doing with it?'

'Nothing. But I could if I had to.'

A patient had once brought a gun into Dean's last practice, so he had learned to take any mention of a weapon very seriously. They'd even had a panic button installed after that, which had triggered the police to attend immediately. Not that there was anything like that here.

'Is something happening at home, Lydia? Is that why you feel you need a knife? For protection?'

She shook her head.

Dean turned his chair to face her dead-on, keeping some distance between them but wanting her to know he was fully engaged. 'Do you feel that I am a threat to you? Would you prefer to speak with a different doctor?'

She shook her head again. 'I'm not going to hurt you, or myself, if that's what you're thinking. The whispers say someone's trying to kill me. But they don't think it's you.'

The 'whispers' rang a bell. A very specific bell.

'I'm just going to check something on my screen for a second. Is that okay?'

She nodded, and Dean pulled his chair closer to his desk. He went back through Lydia's notes and found what he was looking for after a minute. She had suffered from paranoid hallucinations two years previously, but they'd receded when she'd been prescribed anti-psychotic meds. He would bet good money she was the patient Lucien had been worried about in the staff room on his first day at the surgery. And apparently the hallucinations were back.

'Have you been taking your Olanzapine as normal, Lydia?'

She avoided his gaze.

'Have you stopped taking it?'

Her lack of an answer likely meant yes.

'Have you been attending your CBT sessions?'

'I'm still on the waiting list for those.'

Damn. Those waiting lists could be months or even years long.

'Have you been having problems sleeping lately? Or eating?'

She squeezed her bag tighter. 'This is the first time I've left the house in weeks.'

Dean's heart sank. He felt terrible for her. She looked pale and drawn and absolutely exhausted.

'You've been really brave coming here today,' he told her. 'It must have felt like a huge step, and you did exactly the right thing. I don't think you're coping very well, and I think you need some help.' Dean stood. 'I'm really proud of you for coming in. Listen, you stay here. I'm going to get you a drink of water, and then we'll see what we can do to help you.'

Dean found Helen out in the corridor. 'Can you keep an eye on my patient for a second? I'm going to use the HCP line and call an ambulance for her. She's suffering from auditory hallucinations, she's paranoid and she semi-threatened me with a theoretical knife.'

'How is a knife theoretical?'

'She said she has one in her bag, but I'm not convinced.'

'Well, that's a dangerous assumption.'

Dean strongly suspected his hunch was right, but it was better to be safe than sorry.

'Okay. Stay outside the room, but watch the door. I'll ask her if I can check her bag when I get back.'

Dean made his phone call from the reception desk and poured Lydia a drink from the water cooler. His mobile phone vibrated in his pocket and he automatically checked it. It was Rafael's school. It must be an emergency, or they wouldn't call him at work.

He answered immediately, his heart in his mouth. But

his panic soon faded when they simply asked him to verify his home address. Apparently they had the postcode wrong. He corrected it, then rolled his eyes as he quickly ended the call and rushed back to his room.

Only to find it empty, and no Helen either.

'Er…where is my patient?' he called out.

'Would that be the one who's absconded to the car park?' Helen shouted from the end of the corridor.

'What?'

Dean dropped the cup of water and ran. He found Helen standing in the back doorway, waiting for him, and they ran outside together to the grassy lawn by the car park. Dean shaded his eyes from the sun with one hand and squinted at Lydia, standing under a weeping willow.

'Fancied some fresh air?'

Dean crossed the lawn towards her and nearly tripped over her backpack, his foot catching in the strap. She laughed at him, seemingly shocking even herself, and Dean smiled back.

'Since it's nearly killed me, may I have your permission to have a look through your bag?'

'Go for it,' she said, then sat down cross-legged on the grass.

Dean carefully looked through the almost empty bag. There was no knife that he could see.

'So, why are we out here?'

'Did you call the police on me?'

'No, I didn't. I've called for a ride to take us to the hospital. They have specialists there who can help you.'

'Us?'

'Yes, I'm coming with you.'

Some of the tension seemed to leave the frame of her

shoulders. She pulled up some grass from the lawn and tossed it away from them.

'Who says I want you to come?'

'No one. But I want to make sure you get there safe.'

She threw a few more handfuls of grass, then seemed to run out of steam.

'Was there a reason you left the consulting room?' Dean asked.

'The whispers were too loud in there. I needed to be outside.' She turned her face up to the sun. 'The wind in the trees sometimes drowns them out.'

Dean sat back against the tree and listened to the rustling willow. The dancing tips of its branches almost touched the lawn in a green curtain, shielding them from the world.

'I'll sit here with you for a while. But we'll need to get up when the ambulance arrives.'

Lydia didn't answer, and when Dean looked over she was swaying back and forth slightly, with her eyes shut and her hands over her ears.

She must be experiencing the auditory hallucinations again.

Dean felt terrible. If he hadn't answered that call from the school he would probably have been back with Lydia, and she never would have ended up panicking and running out.

He waited patiently until Lydia took down her hands and opened her eyes. 'You okay?' he asked.

She gulped and looked away. 'I've been better.'

At that moment the ambulance pulled around the corner into the car park.

When Lucien arrived at the surgery, Helen accosted him.

'Did Dean contact you?'

'No. Why?'

'I'll let him tell you all about it later. Long story short: he's at the hospital with a patient, but he should be done soon.'

'I hope so—it's Rafael's party today.'

'Oh, it'll be fine. That's hours away,' said Helen.

But on his break Lucien found himself distracted by wondering whether Dean was home yet or not, so he decided to stop wondering and just text him.

How are you doing? Helen's wondering where you are. I couldn't care less, obviously...

Dean immediately replied.

I was just about to message you. Lol, btw. We're waiting to be seen. There's a big backlog.

Lucien sighed. It wasn't hugely surprising news, but it was unfortunate on the one day Dean needed to get back.

Sorry to hear that. Who is the patient?

It's the patient we discussed the other day. The one you were worried about.

Lucien's body tensed, and he sat up straight in his chair.

Is she okay?

I'll explain more later, but she's safe. She says hello. Or she would if she wasn't currently ignoring me and playing on her phone.

Damn it. Lucien should have done more for her when he'd had the opportunity. He hadn't stopped thinking of her since her aunt had spoken to him in the shop. But he was always trying so hard to avoid crossing that line.

She's my patient. I should come in and swap places with you, then you can come back and get on with the party.

No... I appreciate the offer, but I'm here now. Despite what I just said, we are actually getting on. But things are a bit delicate. I want to stay.

Lucien loved it that Dean was so dedicated. But it couldn't help but remind him of his mother, the uncrowned queen of crossing that line. He'd loved his mother for how much she cared, how big her heart was, but sometimes, as a child, his not being the main focus of that heart had hurt. And now Dean was doing exactly what Lucien's mother would have done. Missing his son's birthday party by putting the patient first.

Dean went on.

I'll have plenty of time to do everything. Don't worry.

When Lucien didn't reply, Dean typed:

You still there?

I'm here. Listen, Lydia can be tricky to deal with. But I'll tell you one thing I learned about her. She hates being treated with kid gloves. So don't talk down to her, and don't ever lie to her. Talk to her like an adult and be brutally honest.

Okay. Thanks, Lucien.

Message me if you need anything at all.

I will!

Lucien had a bad feeling that Dean was being way too optimistic about making it back in time to do everything he'd planned for the party...

Dean brought two horribly weak teas from the cafeteria, and carefully handed one to Lydia. 'Have you been able to talk to anyone about the way you're feeling? Family? Friends?'

'My mum always tells me to stop being so self-absorbed. And that she knew from day one I'd be more trouble than I was worth.'

Dean fought a flare of anger. He always tried to be kind in the face of cruelty. Her mother might well have her own issues. But to say that to your own child...

Lydia really didn't have anyone to advocate for her.

Dean settled down next to Lydia and tried to stop obsessing over Rafael's party. Up until six months ago, all Dean had had to focus on was his job. The old Dean hadn't thought anything on Earth could be more fulfilling than advocating for his patients. But now he'd found something else that made him feel just as worthwhile, if not more.

Had he been a better doctor pre-Rafael? Was he now giving his patients less than they deserved as well as his son? He still wanted to be the best doctor he could be, but not if that meant short-changing Rafael. Surely it was possible to do both.

A little later Dean looked at his watch. Lydia had gone to use the bathroom ten minutes ago.

Something didn't feel right.

Dean walked around the corner and knocked on the bathroom door.

'Lydia?'

No answer.

Dean wasn't above braving entry into the women's bathroom if the situation called for it, but a gentler approach was probably best here.

This time he tapped gently on the door. 'Lydia, I just need to know if you're in there. You don't have to talk to me or come out.'

'I'm in here.'

'Cool.' Dean felt a wave of relief. 'Are you okay?'

'The fan in here drowns them out.'

Dean nodded in understanding. She was hearing the whispers again.

'I just want to go home.' Lydia sounded exhausted.

'I know. I'm sorry this is taking so long.' Dean made a decision. 'If you're happy in there for a minute, I'm going to see if I can hurry things along a bit.'

Lydia answered by turning on the hand-dryer.

Finally Dean located the right person to talk to, and cornered him at the desk. The man looked at his screen for a moment before responding to Dean.

'There are a number of patients that need to be seen first. She may not be seen today.'

'It's fine, Dr Vasquez.'

Lydia appeared from behind Dean.

'It's okay. I'll just go home. I can come back another day. Maybe Mum will come with me.'

'Absolutely not. Leave this to me.'

Dean sent Lydia back to her seat, out of earshot, and

then turned back to the man, making sure he spoke calmly and clearly.

'She needs to be seen today. My patient is suffering from auditory hallucinations and has a history of psychosis. She needs help now.'

He stared at Dean for a long moment and heaved a huge, soul-deep sigh.

'There might be something I can do. Hold on.'

An hour later, Lucien received a message from Dean.

They're assessing her now. Psychiatric evaluation.

Is she coping okay? At least she's being seen. Does this mean you're free to leave?

Not yet. I told her I'd be here when she finished. I can't leave her alone. She doesn't have anyone else here. I'm responsible for her. I feel so guilty. I was on the phone and she slipped out of the clinic.

Yes, Helen filled me in about that. But it wasn't your fault. You sit tight and let me know if anything changes.

Lucien checked his watch. Time was really ticking down now. Dean was never going to make it back in time to set up the party.

Lucien didn't want to stress Dean out further, so in a break between patients he pulled up Google on his monitor and searched 'party for seven-year-old'. He read for a minute, his eyes growing bigger by the second.

Yeah, he was never going to be able to do any of that by himself.

'Helen! I need serious help,' he called.

Helen rushed in, holding a steaming bowl of instant noodles and a spoon.

'Sorry, I didn't know you were eating.'

'Spit it out, Lucien.'

'Dean's still stuck at the hospital. We might have to throw Rafael's party for him.'

Helen's eyes widened. 'Oh, fudge…' She thought for about three seconds. 'Okay. Look, I'm going to call an emergency locum. I'll switch all your remaining appointments to them. Then we can both handle this situation together. You may have years of experience in medicine, but you don't know real trauma until you've been surrounded by fifteen screaming kids, high on juice and chocolate cake.'

She swung Lucien's monitor to face her, rolled her eyes at the Google search and clicked over to his schedule.

'You'll have to see the next two patients—it's too late for changes. I'll get hold of the locum.' She rushed out, calling back over her shoulder, 'You can't learn anything you need to know about kids' parties online. You need an expert in the field. And that's me!'

Thank God for Helen.

Just as Lucien finished up with his last patient of the day, his phone dinged with a message.

They're referring her to the local crisis team, but they won't be here for a couple of hours. I'm going to stay and wait with her.

Lucien sighed.

With any luck they'll turn up sooner than that and I can rush home.

   Lucien answered.

Don't worry about Rafael's party I can handle it.

What? How?

You tell me what you had planned and I'll do it. With a little help from Helen.

Lucien, you can't do that.

Of course we can. It won't be as good as you doing it, but it'll be better than nothing.

This is my first time doing a kid's party too, don't forget. I was probably going to make a mess of it anyway.

   Lucien had forgotten.
   This was Rafael's first birthday with Dean, and the first without his mother.
   Lucien's heart hurt. And with that came an absolute determination that he was going to make this party the best he possibly could.
   He got a new message.

Are we making a mistake? Should we cancel the party?

No!

We could postpone for week. I can call round all the parents.

But we're already having it the day before his actual birthday so that his best friend can come. It has to be today. He's all excited about it now. He'll be crushed if we cancel.

Rafael had been practically vibrating with excitement all week about his big party. This morning Lucien had been sure he would either explode or pass out.

He typed out a new message.

I promise it'll be fine.

Maybe. I guess with enough cake and sweets Rafael will be off his head anyway.

That's more or less what Helen said.

Okay. Look, I'm still planning on getting back for the party. So you get things started and I can help when I get there.

Sounds like a plan.

Dean proceeded to send him instructions for decorations, food, games and party bags. He also rang Rafael's school and told them that Lucien would be collecting him.

It had not escaped Lucien's notice that Dean was continuing this whole conversation by text. Most people would have switched to a phone call by now, but Dean knew Lucien didn't love talking on the phone and had noticed he avoided it wherever possible, so he hadn't even suggested it.

It gave Lucien a warm, looked-after feeling in his chest. And along with that, a burst of confidence.

He could handle this.

Three hours later, Lucien saw how wrong he had been.

Most of the children were playing on a deafeningly loud karaoke machine with two microphones. Lucien's face hurt from all the encouraging smiles he had to fake every time a child finished what could only loosely be called a song. Rafael and the remainder of his guests were sprawled on the floor playing a video game, only three feet away from the karaoke machine, all whilst talking, screaming, and laughing hysterically.

How any of them could hear anything was some kind of miracle. Because Lucien couldn't even hear himself think.

Lucien had been lulled into a false sense of security when the party had started off quietly. Polite, well-dressed children had handed Rafael presents wrapped by their parents. They'd even played some games, led by Helen, like musical statues and pass the parcel—the parcel made in about five minutes by Helen herself, whom Lucien was beginning to suspect was some sort of magical fairy godmother sent from heaven.

He'd been stunned that kids still played the sort of games he remembered from his own childhood. And he'd texted Dean to tell him so. He also sent a couple of pictures of Rafael enjoying himself, knowing Dean must feel awful, stuck at the hospital, missing all this.

Dean had replied with a question.

How did the food go down?

Dean had pre-ordered a birthday cake and a mountain of tiny sandwiches on platters, and they'd been delivered about an hour before the party started. Helen had brought a couple of shopping bags full of sweets and crisps with her from the supermarket, dumped them on the table and told Lucien to fill up all the bowls he had and make them look pretty.

Lucien had shown Helen the decorations Dean had bought. Blue and purple balloons, a blue one-use table-cloth with superheroes on, purple paper cups and plates and a huge *Happy Birthday* banner. By the time Lucien had filled some bowls with sweets and crisps Helen had already put up all the decorations and the house had looked wonderful. Everything had gone perfectly to Dean's plan.

But now the food had been demolished, most of the balloons had been popped, and the entire celebration had descended into chaos.

Lucas answered Dean.

The food went down wonderfully. Everything's perfect.

'Is this normal?' he asked Helen, who was wiping up a spilled drink from the food table.

'Totally and completely,' she said with a blissful smile.

'Are you *enjoying* this?' Lucien asked, trying to keep the incredulity out of his voice and failing.

Helen shrugged. 'I've missed the chaos. My kids just want to go off and see a band with their friends on their birthdays now. I'm lucky if they let me take them out to the shops for a new outfit.'

Rafael chose that moment to grab Lucien's knee with a chocolatey hand and pull himself up on to his lap. He fell heavily against Lucien's chest, and somehow managed to get more chocolate on Lucien's shirt.

'Is Daddy still at the hospital?' he asked sadly.

'Yes.' Lucien decided Rafael deserved to smother his shirt in as much chocolate as he pleased. 'Did you want to talk to him again?'

Rafael nodded into his chest, so Lucien dialled Dean's number and listened to it ring, then passed the phone to Rafael, wincing only slightly as it got covered in chocolate fingerprints.

Helen eyed the stains and patted his shoulder. 'Enjoy the mess while you can.'

Lucien tried to keep Rafael more or less upright as he shuffled around on his lap. He seemed to find his second wind as he talked to his dad, giggling and throwing himself back and forth with laughter at something Dean said on the phone.

Lucien smiled to himself. Dean did have that sort of effect on people.

After a few minutes Rafael hung up, thrust the phone back at Lucien and shouted a thank-you as he slid off his lap and launched himself back into the video game with his friends.

Another text from Dean came through immediately.

You'll have to put him to bed later. Do you know how?

Lucien thought about it.

I've witnessed a few bedtimes. I can figure it out.

But Lucien suddenly felt nervous. What if Rafael refused to brush his teeth or go to bed without his dad there? What if he didn't like the way Lucien read him his story?

Lucien shook his head. If he could live through the auction, he could manage to put a kid to bed.

Lucien checked the list of activities Dean had sent him. It was piñata time.

Lucien left the kids with Helen, then got a ladder and hung the piñata from a thick, high branch in the garden. He'd probably have been given this job even if Dean were here, he thought, seeing as Dean hated heights so much.

His hands were freezing by the time he managed to tie a decent knot, and he wished he'd worn gloves.

The kids gleefully bashed the living daylights out of the poor rainbow-coloured unicorn. And when all the sweets had disappeared into hungry, grasping hands Rafael and his best friend ran towards the tree trunk at full speed, as if to start climbing it.

Lucien grabbed Rafael around the waist and pulled him gently away, directing him and his friend back towards the kitchen and the table of treats.

'I'll get the ladder and take it down later. No climbing trees today, please.'

Rafael grumbled, but didn't argue, and Lucien silently congratulated himself on not having caused any tantrums so far today.

There was still plenty of time, though.

'How're you doing?' asked Helen, back in the kitchen.

'Remarkably well... I think?'

Helen nodded in agreement. 'It's a miracle—judging from your previous record with kids.'

Lucien had to agree. Only a couple of weeks ago he would hardly have recognised himself.

Now there was only one job left to do. The whole reason Dean had arranged for the party to be in the evening was so it would be dark enough for fireworks to end the night.

He'd even pushed notes through all the neighbours' doors and made an announcement on the village Facebook group that there would be fireworks that night, so people should get their cats and dogs in.

Lucien set off the fireworks without a hitch—mainly because he was ably assisted by Helen. Nobody got a sparkler injury, no fireworks smashed through anyone's windows, no cars or trees were set alight by a stray spark.

All things considered, the whole night had gone wonderfully.

Only one kid had thrown up, and that had been in the kitchen, so it was an easy wipe-up. Binxie had been happily set up in Lucien's bedroom for the night, and had never minded fireworks anyway.

After the fireworks Lucien sat on the sofa in the living room, exhausted, holding a huge bowl of popcorn on his lap and surrounded by kids coming down from a sugar high. He looked around. Half of them were asleep, and half were still watching a Disney movie on TV, occasionally scooping a tiny handful of popcorn from the bowl, their eyes never leaving the screen.

People did this every single *year*? Several times over if they had more than one child?

Inconceivable.

Helen tiptoed into the room. 'The parents should start arriving for pick-up soon. Help me finish the party bags.'

Lucien nodded wordlessly. He was all talked out.

Thank goodness Dean had arranged the party as a drop-off—he couldn't think of anything worse than having to make conversation with a dozen sets of parents for an entire evening.

'You still holding up okay?' Helen asked, reaching out

for Lucien's hand and pulling him from the sea of children snuggled up by his side.

'I think so.'

'You've gone from being a stranger to being these kids' favourite person in one evening.'

'Not a total stranger. I'm the GP for most of them.'

He'd recognised all the kids at the party. He'd seen most of them for colds, fevers or banged knees over the years. He'd even helped the mother of one guest give birth to his younger sibling when she'd gone into premature labour during a home visit to her farm just outside the town.

'I found out something today about that one.' He pointed at a sleeping kid on the end of the sofa. 'His younger brother is named after me. I had no idea.'

A year ago Lucien having to talk to all these kids would have been impossible. He would have hidden out in his office rather than face that. Of course he didn't have an office now... But he wasn't missing it. He'd been strangely at ease there, in the middle of a puppy pile of thankfully almost comatose kids.

Once all the children had been picked up, and Helen had gone home clutching the single leftover party bag, Lucien was approached by Rafael, chocolate cake on his face and juice stains on his shirt.

'One more call to Daddy before bed?' asked Lucien.

Rafael nodded and climbed on to the sofa next to him.

Lucien dialled Dean's number and listened to it ring, waiting to pass the phone over to Rafael. But this time there was no answer.

He hung up and texted Dean instead.

Any updates?

After a couple of minutes there was still no answer, and no dots suggesting Dean was typing his reply, so Lucien gave up and tossed his phone on to the sofa.

'Looks like he's either busy getting back, or his phone's out of power.'

Rafael pouted and leaned into Lucien's chest. He found his arms going around the kid naturally, to give him a comforting squeeze.

'He'll be home soon.'

Rafael nodded into Lucien's chest.

'He really missed a great party, didn't he? Lucky we took all those videos and photos to show him what happened.'

Lucien looked around the room at the huge mess that still remained. The gigantic cake still sat on the table. Even with all the kids having seconds, they'd hardly made a dent in it.

'And we saved half of the cake, so we can have a special party with him once he gets back. Or even tomorrow.'

'Not tomorrow! Tonight!'

'Well, we don't know for sure if he'll be back in time.'

Rafael sniffled, and Lucien could sense a meltdown coming.

'Remember it's not your real birthday until tomorrow, so if we do wait until then, that's the day that really counts anyway.'

'It is?'

'Yeah!'

'Do I get more presents?'

'Yes—the ones we saved. From your dad.'

Lucien had let Rafael open the presents from his friends, but had thought Dean would want to be there when he opened the ones from him.

'Oh, yeah!' Rafael had evidently forgotten about those, and he eyed them up now.

'See? Tomorrow will be even better than today.'

On his way to bed, Rafael stopped and stared out of the window.

Lucien nearly tripped over him.

'Can we look in the unicorn to see if we missed some sweets?'

The piñata still swung gently from the branch on the oak tree outside.

'We'll do it tomorrow. It's too cold now.'

Lucien managed to get Rafael tucked up in bed, teeth brushed and pyjamas on, in just under forty-five minutes. He was almost too tired to see the words in the storybook Rafael picked out, and made half of it up, which seemed to both anger and delight Rafael in equal measure.

He was almost convinced Rafael had fallen asleep when he suddenly asked a question. 'Do you love my daddy?'

Lucien was lost for words. He was sure they hadn't kissed in front of Rafael yet, but maybe the kid was smart enough to have recognised that something had changed, or he had noticed on some level that they'd become more comfortable and familiar around each other.

Or maybe they were both just utterly useless at being subtle. So inept that even a six-year-old could see through them.

'Henry has two dads. They go fishing. Can we go fishing?'

Lucien knew he actually needed to answer a question at some point.

'I'm sure we could figure that out,' he managed.

It couldn't be that hard to rent some fishing rods and find a lake, could it? He had no clue how to fish, but that was what online video tutorials were for.

Back downstairs, Lucien relaxed on the sofa with a cup of tea. The party should have been everything Lucien had been dreading about living in the same house as a child. But he was shocked by how much he'd enjoyed the day, and how close he felt to Rafael.

Dean and Rafael. He couldn't imagine his life without either one of them. He wanted nothing more than to be part of their lives for ever. He didn't know if Dean felt the same way, but he knew he couldn't lose what they had. Lucien needed them both in his life and he would do anything to keep them close.

After what felt like an entire lifetime spent sitting in various waiting rooms and corridors, Dean had got so bored he'd read an entire issue of *Men's Fitness* magazine from 2003 from cover to cover, and posted three stories on Instagram. He'd even started replying to comments, which he normally avoided doing—until he'd realised that was a waste of his battery. He needed to save it to get Lucien and Rafael's updates from the party. They were the only thing keeping him going at the moment.

The last thing he'd heard was that Rafael was about to go to bed. Dean had officially missed his son's entire birthday party.

He took a breath and tried not to feel like a gigantic failure.

To try and lighten his mood, he subtly pulled his phone out and read through the last few messages from Lucien, laughing under his breath, trying not to let Lydia hear. He didn't want her to know what he was missing to stay with her.

But he wasn't quite subtle enough.

'What is going on? You've been sneaking round corners to talk on your phone and writing messages all night—all the while trying to do it without me noticing. Who are you talking to?'

Dean shoved his phone in his pocket. 'It's nothing important.'

'Yes, it is. Don't lie to me. I hate it when people lie.'

Dean took a deep breath. Maybe it was time to see if Lucien knew what he was talking about, or if Dean was about to make a massive error of judgement.

'Okay. The truth is I'm missing my son's birthday party.'

Lydia's face fell. 'Why on earth are you still here? Go!'

Dean shook his head. 'This is my job, and I take that seriously. I am choosing to be here because I care about you, and you deserve to have someone with you just as much as my son does. And, as it happens, my son is with someone who does care about him right now.'

'The person you've been texting?'

'Yes. There's no one I'd be happier leaving my son with than him. My son is fine. He's happy and safe. My job today is to keep *you* happy and safe. Is that okay with you?'

She nodded.

'Now, do you want to watch a video of my son smearing chocolate cake all over Dr Benedict?'

'Yes, please!'

She laughed and bounded over to Dean's side.

After a minute, she nudged his arm. 'Sorry about the knife thing. I never really had one.'

'It's okay.'

Two hours later Lydia was collected by the crisis team. While Dean had waited, he'd managed to get Lydia into CBT sessions starting in a fortnight, and had found a support group she could go to locally, with other young people with experience of mental illness.

Dean grabbed his phone to text Lucien the good news

that he was one step closer to getting home, but found his phone was finally dead.

He'd give himself a reasonable nine and a half out of ten for being a doctor today. Now he just had to pull up his score for being a dad. And after missing his son's entire birthday party he was not off to the best start.

Dean took a deep breath, pushed open the hospital door, and stepped out into the night. Only for a nurse to rush directly towards him from the car park and grab his arm.

'Are you Dr Vasquez?'

Dean nodded.

'You're needed in the family room.'

CHAPTER NINE

LUCIEN HAD BEEN so careful, trying to do everything right. After he'd put Rafael to bed he'd done some tidying, cleared up all the major messes, and made sure to put all the leftovers in the fridge. He'd manoeuvred the cake into a large Tupperware box which had only just managed to contain it. Then he'd looked at the remaining mess and realised it wasn't happening. He would clear it up in the morning.

The sofa looked plush and warm, and he decided to lie down, watch some TV and wait for Dean to get home. He'd want a full report on the party when he got back, and Lucien was bubbling over with excitement to tell him how well it had gone.

But in the end Lucien's emotional and physical exhaustion and the softness of the sofa won out, and after the cat joined him, purring softly, it was over.

Lucien fell asleep not half an hour after he sat down.

He woke suddenly, convinced he'd heard a noise, but not sure what it might have been. The room was dark, and almost silent but for the TV still quietly playing. He sat up and saw that it was still only ten o clock. Maybe Dean was back? But he couldn't hear anyone moving around, and Dean was never this quiet.

He tipped the cat off his lap on to the sofa and checked the kitchen, before setting off up the stairs and looking in

Dean's room. Nothing. He explored the bathroom, and his own room, before peeking around Rafael's door.

He wasn't in his bed.

Lucien's heart dropped. But surely he was just in the other bathroom. Or maybe Lucien had missed seeing him in the kitchen—he was very small, after all.

Lucien checked every single room again, more carefully this time, calling Rafael's name.

'Rafael? Where are you, buddy?'

Dean had never mentioned anything like sleepwalking, or told him that Rafael had a propensity for wandering around at night. But finally he'd checked every room, and every wardrobe, and he was starting to panic.

He stood in the hall. All the coats were still on their pegs, but Rafael's shoes were missing. He was sure he'd tidied them away just hours before...

Damn it.

Lucien yanked open the door and flew outside, yelling Rafael's name into the freezing cold night. There was no one at the front, but when Lucien ran around the side of the house to the patio he was confronted with the worst thing he'd ever seen in his life.

Lucien stood alone in the hospital's family room, terrified and completely at a loss as to what to do. He fumbled his phone from his pocket and nearly dropped it on the floor before trying to get hold of Dean again.

Nothing.

How had Rafael even got out of the house in the middle of the night? Let alone managed to fall out of the damn oak tree?

All the guilt and fear he'd felt after his mother's death returned and hit Lucien like a truck, and he sat down before his knees gave way. Regardless of the how and why, Rafael was badly hurt—and it was all Lucien's fault. Yet again, someone Lucien loved had come to harm on his watch.

Lucien rocked slightly, staring unseeing at the pattern on the linoleum floor, trying to figure out what on earth he'd missed. How could he have done things differently to avoid this? Maybe he couldn't have. If people got close to him, they got hurt. He couldn't believe he'd been so reckless as to let himself forget that.

He couldn't get the image he'd seen out of his head… Rafael lying on the patio under the tree…his blood mixing with the fallen leaves…

Lucien sent another worried message to Dean.

A sudden thought struck him. What if Dean got home before he saw his messages and went outside? He'd see the blood covering the patio. There was so much blood…

He knew he had to think straight—had to ask the staff if Dean was still in the hospital. Or perhaps it would be quicker to run and look for Dean himself. But then Lucien wouldn't be here if Rafael needed him.

Dean would want him to look after Rafael first.

He had to stay put.

The door to the family room slammed open and Dean rushed in, looking sick with worry, his eyes wild.

'Dean!'

'The nurse told me you were here. What the hell is happening? Where's Rafael?'

Lucien, seeing that Dean was terrified, lost his own fear immediately and went into caretaker mode. He spoke calmly and reached for Dean's shoulder. 'The doctors are in with him now. I'm waiting to hear.'

'What do you mean? Waiting to hear what? Why aren't you in there? How could you leave him alone?'

'I wasn't allowed in, Dean,' Lucien said firmly. 'You know that.'

'I don't care. What the hell has happened to my boy?'

Lucien felt guilt surge up again.

He manoeuvred Dean over to the chairs at the edge of the room and gently pushed him down on to the nearest one. 'Sit down, and I'll explain what happened.'

Dean sat, surprising Lucien by not fighting him every step of the way. Dean was paler than he'd ever seen him.

'It was after the party...everyone had gone home. I put Rafael to bed, and everything was fine. I tried to wait up for you, but I must have fallen asleep on the sofa. Then I woke up. I'd heard a noise—which I guess must have been him going outside. But I didn't know that then. I thought you'd come home, so I looked for you first. Then I checked on Rafael, and that's when I noticed he was gone. I'm sorry... I should have checked on him first.'

Dean shook his head desperately. 'Get to the point. What happened?'

'He went out while I was asleep. The piñata...it was still outside. I'd hung it from the oak tree. He'd said earlier he wanted to check inside, to see if there were any sweets left, and I told him we'd look tomorrow. I guess he couldn't wait... I had no idea, Dean. I should have taken it down myself, but I didn't think he'd climb the tree.'

'He climbed the tree?'

'Yes. I hung the piñata quite high. He fell a long way, Dean. On to the patio. He must have landed on one hand. He's broken his arm badly, banged his head... And he could have been lying there for up to ten minutes before I found him...'

'He was lying alone...unconscious...outside in the freezing cold, because you didn't think to check on my son straight away when you heard a noise in the middle of the night?'

Lucien swallowed and nodded.

A doctor burst in. Lucien recognised her as someone he'd known professionally for years, and knew she happened to be the most experienced paediatric surgeon in the hospital.

His stress levels dropped infinitesimally.

'This is Dean—Rafael's father.' Lucien introduced the two quickly.

Dean shot up. They shared a perfunctory handshake and she gestured for him to take a seat. Dean sat immediately, and the doctor got right to the point.

'We'll need to set his arm. His ulna is broken. It's a clean break, but it pierced the skin and he's lost some blood. He'll need to be given a general anaesthetic before we take him to Theatre.'

The doctor's bleeper went off and she excused herself.

'I'll be back in just a moment to take you to him.'

Lucien felt sick.

'I'm so sorry, Dean. I just wish you'd been with Rafael instead of me.'

'Are you saying this is *my* fault?'

'No, of course not! I'm saying the complete opposite.'

'Because maybe if you had been a better doctor to Lydia then none of this would have happened. You didn't even want me to be here with her tonight. What? Am I not good enough?'

'No, that wasn't about *you*.' Lucien desperately tried to explain. 'When I was Rafael's age my mother used to put her patients ahead of me all the time. I didn't want to see you doing the same thing to Rafael.'

Lucien knew that had come out wrong as soon as he said it.

'You think you can do a better job?'

'No, I'm not saying that.'

'You think you're a better father to Rafael than me? Because, from where I'm standing, missing the first six years of his life and then letting him fall out of a damn tree isn't a great start.'

'What are you talking about? How could I…?'

'Just—please, shut up, Lucien. I can't do this. I can't do it any more.'

'Do what?' Lucien was bewildered.

'Use your big brain for once and work it out. Why do you think I turned up here out of nowhere?'

Lucien stepped back. 'I don't know why…'

'To find his biological father. To find *you*.'

Dean's words seemed to echo off the walls and the shiny linoleum floor of the corridor.

Lucien felt disorientated, and all he could see was Dean's angry green gaze.

'How can he possibly be mine? I've only been with one woman in my entire life, and she didn't have a child. Charlie's a doctor somewhere…miles away. Rafael's mother is—'

'Rafael's mother is Charlie. Charlotte died, Lucien. She's dead.'

Lucien backed away further.

He saw Dean's fury finally soften, and he reached out towards him. But it was too late. Lucien couldn't bear the thought of Dean touching him. And wasn't that a kick to the heart?

'Wait!' said Dean, his voice breaking on the word. 'Look, I was going to tell you today…after Rafael's party. I just didn't want to ruin it.'

'Well, you've done a pretty decent job of that anyway.' Lucien paused as he realised something. 'Is that why you spent the whole night here? To avoid having to tell me the truth?'

'No!'

Dean looked absolutely heartbroken. But Lucien shook his head. If he believed what Dean was saying now, then Dean had been lying to him since the second they'd met.

Was any of it real? Or was their whole relationship a lie? What possible reason could Dean have to do this to him?

Overwhelmed, Lucien knew he needed to get away. He was desperate for air…and most of all desperate to be away from Dean.

And just like that, Lucien left.

Dean's worst fear had come true. He'd been abandoned—again. By the one person he'd hoped would never leave.

Part of Dean already regretted everything he'd said to Lucien. But there was no way he could leave Rafael and follow him—and in any case he was still too terrified and angry to speak lucidly.

The doctor returned.

'Please take me to my son,' Dean managed to force out.

The doctor nodded and led him quickly down a corridor.

Dean knew it was unreasonable to be so angry. Lucien wasn't really at fault for any of this. But Dean had so much pent-up fear inside him it had to come out in some direction.

He'd hoped to feel some sort of relief when the truth of Lucien's identity finally came out, but no part of him could feel relief or even process what had happened while Rafael was lying in a hospital bed.

Rafael was in a private room. His eyes were red-rimmed, but he was awake, and he started crying quietly when Dean rushed to his side.

'Oh, baby, I'm so sorry I wasn't here. I came as fast as I could.'

Dean ran his hands quickly over his son's face and un-injured arm, then kissed his head.

Rafael sniffled.

'How's your arm feel, sweetheart?'

'They're going to give me a blue cast.'

Rafael's voice was so weak it broke Dean's heart, but he smiled widely for Rafael.

'It'll look amazing.'

A chair appeared from somewhere behind him, and Dean accepted the seat without taking his eyes off Rafael. He stroked Rafael's hair with one hand and held his tiny warm hand with the other. Rafael had been given some painkill-ers, but they had to wait for a slot in Theatre.

Once Rafael's gaze was firmly on the action film play-ing on the screen in the corner of the room, Dean allowed himself to quietly break down…just for a moment. Silent tears ran down his cheeks and he subtly wiped them away with his sleeve.

Rafael coughed, and Dean grabbed his son's hand, hold-ing it firmly.

He couldn't help but feel an empty space next to them both, where Lucien should be.

CHAPTER TEN

LUCIEN HAD ONLY spent a minute outside, breathing deeply as Dean had taught him at the auction, before he'd calmed down enough to walk away from the hospital. All he wanted to do was rush back inside and be with Rafael, but he couldn't bear to see Dean.

He was angry. With Dean, but even more so with himself.

He got a taxi home as quickly as possible, and the first thing he did was grab the garden hose and clean the blood-stained patio. Over his career he'd seen his fair share of blood and bodily fluids, but washing Rafael's blood off the flagstones into the roses made him so nauseous he had to lean against the cold brick wall for a minute to collect himself.

After that, he knew he just needed to be alone. Alone somewhere that wasn't inside a house surrounded by Dean's belongings, his smell, and memories of every tainted moment Lucien had spent falling for him.

Not to mention every moment Dean could have told him the truth and had chosen not to.

After striding mindlessly through the cold on autopilot, he found himself outside the tumbledown church. He gazed up at the crooked tower, his breath clouding above him.

This was how it felt to be betrayed.

He'd avoided close relationships for so long—by accident

or by choice he wasn't sure. But he'd managed to steer clear of all the heartbreak and emotional complications he'd seen his colleagues deal with so often. He'd almost let himself feel he was above all that silly emotional nonsense. He was too cerebral…too ruled by intellect.

More fool him.

He shoved open the church door, only to find it was no warmer inside. He pulled his coat more tightly around him. There were so many thoughts rolling around in his head it was impossible to focus on one, so they swirled inside him like a murmuration of starlings, fighting one another for attention.

His heart raced as he relived Dean's words at the hospital. His hands curled into tight fists, and he wished there was something he could throw across the room, just to see it shatter. But he was hardly going to throw a stack of dusty bibles, or a rusting sacramental chalice, and a wooden pew might be a bit optimistic even accounting for rage-induced strength.

Anyway, that wasn't him.

He let out a huge, shuddering breath and felt the anger leave him. And found he was only left with pain.

Dean had lied to him. Lucien had a son—a perfect, beautiful son—and he'd missed out on years of knowing him.

Rafael was his.

Rafael was hurt.

Rafael was hurt and it was Lucien's fault.

He'd done it again. He'd let someone get close, and his own stupid mistakes had almost got someone he loved killed. He was better off alone, and Dean and Rafael were certainly better off without him.

Lucien couldn't face climbing the steps to the tower so he sank down on to a pew instead. Leaning forward with his head in his hands, he cursed his traitorous heart. He couldn't bear the thought of seeing Dean, but Dean was the only person he desperately wished were with him. Dean with his strong hands, his calm voice, his beautiful green eyes that burned deep into his soul.

Ugh.

Lucien sat in the cold church for hours, until his backside was numb and he had trouble feeling his fingers and toes. He figured he wasn't the first person who'd tried to repent of his sins with some good old-fashioned penance within these four walls.

There were still dozens of abandoned candles at the front of the church. Dust-covered votive candles that had never been lit in memory of anyone—at least not for a couple of decades.

Lucien finally felt the urge to get up, and he rubbed his hands together to get some feeling back. He strode up the aisle, closed his eyes and blew the dust from the candles, then fished around in his pocket for his lighter and picked one up. Once it flickered into life, he stared at the tiny strong flame until the shape burned itself into his retinas, then he leaned on the votive stand with both hands, bowed his head and prayed.

He might not have prayed in years, and he didn't even know what he did or didn't believe in, but now he prayed— to God or Mother Nature, to luck or fate, to anyone who was listening—that Rafael and Dean would forgive him. He prayed so hard that his fingers hurt from grabbing on to the stand so tightly.

After a minute, he breathed deeply in and out, focused again on the shape of the flame that he could still see in front of his closed eyes, and felt a strange sense of calm overcome him. He was still scared, and he was still confused, but he knew where he needed to be.

Being alone had always used to be the cure for anything, but that just wasn't going to cut it any more.

Why was he even angry in the first place? The most perfect family in the world was right there, waiting for him. He realised now that had always been true—even before Dean had let slip his biological connection to Rafael. And maybe he could be part of that family—maybe he could have it all.

He would always feel responsible for what had happened to Rafael. But it wasn't about him, or his guilt—he was irrelevant. The only thing that mattered was Rafael being okay. And Dean. He needed Dean to be okay too. And right now Lucien was in completely the wrong place. He needed to go to them and do whatever was necessary to make that happen.

Lucien didn't know what Dean would say when he found him. He didn't know if Dean would be able to forgive him. But when Lucien put all his confusion and fear aside he knew he had to be brave and take a risk if Dean still wanted him. And Dean might have concealed the truth about Rafael, but when Lucien looked inside himself he knew Dean hadn't lied about his feelings.

Lucien smiled down at the dancing flame. As always, this place had done its job and helped him see everything more clearly.

He couldn't imagine his life without either Dean or Rafael.

The birthday party might have proved to him that kids could be a nightmare, but he loved a particular one. Getting to know both Dean and Rafael had made him an infinitely better person, more comfortable being his true self than he'd ever been before. And Rafael being his was the best thing that had ever happened to him. He could have everything he wanted if he was just brave enough to take it.

A few hours later Rafael had been given a general anaesthetic, had had an X-ray taken, his broken bones put in alignment and his arm set. Now he sat up in bed, brand-new blue cast in place, still watching the television. Totally casual…as if they hadn't all just been through the most stressful day of their lives.

A nurse's aide came in with a small pot of red jelly, a spoon and a new cup of water. As the aide left, Helen knocked on the glass door and waved at Dean from the corridor.

Dean jumped up and squeezed Rafael's shoulder. 'Don't eat that yet. I'll be back in a second.'

Dean joined Helen in the corridor, but left the door open in case Rafael needed him.

'What are you doing here? It's the middle of the night.'

'It's daylight, Dean. It's five a.m. And there are no secrets in Little Champney. I got a call first thing, telling me what had happened, and I drove right over. How is he?'

Dean blinked at the nearest window. She was right—the light outside was getting brighter.

'He has a broken arm, but I think I can take him home today or tomorrow. He just needs to sleep.'

'And how are you? You must have been through the wringer.'

'Me? God, I'm fine. Forget about me.'

Helen gave him a disapproving look. 'You're no good to him exhausted. You look bloody awful.'

'Ouch, don't spare my feelings or anything.'

Helen ignored him, stepped quietly into the room, and grabbed Rafael's notes from the foot of the bed.

'You should sleep,' she said, leafing through the notes. 'I'll sit with Rafael. Oh, and you should check on Lucien too. Apparently he didn't look so hot when he left last night.'

'I'll do that,' he murmured in reply.

Helen rubbed Dean's arm. 'I'll be back in ten minutes. Give the poor kid his jelly.'

Back by Rafael's side, Dean spooned up some jelly and offered it up to his son's mouth.

'I can feed myself,' said Rafael, his voice croaky, but stronger than it had been a few hours ago.

'That's funny, because I'm pretty sure I remember Helen's kids feeding you sweets all evening at the auction.'

'S'not the same.'

'I know.' Dean rubbed the back of Rafael's hand softly. 'But just this once let me do it. You need to rest as much as possible.'

Rafael rolled his eyes like a teenager, but let Dean continue.

Dean had completely missed out on feeding Rafael like this, so he was going to make the most of it while he could.

Rafael accepted a few spoonsful and then waved the spoon away. 'Where's Lucien?' he asked.

Dean blinked. 'Well, he's giving us some space...' Dean ate a spoonful of Rafael's jelly himself. 'You know he saved your life today?'

'He did?' Rafael stared up at Dean, wide-eyed.

'Yes. First off he found you outside, in time to stop you freezing to death.' Dean adjusted the blanket over Rafael. 'By the way, we're due a serious talk about how leaving the house at night alone is *not* okay, and how climbing a tree in the dead of night is extremely unwise.'

Rafael nodded sheepishly, and Dean squeezed his arm and kissed his hand.

'And then he got you to hospital and made sure you were safe and looked after.'

'Is he angry with me?'

'Who? Lucien? No, of course not.'

'He said I had to wait until the morning to check the piñata.'

'Yeah, he told me. Why didn't you?'

Rafael didn't answer.

'Can I take a guess?'

Rafael nodded.

'I think, maybe, you were cross about me missing your party. Which is totally understandable. And that made you act up a little bit.'

Rafael scratched his nose and stared at his jelly. 'Maybe.'

'I'm so sorry I missed it, Raf. And I'm so sorry you're spending your birthday in hospital. We can have another party when you get out of here. And it'll be ten times better than the one I missed.'

'The one you missed was really good.'

'It was?' Dean smiled. 'I'm glad. That means I'll have to work even harder to make the next one ten times better, won't I?'

The doctor swept in with a nurse, who checked Rafael's temperature, pulse, and blood pressure.

'Okay, Rafael, you're doing wonderfully,' said the doctor with a smile. 'At the moment what he needs is sleep, Dr Vasquez. So now would be a good time for you to go home, shower, rest…then get some of your son's things and come back in a few hours.'

Dean could recognise a doctor telling a parent politely to get lost. He'd done it himself plenty of times. But now it was his turn to completely ignore a professional.

'There's no way I'm sleeping, or leaving his side for long. But I will run home and grab some stuff.'

Ten minutes later Rafael was asleep. Dean stroked his hair softly for a little while longer, not wanting to leave him. This had truly been a wake-up call for realising how much he loved his son. The ferocity of his love for Rafael scared him a little bit. But now that he knew his son was stable, and not in any immediate danger, there was something he needed to do.

Dean found Helen waiting patiently out in the corridor. She promised not to leave Rafael's bedside for a second. And once she'd sworn that she would call him immediately if anything happened whatsoever, Dean gave her a long hug and left the hospital.

Dean unlocked the front door of the house. He could feel that Lucien wasn't there as soon as he entered the hall. The house was too quiet, too cold.

'Lucien?' he shouted anyway, just in case.

But there was no answer. He jogged up the stairs, checking inside all the rooms on the way up to his bedroom.

Nothing.

Why had he kept his secret for so long? Dean asked himself. Towards the end he knew he'd been lying for his own sake, not Rafael's. He'd been terrified that Lucien would leave, and now his worst nightmares had come true. He'd been abandoned again, by the one person he'd hoped would never go.

He wanted to crawl into his bed, hide away and lick his wounds, as he always did.

Dean sank on to the bed and plugged in his phone charger. He checked his notifications and finally saw all the increasingly desperate texts Lucien had sent him.

They were hard to read, but somehow they made him fall in love with Lucien all over again.

Dean, please, I don't want you to panic, but Raf's had an accident. I'm at the hospital with him now. Find me as soon as you see this. Obviously. What else would you do? He's going to be okay, so please don't be scared.

I'm so sorry. It's all my fault.

Not that it's about me.

But I am sorry.

I guess your phone must be out of power. Or out of signal.

Damn, you're going to be so scared when you get home and find the place empty.

Maybe I can get Helen to be there to meet you. But she's not picking up either. Damn it.

I'm so sorry.

There's still no news, by the way. I'm just sorry in general. Not because I was about to tell you bad news.

I'm making this worse with every text, aren't I?

Just get here, please. I'm in the family room.

I miss you.

Anyone who could make him smile while reading a live commentary of the worst night of his life was someone he could not let go.

As Dean sat alone in the empty house, he let the night's trauma and all his doubts slip away. He only remembered what Lucien meant to him—to them both. There was no denying it. If Dean still needed proof that Lucien was everything he could wish for in a father for Rafael, then this was it. And while they were at it he might just be everything Dean could wish for in a person to spend his life with.

Not that he needed proof. He'd known it for a long time. Rafael needed both his dads.

Dean felt a rush of courage. He would fight for what he loved. And Dean knew exactly where Lucien would be.

He left through the back door and rushed to the garden. He came to an abrupt stop on the patio, nearly walking straight into the piñata. His heart skipped as he saw the place where Rafael must have fallen. Where the patio was clean. He knew Rafael had lost blood there, and his mind projected it so that he could almost see it there, below him, but there was nothing.

Lucien must have come home after their argument and cleaned it up so Dean didn't have to see it. Strange, the things that could seem romantic.

He messaged Lucien only four words as he hurried down to the end of the road towards the woods.

I'm on my way.

Seconds later, Dean's phone chimed with a video call request. Dean answered immediately, and smiled when he saw Lucien's bewildered, open face. So different from the last time he'd seen him on camera, on the first day they'd ever met.

'You don't know where I am,' said Lucien.

'Of course I do.'

And as Dean saw the flickering candlelight behind Lucien's head he knew he was right.

'How are you video calling me? You hate doing this,' Dean panted as he hurried through the field and slipped across the bridge outside the church.

'I needed to see your face.'

Dean smiled. 'More fool you. Apparently I look awful.'

'No, you don't. How is he?' Lucien asked, looking stricken.

Dean couldn't bear it that he wasn't with Lucien yet, so he could soothe that look away.

'Raf's going to be fine. Everything went perfectly. Don't worry. I'm almost with you.'

As Dean ended the call Lucien appeared at the church door.

Dean ran through the church yard, dodging past the gravestones, and launched himself into Lucien's strong arms.

The second Lucien held him, all the emotions Dean had been holding in for hours streamed out, and soon Lucien's shoulder was damp.

Lucien squeezed Dean tight to his chest, rubbing his back slowly with one hand. 'I'm so sorry,' Lucien whispered into Dean's neck. 'Is he really okay?'

'Yes!' Dean sniffed and cleared his throat. 'The procedure went well and they've set his arm. He's out of the woods.' Dean felt Lucien relax in his arms. 'Thanks to you,' Dean added.

'To me? It's my fault he's in there.'

'How? Did you push him out of a tree?'

'No. But—'

'But nothing.'

Dean pulled back and held Lucien's shoulders firmly, to get a good look at him. 'How are you feeling?'

Lucien smiled fondly at him. 'I'm fine, Dean. I promise.'

Dean drew back. 'Lucien, I have some things I need to say to you.'

Lucien looked worried.

'I have a lot of apologies to make. So bed in.'

Dean sat down on the nearest pew and took Lucien's hand, pulling him down next to him.

'First of all, I'm sorry I shouted at you in the hospital earlier. I was scared, and I got defensive and lashed out. You didn't deserve that.'

Lucien shrugged as if it was no big deal.

'And secondly, I'm sorry I've been lying to you all this time.'

Lucien's gaze dropped, and it was obvious how much that had hurt him. Suddenly Dean was scared to keep going, but he knew he had to get everything out in the open.

'And finally, I'm so sorry I told you about Rafael and Charlie in the way that I did. I never planned for things to come out like that. You'd just found out you have a son, and then you found out Charlie had died too.'

'That was a shock,' Lucien admitted. 'But I would have already known if I'd kept in touch with anyone. It's strange, really…she and I weren't all that close, but I've never known someone so full of life. I can't believe she's gone. Poor Rafael.'

'It's been hard for him. But he's brave.'

'He really is.'

'And I'm sorry your mother made you feel second best,'

said Dean. 'You're right—I would never want to make Rafael feel that way. But we can learn from the past and do things differently.'

'How?'

'We have each other. If I have to put a patient first for one night, then Rafael has you. And vice versa. He's so lucky he has both of us to love him. He won't ever get the chance to feel second best to anything.'

Lucien's eyes filled with emotion, and Dean let Lucien pull him even closer, luxuriating in the warmth of his body wrapped around him.

'I hated lying to you,' Dean said. 'If it's all right with you, I never want to do it again.'

'I would be okay with that.'

Lucien rested his head against Dean's shoulder and found Dean's hand with his.

'So you knew who I was when you applied for the job?'

'Yes. You're the reason we came here. I wanted Rafael to have you in his life, but I didn't know you. I couldn't risk that you would hurt him or leave him. I had to make sure you were safe. I never expected that you would be perfect, or that I would fall in love with you.'

Lucien's fingers tightened on Dean's and they kissed deeply. Lucien stroked Dean's hair, then let his hand linger on Dean's cheek. Dean's eyes watered at the gentle touch, but he blinked his tears away.

'When did you decide that I was safe for Rafael?' asked Lucien.

'Pretty quickly. Then I had to figure out if you were safe for me. I started to get scared that I'd be the one who got hurt or left behind. I'd been keeping the truth hidden for so long… This huge, life-destroying secret. How could you ever forgive me for that?'

'Not life-destroying. Life-saving. And of course I forgive
you. I love you too, Dean. I've never loved anyone before—
I don't think I even wanted to. Or maybe I just thought nobody could love me back.'

'Well, now you know.'

They kissed again. Then Dean kicked gently at the pew
ahead of him and kept his gaze off Lucien.

'How do you feel about Rafael?'

Lucien turned Dean's face gently back towards him. 'I
love him, Dean. I've loved him for a long time. Maybe even
longer than I've loved you.'

Dean's smile grew, his eyes wet. 'He's pretty lovable,
huh?'

'Just like his dad.' Lucien winked.

Dean laughed. Lucien was terrible at winking. It was
more of a blink. But it was probably the most adorable
thing he'd ever seen.

'I don't know if you mean me or you,' said Dean.

Lucien shrugged, smiling playfully, and then his face
dropped. 'Jesus Christ... I'm a dad.'

'Yeah, congratulations. It's a boy.'

Dean held out his hand, and Lucien took it with no hesitation. 'Are you ready to hole up in a hospital room with
me and figure out how to explain to a seven-year-old what
a biological father is?'

'I can't think of anything else I'd rather do.'

And as he walked out across the mossy graveyard, in
the shadow of the crooked spire, with Lucien's warm hand
grasped in his own, Dean felt as if he was home for the
first time in his life.

* * * * *

MILLS & BOON®

Coming next month

NURSE'S TWIN PREGNANCY SURPRISE
Becca McKay

'What are you talking about?' Hazel asked.

But as she neared the urine specimen container set neatly on the side, alongside two testing strips, understanding quickly began to dawn on Hazel.

One strip to test her urine for blood, glucose, ketones…all the usual suspects. The other strip to test for a very specific suspect. The kind of suspect that Libby dealt with day-in, day-out. *Pregnancy.*

Hazel was hardly breathing as she approached the testing strip but even from a foot away she knew the result. She could see the two pink lines as clear as day.

'Libby is this a joke? Because…' but Hazel couldn't finish and from Libby's expression, and the vehement shake of her head, she knew this wasn't the kind of prank her friend would pull.

Hazel picked up the pregnancy test with shaking hands and tilted it towards the light as though that might change the result somehow. But of course, it didn't. Nothing would. Because Hazel was pregnant.

And when it came to the father, there was only one possibility. *Dr Garrett Buchanan*.

Continue reading

NURSE'S TWIN PREGNANCY SURPRISE
Becca McKay

Available next month
millsandboon.co.uk

COMING SOON!

We really hope you enjoyed reading this book.
If you're looking for more romance
be sure to head to the shops when
new books are available on

Thursday 27th March

MILLS & BOON

LET'S TALK
Romance

For exclusive extracts, competitions and special offers, find us online:

- MillsandBoon
- @MillsandBoon
- @MillsandBoonUK
- @MillsandBoonUK

Get in touch on 01413 063 232

afterglow BOOKS

Afterglow Books is a trend-led, trope-filled list of books with diverse, authentic and relatable characters, a wide array of voices and representations, plus real world trials and tribulations. Featuring all the tropes you could possibly want (think small-town settings, fake relationships, grumpy vs sunshine, enemies to lovers) and all with a generous dose of spice in every story.

♪ @millsandboonuk
⊙ @millsandboonuk
afterglowbooks.co.uk

#AfterglowBooks

For all the latest book news, exclusive content and giveaways scan the QR code below to sign up to the Afterglow newsletter:

SCAN ME

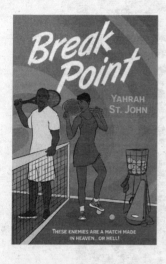
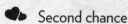
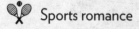
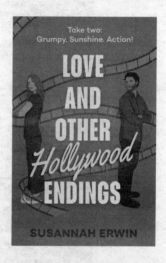
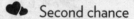

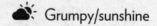

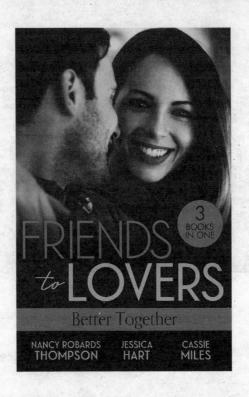